THE

SANTA CLAUS

KILLER

By
RJ Smith

A Storyteller Novel

(MMXIII – 01)

First Edition Fall 2013

Published by:
Storyteller Entertainment, LLC
United States of America

In collaboration with RJ Smith Productions

Copyright © 2012 by RJ Smith

ISBN: 978-0989675321

Represented by

JRK Literary, USA Agent
Robert Snow, UK Agent
Glenda Findley, Editor

Cover concept: Adam McFall
Final design: Richard K. Green

Titles by RJ Smith

Novels

The Santa Claus Killer (2013)
FBI Serial Killer Task Force #1

Cataclysm (2014)

Monsters In The Woods (2016)

Short Stories

The Storyteller (2015)
Written in 1988

Movie Scripts

Destiny
Cataclysm
Storyteller

FOR

HAROLD SPARTI

ACKNOWLEDGEMENTS

To all who continue the good fight… *tramping through the ditches of dreams*… and refusing to surrender their faith in the fantasy of storytelling.

For Friends: Steve Blauvelt, Kainoa Maka, Trisha Cook, Oscar Thomas, Darren Langford, and Gordon Holland.

To my beta-readers, Linda L. Barton, Carol Hovsepian, Debbie Vandyck, and Paul Swearingen, your steady stewardship was well pondered.

To my Facebook acquaintances who listened, engaged, and strengthened the ravings of a dramatist.

This book would've <u>never</u> been written if not for my Manager Julie Stern, and awesome Literary Agent Joyce Keating.

And also: for my UK Agent, Robert Snow.

BUT, *finally,* to that pint-sized boy I once was,
Who crisscrossed the depths of hell,
Yet somehow became a man,
I say these long-past-due words…

Well done, kid... You did just fine getting me here!

RJ Smith
The North Pole
Christmas Day

FOREWORD

WHERE I COME from, Santa Claus would've killed to be in my book... those auditioning would have lined their fat asses up around the block of Woolworths to audition for the part.

Now, they carry their bones down to Walmart and shake barbered heads in feigned disgust.

People have asked:

"What's gotten into you, RJ? Why did you write this horror involving the King of Christmas?"

I say, screw it... if Mr. Chris Kringle has time to keep a naughty list, then my name is número uno to receive coal! Let fatso track me down between deliveries and drag my lazy carcass to the graveyard; good for him.

Everybody has to die sooner or later.

Why not now?

For everyone else, those of you who think the guy behind the beard might have something to hide, this tale is for you.

Growing into my teens on the streets of Manhattan, I wasn't invested in Christmas. The shiny new toys didn't call to me from Macy's glittering windows. The season's opening of Rockefeller Center ushered in the Upper West Side kids... and yes, Christmas was fun for them... it was special...

They bought the scam and drank the Kool-Aid.

I guess, as a young boy, I recalled sitting on HIS lap one winter and tugging on the beard. Then, I knew the hoodwinking I'd received. I understood the con job and how it all played out. So, when I got older, I filed my complaint with the jolly old fat man! He laughed and smiled, and didn't give a crap.

And, that's when I knew something wasn't right. There was a secret.

Thus, the gang and I kept a close eye out for his appearance along the sidewalks and in every store right after the parade on Seventh Avenue. There, he rode into town atop his official red and green glittered sleigh on Thanksgiving Day.

The city would dance, and cheer, and sell their Christmas toys.

But, deep down, I knew a monster lurked under that façade, and, that one day... he would show his real face.

That day is today.

That's what carried you, dear bookworm, to this nightmarish tale of murder, horror, and fright.

Nobody, after all, gazes into the blackness of a shadowy graveyard expecting to find a love story.

You know why we're here!

You stared at the book cover of Santa dragging his bloody sack through Times Square, accepted the premise, and then bought the book recognizing damp, sticky blood would soon fill your stockings!

However, let's not get ahead of ourselves here...

The particulars of how we get through Christmas rests in the pages that follow.

For there, amongst the sleigh bells sounding in the dead of night, a snowstorm is brewing, and just around the corner, a murderer rings his bell.

WELCOME TO THE SHOW

JUST ANOTHER SNOT-NOSED KID, a lousy orphan, an abandoned morsel, left here to die at my feet.

> You better watch out, you better not cry,
> You better not pout, I'm telling you why,
> Santa Claus Is Coming To Kill...

That was his anthem, the tune that got his rocks off better than a five-and-dime hooker. It was also the lone miniature melody he couldn't shake from his throbbing skull. The twelve days of Christmas were heading down the pike like a freight train–Tick; Tock, Tick; Tock–Father Time was stomping through the dead of winter, waiting to turn the calendar of another rotten year.

"Please," a streetwise white boy begged. "Just let me go and I promise to live my life right!"

He was flat on his back staring up at the face of a monster; the kind that Mommy warned would stalk him one day.

"Too bad, so sad," the slaughterer scoffed. "Take your five-finger discounts to the pits of hell."

The boy trembled, fear gripped his spine and urine pooled beneath his hips.

"Just give me a chance!" he bawled, sensing the Fat Lady was about to sing.

"Time's up!" the killer cackled. "There's no more time to lie, cheat, or steal!"

"I wasn't meant to die this way," the boy cried, his arms and legs flailing for freedom. "I could have been somebody!"

Yet, escape was useless; the assassin had him pinned to the sidewalk in the middle of Times Square. To either side, hundreds of people milled about… watching the strangulation, waiting for the moment when they'd witness a murder.

New York was every man for himself.

"But you ended up a fucking nobody!" the murderer growled. "Shit happens and then you die!"

Death, the boy reflected, *will end the pain. It will pinch away all hopes and dreams… and then, my life-force will blink out… like the lights on a Broadway marquee… popping off, one at a time, goodbye, so-long, and farewell.*

That darkness of finality would bring the end to his nightmarish life.

Good Golly! Jolly Molly! A disembodied voice cackled in the recesses of the slayer's mind. *I do believe that boy is about to cry like a bitch!*

Stefan might've sobbed, had his childhood memories not flooded the blurring vision of the killer's face.

I'm on my way to heaven!

But death took time. It never happened like actors portrayed in the movies.

Committing homicide required some doing.

It took muscle, and every once in a while, this murderer knew he had to drag their naughty souls kicking and screaming into their graves.

Chapter 1

The Master Poser

MANHATTAN NEVER SLEEPS.

It gives birth to dreams and stamps them out like cheap, harsh cigarettes.

Frank Sinatra once sang that if you could make it here, you'd make it anywhere. What he failed to mention was the boogeymen who stalked the streets in search of blood.

That's where Richard Blake slouched; ringing his bell at the entrance to Macy's on 34th Street where miracles were replaced by the gore and mayhem that plunged through his mind.

"Bastards," he grumbled. "Good for nothing squares." Every year, he'd shrug on a Santa outfit and watch the fools scurry into the store for their spoiled little brats nestled safe and sound at home. It angered him that while he, the main attraction, stood out here in the freezing cold, panhandling for pennies, those fat little piggies were nestled in the warmth of their beds.

"Nasty little disease carriers, that's what they are!" Grumbling, he reached into his coat and retrieved a pint of Mad Dog 20/20. He adored the red grape flavor—better known as Bum Juice—an inexpensive, low-end, fortified wine that had an alcohol content of 18-percent. It packed one hell of a wallop and washed away his pain and misery. It excited him to drink the Mumble Juice right there in front of the silly fat cows as they dropped their meager coins into his bucket. He called it Mumble Juice because if he drank too much of it, he wandered the streets mumbling to people who weren't really there.

And that was just crazy.

Besides, if he really wanted to be one of the bums he hunted, he had to play the part and drink their Kool-Aid.

First impressions meant everything.

Tossing back a gulp, he scowled at the shoppers. "Ho! Ho! Ho! Have a merry, fucking, Christmas!"

The bargain hunters gasped, covered the ears of their youngsters, and rushed into the night.

"Hey, pal," a fatherly type muttered, shoving his finger into bad Santa's chest. "What's your problem, huh?"

Santa sniggered, and took another swig. "This whole damn city's my problem! You're all stinking gatherers, nothing but spenders!"

The man shoved Santa to the ground, shook his fists, and stormed down the street. "You drunken, stupid idiot, ya need a New York ass-whipping, that's what you need!"

"Asshole wannabe," a passing woman sneered. "You're not Santa Claus at all; you should be ashamed of yourself!"

I should be ashamed of myself. What am I doing wearing this itchy costume again this year? Damn naughty or nice, how many more will piss on my lap and step on my toes?

He staggered to his feet, spat on the ground and stared at a passing Camaro and a teenager who hurled insults from its open window.

"Yo! Dickhead! Where's your lousy reindeer?"

"Rotten thug," Santa answered. "It's because of pricks like you that I'm in this situation to begin with!" Stepping from the curb, he reached to the ground and gathered a snowball. "I'll show you bastards, I'll teach you a lesson or two!"

To those interested enough to stare at the drunken Santa Claus stumbling from the sidewalk and flinging his snowball at the passing car, they might've wondered what had become of the King of Christmas.

But Richard knew exactly what had become of himself... what his mission was, and why he stood out here in the snow to draw in the bums who begged for money and harassed the herds.

So, as his anger tracked straight and true, exploding in the face of a Puerto Rican boy, he smiled triumphantly.

"It's a present from Rudolph, with my compliments from the North Pole!"

Suddenly, the Camaro spun on an icy patch of road and slid towards the place where he stood. What headed his way were four wheels of death and destruction; a horn desperately warned the innocent of its destructive approach. However, for those who knew better, horns and whistles were merely comfort warnings that cautioned the shit wagon was headed their way.

Nothing stopped the candy man when he jingled up your number, calling.

The car crashed into the windows of Macy's just moments after the shoppers leapt to safety.

They screamed in horror as three teenaged boys sprung from the car, attacked Santa, and taught him about street justice.

"You stinking deadbeat fraud!" a white boy shouted, swinging his fist with all his might, striking Santa on the chin.

"Get off me, you little prick!" Santa sniveled a moment before the boy smashed a bottle against the side of his skull. Stumbling to a knee, he reached to the boy's neck, grabbed a crucifix hanging from a chain, and collapsed to the street.

"Kill his sorry-ass, Mighty Whitey!" the Puerto Rican boy begged. "Send his phony ass back to Mrs. Claus in a body bag!"

And that's what might've happened if a black kid hadn't pulled Stefan away at the cacophony of approaching sirens.

"Come on, Stefan! Let's get out of here before you kill him!"

"I got to find my chain, Darius," Stefan yelled. "The lousy deadbeat ripped it off my neck!"

"There's no time," Darius urged pointing to an NYPD cruiser turning the corner. "We have to haul ass!" And so, they abandoned the poser in a puddle of his own blood and hightailed down the dark street and out of sight.

As for the Grinch who stole Christmas, the last thing he remembered were the voices in his head.

Chapter 2

Ushering in the Season

THE NEXT DAY, wind battered the cheeks of three-million spectators lining Macy's Thanksgiving Day Parade.

The tradition began in 1924.

Back then, they released the balloons at the end of the parade until one brought down an airplane.

Now, they fold them up for next year.

Crashing planes are a touchy subject.

The smart viewers lounged at home watching televisions, their feet digging into plush shag carpets, their mouths watering from the turkey roasting in the oven. Nobody wanted to venture into the blustery wind just to welcome a jolly ole fat man from the North Pole.

But, staying at home was for chumps.

Any kid worth his weight in Bubble Yum would tell you, in order to one up their friends, bragging rights came by freezing their balls off while hot chocolate warmed the hand. Boasting that they came, saw, and conquered, meant watching from a heated living room wasn't going to cut it.

Stefan whistled as the Spiderman balloon soared overhead. "Look! It's Spidey!"

The boys went crazy as the masked marauder soared past Macy's followed by the Late Night Float.

"Look," Stefan pointed to the rock and rolling band on wheels. "It has a giant Les Paul guitar on it."

"Imagine that!" Darius grunted, nudging Stefan. "You think it's a sign?"

"Maybe, why not?"

Marco couldn't refuse. "Maybe the universe is warning us not to steal one." It was a reference to an upcoming heist they'd planned.

"Maybe it's a sign?" Stefan again asked.

"Take it easy, Mighty Whitey," Darius giggled. It was a nickname they'd given Stefan.

Then, they cheered louder as the Air Force Marching Band appeared.

"Damn!" Stefan exclaimed. "Those are some ass kicking brothers!" Cheering, he didn't know what war was, but liked the drums just the same.

After a long procession of bands and television stars, pandemonium broke loose and an emerald and gold sleigh appeared. From high upon the float, Santa and Mrs. Claus waved as tickertape fluttered over the scene like a blizzard.

Christmas had officially arrived.

"Can you imagine," Marco joked, "that fat slob screwing the hookers on Forty-Second Street? He'd be pawning his toys to buy those girls their crack."

"Yeah," Stefan chuckled. "Liberty Pawn and Jewelry would put his sleigh in the window with a big fat Santa mannequin sitting on it."

"Red-light special," Darius threw in. "Pawn it or sell it!"

After a moment of hysterical banter, the boys picked up bottles and hurled them at Santa. It was a display of anger that presents weren't delivered to street kids like them.

"Put these in your stockings," Stefan shouted and threw his bottle.

"Hey!" a city cop yelled hurrying through the crowd. "You guys throwing the bottles! Hold it right there!"

But, holding it there wasn't part of the plan.

Before anyone knew what happened, the friends ran through the horde with police hot on their trail.

It was just another day in the city of dreams.

Chapter 3

The Belly of the Beast

STEFAN WAS PISSED at how he'd been treated by New York's finest jerks.

When criminals were arrested in the County of New York, they were searched, degraded, and sometimes beaten before being locked into holding cells pending transport to Rikers Island Jail.

That's where Mighty Whitey now sat with petty thieves, drunks, and most likely, murderers.

He was losing his patience.

The corrections officers had already changed shifts once… and none of the detainees had been shuffled upstairs to the housing units. As far as the prisoners were concerned, the only difference between them and the guards was that the guards hadn't been caught.

Stefan stared through a Plexiglas barrier and cursed knowing the morons weren't actually working. He didn't remember much of the parade, save for throwing the bottle and running for his life. Everything else was beaten from him by the flatfoots who chased him down and taught him the consequences of getting on Santa's naughty list.

"What are you, some kind of tough guy?" they'd barked, daring him to argue. "We have a place for idiots like you."

And they did, too, he found out–a meat locker of freezing human flesh.

Bodies in the morgue are warmer than this, he thought. *My friends are nice and warm back at the apartment, probably resting on the flea-infested couch having a laugh or two.*

"Shit," he moaned, pinching his nose against the putrid stench of urine. It was so rancid he could taste it.

One of these lowlifes is going to vomit on my two-hundred-dollar kicks at any moment.

It was in the middle of those thoughts, that the cell door clanged open and Johnnie Law appeared. In his hands were wristbands, the type found on hospital patients.

"If I call your name, exit the cell, place out your right hand and keep your lying mouths shut."

"It's cold in here," an elderly man protested, his bones rattling from the chill, obviously drunk from one too many.

"This," Johnnie Law sneered, showing the man his wristband, "was your ticket outta here. But now, old man, you wait." He smiled vindictively, pushed the wristband deep into his pocket, and glanced around the room.

"Does anyone else have a hearing problem?"

There were no takers; everyone understood there were no magic numbers in a hat, no prizes squirreled away behind door-number-two.

They knew who the king cobra was in this pit, so they gave nothing–except their rapt attention.

When a snake threatened to strike, you had to avoid the bite.

Stefan was led to a blue payphone hanging on a dingy wall.

"One phone call," Johnnie Law mumbled.

Considering his options, and balancing the odds, he wondered who to call.

"Can I call two people?"

"What're you deaf, kid? You get one phone call and you better make it count."

Putting the receiver to his ear, Stefan dialed the one person who could pull him from the dungeon, his criminal defense lawyer, Terry R. Woodward.

Chapter 4

The Defender of Justice

TERRY STOOD SMOKING a Partagas cigar on the wind chilled terrace of his posh 5th Avenue penthouse overlooking Central Park.

The terrace was his getaway.

Creeping out here late at night, the crisp air cleansed the muck from his lungs. Having danced with demons, he'd whiffed their unpleasant odor and was glad to simply be an observer.

Then, there was Mirabel, his lovely wife.

Yes, indeed, he considered, glancing across the snow-blown scene below. *Life is good.*

He walked amongst the nightmares of society and rubbed shoulders with the worst people in Manhattan. A criminal defense lawyer, he was in tune with the pulse of the real world; he recognized the heartbeat of the street, knowing sometimes, it was a cold-blooded monster.

Years of defending the guilty had born down on him. Yearning to believe in justice again, he wanted to gain that fervor of hope he once held as a young defender of justice. Yet, the lawyer understood those hopes of innocence were lost.

Terry knew justice and truth had nothing to do with actual verdicts. Jury trials were a game. Innocence and guilt depended on which side weaved the best story for a jury. If a lawyer got the jurors to trust them, it didn't matter what the facts were; it was all in the storytelling.

Most defendants were chips to be traded for a later date. The object of the game was to hold other people's chips for that one case which came along every once in a while; the defendant he wanted to save.

But those cases are few and far between, Terry supposed turning to Mirabel who stepped through a sliding glass door carrying Henri IV Dudognon Heritage Cognac.

"Hey, rock star," she said, pouring them a glass, "its celebration time for winning your biggest case yet."

It was true; this was his biggest case.

His client, Pablo Rivera, was arguably the city's most fabled drug dealer, independently ruling the city's crack cocaine and heroin trafficking trade. That meant two things: Rivera was bigger than John Gotti and controlled more cash than Donald Trump.

Terry grabbed the glass and stared into its liquid. "This is two-million-bucks a bottle, a hell of a bonus from the city's most dangerous man."

"Don't beat yourself up, my love, you kept your oath and paid your dues."

"Nah, the jury did the dirty work. I merely told them a fantasy of innocence."

Mirabel sighed, pushed against her husband for warmth, and raised her glass, "To our little white bunny rabbit, then?" It was a reference to a long-ago witticism they shared, that one day he would acquire a cottontail to hop about the office as a reminder of their fairy tale.

"To all things magical," he agreed, placing his arm around her waist and staring into her eyes. "You know I love you, for better or worse."

"I prefer the better over the worse." She lived for moments like this, alone with her man, just sharing the same space. It was magical. This was where she wanted to be–forever. Shivering in his warm embrace and staring into the night skyline, she recalled their humble beginning.

Her husband had climbed the Legal Aid ladder, clawing his way from the depths of nothingness, slaving through eighteen-hour days in the swamps of the criminal courts, defending the poor who couldn't afford an attorney. He had a desire to make a difference, to save them from themselves. But, she knew it was the horse and water tale: Sometimes he just couldn't make them drink.

Today was her husband's day.

It culminated this afternoon in the Federal Courts and Terry was the center of attention. He had beaten back the United States Attorney's Office, the snakes with the longest fangs. A jury of five men and seven women had acquitted his client despite overwhelming evidence of guilt.

And yet, Mirabel knew, the acquittal weighed heavily on the love of her life.

"Why do I feel so guilty? I've let Pablo out to prey on the suckers who buy his dope."

She kissed him. "Your client is free tonight because of your oratory skills and dedication to the law. Right or wrong, innocent or guilty, the United States Constitution guarantees people like Pablo their day in court... to appear before a jury of their peers when accused of a crime. That's the nature of the beast. It's how the system works."

"It doesn't mean I have to feel good about it," he said sipping the cognac."

"No, you don't."

He stared into her bright green eyes and rubbed a palm against her cheek. "On this cold day, the system worked just fine for Pablo Rivera, accused, but acquitted, and most assuredly, New York's most renowned gangster."

She giggled and hugged him.

Then, just as the world seemed bearable again and things were perfect once more, his cellphone rang.

"God damn it!" he growled staring at the display. "It's the payphone from county jail."

Chapter 5

Nightmares & Dreamscapes

AFTER HIS PHONE CALL, Stefan was locked into an eight-foot cinderblock cell.

There, in the frigid loneliness, he stretched out upon a wretched, threadbare mattress and pulled an itchy blanket over his head. It was similar to those utilized by stables to warm horses in the dead of winter.

He fell into a recurring nightmare.

They'd intensified recently, pushing him from slumber into a clammy, panicked sweat.

Nobody escaped the lunacy of dreams.

This particular frightscape extracted a memory of years before when his twelve-year-old eyes watched helplessly as his father beat him to a pulp.

And, his mother got revenge.

"You good for nothing little brat," Daddy Dearest screamed in a violent rage. He was delirious with drunkenness and had slammed Stefan's head against the wall.

"Please, Daddy, stop!" But, he understood father's motives. Once monsters like him got their hooks into you, they stomped and stroked and sometimes...

Off came the belt, "I'll show you who the man of this house is!"

That belt seemed twenty feet long and Stefan knew it was going to hurt... he'd felt its leather slicing into his flesh many times before.

His dad was a butcher and parked his refrigerated truck down the street.

Inside, treats waited for later pleasures.

In the dream, he covered his eyes with trembling hands, helpless to avoid peeking through his fingers at the preview of things to come.

"No, Dad. Please, don't hurt me."

Then, suddenly, his mother appeared through the bedroom door with a knife in her hands.

She's going to shove that knife into his heart, he thought; cowering in the corner, he watched as daddy moved closer, raising the thick leather belt over his head.

Crack! Whip! Crack! Snap!

"Mommy!" he screamed, the leather biting into his pale white skin. "Mommy, help me!"

The strikes stung, the belt leaving a raised red welt across the cheek. And then, his right eyelid began to swell and his vision blurred.

Mother lunged. Her face twisted in fury the moment the monster had grabbed her boy's legs towards the bed. She was quick... swinging the knife with all she had... allowing it to find its mark deep inside his chest.

Cruuuuuuuuunch!

A splash of bright red blood drenched her face and jogged along her neck as it spurted from the wound.

"I told you," she shrieked. "I warned you!"

Yet, that isn't true, Stefan thought. She had never cautioned father that a knife would slam into his ribs. This was something new.

One thing was for sure, Daddy wouldn't drive his meat wagon another night. He'd run out of tokens and the turnstile of life would no longer rotate for the psycho.

His mom was making sure of that right now.

"Get away from us!" she screamed, yanking the blade from dad's chest and watching as consciousness faded from his eyes.

Stefan imagined she'd rip the heart from the chest and take a big old bite, like chomping on a New York apple.

Then a voice woke him from dreamland.

"Wake up, come on, get out of bed!"

Emerging from the dream, he tried to grasp where the words originated, yet there was only darkness.

"Stefan Berks," the voice barked. "Wake up!"

His eyes flashed open and he realized… there was no killing zone; gone was his demonic father who attempted to take his life. And then… it all came crashing back. The barking voice in dreamland was a guard standing in the jail cell.

"Court time, get yourself together."

Stefan swung his trembling legs off the steel bunk, glad that nightmares had an ending. Little did he know; the frightscape had just started.

Chapter 6

No Justice! No Peace!

THE MANHATTAN Criminal Courts building housed the upper ranks of the city's legal system.

Located on an entire block, it was home to the Criminal Courts, the District Attorney's Office, Legal Aid, the NYPD, and Departments of Corrections and Probation.

This was Lady Justice central.

When builders began construction in 1938, they toiled three years to complete the fourteen-million-dollar project. It rapidly became home to the most dangerous degenerates from the poorest boroughs of New York.

Bernie Madoff received his 150-year sentence here, where on any given day, rain or shine, amongst the hundred-dollar haircuts and thousand-dollar suits, an observer was sure to capture the sight of misery, pain, and contempt... in the courtrooms' holding tanks. Inside those iron cages, flat broke folks... *those who struggled day-in and day-out to put food on their tables...* had no say here.

This was morality central, where the rich and powerful hoodwinked the underprivileged into court costs, plea deals, and loss of liberty.

God BLESS America!

Courtrooms had little to do with freedom, the brave usually died broke, and money turned the hand of God.

For those wealthy enough to have an advocate on their side, well... *they* sometimes got a fair shake from Lady Justice.

Everyone else got the blindfold.

That's where Reverend Williams came into play. He was a modern-day *David* who would fight YOUR *Goliath* for a thick padded envelope of hard-earned cash. If anyone could sway the hand of vengeance, surely it was the glory of the reverend and his poverty-stricken protestors. With him on the soapbox, sound bites hit the evening news.

When Marco and Darius approached the courthouse steps, they heard the boisterous reverend before observing him screaming into a bullhorn on the courthouse steps where dozens of protestors gathered.

"Just another scam artist," Marco supposed, "lining his pockets with donations from the poor."

The real reverend, Mr. Sharp Shooter, no longer saw to such trivialities as leading protests, as his schedule was heavy chatting up millionaires on a cable TV show. Some said AL abandoned them for the lure of big money… and boy, wasn't *that* a hoot.

"It is our people's happiest moments," Reverend Williams preached to his crowd. "That is the nightmare of those who scowl at the sight of us, their ludicrous stranglehold choking our hopes and dreams."

Signs waved high above the protestor's heads, their voices shouted amen and hallelujah, lost in a frenetic moment of poking their finger in the eye of the system.

"No justice, no peace!" Darius shouted.

Marco snickered, raised his fist, and yelled to the reverend, "Power to the people!"

"No justice," the protestors repeated. "No peace!"

Glancing to his friend, Marco shook his head. "See what you started?"

"Yeah, I'm stirring up a hornet's nest."

Darius knew the legal system rarely trembled; it did not cower in the corner from ear piercing picketers or Bible toting preachers. What the legal system did quite well was maintain the daily manufacture of its agenda.

That hadn't changed much since England ran the show with a bunch of white-wigged cross-dressers.

That was *then*, this was *now*.

The reverend knew that Manhattan prosecutors had only one agenda. They wanted poor citizens–black people who sold drugs–locked up in Rikers Island jail. For every prisoner lying in one of the 14,000 jail beds, consuming the good mayor's green bologna sandwiches, Gotham generated $150 a day in court costs, probation fees, and other trumped-up financial levies.

Yes, indeed, incarceration was big business.

Darius chuckled at his thoughts while leading Marco through the courthouse door and into the lobby where they stopped to gaze at twin grand staircases rising impressively into the bowels of the structure. "Are you sure you don't have any warrants out on you?"

Marco laughed. "There isn't anything."

"Come on, bro!" Darius stated, pulling on Marco's New York Giants jacket and jerking him up the stairs. "We're going to be late for Stefan's hearing if we don't haul ass."

Climbing the stairs, they stared into the empty, drawn faces; each boy wondering what troubles had brought the *sad sacks* to this place of misery. At the top stair, they moved into a hallway where an old black woman sat on a hard wooden bench.

Darius locked eyes with her momentarily as she dabbed her cheeks with a handkerchief. Beside her, a lawyer spoke urgently while glancing at his cellphone.

"Look, your grandson will do a couple years up in Sing-Sing, maybe Attica, then he'll get out and come home, no worse off."

"Easy for you to say," grandma mumbled, "you're a miserable leech-sucking lawyer and have no problem sending poor black men to prison."

Damn right! Darius thought glancing away in embarrassment. He felt like an intruder, stomping amongst things that didn't concern him. "Damn shame," he mumbled pulling the courtroom door open.

The interior of the courtroom was oppressive... its atmosphere was filled with uncertainty and an undeniable sense that anything might happen. Anyone who's ever been to a traffic hearing felt that sensation of dread.

But, being a defendant in a *criminal* court, where the outcome was unpredictable was a life changer. That was especially true when that courtroom was filled to capacity with Santas holding protest signs and a camera crew from WABC Eyewitness News.

"Damn, this shit is going to be on the news," Darius whispered. "That can't be good for Mighty Whitey."

Marco glanced at the Middle Eastern cameraman pointing the camera at the Santas who filled the back three rows. Nobody threw bottles at the Thanksgiving Day Santa and got away without the publicity that was sure to follow.

The judge looks mean, Marco thought. Perched like a bald eagle staring at a field mouse that dared to make a run across an open field.

"Man," Darius whispered. "They're going to throw the book at him."

The Santas grumbled as a bailiff led Stefan into the courtroom. Chained from waist to foot, he sat at the defense table beside a high-class lawyer.

"Mr. Woodward," Judge McElroy chuckled. "It's nice to see you down here in the trenches. By the looks of the spectators today, I'd say you have your hands full."

"Yes, Judge, every Santa Claus in Manhattan seems to be present. Terry R. Woodward present on behalf of the defendant, Stefan Berks."

The courtroom fell silent in recognition of the attorney the *New York Daily News* had called the *'Prince of the City'* and PAGE SIX of the *Post* dubbed *'The Defender'*.

Terry considered both titles ridiculously outrageous. He wasn't one to give credence to such public grandstanding.

"A big pro bono case, huh?" the judge snickered. "Lots of media attention on this one. It'll be a good day at Woodward & Gottlieb!"

When Terry waltzed into his courtroom, the judge always found himself hitting the brandy a little too hard back in chambers.

"Yes, Judge," Terry answered. "Pro bono in Toto, and let the record reflect I submitted a motion to dismiss on behalf of my client."

"I'm sure you have. Let's get to the meat and bones of the matter, shall we?"

"We want justice," a Santa Claus yelled as his buddies cheered the statement with raised signs.

"Who are you, sir?"

"Jack Berrymoore, Your Honor, I'm the Union President for the Borough of Manhattan Santa Claus Unity!"

"What can I do for you? And why are you disrupting my courtroom?"

"For starters," Mr. Berrymoore demanded, "you can keep that thug locked up for ruining the parade!"

Chapter 7

Clipped & Shipped

JUDGE MCELROY WASN'T HAPPY when he emerged from chambers and collapsed onto his leather chair overlooking the courtroom.

After a short recess wrangling over the motion to dismiss, he felt like his balls had been clipped and shipped to the Bar Association for filing.

Detective John Arias would have agreed should anyone have asked his humble opinion. He hated courtrooms and despised the petty give and take. It was his job to make the arrest, gather the facts, and submit the charges to the prosecutor. As far as he was concerned, cops and courtrooms shouldn't dance the tango.

John Arias wanted to laugh; just let it all out.

But, if he did, he'd be riding a desk pending a mental evaluation at the Psych Department. He hated the inkblots. They resembled butterflies or dead bodies.

So, he kept his mouth shut, as most good cops did, despite the nonsense being played out before him.

"It'll be New Year's Day before we get outta here," Arias whispered to his partner, Robert Romero, who sat beside him scratching out a *New York Times* crossword puzzle. Published daily, it became increasingly more difficult throughout the week, with the easiest on Monday and most difficult on Saturday.

Today, Romero was stuck on a five-letter word hinting a famous line from TV show, *The Apprentice*.

'The Donald likes to say, you're _ _ _ _ _.'

Glancing to his partner, Arias chuckled, pointed to the blank boxes, and blurted, "The answer is *FIRED*, Einstein."

Romero snickered. "These Santas should be fired. Their fake beards look like they came off the rack at Walmart!"

Arias cleared his throat to mask a chuckle.

Romero wasn't a funny cop and didn't cross his T's or dot his I's. He was a dope who didn't know how to build cases against suspects. Piece by piece, line-by-line, building a criminal case was similar to assembling a jigsaw puzzle.

He wasn't good at either one.

Nonetheless, obtaining guilty verdicts was the business of the District Attorney's Office, and holding a case together was an entirely different matter. Getting a conviction meant the D.A. had to convince crime victims to miss a day of work, place their lives in jeopardy, and testify in open court against the very people who tried to rip their heads off in the first place. Most victims didn't follow through; it was the nature of the business.

That's why many cases ended in plea agreements.

Human beings, Arias knew, lived in the here and now and forgot about yesterday with each swooping pass of a clock's hand. Having caught the Stefan Berks case, it hung around his neck like a brick.

"What's the point?" Arias whispered, his arms folded in irritation. "The judges are giving away the store and greasing the revolving door with their manicured fingernails."

"That's the way the gavel falls," Romero whispered, glancing at the Santas. *It is a cluster fuck; every Santa in the city is here except for the one that needs to be.*

"Does the District Attorney's Office have anything to offer?" Judge McElroy interrupted. "If not, I'm going to rule on the motion to dismiss."

The prosecutor stood from his chair and unrolled a printout. "This is the defendant's rap sheet, Judge. Mr. Berks has been arrested sixteen times in the County of New York for assaultive crimes..."

"So, what's your point?" the judge interjected. "Where is the victim of *this case* before the court? The defendant has been in custody a week now for an incident that borders on criminal mischief."

"The victim," the prosecutor snapped, "has a prestigious job as the official Macy's Santa Claus and doesn't feel being here would look very good on television."

Terry jumped from his seat, not believing his ears. "Judge, we just went over this in chambers! The prosecutor could have subpoenaed the victim. They didn't, for whatever reasons. Therefore, we request a *GRANTED* ruling on the motion to dismiss."

"Objection," the prosecutor complained. "The State is working on getting evidence."

"There is no case, Your Honor," Terry argued. "There's no sworn deposition from Macy's or their Santa Claus. Nobody has come downtown to file, despite a prior postponement by this court, and, therefore, the defendant has no viable means to face his accuser as set forth under the Sixth Amendment of the United States Constitution."

"Ah, yes," the judge mumbled, "the Constitution. Let us not trample on that wonderful document."

The Santas stood and booed the lawyer.

"Lock him up!" Mr. Berrymoore yelled, gaining the attention of the media. "Send a message to the public, Judge!"

The judge wasn't upset with the turn of events.

In fact, he was relieved this lame duck case was dead in the water. So, bashing the gavel on the bench, he raised his head and offered his agreement.

"In all criminal prosecutions, the accused shall enjoy the right to be confronted by witnesses. But in this case, I have seen nothing but stalling on behalf of the State. In *Strunk v. United States*, 412 U.S. 434, the Supreme Court ruled that if the reviewing court finds the defendant's right to a speedy trial was violated, then the indictment must be dismissed or the conviction overturned. This Court finds that since the State has not secured a complaint or testimony of the victim and has not presented the witness in court, then said inactions violate the defendant's right, thus, this court has no choice but to dismiss all charges."

"Your Honor!" the prosecutor protested. "This is unreasonable!"

The judge grinned.

"Tell your Santa this isn't the North Pole and the naughty list doesn't apply here. With or without the blindfold, Lady Justice remains blind."

"But, Judge. This is a nationwide story!"

"Merry Christmas, Mr. Berks." the judge shrugged banging his gavel. "You just got a free ticket out of jail."

Chapter 8

Mortal Thoughts

THE SON OF A BITCH got off.

That's what the killer supposed while tailing the courtroom Santas down Duval Street with the scent of Chinese food chasing after him.

I'll be dammed, before I eat food from these slant-eyed bastards frying up their cats and dogs!

> *Humpty Dumpty sat on a wall,*
> *Humpty Dumpty had a great fall.*
> *All Santa's reindeer,*
> *And all Santa's men,*
> *Couldn't put slant-eye together again!*

The killer laughed right there on the street.

Humpty was his mother's favorite nursery rhyme.

Now, as she screamed it in his head, the witch changed the verses to give the memory some meaning.

A one... two puncharoo!

So, as Mammy screeched in the killer's head, he hummed right along. At the conclusion of the rhyme, the monster brought his attention back to the matter at hand.

"Goddamn little snot," he muttered, thinking of the punk who just walked out of the courtroom and the smart-assed Santa who dared address the judge. *I could slash his throat right now! Just sneak right up behind him and rip his innards from that nasty little body.*

No, you won't, Daddy's voice counseled, *not in broad daylight. Not right here on the street!*

I could do it. Just like that freak Andrew Cunanan did, when he gunned down Versace on the steps of his South Beach villa. I wouldn't make the same mistakes, of course... Imagine, hiding in a houseboat not two miles from the scene of the crime.

Stupid little sissy, Mammy whispered. *Fool us once, shame on you, trick us twice, we'll screw you nice.*

"Shut up, Mom!" the killer shouted to the empty street.

Then, out of nowhere, a cop appeared.

"What's that buddy? Is everything all right?"

Of course, it's not all right, Daddy's voice taunted. *It has never been right. Not since the day he was born, kicking and screaming to his mother who tried to strangle him in his sleep.*

"Ha! Ha! Ha!" the killer laughed.

That never happened! Mammy argued.

"Nothing can ever make things right," the madman grunted, forgetting the cop standing before him. "The way people stare into my eyes as if I'm an unwanted outsider charging through the gates of their empire."

Now you did it, Daddy scolded, *stinking bacon in the making!*

"What's that, pal?" the cop asked, his face twisted in suspicion that maybe this guy was hopped-up on a hit of Methamphetamine.

"Sorry," the killer muttered. "I was just thinking out loud, that's all."

"Well, watch your language," the cop warned, his hand resting on the butt of his nightstick. "There are children around here."

The murderer felt resentment escalating from a volcano of rage his psychiatrist had tried to suppress with Xanax bars and mood suppressors. Xanax was his least favorite medication; it made him sluggish and angry and allowed his rage to boil from his secret place.

Measly children, what the hell is it about these people and their excuses of civility because of little ones?

Ring around the rosy, a pocket full of posies, Mammy rhymed, *we all fall down!*

Suddenly, the voices of the courtroom Santas snapped his attention back to the present. They were making way along Canal Street, wide smiles lining their faces, laughter booming from their lungs. He'd known posers like them as an innocent child. They'd bounce him on their knee while grinding yellow teeth behind itchy white beards.

"Dirty sons of bitches," he mumbled. He'd show them how naughty or nice things could really get. *Yes, sir-eeeeee! Let the season of giving begin!*

Today, he'd rushed down to the courtroom and watched the wheels of justice break down before his angry eyes.

Incompetents, Daddy taunted. *They can't do anything right. They have to pay their due, Son, yes they do!*

But first, the killer had to make the Santa imposters pay for stealing his moment, for making him look like an idiot in the court of law.

Santa Claus, Mammy cackled. *Imagine that!*

He would start the season off right with the group of overweight Santas waltzing along the streets as if they hadn't a worry in the world.

How dare them! Daddy screamed. *Speaking out for your justice!*

But it isn't his justice, is it? Mammy argued. *After all, he wasn't THE Santa Claus in the parade the boys threw their bottles towards.*

But none of that mattered.

This was about payback for the beating they'd given him on the corner of 34th Street ten days prior.

Maybe, Daddy suggested, *you can start paying everyone back right now.*

The killer would teach them the same way he taught the kittens that invaded his tunnel only to scream until he snapped their skinny little necks.

"Here, kitty, kitty, kitty," he whispered following the Santas along the sidewalk and down into the subway. "Come and get it!"

This was the day New Yorkers would realize they had a special kind of killer amongst them.

He was *The Santa Claus Killer*.

Chapter 9

The Avenging Angel

SERGEANT MICHAEL MURPHY thought he'd seen it all before. He tried to recall a time when bodies didn't show up during the holiday season.

But this is unusual.

Detective Operations had punched his number and here he stood staring at an eyeless Santa Claus sprawled dead on a park bench in Herald Square Park. It was a tourist hotbed, not a dumping ground for bodies. The park was a rest area for thousands of shoppers and midtown office workers. It served as a stage for product launches, musical performances, and film shoots.

The area surrounding the park and along 34th Street was a retail hub. The most notable attraction was Macy's flagship department store, the largest in the United States and, according to the Guinness Book of World Records, the biggest in the world until being surpassed by a Korean store in 2009. During the holiday season, hundreds of thousands flocked here to witness the famed Holiday window displays. It was central to Madison Square Garden, Times Square, Korea Town and was serviced by the B, D, F, M, N, Q, and R trains.

Murphy knew the killer could have come from anywhere. *This is Main Street, U.S.A.* "It doesn't just take the cake," the detective mumbled. "This ends the entire party." Scanning the pulsing crowd, he shook his head in disgust before staring back to the corpse.

"Welcome to prime time, buddy."

Mike could already see the headline in the paper.

Live from New York! No miracles on 34th Street!

The detective was just out of high school when his father attempted to shame him onto the force. There was an expectation from dad, a standing order really that his boy would storm into the NYPD Police Academy and get down to business.

The son of Captain J. P. Murphy, Mike was a shoe-in for quick advancement and absolute graduation from the police academy.

But he had other plans.

Coming up slowly through the Corrections Department, he worked inside the Tombs, one of the oldest and worst city jail anywhere, before he transferred to Rikers Island on the East River where he gained great insight into the workings of the criminal mind. Working the second shift, three to eleven, in unit C-74, he came into close contact with several goons from hell.

However, for Mike, everything changed on a lazy summer afternoon. His shift commander called him into an empty cell, sat him down on a steel bunk, and mumbled his father had been killed by a mugger's bullet in St. John's Park just down the street from the 1st Precinct. That day, in the midst of his carefree years, crime became personal.

He was no longer a bystander.

That summer, Mike the jailer, became an avenging angel of the New York Police Department.

He recalled the last Fourth of July he'd spent with his mom and dad during a family barbecue at their house in Rye, NY. He'd go there every holiday to escape the city and its crime. When the food was eaten and the small talk waned, they strolled to Playland, an amusement park of magical proportions that lingered in the memories of those who grew up in nearby neighborhoods. It was the only government-owned amusement park in the United States.

Mike summoned a memory of his father sweet talking mom into riding the Dragon Coaster, a wooden track eighty feet off the ground and speeding along at forty-five miles per hour.

Mother would always give in to his dad, so long as he glanced in her direction with a wink and grin.

"One day," she'd warned, "the ride will leave the tracks, go airborne, and put us in our graves."

Of course, that never happened and, Mike suspected, she never really believed it would. But, for Dad's sake, she pretended.

That love was all stolen away.

The mugger might as well have torn Murphy's heart from his chest and ground it into the concrete sidewalk. As for what came after... the funeral was gut-wrenching. There was never a debate where his dad would end up. As everyone knew, if you were a parishioner of Saint Patrick's Cathedral, you met Saint Peter at Calvary Cemetery.

Back then, cops were angels and captains were gods.

That was ten years ago. The force had changed, the guard had distorted, and a new breed had invaded the ranks.

And here Murphy now stood, a thirty-five-year-old seasoned Manhattan South Homicide detective.

Staring at the body, he shook his head.

Saint Nick is dead at my feet, and only a fresh forty-eight hours to solve the whodunit.

His thoughts were interrupted by the voice of his partner rising above the commotion of the burgeoning crowd.

"Hey, Opie!" Lieutenant Rico Martinez roared ducking beneath yellow crime scene tape. "Whaddaya got this time?"

"Dead Santa with his eyes poked out," Murphy retorted, "and nine missing reindeer."

Rico chuckled. "You're kidding, right? Please tell me this is some sick fantasy rambling through your Irish head."

But, there was no escaping what Rico saw as his partner lifted the tarp and pointed to Santa's caved-in skull.

"Blunt force trauma. He was stabbed in the eyes, too. Not much else to go on. No witnesses and no leads."

"Of course not, do we have an ID?"

Murphy reached into a brown paper bag with latex gloved hands, pulled out a wallet and handed over a union identification card.

"Jack Berrymoore," Rico muttered staring at the picture. "What in Christ's name is the Borough of Manhattan Santa Claus Unity?"

Murphy shrugged. "According to that card, he was the President of the Union that governs Santa Claus work."

"Really?" Rico muttered pulling on his own latex gloves and bending over to inspect the corpse. "Beautiful, we just got hit with the Santa Clause!"

Chapter 10

𝓐 Wink & 𝓐 Nod

𝓟ADDY RILEY'S Music Bar was packed.

City politicians, lawyers, and cops crammed the bar to remember Detective Jacob "Mac" MacMillan, whose wake was taking place under their open noses.

Paddy's was the quintessential Irish pub that existed in most American cities. The watering hole belonged to the warriors who fought the good, bad, and sometimes rotten battles of the metropolis. Lawyers, judges, and cops; they all drank and cried right here.

There was an understanding within the pub that no matter which side of the law one practiced, this was neutral ground. It was the bullpen, a wrangling arena for arguments to be made and opinions to be heard... whether attendees liked it or not.

Now, displayed upon a small stage in the dimly lit corner, Mac's corpse lay stretched out in a simple oak casket. It was surrounded by personal effects and various balled up handwritten notes. Nobody knew exactly who penned the notes, or what was etched upon them. But every so often, if someone happened to turn their head just so, the corner of their eye would glimpse a ball of paper soaring through the air and into the coffin.

Crowd screaming, extra point good!

Above the casket, a walnut mantle overflowed with Irish knick-knacks, charms, and dozens of untouched brimming shots of Jameson Irish Whiskey. These were placed there to assist the soul on its journey through hell.

Yep, the detective's soul, if he had one, was going out in much the same way it lived; Irish to the core, but surrounded by strangers. Of the hundreds of attendees present for his lavish send out, only a handful actually knew the deceased or gave two shits about his extinguished life. When complimentary booze was poured, the Irish, and everyone else, were sure to show up to rub their noses and wink a silent understanding.

As the old saying goes: *He who loses money loses much!* And thus, if you kept pockets full of cash and still got to be cheerful and right… life was all gravy!

And, wasn't that a goddamn blessing?

After all, this was the last call for a fine Irish boy who tried, yet failed, to make good the luck of the Irish.

Terry Woodward and his partner, Michael Gottlieb, were sitting by a stone fireplace sipping Guinness from freshly frosted mugs. They were listening to the District Attorney mutter his holier than thou utterances of justice and karma.

But, nobody gave a damn either way.

As far as Lady Justice was concerned, Terry thought, recalling what the judge had said, *she wears a blindfold, and that speaks volumes about her wisdom.*

So, as the D.A. slurred his speech and made a fool of himself; Terry tuned out and gave all his attention to the Guinness, for at least what swilled in the mug allowed peace and tranquility.

"Are they going to make a toast?" he grumbled, obviously bored and ready to make a hasty exit.

"That is doubtful," Gottlieb answered glancing to his partner. "Not as long as free drinks flow down their gullets."

There was no doubt about it, ignorance was bliss.

Terry knew the corpse in the corner was as crooked as Tony Bennett's nose. What wasn't breaking news was information on Mac's pending arrest, which was scheduled diplomacy. Of course, all that was *before* he placed a .45 caliber service pistol into his mouth and pulled the trigger blowing his brains and all speculation about guilt right out the back of his skull. One thing was for sure, good ole Mac was out of his corrupt mind, literally.

"Listen up, you lucky schmucks," Captain Anton McKenzie roared, standing atop a chair in the center of the room. "Let's send Mac out right." Raising his glass, he was about to utter a toast when the door swung inward revealing Rico and Murphy. "Damn it, Rico! Can't you and Murphy arrive on time for a feller's final round?"

"Sorry, Captain," Rico muttered shuffling through the crowd to the barkeep and an awaiting Jameson.

Terry, on his third Guinness, watched as the dynamic duo drew the stare of their commander. Although the lawyer considered Murphy a friend, Gottlieb held the NYPD in contempt.

Excusing himself from his partner, he trooped over to Murphy, "What's going on, Mike?"

"Sonuvabitch," the detective jested, grabbing Terry by the shoulders, "they still let rats in this place, huh?"

"I'm not the one getting my ass chewed out. Where have you guys been, anyway?"

"Fighting crime, counselor," Rico offered sarcastically. "Something you spend your days defending!"

Murphy chuckled, elbowing Terry in the ribs. "We're investigating a deceased Santa Claus found in Herald Square Park."

"Santa Claus, huh?" Terry snorted. "That's interesting."

"It sure is," Murphy replied. "People are getting bolder all the time."

"Today we ferry off a brother," the captain continued, "a defender of the brotherhood, down the gutter and into the ground, a fair soldier, and a better man, regardless of the press."

Everyone tipped back their glasses then, for they knew the verse, took the pledge, and were happy it wasn't them lying in the casket with unblinking eyes.

McKenzie stepped off his roost and led the attendees to the body where they sang the second best Irish sendoff song of all time, *Parting Glass*.

Leaning on one another's shoulders, and rocking to and fro, the room full of hardnosed legal defenders sang, way out of tune, but singing just the same.

There was only one thing missing on this fine night. Detective Jacob "Mac" McMillan and the tears not shed for his early departure.

Life, after all, continued moving.

Chapter 11

Gremlins of Doom

IT WAS MIDNIGHT, and Lieutenant Rico Martinez was back at the homicide office studying suspect logs while sipping stale coffee from a chipped Yankees mug.

Battling a migraine brought on by the Guinness, he glanced at an ABC Newscast blurting from the television hanging on the wall.

> "Manhattan Homicide Task Force detectives are seeking information on the identity of a killer who murdered the Union President of Manhattan Santa Claus Unity earlier this morning in Herald Square Park across the street from Macy's. Police say there are no leads and they need the public's assistance in tracking down *The Santa Claus Killer*."

For Chrissakes, the media already has a name for him? Turning his attention back to the pile of crime records sitting on his desk, he shook his head and stared at the names jumping off pages of suspects. *These are just regular customers. Frequent flyer felons continually rounded up for questioning, rarely getting booked on criminal complaints and hitting the street in search of more sheep to fleece.*

The judicial door kept on revolving.

But things were heating up at the Task Force.

The war chants had begun to rumble from Deputy Inspector Morrison's office and Rico was perplexed as to why the inspector had his panties up in a bunch.

Miracles were sparse in homicide, where mayhem and murder resided. Suspects rarely opened the squad room door, peeked around the corner, and introduced themselves.

They didn't waltz into the jail and inform the corrections officers they were wanted for murder.

Killers had to be hunted down like dogs.

Rico grunted and rubbed his temples. "Damn it. Why is the Deputy Inspector so pissed about this one murder?" Picking up the department's Compstat Historical Report, he saw murders had been dropping steadily since he'd joined the Task Force back in 1990. And since becoming supervisor of Manhattan South Homicide, gone were the thousands of murder cases that used to roll in. Now, there were just hundreds of annual homicides citywide. Notwithstanding those facts, the gremlins of disaster were tormenting him with visions of the ass chewing sure to occur should an arrest be slow to come.

Deputy Inspector's Office... all juiced up over the murder of one fat Santa Claus.

He thought that was odd.

However, with his thirtieth anniversary and retirement from the NYPD approaching, he found himself daydreaming of the new position offered by his brother down in Florida.

"Forget Manhattan," Miami Beach Police Chief, Ray Martinez had suggested during their weekly phone calls. "My Deputy Chief is retiring and we could use your man-hunting skills down here."

RICARDO MARTINEZ
Deputy Chief of Police
Miami Beach, P.D.

He could envision the brass nameplate attached to the office door, the window looking across Ocean Drive offering a view of crashing waves pushing ashore.

The kids laughing in the surf, what a life, he thought, imagining his wife, Liz, and three teenaged boys, Marty, Luis, and Carlos, sunbathing on South Beach. Maybe they'd even spend weekends at the theme parks in Orlando.

Disney, Universal Studios, Sea World... they were just four hours north of Miami.

He imagined Liz tossing back coconut rum on weekends as the boys stalked tropical high school girls who'd be giving the boys the once over.

"And besides," his brother had pushed, "you'll have a full pension from the NYPD, and Miami Beach pays the Deputy Chief above six figures."

"Jesus, Ray, you make it seem so simple," Rico had said, a smile turning up the corners of his mouth.

"Just talk it over with Liz and the boys," Ray pleaded. "It might be time to get out of the city that never sleeps!"

"I don't get much sleep myself," Rico chuckled.

That evening, as Liz sat surrounded by her sons, they heard Rico's argument for a planned escape from New York.

"Miami Beach?" Liz shrieked. "Yes... and hell yes, and more yesses!"

The boys had smiles implanted on their faces.

"When do we move?" Carlos, his sixteen-year-old, yelped. Beside him, the twin fifteen-year-olds had mischief in their eyes.

"Heck, yeah," Marty shouted. "That means we get Cuban girlfriends!"

"And deep-sea fishing," Luis added. "Are you going to get a boat, Dad?"

That sealed it for Rico, seeing his family lighting up with happiness. He was getting out of Manhattan.

It was just a matter of time now.

The clock was ticking; his papers were pushing through command.

"It's been nice," Rico mumbled in memory of his career.

He'd been raised in the Bronx, a roughneck, hardnosed Puerto Rican who always knew he'd become a cop. Police work throbbed through his veins; and he experienced the rush of catching the bad guys, tracking them down in the alleys and streets of Fort Apache, the Bronx. He was a detective who wore black leather jackets and stepped with confidence when stomping a crime scene; suspects were known to say his eyes stabbed into their soul.

I'm a spirit hunter, the goddamn Murder Police! He reminded himself, *at least until January first.*

That was the date he'd turn in the badge and gun, waltz into the city sunset, and forget about Manhattan Homicide's dead bodies. The only corpses he'd have to worry about in Miami were:

BEACH BODIES

What's the worst that could happen on the beach? He thought, *a bloody shark attack, maybe an accidental drowning once in a while?*

Rico chuckled at these considerations.

With his luck, there'd be a serial killer stalking tourists. When that happened, in any city, the murder police would stalk the scent, stomp along the shadows, and peek behind every door. Some murders were investigated more than others... although nobody would admit to this. When the victim was a dirt bag, notes didn't get taken, questions didn't get asked, sometimes eyes turned the other way, and reports came up missing.

That is the nature of the beast.

His superiors didn't care about sleazebag corpses with needles sticking from their veins.

They got what they had coming.

Nobody adores snake eyes, Rico always said, *but the dice has to be rolled. Every number has a story and sometimes that story meant crapping out.*

"It's all part of the game," Murphy would say. "If you want to play in the biosphere of crime, you have to be in the biosphere."

Dammit, how could my last case be a dead Santa Claus? It was downright dirty.

There are no leads or tips, but plenty of questions from the deputy inspector's office, and that means crap is going to run downhill. City Hall will want a warm body brought in... and fast.

It was in the middle of that realization when his newest sleuth, Detective Robert Romero, walked into the office and dropped a file onto the desk.

"That," he grumbled and pointed to the file, "is the coroner's autopsy on our Herald Square Park Santa."

Rico glanced at the report, flipped through its pages and snorted. "What the hell is this– *'Death by Bludgeoning'*–we already know Santa was beaten to death!"

Romero shrugged, "We got no prints, no nothing. We're going to need the Virgin Mary to intervene."

"I don't care if Jesus Christ himself comes down off the cross. The best friend of children is in the morgue and you give me this crap?"

"Hey, give me a break, will ya? That's all we got!"

Rico was hot under the collar! He had requested Romero be transferred to his squad as a favor to John Arias. Romero was a crackerjack in the vice squad and Rico always sought out the newest talent in the NYPD.

"Don't wrap this bullshit in a red ribbon and call it a present! Do I look like Santa to you?"

"No, Sir," Romero answered.

"Then get out there and find a suspect!"

Watching Romero hurry from the squad room, Rico knew it was full speed ahead to find the newly dubbed media darling, The Santa Claus Killer.

Chapter 12

Page Burst Heist

THE FIRST WEEK of December found Stefan staring at a Les Paul guitar hanging on the wood paneled wall of Rudy's Music store on 48th Street in Times Square.

In 1974, on Rudy's first visit to New York, he went directly from John F. Kennedy Airport, with a suitcase in hand, to the world famous shrine of music… 48th Street.

So in 1978, with his wife by his side, Rudy opened Rudy's Music Store and turned his passion for guitars into a palpable reality. It wasn't long before the business became a highly respected guitar shop to string benders around the globe.

Now, as Stefan stared at the guitar, his stomach growled with thoughts of a Burger King Whopper & Cheese. Of course, there wasn't anything whopping about the burger anymore, the franchise had long ago ruined it.

Now, Burger King & Whopperland was a joke.

"Hey, there," a sales girl, Trisha Laughlin, interrupted. "What are you looking for?" Eying him coyly, she was sizing him up, knowing he wasn't a buyer, but more of a browser, and a cute one at that.

She wasn't accustomed to cute boys wandering into the store. What she was familiar with was the tedium of marketing instruments to music industry snobs. She could never quite figure out how a *sweet*, struggling guitarist from the East Village turned into such an *elitist prick* after signing a record deal.

Staring at the boy before her, she attempted to place him into one of her little compartments; maybe file his traits away for future reference. The problem was... she couldn't quite size him up.

He was a blank wall.

"Hey, back at ya," Stefan replied, pushing blond locks behind his ears.

"You like Les?" Trisha asked, unwrapping a piece of Bubble Yum and popping it into her mouth.

Stefan gawked at her, entranced, like viewing one of those porn flicks Marco and Darius swiped from the triple-XXX store over on 44th Street.

"Hello?" the girl asked. "Is anyone home in there?"

"What?" he asked, her question snapping him back from the front row fantasy.

"Les Paul? Do you like him?"

"Sure, I guess so."

She giggled, noticing the bulge in his pants, the confusion on his face. "You have no idea who Les Paul is, do you?"

"Of course, I do! I'm looking at the guitar, right?"

She pushed forward. "I'm Trisha and I obviously work here. What's your name?"

But, before Stefan could answer, Marco interrupted.

"Look at that old plate," he pointed at a license plate hanging above the doorway with 'Gretsch' stamped on it. "Sometimes I wonder about the places those things come from."

"I lived in a place like that," Stefan responded, glancing at the green metal plate. "Peekskill is a fairy tale compared to where we are now."

Trisha giggled and shook her head, "It's not a place. Gretsch is a classic orange hollow body electric guitar. They stopped making them in the late 1970's, but they're coming back thanks to Brian Setzer of the Stray Cats who played one in his music videos."

"The *Strays* were cool," Marco exclaimed, "but Slash rules the strings."

"Well, Mr. Rock and Roll," Trisha turned to a paying customer. "You guys just don't break anything."

Stefan watched her strut to the customer and then glanced at a Jimmy Page Number Two by Les Paul. *It's Just an old piece of wood, from another place and time.*

"You ready?" Marco asked, fetching him back to the present, like lending a hand to someone who's lost their way in a dark room and couldn't find the way out.

"Yeah," Stefan replied, aware of what was to happen, but wishing it could be stopped. They planned the theft just minutes before entering the store and were going to pretend a fight, drawing the employees' attention–and anyone else– away from the guitar rack. Darius would snatch the $10,000 Page Burst VOS and run for the door. It was ordered by a musician who lived on Church Street. He'd previously cased the store and picked out the guitar he wanted. On the streets, if you wanted to get your hands on the really good stuff cheap, you made friends with the street trade who'd snatch just about anything and sell it to you for pennies on the dollar.

That was the plan.

Marco threw Stefan to the ground and began wrestling with him.

Trisha and the customer rushed over to separate them as Darius grabbed the Page Burst and bolted for the door.

Chapter 13

Guilty as Charged

ACROSS TOWN, Judge McElroy was lost in thoughts of smiling children while pulling on a Santa hat, and rushing down the courthouse steps.

Stepping onto Centre Street, he stopped at a Sabrett vendor's cart, grabbed a dog with onions, and hurried across the road to Collect Pond Park. As far as he was concerned, there was no better feeling than ending a tedious day of law and order with a hot dog and stroll in the park.

"Good evening, Judge," a county court bailiff nodded climbing onto a Schwinn bicycle and strapping on a helmet.

"Night, Mike. See you in the morning."

The balding, elderly bailiff nodded. "Full calendar tomorrow, it's like Motel Six at the jail; we keep the lights on for them."

"Yes, we do," the judge replied, "and they keep coming back." pushing through the square and onto Lafayette he saw Eyewitness News Reporter, Tim Smith, lurking on the steps of the Family Courthouse. "

Your Honor," Tim said approaching. "Are you aware there's a killer stalking Santa Clauses along the east coast?"

"Is that right, Tim?"

"That's correct, Judge," the reporter stated. "And now we have a dead body in Manhattan. It might not be good walking around the city in that get up of yours!"

The judge smiled and hurried away. The last thing he wanted was to be quoted at six o'clock acknowledging such a preposterous story.

Tim gave chase. "Have you heard anything about the possibility of a murderer hunting the streets? Aren't you concerned walking around robed as Santa?"

"I don't know anything about it," McElroy replied with a dismissive smile. "Try to stay warm!"

Damn them!

It infuriated him that the scavengers manipulated his privacy. His stretch functioning for the county concluded ten minutes ago, at exactly five P.M. The judge was delighted to leave his gavel at the bench. Tonight, he was making an annual journey to the *Herbert Irving Child and Adolescent Oncology Center* on Fort Washington Avenue.

Beaming with the knowledge this would be the fifth year frolicking as Santa Claus; he forgot the reporter and lost himself in visions of the evening ahead. The kids would squeal in delight with smiles as wide as the Grand Canyon. Considering this, he whistled *'Silent Night'* and descended the Canal Street subway stairs where he'd soon hop aboard the Q-train to Herald Square.

Reaching the subway platform, he shivered from the chill and sat on a concrete subway platform bench. Stillness from the dark tunnel filled his ears and then he realized... this was his least preferred portion of the commute, waiting for a train that was once again running behind schedule.

You better watch out, Judge.

Criminal jurists were always cognizant that the jail released predators every day. And, occasionally–every now and then–just when he least expected it, criminals turned up beside him on barely lit street corners.

It wouldn't be the first time he met a defendant on the street. *And, maybe,* his mind whispered, *one is creeping along this abandoned subway platform looking for judges to throw onto the third rail.* A sense of foreboding flowed through his veins and goosebumps crept up his spine. Sensing surveillance, he felt like he was being hunted down by the maniacs who traversed the underground. Feeling a change on the breeze, the judge's gut cautioned of something out of place. It was a dreadful feeling of the unknown, stalking him, warning that something lingered in the darkness... ready to pounce at the first opportunity.

Then, from the corner of his eye, he glimpsed a wayward stare of terror, just a sideways gesture of acknowledgement from the killer as their eyes locked in recognition of something more than a transit through the night.

"Crap!" McElroy mumbled, understanding what the gaze meant. "What do you want?"

No sooner than he questioned the fiend, he saw the knife descending and tried to dodge from its path.

But to everything an end must come.

It was an understanding that arrived just moments before the blade slipped into his lung. Falling onto the platform, his gushing blood splattered the concrete.

"What is it?" he cried, staring at the gaping hole in his chest. "What have I done to deserve this?"

But, there was no karma to be paid into the collective consciousness of those who summoned such explanations.

Murder had no rhyme or reason.

It just was.

The killer watched that realization working its magic, the victim trying to make sense of the nonsensical.

He could always see it in their eyes–the exact moment when the soul began ascending into the land of the departed.

"We have a verdict, Your Honor," the murderer taunted seizing the jurist by his hair and dragging him onto the tracks. "You're guilty as charged."

And then, McElroy realized, the madman began humming *Santa Claus Is Coming to Town.*

Sometimes, Christmas brought death. And, occasionally, it was Santa Claus himself who passed down a sentence.

Chapter 14

Flop House Haven

NIGHTFALL BROUGHT thunder and lightning above the condemned Washington Heights apartment building.

During storms like this, the ceilings leaked rainwater down mold-infested walls. The wind rattled broken windows, and cracked pipes struggled to contain whatever nastiness ran through them.

Nonetheless, on this night, nobody detected the dripping raindrops because Darius and Marco were comatose in their dreams, stretched out upon the filthy floor.

They were worn out following a day of running through department stores collecting five-finger discounts.

Beside them, Trisha stared at Stefan in his sleeping bag.

They were an unlikely duo, but since first encountering one another at Rudy's, a spark ignited after Stefan tracked Trisha down one night as she'd locked up the music store.

"Hey, Trisha, remember me?" he inquired.

Just like that, as if he hadn't been involved in the theft of an exclusive guitar from her father's storefront.

"How could I forget? You and your associates made off with a very expensive guitar."

"Yeah," he admitted, staring down the street. "We sure did."

Reluctantly, Trisha smiled now at the memory. She hadn't complained or argued how disappointed she was. The girl was happy to see him again.

"Want to walk me home?" she recalled asking the boy, his hands pushed deep into his pockets, a look of embarrassment on his face.

"Sure," he grinned. "I'd like that a whole lot."

And, that was that!

They strolled along the East River gossiping for hours, laying everything bare as the day they were born.

No secrets, no lies.

She told him of her well-heeled Long Island upbringing and learned that his life was the opposite of her own.

It was the tie that bound them.

Just as the old adage specified, opposites did attract.

Trisha fell into young love…whatever one might assign the spirits of carefree youth. The fact was, she realized, they had become inseparable. During the day, working in the guitar shop, she thought of him running the streets trying to make his way with what little he had.

Shaking her head at the sight of Stefan, whimpering in the sleeping bag, she knew he was lost in the recesses of nightmares.

"Darn it, how'd you capture my heart?"

She recalled making the mistake of telling her parents about him. And, right on cue, Rhonda and George did their best to convince her that he was no good street trash.

"Just leave him," mother had insisted.

However, fairytales didn't play out in such a manner.

And so, the days moved into weeks, which turned into months, and Stefan fell more in love. Watching him now, trembling on the old wooden floor, which creaked under their weight, she imagined one day the floor would just collapse.

"No," Stefan muttered, his dreamscape expressions twisting in a mask of terror, "please let me go!"

Mentally, the demons attacked. He was a fly clinging to a slimy subway wall, its wings trembling erratically. His limbs were gone, replaced instead by six hairy legs.

"Help!" he screamed, his eyelids twitching.

In the nightmare, his words emerged as nothing more than a buzzing tone. In the distance, a single light flickered, and he saw something along the edges of sight. It was different from anything he'd ever perceived before…

hundreds of images, all displaying the same thing, much like a computer set to *tile* a photo on its screen.

He was looking through the eyes of the fly.

Then, he overheard footfalls echoing in the darkness and saw a Santa Claus step into view dragging another bloody Santa along the subway tracks.

"Ho! Ho! Ho!" Santa blurted in the darkness. His voice reverberated through the channel. "You better watch out, you better not cry, ya better not pout, I'm telling you why. Santa Claus is coming to town!"

The fly pulled itself from the wall and winged towards the shadow dragging the other through the subway.

Back in the apartment, Stefan muttered nonsense in the safety of his dream, trying desperately to shake awake from the nightmare while Trisha stared at his shuddering body.

"Stefan?" she whispered. "Baby, wake up!"

However, he couldn't move. There wasn't a switch to flip or a lever to yank to allow escape. He was trapped down in the subway in the body of a fly buzzing the head of a killer who lugged the body through a hole in the tunnel wall.

Swatting at the annoying fly, The Santa Claus Killer attempted to smack it into oblivion. "I'm making a list and checking it twice. I'm gonna find out who's naughty and nice!"

That's when Stefan saw the knife sticking from the other Santa's chest. Behind the moaning body, a blood trail streaked along the pebble pathway between the tracks.

"I see you when you're sleeping," the killer huffed while dragging Mister Law and Order. "I know when you're awake. I know when you've been bad or good–"

"Help me," McElroy begged. "Please, help me!"

However, there was no help, because as the fly buzzed the killer once more, the murderer swatted it against the concrete wall, where it fell to the ground.

"So be good for goodness sake!" the murderer shouted glancing at the shit-eating fly. Raising his boot, he stomped it into obscurity.

Stefan snapped awake at the apartment, his face clammy with sweat, fear filling his eyes.

"Come on, baby!" Trisha urged, her hand shaking Stefan's shoulders. "It's just a nightmare."

But it was much more than that; it was a frightscape!

Shaking terror from his head, Stefan sat up and hugged her, before glancing to Marco and Darius who stood staring at their buddy.

"He's coming!" Stefan muttered. "The meat man is coming to take my life!"

Chapter 15

Good Ole Bible Thumpers

MORNING CLEARED out the storm and Times Square was once again crammed with the hustle and bustle of holiday tourists.

And, of course, plenty of violent thugs.

They never left Broadway.

The eyes of killers roamed the streets every minute. Waiting, hoping, and calculating that one of the sheep would wander down an alleyway to sneak a piss behind a putrid dumpster.

Not far from here, Stefan, Darius, and Marco bounced from the Eighth Avenue subway station.

"Check out all the suckers," Darius jived, glancing at the would-be victims. "They're like sheep to slaughter!"

"Today, we're gonna clean up," Marco stated. "And fill our pockets with holiday greenbacks."

The train ride from 168th Street was occupied with enthusiastic conversations of pickpocketing the Broadway *sheeple,* and the movie, *Nightmare on Elm Street.*

"Stefan," Marco stated. "Just because Hollywood makes nightmare movies doesn't mean yours are coming true."

So, there it was, Stefan thought. *Proof my closest friend thinks I'm bonkers.* "The dream felt so real! I could almost feel the dampness of the subway tunnel, the filthy stench in my nose, and the rush of air as Santa swatted at me!"

"At you," Darius teased, "or the fly?"

"It seemed real," Stefan insisted. "How could I have imagined all of it in a dream?" But, he recognized, the reverie didn't just *seem* real, it *was* real. Glancing to a storm drain gutter, he imagined a skeleton's hand reaching through the grate to yank his flesh into the recesses of hell.

Knock, knock, a disemboweled voice whispered.

"Who's there?" Stefan inquired, spinning around to the sound and finding nothing.

It's your Daddy!"

Glancing to his friends, he noticed them staring, worried amusement lining their faces.

Knock! Knock! Motherfucker!

"Man, you're acting crazy," Darius chuckled, snatching Stefan's thoughts from his fantasy. "Are you talking to yourself now, too?"

"No. I didn't say anything!"

Little Miss Muffet, sat on a tuffet,
Eating her curds and whey!

"Who said that?" Stefan cried in panic. "Where did that voice come from?"

Marco watched his friend spinning in circles on the sidewalk, searching for something that wasn't there. "Dude, nobody said anything! You're tripping!"

"He's daydreaming," Darius offered. "Right here in the middle of Times Square!"

"I'm not tripping!"

Darius giggled. "So, you believe an imaginary killer is talking to you?"

"He's not imaginary. I just heard him quoting Little Miss Muffet!"

"Stefan," Marco offered, "you're imagining all this crazy stuff. It's *not* real!"

"But, I saw the judge, just as sure as we're standing here on the street."

For tourists wishing to slow down long enough to peer at the sight of the boys, one might presume they were just a band of friends.

But, for a pair of twin, Iowan boys, who stood there watching, they were transfixed by something else.

"Mommy, Mommy!" one of them shrieked. "Look at Mickey Mouse!"

It was a reference to the Disney shirt Marco wore.

"Honey, don't stare!"

I'm gonna find you, boy! The voice interrupted the scene. *Maybe lay out these little ones for everyone to see.*

"Please!" Stefan yelled to the empty space around him, "Stop talking shit to me!"

"Hush your nasty mouth," a Midwestern mother scolded while covering the twin boys' ears. "Is this how your mothers raised you?"

"No, lady," Darius spat back. "Our mothers taught us how to eat from garbage dumpsters."

The woman turned several shades of red and pulled her children away with a backward glance that would've melted the ice from Frosty the Snowman.

"Darius," Marco teased, pointing down the street. "Look at what you did, scaring off the tourists!"

Everyone laughed then, knowing the vacationers would carry the story to their prayer circles and mutter litanies of damnation.

Silly little sinners, the voice taunted Stefan, *that's what all of you are!*

Stefan glanced up and down the street, seeking an explanation for the horrid little voice in his brain. His eyes stopped on a newsstand, and a picture on the front page of the *New York Times*.

"Marco! Get over here and look at this!"

Hurrying to Stefan's side, he stared in shocked surprise at the photo of Judge McElroy.

Picking up a copy, Stefan shoved it towards his friends. "I told you guys I saw him down in the subway!"

"You going to pay for that paper?" a Pakistani newsstand attendant grumbled. "I don't want grubby fingerprints on my papers!"

Darius, ignoring the man, stared at the newspaper. "I guess nightmares do come true."

"A nightmare in Manhattan," Marco agreed.

See? The voice mocked Stefan. *They're starting to come around!*

Beneath the *Times'* photograph was this caption:

'Police Seeking Missing Judge'

And soon, there will be more, the voice advised.

Stefan didn't know from where the voice came, but he knew it was responsible for the death of the judge.

And, he knew something else:

The Twilight Zone was living in his head.

Chapter 16

Winter Wonderland

TWLEVE HOURS LATER, the Holiday Train Show was hopping. Every year, the New York Botanical Gardens hosted the event in the Enid A. Haupt Conservatory.

Rico and his wife were fans.

The happening showcased more than 140-to-scale iconic New York buildings and structures constructed of plant stems, tree bark, twigs, seeds, fruits, and pine cones.

Above Rico's head, thousands of twinkling Christmas lights lit the scene. Staring at the handmade structures, he knew some of the erections were recreations of the original Radio City Music Hall, St. Patrick's Cathedral, Penn Station, Yankee Stadium, the New York Public Library, and, of course, the Brooklyn Bridge.

"Let's get a drink, babe," Elizabeth purred into Rico's ear. "You need to unwind a bit from work."

"It's that obvious, eh?"

"Clear as the gun hidden in your waistband."

Bar Car Nights was the premier adult event at the show. Held on Saturday evenings, it boasted complimentary cocktails under the magical glow of the event.

"I needed this," Rico admitted, wrapping his arm around Liz's waist as they strolled through the conservatory. The couple had been a dual member of the gardens for years now. "I sure hope the Mayans are wrong, or this party will all end in a few weeks on December 21st, 2012."

"Oh, Papito!" Liz giggled, snuggling in close to her man. "You don't still believe in that nonsense, do you?"

But, Rico did believe something was about to happen. He'd spent many sleepless nights watching the History

Channel's *'Ancient Aliens'* with the kids. As far as the boys were concerned, it was just a matter of time before THEY landed on the White House lawn.

Tossing those thoughts aside, he smiled at his wife.

"What I believe is that my thirty-year career at the NYPD is just about over."

"Thank the Lord Jesus for that," she smiled. It was a bittersweet realization. She knew how her bread was buttered and understood her husband was happiest when he handcuffed a suspect who'd killed an innocent victim.

Rico hugged her and gently rubbed his palm along her cheek. "You and I are going to have a wonderful night."

"Oh, Ricardo, you have a way of making Christmas, this place, and our life... so special."

"That's because it is special and will only get better when we flee for the shores of Miami Beach."

"I can't wait," she smiled.

"We'll be on the beaches of Florida next year. I don't care what those crazy Mayans have to say about it."

I love him, she thought, *more than the day I married him.* "You complete me," she whispered.

It was a line from her favorite movie, *Jerry Maguire.*

"Shut up," he responded, hitting her with the movie's follow-up line. "You had me at hello."

They fell into an embrace beneath a Brooklyn Bridge mock-up where an electric model train moved along the tracks far above the attendee's heads before disappearing into shrubbery.

It is magical. Rico thought. *This place, filled with the hopes and aspirations of those waltzing amongst a fantasyland of peace and tranquility.*

"Look!" Liz squealed, pointing in delight. "It's the original Yankee Stadium!"

The display was a showstopper. The real stadium over in the Bronx–*the house that Ruth built*–had since been torn down in exchange for a modern home for the Yanks.

Rico sipped his cocktail and smiled. His existence outside the department had significance; a deep-rooted importance which allowed his spirit freedom after dealing with death and the destruction of life.

Now, making way along the exhibition, Liz and he came upon the New York County Courthouse built from plant parts, nuts, bark, and leaves.

"Jesus," Rico grunted. "It looks just like the criminal court steps I climb to throw the book at the guys I arrest."

"Not tonight," Liz ordered. "Lieutenant Rico Martinez is off duty and I'm happy the Homicide Hunter is not here."

Her twenty-five years of love was conditional, he knew, so long as he left the job at the precinct and came home a citizen. Grabbing her hand, he pulled her through the Christmas wonderland.

"Tonight, I am your fairytale prince."

"And I, your princess," she whispered.

Suddenly, his cellphone rang in its holster and Rico knew—*even before his reflexes reached for it*—that murder called out his name somewhere in the gutters of Manhattan.

"Don't answer it," Liz pled. "Just let it go to voicemail." Nevertheless, even as she asked, she knew the lieutenant commander of the Manhattan Homicide Task Force had to take the call.

"Honey, you know I have to answer it." He said apologetically staring at the image of Murphy on the phone's screen.

Pressing *ACCEPT CALL*, he asked, "What's up, partner, this better be worth my marriage?"

"Purchase Liz some long stemmed roses," Murphy's voice replied. "And then… climb into the car."

Rico glanced at his wife, and noticed her eyes were moist with silent damnation for his job and the City of New York.

"Where is the car taking me?"

"One Hundred Center Street," Murphy responded. "We found McElroy on the courthouse steps."

Chapter 17

Blind Justice

MANHATTAN CRIMINAL COURT was cloaked in darkness and was hectic with first responders.

It was an entirely different place at midnight.

As Rico stepped from his unmarked cruiser on the corner of Centre and Leonard Streets, he grumbled at the sight of the media correspondents shouting questions from behind the yellow crime scene tape.

"Lieutenant!" crackerjack Eyewitness News Reporter, Tim Smith, yelled. "When can we expect a comment?"

"As soon as I find a suspect I'll release a statement."

"Hey, Rico," NBC Nightly News Reporter, Les Bolt inquired. "Is it true a killer is stalking the city?"

"Come on, Les, you know I'm not gonna comment on a hyped story for the network's lead piece."

"So," Les persisted with a grin, "you're confirming there's something to hype?"

Rico turned to his longtime media acquaintance, "Les, *gimme* a break, will ya?"

"Just attending to business, buddy, you know I wouldn't nail you to the cross."

"Famous last words," Rico answered. "We can both name a governor who fell on that sword."

"Yesterday's news," Les snickered. He was a heartbeat from Brian Williams' position, should the host decide to retire, and many silently cheered Les on.

Rico knew that he and the reporter had a long affiliation that offered assistance to the other in their time of need. "You have my number, Les, hit me up later and I'll slip you something exclusive before the wolves get anything. Right now, I have to move up the steps and see what waits."

"It's the missing judge, right?" Les called. "Is this the messy work of a jurist-stalking madman?"

So, Rico thought, *that's the story the networks would sell the public in the morning, a madman stalking Manhattan Judges.* "Yeah, it's him, but you can't attribute that tidbit of information to me."

"How about... sources close to the investigation?"

"You're a beaut, Les," Rico remarked with a shake of his head. "Just shoot me in the back."

"I wouldn't be where I am if it weren't for awesome friends like you."

"Confidence man!" Rico murmured making his way towards Murphy who stood on the Criminal Courthouse steps. "What are we looking at?" he asked kneeling beside the body and pulling back the tarp covering Judge McElroy's body.

"The man who gave out one hundred thousand years," Murphy mumbled. "He's naked, has been beaten to death, and is deprived of his gleaming eyeballs."

"Jesus Christ," Rico commented glaring at the eyeless, beaten cadaver. "What animal would do this and throw him on the courthouse steps naked?"

"Take your pick, Lieutenant," Murphy retorted pulling on latex gloves and removing a taped envelope from the judge's chest. "The corpse was found by a drug dealer just released from night court."

"What's that?" Rico asked, pointing to the bloodstained envelope Murphy opened.

"A message from our killer," Murphy said scanning the handwritten note. It looked perfectly scripted by an educated hand. Showing it to Rico, the detectives stared at the message.

Justice may be blind, but I see what people fail to notice!

"It appears," Rico observed, "the nutcase is answering somebody's question."

"You may be right," Murphy agreed. "I'm sure the rest of his manifesto will tell us exactly what he wants from us."

"Fuck me," Rico muttered, reaching into his pocket for a pair of gloves. "I promised Liz I wouldn't stay with this case all night."

"I hope you bought those flowers," Murphy reminded, "because this is the real *First Forty-Eight,* and we're not on the A&E Network." It was a reference to the hit TV murder show. "The networks are sending this scene out live and in color."

"I know," Rico answered. "Les just shortstopped me, and, Liz wants your balls on a platter for interrupting her magical night out."

"Is that right?" Murphy chortled, readjusting his privates. He had been kicked by that loco Puerto Rican chick once before and the memory remained with him.

Rico inspected the judge's empty eye sockets.

"The eyeballs were stabbed out like the Santa body in Herald Square Park."

"An ice pick maybe?" Murphy guessed pointing out the scratches surrounding the sockets. "See these abrasions? They almost look like fingernail scratches. Could be trace evidence. Maybe we'll get a match from CODIS." The Combined DNA Index System was established and funded by the FBI to enable forensic laboratories to create searchable databases.

"If our suspect left his DNA," Rico agreed, "then Homeland Security might have a profile in the system. Then, he noticed something McElroy grasped in his dead cold hand. "What's he holding?"

Murphy uncurled the fingers, discovered a crucifix chain, and lifted it into a clear plastic evidence bag with the tip of his pen. "Hey, guys," he yelled to the patrol officers monitoring the perimeter, "let the M.E. into the scene, will ya?"

"It's going to be a long night," Rico said.

"And a longer morning," Murphy nodded, "especially when our friend, the Deputy Inspector, learns the identity of this DB on the steps."

"I already know who the dead body is," Deputy Inspector Morrison grumbled shuffling over to the corpse. "You mucks better get this case rolling before the crack of dawn!"

And just like that, their chance of solving the case depended on whether or not they could track down a suspect in the first forty-eight hours. In those first hours following a murder, the evidence was fresh. Witnesses still remembered what they saw or heard, and it was more likely DNA and other samples survived that timeframe.

Any time after the First 48:

The chances of finding a suspect waned.

Chapter 18

Squirrelling Around

THE BLACK PANTHER exited the subway at 59th Street at Columbus Circle.

Named after Christopher Columbus, the marble statue at the center of the loop was erected as part of New York's 1892 celebration of the 400th anniversary of Columbus' landing in America.

The scent of baking bread filled Darius' nose as he pushed past the statue–he never seemed to notice it standing sentinel before his very eyes–and squinted in the direction of the bakery, his mouth watering with hopes of an afternoon apple turnover. That was his favorite because of its flaky dough filled with sweet, buttery apples.

Who the hell came up with that taste?

The ground lay blanketed from a short-lived snowstorm, the kind that allowed him to dream of winter and a cup of hot apple cider.

Two days had passed since the boys read the *New York Times* article of the missing judge; and, just this morning, Darius overheard a WABC News report that his naked body was discovered on the courthouse steps.

Crap, what if Stefan really dreamed of the murder?

As far as Darius was concerned, there was something very fishy about the whole situation. Born in Yonkers, a side street unmentionable ghetto, it was the place where he'd spent his childhood. Known on the street as the Black Panther, he could turn a dime to a dollar with little effort by pickpocketing, shoplifting, and scamming the street traffic.

His sleight of hand was so rapid that Midtown Vice Squad banned his Three Card Monty table from Times

Square. There was a baby born every minute, But a sucker came close behind. Today, he was anxious to meet Marco and Stefan. They'd planned to meet up with a handful of Central Park West trust-fund kids to rough things up during their weekly football game.

So, now, he hurried through Columbus Circle and past the towering effigy. He hadn't a clue that this was the point at which all distances to and from New York City was officially measured and he could care less what the statue was or wasn't. Like most New Yorkers, he considered sculptures mere attractions for camera wielding tourists.

Entering the park, he followed a pathway through the barren trees where a squirrel whizzed across the trail, scooped up an acorn, and began to crack it open just steps from where Darius stood.

"Hey, little guy," he whispered, spellbound by the unconcerned creature, sharing the same space, lost in its own thoughts. Then, as rapidly as it appeared, the fur ball scurried up an oak tree and disappeared from sight.

"Wow… that was seriously cool."

Then, he glimpsed something moving through the tree line. "What the hell is that?" Picking up a rock and flinging it with all his strength, he watched it crash into the trunk of a maple tree.

"Hello? Who's there?"

It's nonsense, his mind reasoned. *Storybook fears of killers stalking the park in search of flesh.*

Turning back onto the path, he shook his head and chuckled at the childish fears. It had been years since such thoughts of boogeymen had peeled back the layers of his brain. "I'm starting to think like Stefan, seeing monsters around every corner."

Suddenly, birds flew from the trees, their cries shattering the peace and tranquility of the park.

Here it comes; it's creeping 'round the corner.

Abruptly, a tree branch snapped and a hideous laugh echoed from behind him.

"Looking for me?"

Spinning to the voice, Darius saw the scariest Santa Claus he'd ever seen.

"Ho! Ho! Ho! It's the season to be jolly!"

"What the hell are you?" Darius yelled a moment before a blackjack slammed into his skull knocking him to his knees.

I tried to warn you, his mind mocked, *that the psycho was coming to ring your bell!*

Santa bent over Darius, bound his limbs with duct tape, and rapidly dragged the boy through the woods.

It was something you'd imagine to see in a horror movie; hard... senseless and scary as bat shit!

"Please, mister," Darius begged, his head aching from the crushing blow. "Please, man!"

"I'm making a list," Santa countered, dragging him through the snow. "I'm checking it twice, and I already know who's naughty and nice!"

Chapter 19

Rag Tag Friends

THROUGH THE TREES, Central Park's Sheep Meadow was absent the frolicking children who'd normally fill its greenery with shrieks of delight in springtime.

Gone were the blooming flowers and lounging teenaged lovers sprawled on blankets beneath the tree canopy.

What replaced those visions of spring was a ragtag assortment of spoiled teenagers playing tackle football in a foot of snow. They'd assemble here every week after Saint Patrick's bells silenced themselves following Mass.

"Hut one!" Stefan shouted, looking over the well-heeled players of his offensive line.

Juan, an overweight Mexican kid, was ready.

He knew how to win food eating contests, but wasn't the best at catching passes. But this time, things would be different. He'd catch everyone off guard, run right down the field, and score one for the team!

"Hut two!"

"Watch for the deep pass," Marco cautioned his teammates.

"Hut! Hut! Hut!" Stefan shrieked, as Juan hiked the ball, pushed through the defensive line, and ran for glory down the field. Scrambling into the pocket, he looked to the end zone and let the football fly.

"I got it," Juan yelled confidently, stretching his pudgy arms for the football and pulling it down moments before crashing to the ground just inches from the goal line.

The opposing team piled on, laughing and poking fun at the lardass who came up short.

"Damn, J-Man," Stefan teased. "You should've joined the Girl Scouts and sold cookies instead of attempting suicide on the field."

Everyone laughed.

"How could you fall," Marco teased, "just an ass-crack from the goal line? Nobody was even near you!"

Juan shot him the finger. "You should've kept your ass in Puerto Rico and you'd be dick deep in Chicano poontang right now."

Those were fighting words, had anyone else except Juan muttered them.

"You did just fine, J-Man," Stefan chuckled. "At least you tried and for that you should be proud."

Suddenly, the game was interrupted when a deafening scream echoed from the woods.

"Marco! Stefan! Help me!"

"What the hell?" Marco exclaimed. "That sounds like the Black Panther!"

The teenagers scrambled through the woods in search of the disembodied scream.

"Darius!" Stefan shrieked, penetrating the tree line with the boys close behind. "Darius, where are you, bro?"

Nothing… only an eerie silence filled their ears.

"Holy shit!" Juan remarked, pointing towards a trail of blood staining the freshly fallen snow.

Marco saw footprints leading through the woods. "Darius, can you hear me?"

"Please, help me!" Darius' frightened voice echoed through the windswept tree line. It was a scary, high-pitched squeal, the type that would cause their girlfriends to flinch with fright at a late night horror flick.

"It came from that way!" Juan pointed in the direction of Central Park Driveway, which looped the field.

They sprinted through the trees hell bent on vengeance for whoever triggered one of their own to scream for his life in the loneliness of the woodlands.

"Darius!" Marco shouted leading the boys out of the trees and onto a road where a man dressed as Santa shoved Darius into the back of a van.

"Marco!" Darius screamed. "Help me, bro!"

The boys sprinted for the van. However, before they could reach the vehicle, the abductor slammed the hatch, jumped inside and sped through the park as the boys chased after its bumper.

"No!" Marco yelled, falling to the ground with his hands in his face, "No!"

What Marco didn't see, and everyone else did, was Darius' fear filled gaze staring through the back window; his cheeks streaked with tears.

"Shit!" Stefan yelled. "Did anyone see what was written on the side of that van?"

"Manhattan's Best Meat," Juan offered, terror lining his expression. "That's what it said."

Chop, chop, slice, slice, the voice in Stefan's head whispered. *Gonna cut him up real pretty and nice!*

Marco glanced at Juan. "Is that what it really said?"

"I swear to God it did! It was a butcher shop van!"

Stefan ran into the woods searching for comfort.

"Stefan!" Marco yelled after him, "Stefan, come back!"

But nothing could stop Stefan's feet as he sprinted along Traverse Road in search of safety from his nightmares.

One thing was certain; the meat man had been stalking him since the day he was born.

Chapter 20

Connecting the Dots

RICO AND MURPHY searched through Judge McElroy's case files on the seventeenth floor of the Criminal Courts building.

There were thousands of active cases scheduled to come before the judge, and ten times that in the County Clerk's office.

Here, in judge's chambers, the décor was rich with the vestiges of a storied judicial career of locking up the filth that preyed on the city's law-abiding citizens.

Murphy knocked his knuckles against a six-foot-tall knight in shining armor where it stood sentinel at the entrance of the justice's chambers.

"What do you think this piece set McElroy back?"

"A couple of grand, at least," Rico muttered, thumbing through a stack of recent court cases.

"Damn and we struggle to pay our mortgages."

Rico shrugged. "Shit rolls downhill, partner."

"It is guys like the dead judge who shovel most of it our way."

"One thing's for sure," Rico agreed tossing files onto his growing stack. "The suspects are piling up like dirty old men in Heidi Fleiss' little black book. After an endless barrage of amassing these criminal cases, and listing possible killers, we have more questions than answers."

Murphy walked to the window and stared out across the East River. "The Judge sure had a great sight, I know people who would kill for a view like this."

Rico threw another file onto the pile and walked to the window. "Must've been nice, eating lunch and gazing at the Brooklyn Bridge."

"I don't get it. Why risk everything to knock off a County Court Judge?"

"McElroy wasn't whistling Dixie on Broadway," Rico answered. "They called him the *Million Year Man* for a reason. That's got to make a few haters want revenge."

"Sure," Murphy agreed. "He was known for wanting to hand out a million years of prison time before he retired; haters I get, but even the craziest of criminals know the hands off rule."

"No killing cops," Rico mumbled, "prosecutors, witnesses…"

"Or bench warmers," Murphy finished, scratching his head and turning his attention back to the files. Shuffling through recent rulings he was about to crack open a manila file when a blue-haired lady interrupted.

"Hello, detectives," she said, eyeing Rico suspiciously. "I'm Ethel, secretary to Judge McElroy here in the criminal part."

"Glad to meet you, Ethel," Murphy responded extending his hand. "I'm Sergeant Mike Murphy and this is Lieutenant Rico Martinez."

Rico was familiar with the studious old guard. He'd battled the old shrew one too many times when he'd sought to gain a signature on a questionable search warrant.

"Ah, yes," she replied with a grunt, "the bad boy tramper of Miranda waivers."

She referred to Rico's ongoing refusal to read defendants their Constitutional Miranda Rights before he smashed their heads into the pavement, forcing confessions.

Ethel was not one of his fans. She'd pounded it into him that the U. S. Supreme Court held admissions of guilt, elicited under intimidation, were unconstitutional and inadmissible in a court of law.

"What about the people they attack?" Rico had once yelled. "Don't *they* have rights?"

"Of course, they have rights, in a court of law."

"Bullshit," Rico caught himself mumbling–*but none of that mattered right now*–while staring into the wise old eyes of the soon to retire hag.

"Maybe," she said, handing Murphy a case file, "you guys ought to peek at these recent court cases. Are you familiar with the Santa Claus attacks nationally, the ones reported in the papers over the last few years?"

"Sure," Murphy answered. "A recent murder involving one of the victims is our biggest case right now."

"What's this got to do with the Santa case?" Rico questioned, shoving his hands into his pockets and staring at the floor like a third grader avoiding the stare of a pissed off teacher.

"Well, Mr. Detective... the last time anyone saw Judge McElroy alive he was walking through the park dressed as Santa Claus."

"Santa? Are you kidding?"

"Of course, I'm not kidding. He was on his way to a benefit for kids with cancer."

"Any idea who saw him last?"

"That's easy, our very own bailiff, Mike Owens. He informed me he talked with Judge McElroy as he left court that evening."

"Where is Mike right now?" Murphy asked.

"I'm not sure, but I can get you his cell number."

Chapter 21

Lair of the Cats

ᏴENEATH THE CITY STREETS, the dissonance of trains screeching along their tracks assaulted Darius' ears.

Agonizing pain pierced through his shoulders at his slightest movement. The throbbing ran down his spine, causing him to grit his teeth.

"Hey! Please let me go!"

The Black Panther was captive in the darkness.

A blindfold shielded his vision and only Nat King Cole's *'The Christmas Song'* answered his cries as the thunderous clang of the subway faded in the distance. He could have sworn he heard someone muttering to the lyrics of chestnuts being roasted on an open fire. It wasn't more than a whisper, really; lips smacking, a voice fumbling with long-forgotten lyrics.

"Hello, help me! Please, somebody, answer me!"

He was about to pass out from the pain; the torture, it was similar to what spikes felt like if driven into flesh and punched through bone.

"Help you?" a gruff voice chuckled. "Why would anyone want to help someone like you?"

Darius' breathing quickened, his pulse raced and for the first time in life he was scared, *really* scared. Behind the blindfold his eyes twitched in fear, his fingers trembled and he imagined what came next might be worse than the pain shooting through his shoulders.

Then, the volume of the song rose, Nat King Cole shrieked in his ears... and that's when the Black Panther knew something else: Turning up a radio was something a serial killer did to drown out screams of a victim.

"Please, mister, puhleeeaaase!"

Shooting pain gripped Darius' collarbone as he twisted, desperately attempting to free himself from whatever held his body captive.

If only I could see him, then maybe I could make him understand.

Yet, he knew deep down inside where reason resided, there was no understanding madness. There would be no dramatic rescue on the Six O'clock News.

No superhero would charge into the lair and save him.

And then, as if on cue with a director's command in a Wes Craven slasher flick, the radio rose even louder to drown out his cries.

Darius screamed. "Turn it off, turn it off!"

"You know that Santa's on his way," the sinister voice began to sing. "He's loaded toys and goodies on his sleigh."

The monster screeched in a horrifying, devilish scream reminiscent of Michael Jackson's *Thriller* video and Vincent Price's wicked laughter, which boomed from the soundtrack just before the track ended.

"Holy fuck!" Darius screamed. "Get me outta here!"

"I don't want to hear you," The Santa Claus Killer grumbled. "Just shut your ill-bred mouth!"

"Help me, somebody!"

Suddenly, the blindfold was ripped from Darius' face and Santa's scowl invaded his vision.

Holy shit, take a look at this guy!

The man smelled like decaying bodies, a foulness Darius hadn't whiffed since Marco and he had stumbled onto a prostitute's corpse in a crack house months before. Anyone who's walked past a supermarket dumpster has winced at that horrid stench.

"Hello, young man," Santa shrieked. "Remember me?"

Darius stuttered in fear. "Who-oo ah, ah, are you, mmm-man?" His bladder let loose and urine ran down his legs pooling on the filthy floor.

"You don't remember me, then?" Santa frowned with disappointment. "Tsk, tsk, tsk, I would have thought you'd man up and take some responsibility!"

Darius understood all too well, who the rancid man was. "Just leave me alone! I don't have any problem with you."

"Come on, now," Santa snickered shuffling to a workbench and picking up his hatchet. "There's no need for silly fat lies. After all, this is your big day. Yes, it is."

Darius was gripped in horror's embrace as he glanced around the abandoned subway cavern.

Newspaper articles covered the walls and...

Oh, my God!

Dozens of dead cats hung from fishhooks, their eye sockets empty, the flesh rotting from their skeletons.

"Oh, no!" the Black Panther bawled, shaking in fear and staring at his reflection in a broken mirror hanging directly across from where he hung suspended on rusted chains. Huge meat hooks had been punched through his shoulders, holding him by the collarbone.

"No sense trying to move," Santa stated while sharpening a hatchet. "You have beef hooks in your back. Nobody ever gets *off the hook* that easy!" He laughed insanely at his own joke.

"What do you want?"

"Nothing more than you can give," he answered, pointing towards the newspapers. "Just like the others gave."

Darius stared at the yellowed articles attached to the stone walls.

THE DEATH OF SANTA CLAUS
Washington D.C. Police on the Case

SILENT NIGHT, DEADLY NIGHT
Charleston S.C. Cops Find Slain Santa

Santa hurried towards Darius with a smile on his face and the hatchet swinging at his side.

"It's time to tell Santa what you want for Christmas."

"No man! Get away from me!"

Santa crept towards his victim, his rotten black teeth stabbing through cracked lips.

"It's time to pay the piper!"

Each step, the killer knew from past experience, would bring a piercing, gut wrenching scream from deep within the boy hanging on the hooks.

"Nooooooooooo! Don't you come any closer!"

But there was no getting out of this.

This was how things ended.

The way darkness found millions every year.

A knife, gun, hatchet… the tool might change but the method remained steady. MURDER in America was as commercial as apple pie and, well, Santa Claus.

"Momma!" Darius yelled. "Jesus…"

Santa hobbled beside the swinging body, sniffed the boy's stench, and smiled.

"You're going to taste great, boy!"

The last thing Darius experienced was the madman's stench and the pain of chopping steel as Santa hacked him to pieces while mumbling parody lyrics of *Jingle Bells*.

And then, there was nothing, except the sound of blood dripping onto the stone floor.

Chapter 22

Snooping Billionaires

MURPHY LOVED STARBUCKS.

Usually a tall caramel Frappuccino lightly blended worked its magic, but today he went for a heart attack dose of caffeine...the grand energy booster.

Five hour energy my ass!

"Remember," Rico asked. "Mayor Bloomberg and his gestapo attempting ban on large sugary drinks?"

"He'd have to lock me up," Murphy chuckled, "and toss away the key to get my cup of Joe."

"Frigging dictator is what he was," Rico griped. "Can't we bring back Rudy? Now that was a mayor I could *and did...* follow into the trenches."

Rudolph William Louis "Rudy" Giuliani was the 107th Mayor of New York City from 1994 through 2001, and as far as Rico was concerned, he was a hero way before Queen Elizabeth bestowed the real honor on the mayor who should have been America's President.

The Honorary Knighthood was a direct result of his heroic leadership during the 911 attacks.

"Times are shifting, partner," Murphy jabbed. "You're out of touch and lost in memories of the good ole days."

"Just drink your coffee," Rico ordered, "before the new mayor walks through the door and snatches it from your cold trembling hands."

Murphy chuckled and glanced through Starbucks' windows at the people navigating Canal Street. It was situated two blocks from the criminal courts building.

"Did the bailiff say what time he'd get here?"

Before Rico could answer, Mike Owens ambled through the door shaking snowflakes from his hat.

"Lieutenant Rico!" he bellowed to his old friend. "Are you staying out of trouble with the brass asses?"

Rico shook his hand. "Hell, no... *brass ballbusters* is what they are. You're looking pretty good for an old man!"

"Gotta love the court system," the bailiff chuckled, removing his service coat and throwing it over a wooden backed chair. "They'll let me drop dead standing beside the judge!" Removing his leather gloves, he called the waitress behind the counter. "Let me get the usual, Crystal."

"Sure thing, Mike," the strawberry blonde responded. "I'll be right over with mocha."

It's time to get down to business, Murphy thought, *while the aging bailiff still has a pulse.* Pulling out an evidence bag containing the crucifix chain, he showed it to Mike.

"Ever seen this before? We found it on the judge."

"Nah and I doubt old man *Lead Bottom* would be caught dead wearing that old guilt enticer."

"Ha!" Murphy snorted. "Why's that?"

"His Honor only wore the Star of David. He converted to Judaism after quite a bit of bitching and moaning from that commandant wife of his."

"Unbelievable!" Murphy smiled. "Is there anything sacred to booty whipped married men?"

The elderly bailiff laughed. "You must not be hitched, Son, because if you were, those words would've been knocked from your noggin long ago. Trust me; resistance is futile to the destroyers of peace and tranquility."

They laughed in appreciation of that one liner.

"Mike," Rico asked, "you were the last to see Judge McElroy at the courthouse, isn't that right?"

"Oh, yeah, sure, we met up just inside Collect Pond Park. He was inhaling a Sabrett like a starved Ethiopian while dressed as Santa Claus. I guess his wife still allowed him to play the part. It was a hell of a sight."

"Why's that?" Murphy asked, making notes.

"Well, if you knew Lead Bottom like I did, after working his courtroom for twenty years; you knew two very important things about him."

"Lead Bottom?"

"The judge was shot in the ass while hunting in the Adirondacks. They say he walked for miles, without complaining. Anyway, he wasn't the smiling, happy go lucky type… that's the first thing."

"And the second? What's that?"

The bailiff grinned. "Old Lead Bottom was certainly no Santa Claus and he was one cheap cocksucker."

Murphy glanced at Rico in silent understanding.

This was their first insight into how others privately viewed the judge, and both detectives understood these sharp views needed to be explored much deeper.

"What do you mean, Mike?" Rico prodded. "That he was certainly no Santa Claus?"

"Look, you know that McElroy was Manhattan's Hanging Judge? A real defender of the victim, he always sent the scumbags to Downstate Correctional to begin serving hefty prison sentences."

Rico knew all about the maximum-security prison. It acted as a classification reception center where newly convicted criminals were housed for weeks before transferring to permanent, long-suffering penitentiaries.

"His Honor," the bailiff continued, "was certainly no Santa Claus. In fact, we often thought he'd carry coal up to those prisoners if the state would let him, and he might have personally handed it out to the lifers in their cells."

"Right," Murphy chuckled. "But on the day you saw him outside the courthouse, eating his hot dog, he *was* dressed as Santa."

The bailiff shrugged. "He was playing a role, that's all… for those poor kids stuck in their beds at the cancer hospital."

"Ethel said he went there every year," Rico confirmed. "Do you know how he got there?"

Mike pondered the question, trying to recall a long lost memory. Then, almost as if he'd been smacked in the head, he smirked.

"Yeah, right after we joked about the jail being a Motel Six and how we were leaving the lights on for the criminals, the judge continued through the park towards Lafayette Street. I saw him talking to a reporter from Eyewitness News."

"Do you know who the reporter was?"

"Timothy Smith, the crime correspondent who hangs around the courtroom like an ambulance chaser seeking life altering injuries."

"Tim Smith," Rico reiterated. "You sure it was him?"

"Absolutely, I rode my bike past him and the judge who were standing in front of the Family Court."

"You ride a bike?"

"Sure, why not. I have to keep my heart ticking or else the fat lady sings."

Chapter 23

Rhyme & Reason

THE MURDERING FIEND pushed his shopping cart along Canal Street's desolate subway platform.

The basket brimmed with black plastic bags dripping blood onto the concrete walkway.

Glancing to a digital clock embedded in the wall, he noticed it was after midnight, and dear old Santa couldn't resist delivering his gifts.

You forgot to put the monkey suit on, Mammy's ghostly voice scolded, *how the hell are you going to deliver the presents without your outfit?*

Richard wasn't dressed as the king of Christmas right now. He figured it would look fishy to the *neighborhood watch* crowd. He'd spied their kind once or twice before.

They'd hide behind heavy curtains while snooping through windows at private things which were none of their business.

"Just like that time in Key West," he mumbled, "when I caught a peeper watching me do my deed; nasty little John Walsh tipsters."

He enjoyed playing the game, trying to blend in and catching them off guard. Sometimes it worked to his advantage to appear as a homeless, isolated, bum... stumbling aimlessly down the street.

You'll be the man of the hour, Daddy whispered in his head, *and the toast of the town.*

It's going to be a wonderful Christmas, Mammy agreed.

But Richard didn't care one bit about the hogwash his parents ghosts constantly uttered interrupting his thoughts and invading his privacy.

"Uh-uh, I don't care about you people one bit!"

What he did care about were the expressions of fear sure to line the boys' faces when they un-wrapped the gifts.

"Three blind mice... see how they run!"

But there aren't THREE anymore, are there? Mammy cackled, her shrill... *hehehehehehehehe...* jabbing into Santa's thoughts like a knife stabbing a side of beef.

The killer laughed at their silliness while making his way up the subway ramp. All the while, his parents yapped to one another.

And then there were TWO, Daddy chuckled.

Three minus one... equals two, Mammy agreed.

"Everything would have been just fine," Richard growled, "if the bastards hadn't invaded my space... all I tried to do was... get better."

Indeed, things had been improving.

He hadn't killed anyone in years.

And most importantly, the sessions with the psychiatrist were working. Nobody was interfering with his life.

That was, until the brat and his friends leapt from the car and beat him to a pulp outside Macy's. That's when the voices of Mammy and Daddy roared back with a vengeance. The beating got their ghostly dander up and offered the spirits something to talk about.

Dirty rotten thugs, Mammy whined. *They'll be sorry... just like the judge who let the boy walk free!*

Richard despised the mumbling control freaks that brought him into this world. There was a time when he believed all he had to do was end their lousy lives to shut them up. And that's what he did... cutting their throats and shutting their mouths... once and for all.

But *that* act made things *worse*. He hadn't planned on their ghosts coming back to haunt him.

Yet, here they are... yammering on and on!

Don't forget what's in those big plastic bags! Daddy whispered.

Glancing at the bags, Richard *laughed*–no, that's not right–he *shrieked* with joy.

Just like in the movies, Mammy muttered, *the black guy always gets knocked-off first.* She cackled like a loon out in the woods. Day-in and day-out, Richard recalled the birds hooting... *on and on...* until, one day, he silenced the *loonies* with a slingshot and BB's. One by one, he picked them off, watching as they fell from the trees splattering their guts onto the ground.

"Yap! Yap! Yap!" Richard sarcastically grumbled. His muttering parents wouldn't shut the hell up no matter what he did. So he pushed his cart into elevator #325 and pressed the S-button to ferry him up to Canal Street. Glancing at the surveillance camera nestled in the corner of the elevator; he smiled a rotten grin.

After the Saudi's attacked New York on that fateful day of 911, the MTA installed over 507 cameras just like this one whose video feeds were transmitted to the NYPD Command Center.

But that doesn't matter, he thought, *because all the Homeland Security snoopers could see was a bum pushing garbage. And nobody cares about lazy rats like them.*

The elevator door whined open and he pushed out onto Canal, which was absent the haters, tipsters, and goddamn witnesses who could end it all at a moment's notice.

Now, only cat sized rats scurried through the lonely dark city in search of food to fill their infected stomachs.

And bums like you, Daddy chuckled, *no good freaks that roam the streets and murder hard working folks.*

Mommy Dearest couldn't refuse. *Why'd you kill us, Son? What did we ever do to deserve being hung like pigs in the freezer?*

The giver of gifts ignored her annoying complaints, hurried along the sidewalk, turned down Mulberry, and pushed his cart of presents around the corner to Bayard Street. There, he scurried to the entrance of *Manhattan's*

Best Meat Market and glanced at a pile of trash bags sitting at the curb awaiting the morning collection.

There's much better stuff in there, Daddy snorted, *than what lies in your shopping cart!*

Glancing up and down the street, the killer reached into his pocket and slipped a key into the butcher shop lock.

Better hurry up, Son, Mammy enticed. *Your meat is starting to rot!*

The gifts he needed to deliver were beginning to stink like his parents' corpses, just before he hung them on their hooks.

Chapter 24

Shoulda! Woulda! Coulda!

$\mathcal{D}$AYS PASSED since Santa stepped from the shadows, swung his hatchet, and stole the Black Panther's life.

As it turned out, Darius wasn't as fast as a panther.

"We should call the cops," Stefan urged.

He was following Marco up a set of rusty, groaning, fire escape stairs hugging the building's facade. In the distance, firewood smoke billowed from chimneys.

"You think we could still do it?" Stefan continued.

They stepped onto the snow swept roof where they often assembled to stare into the sky while baring their broken souls to one another.

"Do what?" Marco asked. "Call the cops?"

"Yeah, just dial in an anonymous tip to crime stoppers."

"It would've been better if we did that yesterday," Marco shrugged, striking a match and lighting the end of his Newport cigarette.

"Yeah. But, maybe we can still do it."

Marco stared into his buddy's eyes. It was the first time Stefan had questioned him on anything and that made Marco realize something. Gone was the scared little kid he found years ago and in his place stood a man.

"Don't hate the player, Stefan," Marco snickered, "hate the game." Reaching over, he lit Stefan's Marlboro that hung from his lips. "The lunatic Santa is the one who has to answer the cop's questions, if he lives to tell about it."

"We should have left him alone at Macy's!" Stefan admitted. "He'll always be a lowlife, no matter how many times we kick his sorry-ass."

Marco picked up a rock and threw it towards the frozen river. "Maybe, if we go on over there, we can find that child abuser and kill him this time."

They stood there on the roof, smoking their coffin nails–the smoke drifting from their noses–sizing up one another while holding their positions.

"It would be payback for everything," Marco continued.

"You think Darius will get away from him?"

Marco shrugged, walked to the roof ledge, and stared into the distance. "I think Darius will kill the guy for pulling this crap."

Stefan wasn't as sure as he pulled out an iPhone 5 and dialed Darius' number.

"YO! Wassup peeps?" Darius' voicemail squealed. "I'm probably getting my rocks off right now so leave a number."

Stefan pressed *end call*, "What are we going to do?"

"I don't know, but we have to find Santa. This reminds me of losing my Dad, when he went to prison for beating my Mom. I didn't feel anything for him. I didn't miss him or hate him, or care that he was gone. I was just numb. But a few years later, my Mother got a call from Eastern Correctional Facility saying my Father had dropped dead of a heart attack." He paused then, shook his head, and gazed at the river below. "I cried for days. I never forgave my Father for hurting my Mom, for leaving me, but most of all, for giving up on us."

Stefan placed his hand on his friend's shoulder, not saying anything, just listening, understanding.

"It killed her. It took the life right out of her, you know? She was never the same after that."

Stefan was filled with sorrow for his friend.

"What happened to her?"

Marco pointed to the George Washington Bridge spanning the Hudson River, reflecting the moon on its icy surface. "One night, on her way home from Jersey she walked through the snow, across the bridge and climbed atop the railings."

There wasn't anything to be said. It was just the two of them tending to wounds that would never heal.

"Later, I found out the cops just let her go, they watched her leap into the abyss. To them, she was just another Puerto Rican lost to the currents of the river."

"Pigs," Stefan mumbled in anger.

"She jumped," Marco continued, motioning a downward swoop with his hand, "right into the frozen river, taking with her my heart and any feeling I ever had for anything."

Then, silence embraced them for a moment as they stared at the river and the secrets they knew it held.

"Since that day, I've hated my Father for a lot of reasons, but most of all, for killing my Mother and tearing her from my life." Glancing back to Stefan, he nodded. "It wasn't her that abandoned me, Stefan. It was my Father!"

"I know, bro, I know."

"That's enough for the both of us," Marco agreed.

There, standing on the rooftop with the winter moon shining down on them, Marco knew something else, too.

"Sometimes, Stefan, the people who abandon us are not the people who walk away; it's destiny."

"Yeah," Stefan retorted.

Marco put his arm on his friend's shoulder. "Tomorrow, we look for Darius, because we know what it means to be alone and we won't abandon him."

"No," Stefan agreed. "We'll never abandon the Black Panther." He knew they had demons to battle that night as they stared at the waterway. They were two friends, lost along the twists and turns of life, trying to find their way. "It looks like we're going to get some more snow."

"Yeah, is that right?" Marco grinned. "Maybe tomorrow we can check out the Rockefeller Center Christmas tree, kind of get a feel for the holidays!"

"That would be awesome," Stefan nodded.

However, between the two boys existed a nagging sense of doom lingering on the night breeze, a warning that their lives were about to change... *forever*.

"There's a cold wind coming," Marco said. "We have to be careful not to lose our way!"

Chapter 25

Here Comes Santa Claus

THE BUTCHER SHOP sat on the corner of Bayard and Mulberry in the heart of Chinatown.

In daylight, tourists could be glimpsed laying down mounds of cash for the hottest designer knock-offs.

Louis Vuitton… Chanel, and Dolce & Gabbana.

They all fell off the back of trucks.

Inside the loneliness of the slaughterhouse, devilish undertakings were cloaked by nightfall. A dim light flickered in the carving room as Richard stomped past a hardwood butcher block and into a commercial walk-in freezer dragging his large plastic bags.

Better be careful, Mammy muttered. *It's a little too close for my liking!*

"Things were going so good," Richard mumbled in regret of his current circumstance. "For close to a year my sessions with the psychiatrist worked out just fine."

Bullshit! Daddy screamed. *You hung him in the freezer beside a leg of lamb!*

"Don't you two ever stop?" Richard shrieked to the ghosts. "When can I live life without you butting in?"

Just admit it, Daddy demanded. *Tell us what you did.*

It was late one night just days after the boys beat Richard's ass outside Macy's. The moon was full in a clear dark sky and he could have sworn a moment of peace and quiet calmed his thoughts. There were no voices of damnation. No recriminations or finger pointing.

It was tranquil.

And then, hours later, he went to his weekly scheduled session with the good old doctor who knew too much and prodded too deeply into his private thoughts.

"Tell me about the beating," the nutcracker probed handing over another cheap Dollar Store tissue.

They'd been through it on the phone, about how the kids jumped from the car and beat him into the pavement.

How the *boy* had embarrassed him.

"I don't want to talk about it."

Nevertheless, that wasn't what the Mind Invader wanted to hear from someone placed in his care by the New York County criminal court system.

The shrink picked up the phone.

"I'm going to have to call the probation officer. You don't want to go back to Rikers Island, do you?"

Kill his head-shrinking ass, Mammy ordered. *Bring him on over to the shop and hang him up.*

Richard didn't remember how it happened, that exact moment when he charged the doctor and beat him to death with the receiver of the phone. And then, later, in the dead of night, how he removed the headshrinker's eyes so they couldn't stare at him from beyond the grave.

The fiend shook his head now, released the horrific memory, and glanced at the dead doctor hanging on a meat hook in the center of the walk in freezer.

"You dumb idiot, look at you now; the hospital will be looking for you!"

It was a disgrace, too. Because the meetings *were* starting to get through to Richard; he *was* getting better.

Gone was his need to strangle little kittens who stared with damning gazes that scorched his soul when they leered in his direction.

"*We know what you are,*" the cats purred.

And so, they too, ended up in his lair, with their eyes ripped out and their tongues removed from their mouths.

That'll fix them, honey, Mammy murmured. *Nine lives my ass!*

That was a week ago.

He blinked away the memory and grabbed the garbage bags, turned out the freezer light and ambled back into the carving room.

Better get a move on, Son, Daddy uttered. *Don't want to be late for this delivery.*

Walking to the rear exit of the butcher shop, The Santa Claus Killer pressed a red button that opened the loading dock door.

"Almost back home," he mumbled to the bags. "You're going to make a perfect gift for those devilish friends of yours." Dragging them onto the loading dock, he opened the meat wagon hatch and tossed them in.

Not much of a one horse open sleigh, Mommy Dearest spat. *What kind of Santa drives a butcher van?*

Richard grumbled, stepped into the wagon, and drove through an alley, which would start him along his way to Washington Heights.

Smiling, he mumbled a favorite tune.

♫ *Here comes Santa Claus,*
Here comes Santa,
Right down Santa Claus lane! ♫

Chapter 26

Special Delivery

A FAT RAT SCURRIED across the flophouse floor, its bulging eyes nervously darting about like a crackhead searching for crumbs to banish the monkey clinging to the back.

Tick... tick... tick...tick...

The rat's nails scratched along the floor as it bounded onto the cracked coffee table and nibbled on a half-eaten quarter-pounder with cheese.

Quarter-pounder... *what a joke!*

Had a crackhead been present he'd have sworn the rodent smiled as its jaws tore the burger to shreds.

Hearing the building's entrance door squeaking on rusty hinges from somewhere downstairs, Marco snapped awake on the bedbug-infested couch.

"Stefan, is that you?"

Only silence answered.

Dim moonlight shone through the broken window and he noticed Mighty Whitey's sleeping bag lay empty in the corner of the room. That's when he heard heavy footfalls echoing out on the creaking wooden staircase.

Rolling off the couch, he blinked sleep from his eyes and grabbed a battered Smith and Wesson .38 revolver from the table.

It can't be Stefan.

He knew this because they both purposely avoided those particular steps. It was a failsafe warning system of advancing danger.

"Stefan. Where the hell are you?"

The rat leapt from the table and scampered through the room desperately fleeing as its *danger senses* rang in its head.

Marco spun towards the creature and watched as it scurried through a hole in the wall, and then...

He sighed in relief.

"Disgusting, rat infested shithole."

Footsteps shuffled closer, they were moving down the hall and approaching the apartment door.

Creeping towards the door, Marco leveled the gun before him, his finger tickling the trigger... waiting. He imagined that Jason from *Friday the 13th* might be about to knock down the door. Goosebumps of anxiety crept up his spine. Sweat rolled down his brow, and for an instant, *just a fleeting second...* he sensed the icy tendrils of death lurking.

Suddenly, a movement from the window caused him to spin, aim the gun, and fire a shot.

Stefan leaped to the floor, covered his ears, and stared at the hole in the wall where his head had just been.

"Damn, Marco! What are you trying to do? Blow my head off?"

"Stefan?" Marco panicked. "Are you okay?" He lowered the gun, ran to his friend, and examined his body for the gaping wound sure to be oozing blood. "Are you hit? Did I shoot you?"

Stefan stared at his friend in annoyance. What he wanted to do was reach back into the last century, swing with all his might, and connect the most powerful bitch slap ever known to man.

That's what I should do, just let one fly and slap the taste out of his mouth!

"No, you didn't hit me. But that was close! What the hell were you thinking?"

Then, from just outside the apartment door, they overheard a thump and a deep bellowing chuckle.

Page 96

"What the hell is that?" Stefan whispered picking himself off the floor and hurrying to a hazy peephole burrowed through the door.

"That's what I'm trying to tell you!" Marco whispered. "There's somebody out there!"

"You're trying to tell me with a bullet?" Stefan spat peering into the dark hallway. "There's nobody out there, but I think there's something at the foot of the doorway."

"What is it?" Marco asked, pushing his friend aside and peering through the glass. "It looks like trash bags." They lured him, like a horror flick actor who opened the entrance to discover a killer with a hatchet on the other side. Glancing to Stefan, he turned the doorknob.

"Get behind me, bro, just in case I have to shoot somebody." It was distress and swagger mixed with nerves that offered wishful courage to utter such things.

Turning the deadbolt, it disengaged with a click as Marco inched the door open on squeaking hinges. The hallway was pitch-black and he couldn't see more than ten paces into the darkness. However, what did come into view were two large bags and dark blood on the floor.

"What the heck?" Stefan shrieked shielding his nose against the stench.

Marco leveled the gun at one of the bags and pulled free a red twist tie that held it closed. What rolled out onto the floor and into their nightmare was the rotting, eyeless skull of Darius!

Both boys screamed like two bitches running through the woods late at night...

Chapter 27

Sticks & Bones

CHIEF MEDICAL EXAMINER, Dr. William Heung, was arranging body parts on his autopsy table when he discovered the bloody hand written note.

Sticks and Stones may break my bones,
...but names will never hurt me.

It was scribbled onto a yellow sticky-pad taped to the torso of Darius Williams, *AKA*, The Black Panther.

"He's toying with us," Captain Anton McKenzie growled. "That scumbag is taunting the entire department."

Two plus two, must land on four. It could never add up to anything else. That was especially true when homicide similarities began to emerge.

There is a pattern here.

And Anton knew patterns *turned* into serial killings.

Murphy and Rico stood mute leaning against the morgue's puke-green tiled wall. They understood why the division commander stood over their victim. Manhattan South Homicide couldn't afford another scandal like that of the former police commissioner. He had dispatched high-ranking supervisors, in the dead of night, to search for a cellphone and jewelry his girlfriend believed stolen from her purse while at a news station. Detectives fingerprinted, photographed, and threatened arrest of manufactured suspects in their households. The problem was, a theft never took place, and homicide detectives were improperly coerced into ushering forth special favors. The cellphone was found in a garbage can near the TV studio, and the jewelry at the bottom of the lady-friend's purse.

It was all laid bare in the *Daily News* for all to read.

"No more scandals or mishandling of cases," the deputy inspector had passed down the chain of command. "Everything will be by the book and no half-assed leaks!"

And so, here was the commander breathing down their backs at Five O'clock in the morning.

"First, Santa," Murphy said. "Then, the Judge's corpse and that handwritten note of justice being blind, I just don't get the connection."

But there had to be one, everyone agreed.

"Well," the captain barked, "you can bet your Irish shamrock that Deputy Inspector Morrison will be shoving a stick up my ass on this one. The case is bothering him."

The Medical Examiner placed the note into an evidence collection bag. "All three of your victims have one thing in common."

"What's that, the missing eyes?" McKenzie guessed.

Dr. Heung nodded. "The assassin is utilizing the same piece of steel to punch out the eyes in all three of your cases. Something similar to an icepick, and on this note, there's a fingerprint on the corner, but I doubt the Latent Prints Department will match it to a suspect."

"Why is that, Doc?"

"It's the same type of note we found on the body of Judge McElroy," Rico argued with the M.E., "and most certainly the forensic department will match that handwriting."

The Medical Examiner shook his head. "The analysis of fingerprints requires comparison of three basic patterns; arches, loops, and whorls. As you guys know, the most common fingerprint pattern is the loop. If you look at this print, the ridges start at one side of the finger, loop around the tip, and come back to the same side they started on."

"Then why won't we get a hit on it?" Murphy asked.

The doctor took a pen and traced the exterior of the plastic baggie containing the sticky-pad. "If you look at your own hands, the chances are you have at least one fingerprint of this type. Over sixty percent of all fingerprints are loops."

That's exactly what everyone saw.

"The problem is, whoever left his print used the victim's own fingers to handle the note."

"Are you freaking kidding me?" McKenzie fumed. "The killer used the victim's hand to tape the note to the body?"

"Yup," the M.E. nodded. "I compared the corpse's print to the one you have on the note. They're the same. You have a smart suspect running around out there."

Murphy shook his head. "That leaves us with the two homeless teenagers. Maybe they can tell us why someone would want to chop up their friend."

"Where are they now, Murphy?" McKenzie inquired.

"They're cooling their jets down at Two-Thirty East Twenty-First Street."

"Keep me posted. I'm going home to catch a few hours sleep." The captain had been burning the midnight oil on a half dozen cases and was about to pass out on his feet.

At least somebody would get some sleep.

For Murphy and Rico, sleep was a commodity that would escape them until their *First 48* wound down to zero.

Chapter 28

Cat's Outta the Bag

$\mathcal{D}$ETECTIVE RICO MARTINEZ watched Arias snaking his way through Manhattan South's squad room.

"Hey, John," Rico nodded, seeing his longtime friend. "What brings you up to the big leagues?"

"Sleepless nights, Lieutenant, plus a few suspicious ramblings of mine have been confirmed by the morning news."

"Is that right? I didn't take you for a news junkie."

"A bloodhound detective at your service, how is the new kid, Romero, working out?"

"Not bad. He's got a chip on his shoulder the size of a baseball, but who doesn't at that age?"

The two men had a history. Back before either had considered serving decades in the department, they'd suffered through the academy by the skin of their noses, with the help of multiple drunken nights in Paddy's.

"I think I have some pertinent information," Arias offered, "on Judge McElroy's murder."

"Is that right? How did you come upon it?"

The realization literally slapped Arias across his face just an hour prior while gulping his third cup of coffee. He had flipped on ABC News and found the video of Murphy leading Stefan Berks to an unmarked unit. And then he watched the report of the black kid found chopped to pieces in black plastic bags.

"They're all connected to one room," Arias whispered in Rico's ear. "The dead Santa Claus, McElroy and the black kid you found a few hours ago."

Rico froze. There were moments in life he could point to, nod his head and have one of those... *ah-ha* moments. This, he realized, wasn't something he wanted others to hear.

"Why don't we step into my office, never know where the leaks are in this department."

Hurrying through dozens of cramped cubicles assigned to nosy junior detectives, they pushed into a sparsely furnished corner office.

"You need a decorator in here," Arias joked. "Where's all your stuff?"

"I've been lugging it home; I'm taking the long walk in three weeks."

"Really! Liz convinced you to throw in the cuffs?"

"Just trading them in, Miami Beach P.D. gave me four stars and a white shirt."

"No shit? Deputy Chief in Miami Beach, bet your boys are going to love that, huh?"

Rico collapsed into his metal backed chair behind an old steel desk and pointed to an empty armchair.

"Have a seat. Tell me what the hell you're talking about with this connection."

"Remember me telling you last week that I was in court for a case I caught that had to do with this kid who threw a bottle at the Macy's Santa Claus?"

"Sure," Rico interrupted. "Sometime after Mac's funeral, the Berks kid, right?"

"The whole city was at Mac's funeral, eh?" Arias recalled. "I got drunker than two Scottish whores."

"Get ready to do it again; we're having my farewell party there."

"Gonna be sorry to see you go. Who's going to take your place?"

"Dunno," Rico frowned. "Maybe they'll give Murphy a step up, but he should be in other places, like the U.S. Marshalls Office or something like that."

THE SANTA CLAUS KILLER

Arias grunted. "Anyway, as you know, the bottle throwing case got tossed because the victim didn't want to dirty his hands."

"No appearance in court," Rico nodded.

"Correct. He thought it would tarnish the image of Christmas if the official Santa Claus had to show his face in a courtroom."

Rico laughed, reached into his pocket, pulled out a Kool and lit it. "He might have something there."

"Isn't it illegal," Arias pointed out, "to smoke in city buildings?"

"So, arrest me." Rico said inhaling deeply. "Smoking is also illegal in all New York parks, beaches, and even in the plazas on Times Square. Screw 'em."

Arias went on. "Here's the thing. The courtroom was full of Santas in support of the arrest."

"How does this help me?" Rico asked flicking his ashes on the floor.

Arias shook his head. "The funniest thing was, this Santa who you found on the park bench…"

"Jack Berrymoore," Rico interrupted.

"Yeah, that's him. Anyway, he stood up in the courtroom and…"

"What?" Rico exclaimed and leapt from his desk. "Wait a minute! Are you telling me Berrymoore, my first murder victim, was in the courtroom that day?"

"You bet, along with McElroy, the black kid who wound up dead this morning and this teenager, Stefan Berks."

"How long have you sat on this?"

"Like I said, it dawned on me this morning when I saw a photo of Berks on the news. I remembered him from the courtroom, and then I realized all three of your victims were in that courtroom!"

"Mother of Christ! You know what this means, John, don't you?"

"My guess is your killer was in that courtroom, too!"

No sooner than Rico realized the connection, junior detective, Robert Romero hurried into the office.

"Hey, Rico, I think all three homicides are connected."

"No shit, Sherlock!" Arias snapped. "What took you so long to figure it out?"

Chapter 29

Close Encounters

FOLEY'S PUB AND RESTAURANT was named after Red Foley, a legend among New York sports writers.

The pub boasted one of the best sports memorabilia collections in the country. Signed mementos from Joe DiMaggio and Bill Parcells hung on the walls.

But none of that made the joint famous.

What made Foley's a renowned watering hole was when its owner refused to play *'Danny Boy'* on Saint Patty's day.

That little stunt caused more than eight-hundred newspapers worldwide to scream from their ivory towers.

> *An Irish Pub?*
> *Without Danny Boy?*
> *Unheard of!*

The news reverberated around the globe making Foley's a destination for international tourists and, more importantly, Manhattan reporters.

That's what brought Santa Claus to be seated in a whiskey leather booth staring at the back of Tim Smith's head as he downed a glass of Irish whiskey.

"You have a hell of a job, Tim," the bartender supposed refilling the newscaster's glass. "Robbery, scandal, and death every night, live and in color, on TV!"

An erotic brunette with Radio City Rockette limbs leaned over, licked Tim's neck, and whispered into his ear.

"I got a story for you, baby."

Tim spun to his assistant, clutched her buttocks, and kissed her luscious lips. "I bet you do, Sweetie Pie!"

"I'm going to slaughter that bitch!" Santa muttered rising from the booth, seizing his empty glass, and hurrying past an elderly couple seated at a table.

Lucky little metrosexual, Daddy's ghost taunted, *why can't you get a piece of ass like that, huh?*

Santa stared at her legs and imagined them wrapped around his waist as they bucked in his fairytale.

Because your son is a girly man, Mammy responded to her husband. *Just like your brother and his South Beach Cuban lover!*

The giver of gifts bit his tongue to hold back a few choice words he craved to roar in angered complaint.

See? Mammy spat, driving home her point. *His sorry-ass can't even speak up for himself.*

Santa disregarded the ignorance of her manner and stepped onto the black and white tiled floor at the bar.

"Hey," he interrupted the correspondent, a deceiving smile lining his face. "You're that guy from the TV, Tim Smith, right?"

The newsman released the girl.

"Tim Smith," he confirmed, holding out his hand, "and you must be, Santa Claus, huh?"

The bartender walked over, eyed the costume, and picked up Santa's glass. "Can I get you anything else, Santa?"

"Pabst Blue Ribbon, and set one up for my friend."

"Thanks," Tim smiled. "I didn't catch your real name?"

Tell the man your name, Mammy whispered. *He'll crack right up once you say you're The Santa Claus Killer.*

But before he could answer, the noontime Eyewitness Newscast appeared on the flat screen over the bar.

"Hey," Tim hollered to the bartender. "Give me a break with the self-portrait, will ya?"

"Early this morning," the news anchor began, "detectives from Manhattan South

Homicide were called out to Washington Heights where they discovered dismembered body parts of a teenage African American boy. For that story we take you to Eyewitness News', Timothy Smith." A pre-recorded news report replaced the anchor and showed Tim Smith standing outside Manhattan South.

"Matty," Tim shouted again, "turn that crap off, please!"

"Sure thing," the bartender replied, turning the channel over to Sports Center.

"What's wrong?" Santa chuckled. "You don't like seeing yourself on TV?"

The correspondent glanced curiously at the grinning Santa. *There's something unnatural about that face.* It reminded him of Jack Nicholson's portrayal of the Joker in *Batman. Except this is Santa Claus.*

"It's kind of like watching reruns, you know? I already know the outcome."

"Yeah," Santa replied. "I get the same feeling when the TV displays me on the screen."

Timothy chuckled. "We're two peas in a pod, eh?"

The killer was intrigued sitting beside the reporter. *After all, this is the guy who's gonna make me famous.*

"What did you say your name was?" the reporter once again inquired.

Imagine what he would think, Mammy muttered, *if you told him you're the real deal.*

Santa reached out his hand. "My friends call me the butcher."

"Oh, yeah?" the reporter chuckled. "Why is that?"

"Because... I'm the one who cuts up bodies."

The reporter shook his head and slapped his new acquaintance on the back.

"That makes perfect sense," he laughed, "a Santa Claus who butchers cows, chickens, pigs, and lambs!"

"You think that's funny, huh?" Santa smiled.

"Absolutely! I've never met a Santa Claus who was a butcher before."

"Well, now you have."

"A toast, then," the reporter offered cheerfully lifting his glass, "to rib eye steaks and chicken cutlets!

"And Christmas," Santa said. "Never forget about the day of gift giving."

Chapter 30

Sweating Bullets

Rico STORMED THROUGH the squad room and pushed into Interrogation Room Number One.

"How's it going, Murphy?" he asked, glancing over at Marco handcuffed to a steel table.

"Amigo! Que me salga formar este tipo irlandés loco!"

"Don't call me a friend! I'm not your homeboy!"

Murphy chuckled and pointed to the kid.

"Your rice and beans eating buddy gave me nothing; he's selling us a knockoff Chinatown circle jerk about Santa and a bunch of goddamn elves."

"I'm telling the truth! It was a guy dressed as Santa who kidnapped Darius from the park!"

"And what did he do? Fly away on a sleigh pulled by reindeer?"

The interrogation pissed off the detective.

After hours of pulling teeth and flinging threats, the street smart *Dead End Friend* merely shut his mouth.

"I want a lawyer!"

"Come on, kid!" Rico coaxed. "Help yourself out here! My partner and I've been working bodies long before you were a sparkle in Mommy's eye!"

"Leave my old girl out of this!" Marco warned. "I don't care if you believe me or not!"

Murphy slammed a photo of Stefan on the table. It was found in his pocket by crime scene investigators. The picture displayed him in Times Square wearing the chain now held in the homicide evidence room.

"Tell me why your buddy is wearing a chain found in the clutch of a cadaver?"

"Hey, man. I already told you! Macy's Santa snatched it from Stefan's neck during a fist fight."

"And I'm the Easter Bunny," Murphy grumbled.

"You're sure as white as one!"

"We better get hopping, then," Rico joked glancing out an iron barred window to the falling snow. "A storm has descended on the city and the weather gods are predicting a blizzard." Turning to Marco, he changed the subject. "Let me ask you one question, make one simple little request."

"I asked for a lawyer. Aren't ya supposed to stop sweating me and get a public defender?"

"Sure, if you were an actor on an episode of *CSI New York* and not a real life murder suspect."

"But I haven't killed anybody! I have rights!"

"What's that got to do with anything?" Rico chuckled. "Haven't you ever heard of accessory after the fact?" Walking to the door and pulling it open, he watched the boy's reaction as Arias walked in. "This detective was in the courtroom the day you and Darius Williams showed up to support your friend, Stefan."

"Sure." Marco stated. "I remember him, so what?"

"You jumped out of your seat and screamed," Arias confirmed, "when the judge dropped all charges against your buddy for throwing the bottles."

"Yeah, I was there, I screamed when the charges were dropped... and Stefan is my buddy. What's that have to do with Darius being chopped to pieces and left at our doorstep?"

Rico turned to Murphy. "John just informed me all three of our murder victims were present in that courtroom."

"Is that right?"

Arias laid it all out, how he'd come to be assigned to the attack on Macy's Santa, the absence of cooperation and the dismissal of all charges.

"But that's not the best part," Rico grinned. "No, sir, the juiciest twist and turn of fate is yet to be told."

"Go on," Murphy prodded. "What am I missing?"

Rico slammed his hand onto the table. "As for my one question, Marco, do you want to explain why, right after your friend was released from jail, people present in that courtroom ended up in the city morgue?"

"I don't know, man!"

"Well, maybe you were pissed Mr. Berrymoore opened his unionized mouth."

"Who? I don't know that name."

"He was the Santa in court," Rico reminded, "the guy who screamed for Judge McElroy to lock up your buddy."

"But Stefan was cleared, why would I care about a square like him?"

Then, a knock at the door interrupted the questioning and Terry. R. Woodward marched into the room.

"I believe you guys are holding a client of mine."

Chapter 31

Whiteout Conditions

SANTA STOOD at the entrance of ABC's World Headquarters on Columbus Avenue and 66th Street.

Flurries fell from heavy grey clouds and it was beginning to look a lot like Christmas.

In Santa's left hand was the Priority Mail package, and in his right, a Louie Vuitton briefcase. He'd come to deliver the box to Timothy Smith who'd hopefully broadcast a *frightscape* message to the island of Manhattan.

"And maybe," Santa mumbled wiping melting snowflakes from his brow, "the reporter will post the report on the World Wide Web!"

You have a very special delivery, Mammy whispered. *You'll make the media realize how crazy you are.*

The voices had started yapping earlier that morning over a bowl of Wheaties and a Twinkie.

It pissed Richard off that *Hostess* went out of business due to a nationwide worker strike crippling the company's ability to deliver its fat filled products. In response, the CEO shut the doors, sold the brand, and stumbled into winter with millions of dollars. That left the employees holding useless picket signs and dwindling checking accounts.

"Greedy little worker bees," Santa growled. "Don't know a good thing when they have it?"

Oh, they know now… all right, Mammy whispered. *How could they forget the mess they made of everything? All they have to do is look at the closed factories.*

"Just go away!" Santa shouted at the invisible hag. *A simple gunshot can end my misery. One silver bullet to my temple and wham, bam, thank you, Mammy!*

The voices would fade... forever!

Now, that little show would take some guts! Daddy's words rang in his ears. *And we all know you don't have the fortitude for that action!*

Santa sighed in defeat and stared at the entrance. He considered his plan to walk in nice and calmly, then ask for the star reporter to hand over the box of goodies.

Just have balls, Daddy griped, *and waltz right on in there!*

This could be it, Richard thought. *This simple journey to the network might conclude with me in a cell at Manhattan South Homicide.* He knew the detectives would lock him into their dungeon and shuffle him through the courts.

Well, look what we have here, he thought they'd shout. *Take a nice long gander at the monster we dragged from under a rock!*

He couldn't allow himself to become an interrupted broadcast of breaking news. He had things to do, people to see, and presents to deliver. But most of all, there were names on his naughty list.

Timothy Smith was in the top ten!

David Letterman could work with that list, Mammy shrieked. *Top Ten reasons Santa is nuts!*

The coast is clear, Daddy whispered. *Get your lazy, cowardly ass in there and show them what you've got!*

The executioner smeared the snowflakes from his face and glared at the Priority Mail package.

If it fits, it ships. Mammy snarled. *I bet the postal service wasn't thinking of body parts when they shoved that slogan down our throats!*

Richard's mind wandered then, back to the rude, robotic, blithering black woman back at the Post Office.

"Are you going to mail foreign items," the sloth had asked, "animals, weapons, or plants?"

"Weapons," he'd laughed in her face, "who mails weapons in postal boxes?"

"Everybody gets guns in the mail since the Newtown massacre," she answered, rolling green contacts into her head. "Did you know that the Sandy Hook Elementary shooting was the second deadliest in U.S. history?" Grunting, she shook her head in disgust and wiped a tear from her cheek. "That no good child murderer fatally shot twenty kindergarten children and six adults that day and, I tell you, it was a sad day here."

Standing on the street now, Santa recalled being transfixed by her fake green eyes. *I could have used a set like them to add to the collection. Damn, another missed opportunity.*

"So, let me ask you again," the postal lady had sarcastically mumbled in a ghetto voice he'd heard once or twice from the Jerry Springer show. "Are you shipping anything illegal, are there guns in that box?"

Let her look in the box, Richie Boy! Mammy sniggered. *That witch will wave to the heavens and give up her ghost. Lord have mercy! I'm coming!*

For just an instant, Richard considered pulling out his ivory handled switchblade and popping her eyes from their sockets.

How's that for illegal?

She would have screamed for help as the eyes rolled across the cheap, tiled floor.

But Santa didn't do that.

Instead, he gawked at her for a moment, trying to decide which eye he'd pluck out first. "Ha! Ha! Ha!" he laughed, not realizing the Ham hock eater had reached beneath the counter for her hidden Louisville slugger.

"What are you, some kind of nutcase?" she asked, glimpsing the madness in his eyes; enough to send shivers crawling up her spine.

Where the hell do they get these people? Daddy mumbled. *They all think their turds don't stink.*

"Sir," the mailroom queen interrupted, her hand firmly grasping the hardwood clubber. "I'm busy here. Are you going to buy that Priority Mail box in your hand or just stand there *stuck on stupid?*"

He offered her a rotten grimace. "I'll purchase your stare if you don't watch that tongue."

Breaking from the memory, he pushed into the lobby of Eyewitness News, chuckling at the incident.

"Can I help you, Santa?" a Calvin Klein suit called out.

Step right up, Son, Daddy chided; *tell him why you're here.*

Placing the Priority Mail package onto the counter, he glanced through the high-class lobby.

"I have a gift for Timothy Smith."

Good boy, Mammy stated. *I knew you could do it.*

The suit glanced at the box. "I hope your timing improves when you slide down my chimney, you just missed him."

Goddamn, son-of-a-bitch!

"Is there any way you can get it to his desk?" Santa asked with a fake crooked smile on his face.

I should chop off his head!

"I'm eating lunch right now," Calvin Klein dismissed. "But you can go on up to the newsroom and leave your package at his door."

Now you're talking!

"That would be great," Santa grunted, shuffling off towards the elevator. Pressing the UP button, he tried not to piss his pants in excitement.

"Fifth floor," Calvin whined to his back. "Down the hall and to the right, you'll see Tim's name on the door."

Suck a fucking light post!

"Thanks," Santa smiled stepping into the elevator.

"Just don't forget my kid's gifts this year, huh?"

If he had the time, Richard might have taken the man up on his offer to swing on by.

Chapter 32

The Watchers

THE PROBATION Special Offender Unit provided intensive supervision of lawbreakers who posed a threat of committing additional crimes.

Richard Blake had been designated such a menace in Mental Hygiene Court by a Manhattan Judge.

Nobody expected him to get well.

That included his psychiatrist.

It was case file day in the felony unit, earmarked for the most dangerous criminals stalking the streets. For ten years, the unit had meticulously monitored psychiatric probationers under the Kendra Law, which came about when a nutcase pushed someone into the path of an oncoming train.

Kathleen Royce had seen her share of demented probationers. Today, she hid a sick feeling as thoughts of *I told you so* rumbled through her mind.

"Tell us about your case," Senior Officer Tom Brady ordered, pointing to a manila file on Richard Blake.

Standing from the uncomfortable state issued chair, Kathleen marched around the conference table and handed out case sheets.

"Richard R. Blake was assigned to this unit for twenty-seven counts of cruelty to animals."

"Is this the cat fellow?" Tom interrupted. "The doctor who ripped out feline eyes because he thought they were watching him?"

"And talking behind his back," Kathleen confirmed. "It was, and still is, Richard's belief that cats speak to him and force him to carry out chores. The case was notorious in

Manhattan. The media covered the arrest extensively on their evening newscasts. The community was outraged. For some reason, NYPD Deputy Inspector, Harold Morrison, didn't want Blake's head on a silver platter, claiming the defendant was schizophrenic and not responsible for his actions."

"And so," Tom grumbled, "Blake was sent to the psych-hospital where he languished for three years before landing on Kathleen's caseload."

"He's been on the anti-psychotic drug, Haloperidol," Kathleen went on. "But his psychiatrist told me last month he suspected Richard stopped taking it."

"Why isn't the shrink at this meeting?" Tom asked.

"Can't track him down; he's gone missing."

"That's concerning. All we need is for this guy to start killing cats again."

"Or worse," Kathleen offered. "It's been four weeks since I've spoken with Richard, he's not appearing at scheduled meetings, all calls to his cellphone have gone unanswered, and we've been unable to contact his parents at their place of business."

"What kind of business?"

"It's a butcher shop located in the heart of Chinatown."

"Great," Tom complained. "Of all the businesses you could have told me, a butcher shop is the last one I wanted to hear."

"What's Blake's history?" Murray Matthews inquired. He was head of the Warrants Division and therefore would be responsible for tracking down and capturing the target.

Kathleen paced the floor. "He's non-violent to people, as far as we know, but still thinks cats talk to him. Much like the *Son of Sam*, Blake believes they watch, stalk, and advise him to kill other animals."

"What about the parents," Murray asked. "We don't know where they are? They don't answer the door at their home, either?"

"That's right, I've been out there five times and nobody answers. It's off Flatlands Avenue and Eighty-Eighth Street in Canarsie."

"Why are we supervising an offender that lives in Brooklyn?" Tom wondered. "Isn't that the jurisdiction of Region Two Probation and Parole?"

Kathleen was embarrassed. She'd allowed this oversight to slip through her fingers due to a massive caseload.

"I slipped up. I was supposed to transfer Blake's file to Canarsie a few months back, but we got swamped with the new offender regulations."

"So now we're paying for that mistake," Murray griped. "What if this guy kills someone?"

"Okay, all right!" Tom waved off Murray. "Look, not transferring the file is spilled milk. Right now, let's focus on finding the Cat Man."

"What's the plan?" Murray sulked. "Have we filed for a no-knock warrant on the home and business?"

Kathleen reached into a leather binder and pulled out the arrest warrant. "I have it signed and ready to go. But a major snowstorm is blowing through the city today, so we better get moving."

"Then, let's get this guy in lockup," Tom stated, "before he ends up on Nightly News again with his Dr. Doolittle act of chatting up animals."

"Maybe this time," Murray snickered, "the cats will tell him to jump off the George Washington Bridge."

"Wouldn't that be a hoot?" Kathleen snickered.

Chapter 33

Come To Jesus, Son!

THE PRINCE of the city sat in the holding cell with frustration lining his face.

"I assured your mother I'd look out for you, but we must have a come to Jesus moment."

The lawyer met Stefan's mom years before while serving as a public defender assigned to the Manhattan Treatment Court. The program was designed to rehabilitate drug addicts facing felony possession charges.

Instead of jail or probation, Treatment Court placed druggies in residential drug programs.

"Please, Terry" Stefan's mother had begged. "Just assure me you won't allow my husband to hurt my son."

Terry knew she was a junkie who'd rather have a needle in her arm than her four year old kid. Representing her half a dozen times for drug offenses, the lawyer was sad the day he found out she was found murdered in an abandoned building used as a heroin shooting gallery.

"You promised Mother thirteen years ago," Stefan replied. "Mirabel has been more of a mother to me than my lousy Mom ever was."

That was true, Terry knew. *Nonetheless, things are getting out of control for this kid.* He'd watched as Child Services stumbled and mishandled the boy's life. There were handfuls of foster homes, boy's institutions, and placements that always ended in catastrophe.

"So, what happens now?" the boy asked staring to handcuffed wrists. "They think I killed someone, huh?"

Terry reached into his pocket and pulled out a tape recorder. "I have to know everything, Stefan. No lies or stories you think I may want to hear. This could very well be a fight for your life, you understand?"

Silence, and then, "How's Mirabel? Is she mad at me?"

"She's disappointed, and hurt, that you keep placing yourself, her, and me, in these situations."

Mirabel had struggled to change Stefan's life.

For several years, she'd combated the juvenile court system and often spoke of adopting him. The kid was the son she could never have, and yet, he fought the very concept of the love she offered.

"Tell her I'm sorry," Stefan mumbled with shame. "That I didn't kill anybody."

"What about Marco? Did he?"

"No! Terry, we don't know about any of that stuff, I swear to God!"

The defender stared into the boy's eyes and saw sincerity. He prided himself on being able to gaze into his client's soul for truth.

"I'm going to have to let the detectives in here, they're going to have questions and you've got to be straight or they'll know you're lying."

"I've got nothing to say to the Spanish cop! He slammed my head onto the hood of his car."

Stupid Rico, Terry thought. *He just can't go by the book.* A knock at the door fetched his attention back to the matter at hand. "Come on in."

Murphy peeked into the room. "Is your client going to talk with us?"

"Just you, not Rico," Terry countered. "It appears we have another case of police brutality against your partner."

Murphy slipped into the room, closed the door, and sat beside the boy. "Look, nobody ever accused Rico of reading department policy and procedure. Give him a break, he's turned in his papers; the New Year will end his thirty years."

"He can't continue placing hands on my people." Turning to Stefan, he nodded to the detective. "Are you ready to answer Sergeant Murphy's questions?"

"We didn't hurt anyone," Stefan whispered.

"I didn't say you did," Murphy grumbled. "But how'd I find your crucifix chain in the Judge's dead hand?"

"Come on, Murphy," Terry interrupted. "Give me a break, will you?"

"Okay, okay. Stefan, how'd you lose the chain?"

"It was stolen from me, the day before the parade, on Thirty-Fourth Street."

"How'd that occur?"

Stefan glanced at his wrists again. "A drunken Santa Claus threw a snowball at the car which caused Darius to crash into Macy's."

"Did you know this guy dressed as Santa Claus?"

Stefan bowed his head, a thought passing through his mind. He was unsure of the answer to come before the words actually spilled from his lips.

"No, he was just another loser on the street."

"So, how does that get the chain off your neck?"

"Go on," Terry advised.

"After we got into the accident, the three of us leapt from the car and beat the fucker's ass. That's when Santa snatched the chain from my neck."

"So, you just let a bum keep it?" Murphy grunted in disbelief. "If that chain were mine, I'd have gotten it back."

"The cops came. I didn't want to go to jail."

"That should be easy to confirm, Murphy." Terry said. "You can check the precinct and see if a car crashed into Macy's that day."

"That doesn't mean he didn't kill the judge, Terry."

"Why would I? He dropped my case! I don't care about that dumbass judge."

Murphy reached into a case file and pulled out a computer printout. "You have numerous detentions for assault and battery and also just got released from the Thanksgiving Day parade nonsense."

"So, what? If you lived on the streets, you'd have to *fight or fuck*. Shit ain't easy in the dark alleys at midnight."

Murphy studied the boy. There was something nagging the back of his mind. The boy didn't feel right for murder–*assault, robbery and theft...absolutely, but not murder.*

"I'll tell you what, Stefan, let me check out your story, and if someone comes forward confirming what you say, maybe you'll get a free ride on this one."

"I'm going to jail?"

The detective hiked to the door. "In a few hours I'll be able to tell you exactly where you're going."

"But I didn't do anything!"

"We'll see about that," Murphy grumbled and pressed through the door.

Chapter 34

Making the News

$\mathcal{S}$ANTA HATED ELEVATORS.

Not because they scraped and groaned and sometimes crashed to the ground.

That was part of the thrill.

He loathed the winches because of the *nose raisers*–the ones who turned up their *snotlockers* as if he didn't belong– who acted like the world belonged to *them*.

Uppity sons of bitches is what they are.

Now, Richard was pushed into the corner of a mirrored elevator filled with the pretenders.

He wanted to murder the elitist bastards.

Take a peek, Mammy whispered. *Look at how these folks are regarding you! They think you're a real charmer!*

He always was a decent performer, Daddy agreed.

Maybe, she spat, *if they knew he wanted to kill them we might see panic set in.*

"Shut the fuck up!" Santa barked, blinking back his anger. He'd been trying to appear polite to the elevator full of news people.

But now, nobody felt safe standing beside a muttering psycho. That was apparent by the way they suddenly moved to the other side of the car to escape his ranting.

A female reporter whipped out a cellphone.

"I'm calling security; this guy is off his rocker!"

Santa turned to her… his bright red cheeks quaking with rage, white fingers digging into the Priority Mail box. For an instant, he imagined dragging her into his lair, heaving her onto a meat hook and probing her opinions of life and politeness. He wagered she'd have a new viewpoint of how the cookies of life crumbled.

Oh, she'll have a change of heart, all right, Mammy cackled, *as soon as you show her the hatchet.*

Santa was considering how to make that happen. But then, the door slid open and the media slaves escaped down a plush carpeted hallway.

"Lucky little fuckers."

When the door closed again, he reached above his head and pushed the briefcase through an escape hatch.

"Just in case things get out of hand there's nothing wrong with having a Plan-B."

The elevator came to a halt at the fifth floor where it deposited him into an energetic newsroom. The air was electric and he felt the tension hanging over the room. He wanted to squeal in delight at the sight of the reporters who'd soon shout he'd come to smack the sneers off their faces and cut their lying throats.

"Ho! Ho! Ho! Merry fucking Christmas!"

It was a sight to see, witnesses later recalled, an angry, miserable Santa–*the Jekyll and Hyde of Christmas*–walking among New York's media elite.

Have to be careful, Mr. Eye Poker, Daddy warned, *they'll turn the cameras on you and laugh in your face*!

Scanning the newsroom, the killer spotted the Radio City Rockette wannabe and recalled her pawing at Tim Smith inside Foley's pub just a few days earlier.

And he recalled something else, too, his vow to slaughter her for interfering with his moment.

"Can I help you?" little miss *ladder climber* asked moseying up beside him. "Is there something I can do for you?"

Santa grinned and wiped sweat from his brow.

To the moon, Alice! Daddy roared. *The boy just can't hold his nuts!*

It took a moment for Santa to gather his thoughts again, to suppress the urge to slam her head into the Chinese drywall and drag her body through the newsroom.

Extra! Extra! Read All About It!

"Hello? I'm Marcy," Miss Rockette rudely interrupted. "I'm Mr. Smith's executive assistant here at Channel Seven. Is there something I can help you with?"

Tell her to reach into your pants, Daddy chuckled, *she'll find all the help she needs in your mayonnaise!*

Santa fought back laughter and pushed the voices down into his private place.

Goddamn blabber mouth, I'll deal with you later, Daddy, and don't you worry!

Blinking back that consideration, he pushed forward the Priority Mail package.

"I have a present for Timothy, is he here?"

"Not at the moment," she smiled. "But I can take the delivery." Grabbing the box, it tumbled to the floor where it spilled a pile of stinking, rotting eyeballs.

"What are those?" she screamed, gazing in horrified shock at the gaping pupils.

"What do they look like?" Santa sniggered. "Them there glowers are the cat's stare!"

That's when Marcy collapsed into *never land* for a chat with the sandman, for at least in that dreamscape, nightmares couldn't hurt her.

Chapter 35

Circling the Wagons

THE Special Offender Unit and the NYPD Violent Fugitive Task Force were ready to serve the no-knock warrant on Richard Blake's house.

Strapping on Kevlar vests in an empty lot on the corner of Flatlands and Ramsen Avenues, the officers had no idea what they were getting themselves into.

And, the snow was coming down hard.

"Where the hell is Kathleen?" Probation Supervisor Tom Brady asked loading ten shots of 9mm ammo into his Pocket Glock 26's magazine. Officers had three choices of handgun options while on duty: Glock, Smith & Wesson, or Sig Sauer. Tom long ago discovered the *Model 26* could be carried comfortably and safely in a good pocket holster.

"I sent her across the street," Warrant Division Chief, Murray Matthews answered, pushing buckshot into a Mossberg 12-gage shotgun. "She went to the twenty-four hour Mini-Mart to get us coffee."

"You mean the *Crack Mart*?" Tom chuckled, pointing at the red, white, and blue storefront. "That must have struck a spark under her ass."

The store received its nickname from local patrol cops who rounded up neighborhood drug dealers selling vials of crack cocaine under the cover of darkness.

"Kathy wasn't a happy camper," Murray snickered. "She's a rattlesnake before morning caffeine; better hope she makes it out of that store."

The neighborhood had seen better days.

It was a hot bed of drug dealing, muggings, and bloody homicides. But back in the 1900s it was a section of

Brooklyn where Italian and Jewish immigrants settled when arriving in America.

That was a long time ago.

White people had long ago escaped Canarsie finding better lives and added security in Staten Island, Queens, and Long Island.

Nobody wept for Brooklyn.

They just abandoned it.

"It's a goddamn shame what happened to this community," Tom muttered glancing along the filthy streets. "You know, my grandparents grew up not far from here, back when it was safe to walk the avenues."

"Those *were* the days, huh?" Murray agreed. "My favorite uncle–*my dad's older brother*–Uncle Philly? He still talks about the neighborhood when I visit him over at Prospect Park."

"Is that right?" Tom grunted. "He's got to have some serious scratch to be able to live there. That's a long way from these boulevards." At Union Street, and Prospect Park West, stood the Prospect Park Residence. The building was a nine-story residence within walking distance of the Brooklyn Public Library, Botanic Gardens, and the Brooklyn Museum of Art.

"It's the Taj Mahal of senior living," Tom continued. "Maybe, after I put in my thirty years with the department, I'll join him for a walk in the park."

"Or a Broadway show," Murray winked. "He loves the knockers on those showgirls."

"Yeah," Tom laughed, "so long as gravity hasn't started its epic pull towards the pavement."

"You guys disgust me," Kathleen interrupted while distributing black coffee and buttered rolls. "That filthy talk is what sixteen-year-old boys dream about under their covers late at night."

"Hey, that's the nature of the beast." Murray giggled. "You want the boobs; we pay for the surgery... and then lust after them until they fall to your knees."

"Then, you assholes trade us in for newer models," Kathleen acknowledged. "You guys need your balls cut off and thrown to the dogs. Now that would be a treat!"

"Whoa, Rattlesnake!" Tom chuckled. "Do you have a weapon on you right now?"

She pulled on a Kevlar vest, reached for the holstered Sig P-229 .40 caliber and pushed rounds into the clip.

"You better believe it, Skippy."

"Okay, people." Murray bellowed throwing a map on the hood of his car. "We have a one minute jaunt down to Eighty-Eighth Street. At the Little Flower Day Care & Prep School we make a left and go down the one-way to a red brick house."

"The warrant," Kathleen added, "gives us a green light for the entire place, my guy might be hiding in the locked basement."

"There are four stairs," Tom continued, pointing to the blueprints of the house. "They lead to the front door which we have to compromise with the ramming pole."

It was a three-foot long iron-breaching tool resembling a miniature telephone pole with handles on its sides. Usually, two guys used it to knock down the door.

"Any questions?" Kathleen asked. "Speak now or forever hold your peace."

"What's the configuration inside?" a patrol cop asked.

Murray pointed to the blueprint. "There are two bedrooms and a bathroom upstairs, a kitchen, living room and family area downstairs. Kathleen's freak might talk to his cats in the basement. What's the layout down there?"

Kathleen shook her head. "It's inaccessible and the door is nailed shut. During two previous home visits I could never get in there."

Murray glanced at his team. "All right, everybody, saddle up and let's go get this guy."

They climbed into two black NYPD unmarked Crown Victorias with blacked-out windows. It was like arriving at a surprise party dressed as a red headed clown.

"We're off to see the wizard," Murray sang steering onto Flatlands Avenue with Kathleen seated beside him. Glancing to her, he chuckled. "Try not to click your heels together, Kathy…. will ya? We don't want the Wicked Witch of the West showing up."

Kathleen gave him the finger. "Suck me, nice and slow, Tin Man… and watch your steel teeth."

"I always knew you had balls," he teased. "They don't make broads like you anymore."

Chapter 36

Action News

TIMOTHY SMITH blocked Marcy's view of the rotting eyeballs strewn on the newsroom floor.

He thought they smelled like putrid eggs and rotting hamburger. The stench brought back his memory of a decaying dog's carcass in an alley.

"They look like cat eyes," he pointed, "but a few of them appear to be human!"

"Pork, beef, fish, or human," Bureau Chief Mike Anderson was delighted. "This is our lead story this evening! Get a film crew in here and get this cued-up!"

Marcy gagged. "They're from a person?"

Her face was lined with horror–*as if she'd been possessed by a demon in The Exorcist*–and she was about to lose her lunch.

"They're human, all right!" Mike confirmed.

It wasn't the first time he'd seen eyes torn from a skull. The image harked back to a Miami newscast where a naked man chewed on another guy's head. Witnesses claimed the victim's eyes were gnawed from his face just before the suspect was shot dead by the cops.

This atrocity is something different, Mike recognized, staring at the heap glowering on the floor. "Whomever they belonged to aren't among the living any longer." Lifting a pen from his pocket, he bent over the nastiness.

"What do you mean?" Marcy begged. "The eyes are from dead bodies?"

Mike flipped through the eyeballs. "Mother of God, there are four human eyes in the pile!"

A crowd of reporters encircled the scene as the cameraman, Ahmed, arrived with an HD camera.

"Where do you need me to set up?"

The Bureau Chief snapped his fingers. "Tim, get your jacket on! Where are my copywriters?"

Suddenly, a squeal echoed from the lobby where Eunice, a stately receptionist, tore into the newsroom, screaming.

"He's still here, Mike! He's out in reception. The Santa Claus came at me with a hatchet!"

That's when everyone turned to see Marcy collapsing onto the floor again, her eyes rolling into her head.

"Somebody call an ambulance!" Tim bellowed.

But, everyone already held cellphones to their ears and were reporting the activities of the madman stomping through the building.

Then, a hair rising scream gained their attention.

"Nooooooo! I don't want to die!"

"Holy God!" Tim exclaimed before leaping into action. "Ahmed! Roll the camera, we have film to shoot!"

"I'm rolling, buddy," the cameraman shouted sprinting through the newsroom and bursting through its door. There, he came face to face with the villain garbed as Santa dragging an intern by the hair. In his hand was held a hatchet pressed against her pale white throat.

"Please," the intern begged. "Stop him!"

"Come on, now," Tim begged the killer. "You don't want to hurt anyone here today."

Santa giggled and pushed the elevator button. "You believe I came here to hurt someone?"

"Why did you show your face here?" Tim asked pushing a microphone towards the murderer.

How dare this punk, Daddy whispered, *talking to you like a child!*

The elevator door opened and Santa glanced to it.

"Timothy, I simply came to bring you a present from my workshop." Then, he dragged the terrified girl, kicking and screaming, into the elevator as everyone stared in shock.

"Wait! Please?" Tim shouted.

Santa paused just long enough for Ahmed to get a close up of the murderer's sneer.

"What is it, Timothy? What do you want?"

The reporter inched closer. This was the story of his lifetime, the one investigation he'd been working on for years. And here it was, the exposé laid bare at his feet.

"What the hell is it?" Santa screeched. "Fucking ask me your silly questions, Timothy, or I swear I'll kill this girl!"

"No! No! Don't hurt her! This has nothing to do with an unknown young girl like her; we both understand that, right?"

Cut her throat, Mammy insisted, *just chop off her head right here for the camera to record.*

Santa stretched the hatchet above his head.

"One last time, what do you have to ask me, Timothy?"

There was something eerie about the way he pronounced the reporter's name. Like a mother scolding a child for some unknown sin.

Tim-o-thee, Daddy spookily whispered, *a little boot-lickers name, that's what Timothy sounds like.*

"Shut your dirty, fat mouth, Dad!" Santa screamed to the emptiness around him. "He's my business, not yours!"

Ahmed glanced at Tim, their eyes meeting in silent recognition, both understanding a sicko was in their midst.

But damn, it was thrilling news!

Bureau Chief, Mike Anderson, slipped through the door and studied the situation unfolding before him.

"Who are you? What do you want with my staff?"

"He's the *I-95* Corridor Killer," Tim blurted. "I've been following his trail of bodies for years."

"What are you talking about, Tim?"

"He's the slaughterer. The one the FBI Serial Killer Task Force has been hunting from Key West to Maine."

Santa winked at the Bureau Chief, a gleam reflecting from his eye. "You have a crackerjack on the team."

"Please!" the intern struggled against Santa's grasp. "Just let me go!"

Richard's eyes narrowed, his teeth clenched, and his stare turned cold. Raising the hatchet, he chopped the girl's head from her neck.

A gush of blood exploded from her headless corpse and everyone screamed.

"We'll meet again," Santa cackled. Tossing the decapitated head at the Bureau Chief, he backed into the elevator and dropped an envelope on the floor as the doors slid shut.

Instead of mourning the dead girl, the bureau chief thought this story might just fetch his team the elusive Peabody Award for Broadcasting Excellence.

That's the way things worked in network news.

Blood and guts meant more viewers.

And that meant money, *lots of it.*

Chapter 37

We Got Bupkis

CAPTAIN McKENZIE paced the floor.

"This is bullshit."

"Your department is stepping right in it," Terry smirked. "You don't possess probable cause on a Class-B misdemeanor, let alone felony murder."

In New York, a suspect could be jailed for something as minor as simple assault, trespassing, or disorderly conduct. However, without a shred of evidence that a crime had been committed, Stefan and Marco would be back on the streets before nightfall.

"Rico," the commander ordered, "give me something!"

"What can I tell you, Captain? I've checked and re-checked dispatch and responding patrol officers. Nothing ties these punks to the murder of Judge McElroy."

"Also," Murphy presented, "there are multiple confirmations from witnesses that the boys did jump from a Camaro, assault an intoxicated Santa, and ran off as cops arrived on scene."

"Just like my client admitted," the lawyer agreed.

Rico pulled a report from a folder and read from it. "A man dressed as Santa Claus ripped the boy's chain from his neck just before passing out. That's a direct quote."

"So, we're looking for a man dressed as Santa Claus," Murphy chuckled, "in December, running around killing other Santas?"

"Goddamn. That means we got bupkis," McKenzie barked at the millionaire lawyer. "You're representing thugs with *Robbery in the First* tendencies."

"Prove it, Captain. Bring in a criminal complainant and fill out a charge-sheet or let my kids go."

"Your kids, Counselor?" McKenzie spat glaring at the attorney. "Since when do you give a *rat's ass* about trash?"

"It's personal, I knew Berks' mother and I'm taking the Alvarez kid from the other room, too."

"Oh, isn't that a *nice fat* turd," McKenzie hooted. "A two dollar crack whore who abandoned her boy for the rocks in her freebase pipe. You care about that?"

Terry strode over to the captain. "So, you know about her? You miserable, S.O.B! We can take this up to One Police Plaza and work it out before the Commissioner."

That seemed to cool things down, as everyone knew the police commissioner played golf with his friend, Terry Woodward.

"This isn't personal, Terry," McKenzie said backing down. "It's business for me, all of the time."

"Then order your detectives to cut loose the blameless. That *is* your job, right? To protect, serve, and safeguard the innocent?"

"Innocent?" Rico chuckled. "You want us to fling open the holding cells and turn the boys loose to beat someone else into the pavement?"

The defense attorney snorted. "There's no evidence that happened, you don't have a victim, and you fetched these guys in here on a homicide inquiry, not some fictitious, hocus pocus incident!"

The captain walked to the window and stared at the street below. "So, what we do know, other than this story, which equals the twists and turns of an Elmore Leonard novel."

"One thing is for sure," Murphy assessed, "we have three bodies in the morgue, and handwritten notes left at the crime scenes."

On the desk sat a multi-line telephone. One of its buttons lit up and the phone began to beep.

"Lieutenant Martinez?" a female voice crackled over the intercom. "You have a call on line six."

Rico leaned over the desk and pushed the blinking button. "Martinez, Manhattan South Homicide."

"Good afternoon, Detective," a jovial male voice snickered. "You need to hustle up your corn beef and cabbage eating Sergeant and stomp your Puerto Rican ass over to Eyewitness News. There's a lady waiting for you."

"Who is this? I didn't catch your name, buddy?"

"Well. I'm the observer of all things the dirty little people fail to notice."

The lawyer giggled and shook his head. "At least I'm not the only one who thinks you're a nut job."

Nobody else supposed what they heard was comical. It was as if the oxygen had been siphoned from the room. The cops knew the words just spoken were a direct quote from the note discovered on Judge McElroy's body.

And that means a killer is on the line.

"You can wipe that grin off your face, Mr. Woodward," the voice scolded. "You should've never gotten yourself involved with those bastardly little thugs."

"Who the hell is this?" McKenzie growled.

"I'm the jolly old fat man, and I have rounds to make."

Suddenly a click and dial tone replaced the voice.

The silence in the room was deafening.

"We just heard from our killer," the captain offered as Detective Arias burst through the door. He was out of breath and a sense of urgency sprung from his movements.

"A guy dressed as Santa Claus just chopped off the head of an intern at the ABC World News building."

Murphy moved to Terry, placed a hand on his shoulder and nodded. "Perhaps this time, you do have an innocent client on your hands."

"I have the car waiting downstairs," Arias excitedly stated. "Crime scene is on the way and Midtown patrol is securing the scene!"

"Do we know if anyone got a look at the suspect?" McKenzie inquired walking from the office and hurrying through the buzzing squad room.

"The entire newsrooms saw him, and guess what else they witnessed?"

"What's that?" the commander probed.

"A box of decomposing eyeballs."

Chapter 38

The Bad Luck

SANTA PRESSED *'End Call'* on his prepaid TracFone, stepped from the blood-soaked outfit, and heaved it all overhead.

He now wore a Ralph Lauren cardigan and matching slacks. It was all planned out earlier that morning before he sloshed through the streets to purchase the phone from a corner store. He'd picked this particular Korean device because the packaging touted: Double Minutes for Life

That's just hilarious! Richard thought. *It should be...double minutes or death!* He'd learned burner phones were popular among drug dealers by watching *Cops* on the FOX Network. The handset required no activation fees, contracts, monthly bills, and most importantly, there were no credit checks or identification necessary. That meant calls were untraceable.

Just pay the Habib store twenty bucks, Mammy whispered, *and off you go to commit your sins.*

Carrying a hatchet: WONDERFUL!
Dressing as Santa: CUTE!
Calling homicide: PRICELESS!

He removed the Louie Vuitton briefcase from the elevator's roof, opened the latch, and wrapped a sixty-thousand-dollar Rolex President Midsize around his wrist.

Pushing the blood-spattered hatchet into the now empty case, he winked at his striking reflection on the mirrored wall. Nobody, he knew, would dare make eye contact with the scent of money strolling from the elevator.

"Just another newsy, preppy cocksucker," he snickered licking his fingertips and styling his hair into place.

The prince of primetime, Mammy complimented. *Your little act may just make Nightly News.*

"Wouldn't that be a hoot?" he snorted. "NBC covering a murder at ABC, maybe they'll have a beheading war!" Smiling, he cut loose a senseless cackle that twisted his face in a grimace of madness. For a twinkling, he wasn't sure if he could contain himself–savoring the recollection of the intern's blood gushing from her carotid artery– saturating everything within feet of the falling body.

Did you get a load of the newsman? Daddy grunted, *when you threw the head at him?*

"I thought he was going to shit his pants," Richard answered his reflection, spinning like a Vogue supermodel strutting a Paris runway… and then, he kissed the mirror. "You look fabulous, darling!"

You see? Daddy murmured to his wife, *I told you he was a Christopher Street boot-licking slut!*

"So what, Daddy, what's it to you?" Richard yelled at his reflection. "The guys down on the pier actually appreciate me! They don't judge or make meaningless, despicable commentaries."

They do other things, though, Mammy said in disgust. *Out on the end of the pier where nobody cares if you live, die or god knows what!*

The Christopher Street Pier sat at the foot of Greenwich Village. It was part of the Hudson River Park and had developed a vibrant gay social scene for "cruising."

That meant sex, oral and anal… *and* lots of it!

Since renovations of Hudson River Park's new Greenwich Village segment, it retained its role as *the* gathering place for gay men from Manhattan and Jersey who congregated on the pier.

Congregating, my ass! Daddy grunted, *corn-holing is more like it! Slurping on their throbbing ice cream poles!*

Those poor boys, Mammy sighed, *why can't they find themselves a nice girl?*

"Why do you have to condemn me?" Richard shrieked and slammed his fist into the mirror which shattered and splintered into a hundred shards.

Now look what you made him do, Daddy murmured, *that's seven years bad luck!*

"I'll take care of those mouths of yours," Richard promised picking up his attaché case, "just as soon as I get back to the freezer."

The recriminations ceased then as the elevator's floor arrival notification ding sounded and the doors slid apart revealing a security guard holding a gun at his side.

"Sir," he shouted, "did you see a man dressed as Santa Claus get off this elevator?"

In the distance, sirens could be heard as ABC's employees rushed through the lobby and out into the street.

"Yes!" Richard cried in fabricated panic. "He had blood on his clothes and a hatchet in his hand!"

The guard's eyes went wide as he glanced through the empty elevator, taking notice of the shattered mirror. "What floor did he get off on?"

"The third floor, he said he had people to see and things to deliver!" Suddenly, Richard saw swarms of NYPD Officers storming through the lobby barking their commands.

"Get out of the way! Evacuate the structure!"

"The killer's on the third floor!" the guard directed the police, "and he's got a hatchet!"

"For God's sake," an NYPD Sergeant hollered, "get up the emergency stairs and find that guy!

Richard hurried through the lobby, glancing over his shoulder like an adolescent prowling a haunted mansion. Through the exit doors he hurried amid hundreds of fleeing civilians who never knew the reaper of souls walked in their midst.

Nice clean escape, Mammy whispered, *but you left evidence on the roof of the elevator, and that means DNA for the inquisitive forensic unit. Stupid little boy, you can never do anything right!*

Noticing snow had inched its way into a blizzard, the killer hurriedly stepped along Peter Jennings Way where yellow cabs skidded on the slush covered asphalt.

"Got nothing to say, Daddy?" Richard mumbled. "Don't you have an opinion on how your assassin son is pushing towards the twelve days of Christmas?"

Come on, Mr. Blake, Mammy's ghost prodded; *tell our son what you think! Give him the skinny!*

Richard was disappointed. Only silence answered his paces through the whiteout conditions masking the metropolis with a blanket of trampled snow. For no sooner than he stalked along the sidewalk, the blizzard filled in his footprints.

The streets hid many secrets.

Everything else was a whisper on the wind.

Chapter 39

Bloody Sunday

THE FUGITIVE TASK FORCE couldn't see two feet in front of them as they leapt from their cars, rushed through the snowstorm and surrounded Richard's house.

Brooklyn patrol cops rammed the battering pole through the wooden door and led an entry team into the foyer,

"NYPD search warrant!"

Parole Supervisor, Tom Brady, followed them into the house pointing his gun. "State Officers; come out with your hands up!"

Within seconds, Kathleen appeared from the back of the house with two cops at her side. "The rear door was ajar; he is not home."

"Clear!" a cop bellowed from upstairs.

"There are blood trails from here to the living room," Murray pointed to the floor, "which tells me someone struggled for their life."

Kathleen inspected the dark, dried trails. It reminded her of ketchup coagulating around the bottle top. But the smell was something else. Blood generally reeked of iron. It was similar to the aroma of rusting metal, a fading rainstorm, or a jar of pennies. But, *decomposing blood* smelled like hamburger, and in due course, rotting meat.

"Stinks like a cadaver in here, anybody find a body?"

"No, Kathy," one of the Brooklyn Cops answered. "But there is enormous blood spatter in the master bedroom."

"There probably *was* a cadaver here at some point," Murray indicated. "That means our boy has graduated from probation violator and cat chatting animal abuser to homicidal maniac."

"Exactly where is the blood in the bedroom?" Kathleen asked the uniformed cops.

"Come on, I'll show you," one of them answered leading her up a flight of worn carpeted stairs soaked with deep red stains. "The blood is dry on the bed and floors. It's butchery up there."

Murray thought this was a notch above his pay grade and wasn't afraid to say so. "This isn't an issue for the Warrants Division, Kathleen. I have to release my guys from the scene." However, before he could protest further, they saw bloody handwriting on the bedroom wall.

Jack and Jill went out to kill,
To fill a pail with blood...

"Disgusting," Tom muttered at the sight. "There must have been a couple people murdered right in this room." He glanced away from the wall and stared at a patch of dried blood staining the king size Serta Perfect Sleeper.

"Dispatch," a Brooklyn cop urgently radioed, "requesting ten-thirteen backup for homicide investigation at six eighty-eight Flatlands Avenue."

Kathleen felt queasy. The room began to spin and she fell to a knee. It had been years since she'd witnessed anything like this nightmarish scene.

"Kathleen," Tom hurried to her side. "Are you all right? Can you hear me?"

She was gone. As it turned out, the tough as nails probation officer didn't have balls at all. Her mind had shut down... she was lost in a memory of childhood and the image of her dog's corpse which had been torn to pieces by wolves in upstate New York. Its furry little limbs lay matted with gore, which also littered the ground.

"Kathleen, come on!" Tom called from the echoes of consciousness. "Let me get you out of here!"

She snapped back from her childhood and the fog cleared. Standing before her was not the nightmarish remains of her childhood best friend, *Skippy the Dog*, but her supervisor and best friend.

"Tom?" she mumbled, "Tom, what's going on, Tom?"

"It's going to be *A-Okay*, kiddo," he promised leading her back down the bloody stairs.

Privately, however, he wasn't sure.

This was a rotten little nightmare that took on the form of deadly things.

And deadly things stunk.

Chapter 40

The World of News

Rico KNEW that ABC News was owned by the Walt Disney Company.

"Dreams come true, my ass! If you believe that, I have a bridge to sell ya!"

That's what Rico thought now, recalling the year before when Liz and he took the boys on a Disney cruise–*The Disney Wonder*–and was shocked to find that Mickey, Minnie, Goofy, and Pluto were prohibited from talking.

It's like watching a silent film; they just stood there making hand signals, forcing the kids to guess what they were trying to say, without actually saying anything.

It was the strangest thing.

He understood that network news, like shoot-em-up movies, had everything to do with show business.

It's all about illusion, death and destruction.

Both, he and Murphy were standing on the set of *World News* inspecting Commander McKenzie who was busily chatting up Dianne Sanders.

She was the network's anchor.

Murphy turned to Chief Executive Officer, Marc Klein, who was complaining of market share and a murder occurring in his building.

"How do I tell my board of directors that the emperor of Christmas waltzed into our WABC newsroom and murdered a twenty-three-year-old college intern?"

"I don't know how you spin that tale," Murphy responded. "Nevertheless, a life has been taken, so we must investigate; it's the only way to find the killer."

"You know," the CEO abruptly interjected, recalling a memory, "Timothy did warn us a serial killer might be loose in Manhattan, but we didn't take him seriously."

"Is that right? What, exactly, convinced him of that? Up until today, nobody knew a Santa Claus was killing people."

"We assumed he said it in passing. None of us had been tuned-in to a nationwide killing spree, after all."

"When did Tim say this?" Rico asked pulling a notebook from his jacket pocket.

"During the Christmas Party last night. Tim said he believed a dead Santa in Herald Square Park had similar traits to other Santa Claus murders along the eastern seaboard."

"Was that an investigation the network was running?"

"I don't believe so, but Tim works for the local WABC affiliate, so maybe that is something his Bureau Chief could answer. I run the business side of the company, news, programming, and show business entertainment."

As far as Mr. Hotshot CEO was concerned, anybody not in his biosphere of show business *somebodies* were good for nothing *nobodies*.

All you had to do was ask him.

Murphy frowned. He had a crummy taste in his mouth for anything with the aroma of entertainment. His younger brother, Aaron, had busted his ass at New York University for several years learning screenwriting.

Aaron was going to be the next big thing! HA!

That was ten years and sixteen screenplays ago.

Last Christmas, after a development executive ripped off what would've been Aaron's breakout big-budget SPEC script, he climbed into his pending repossession Mercedes, drove onto the Vincent Thomas Bridge and leaped to his death. Authorities later used sonar equipment to find his body in the seaport's murky waters.

That suicide didn't make a splash in the media like another big director's plunge into the shadowy seawater.

Yet, that Hollywood director was somebody. And Aaron was what Hollywood called *'a nobody, nothing writer.'*

"When will the crime scene be cleared?"

"Look, Mr. Klein," Murphy grumbled arising from his memory. "We have a murder investigation to run and that means the entire newsroom is restricted. Nothing comes or goes until we clear everyone."

"Christ," the CEO swore, rubbing a pulsating headache inundating his temples. "First, I have to tolerate B-list actors, and now this?"

"At least you get to green light another project," Murphy spat. "Then cause some other schmuck to lose his hopes and dreams of greatness."

"What are you talking about, Detective?"

"Hello, Sergeant," Dianne Sanders interrupted. "We will, of course, cooperate in every way possible in this tragic situation."

"Yes," Murphy replied. "It is tragic and we will try to stay out of your way."

"No worries," she retorted with a kind glance. "I understand completely, and if there's anything we can do here at ABC to assist your investigation, please don't hesitate to have Marc here jump through your hoops."

"Of course," the CEO fumbled over himself. "Anything I can do to help."

Dianne brushed a lock of hair from her face, turned, and strolled across the studio floor where she took up her perch behind the anchor desk as hair and make-up began their studious labor.

"Nice lady," Murphy commented. "She has class."

"Did you want me to escort you to Tim's office," Mr. Klein offered, "it's on the fifth floor in the Channel Seven studio."

"Quiet on set," an energetic production assistant called out counting down with the fingers of his hand, "we are going live in five... four...three...two and you're on..." he pointed to Dianne who stared at the teleprompter.

"From ABC News Headquarters in New York," a canned introduction began as the detectives watched a camera close in on the network queen. "This is ABC World News with Dianne Sanders."

"Good Evening," she sadly reported. "Today, a riveting human tragedy unfolded right here in our very own building when a madman, robed as Santa Claus, circumvented security, slipped up to the fifth-floor and killed one of our interns in the Eyewitness Newsroom just hours ago." Diane glanced to another camera when its red light blinked. "For that unfolding story, we now take you live to our local correspondent, Timothy Smith, in the newsroom. Tim?"

"That's right, Dianne," Timothy Smith's image nodded from a wall-mounted monitor behind the anchor desk. "The arrival of Santa Claus here on the Upper West Side brought murder and mayhem close to home today as ABC employees stared in horror while one of their own was cut down in the prime of her life."

"It appears Santa made his debut early," Murphy whispered following Rico from the studio to investigate the carnage awaiting their arrival four flights above.

There, entertainment came in the form of blood.

Chapter 41

Cross My Heart

THE LAWYER loved his limousine.

But things that mattered came with time and patience.

Terry hoped Stefan realized this by now.

Upset that the teenager didn't seem to take life seriously, he glared at the boy sitting pug faced beside his friend.

"I just don't understand, Stefan. You have the potential to be a decent young man with a very bright future, if only you'd apply yourself."

"I cross my heart and hope to die. Ya won't have to get us out of jail again!"

"Yeah, right!" the lawyer retorted. He knew about crossing hearts and hoping to die.

They were riding in a Bentley Stretch Limo that cost a ton of heart crossings, disappointments and cold hard cash.

Some things might change, but cross my heart and hope to die is something that never changes!

"One of these days," Mirabel snapped, "you boys will have to take responsibility for your own lives."

"But we didn't do anything," Stefan protested. "Besides, Terry showed the cops who the boss is."

"I won't always be able to save you," Terry frowned. "This time, it was my game to win, but next time… the dice might roll another way."

Marco chuckled. "I'm sorry you had to come out in this weather." Reaching into the drink compartment for a coke, he shrugged. "The cops have a hard on for us…"

"I know about having a hard on for people," Terry cut him off, "Nevertheless, you make your own glitches by stealing, hustling, and running the streets of Manhattan."

"They certainly aren't killing people," Mirabel hoped.

"Who said anything about any of that?"

"I know what you're thinking."

Marco shook his head, opened a Santa Claus Coca-Cola can, and gulped down the syrupy carbonated water. "You're one to talk anyway, huh? Guys like you always get rich from guys like us! The only difference between me and you is I got caught."

Was that an admission of guilt to murder?

The lawyer wondered and glanced to the boy.

"I work for a living, Marco, and you haven't ponied up a single dime for my time or efforts. I just saved you from a long jail sentence."

Mirabel was livid.

It was one thing to venture into a snowstorm to rescue Stefan, but she wasn't about to sit silent as a smart-mouthed hoodlum condemned her husband.

"Watch your tongue," she pointed at Marco's chest. "Stefan wouldn't be in this situation without you, and if it wasn't for my husband, you'd be rotting in a jail."

"Oh, yeah? You people don't give a crap about the Spanish kid. If I wasn't Stef's friend, I'd never be in this car, you'd leave me out on the cold streets, maybe toss a few coins out the window!"

"I didn't say that!" Terry argued.

"You didn't have to," Marco alleged, pushing open the limo's door and stepping into the storm. "I know when I'm not wanted and have a long history of being tossed to the curb like trash."

Stefan followed him out. "I'll call you, Mirabel. Thanks for getting us out of that hell hole."

"Stefan! Wait!" she begged. "Please, come home!"

"Let him go, honey," Terry groused reaching for a decanter of scotch. "He'll either come to his senses or end up dead on the streets."

"Home is where my heart is, Mirabel," Stefan smiled apologetically. "Without Marco, I'm nothing."

"What are you talking about?" Terry grunted. "Get your ass back here and apologize to Mirabel."

Mirabel's jaw dropped in despair as she watched the boy shut the door, sling his arm around his buddy, and stomp off into the swirling snowstorm.

"Go after them, Terry!"

"No way, Sweetie, that kid has made his bed and we have to let him sleep in it. Tough love, that's what he needs right now, just like my dad gave, and his before that."

"But, Terrance," she pleaded.

Shaking his head, the power broker had made up his mind and was not going to give in. Not this time.

Watching as the boys disappeared, Mirabel was frightened she'd never see the boy again.

They were gone, and only their footprints remained.

Chapter 42

Ghosts of Christmas

NOBODY ENJOYED climbing down rotting basement stairs in search of a sociopathic kitten killer.

It was pitch dark and only flashlight beams lighted the path down the steps.

Each footfall creaked.

Then, without warning, the staircase collapsed. The sideboards fractured, the risers disintegrated, and down went Detective Tom Brady and two officers into hell.

"Damn it!" Tom shrieked in pain and surprise as his body hit the dirt basement floor.

"What the hell?" a cop shouted flicking on his flashlight and running its beam over the floor. The earth was excavated and displayed dozen of grinning skulls lying in shallow graves.

"Jesus, Lord in Heaven!" Tom murmured taking in the horror. *Thanks for flying Deadly Things Airlines; we hope your experience was painful and treacherous!*

"Tom?" Kathleen's voice reverberated through the pitch-black cellar. "Are you guys all right down there?"

The stench is close to unbearable, Tom realized. It reminded him of the mildew odor of an old house.

But he'd never seen anything quite like this.

There were skeletons garbed in Santa outfits, the skulls, hands, and feet sticking from the garments.

"Look at the walls, Tom," a cop stated shining his light on a chipping concrete wall.

TO LIVE IS EVIL

That's what was written in dried, streaked blood. And spaced every few feet, newspaper articles had been duct taped haphazardly into a long paper banner.

MURDERER STIKES AGAIN
Miami Police Finds Third Santa Body

"Holy shit!" Tom exclaimed, stumbling over a skeleton. Looking closely, he saw there were fifteen years of headlines taken from cities peppering the east coast.

"Dead bodies," the cop said, "all the way to Key West."

"New York City will have its own headlines in just a matter of hours," Tom mumbled. Reading the articles by flashlight he saw Washington Cops were hot on the trail of someone, and then, poof! The leads were gone.

"Get a load of this!" Tom shouted.

On the wall was this headline:

SANTA DEAD
D.C. Man Clothed as Santa Killed

"Tom?" Kathleen called. "Are you guys okay?"

Far from okay, he was transfixed; his eyes moving from one headline to the next... all stuck there on the wall like a discarded, demented remembrance of secret deeds long ago committed and covered up.

He saved the articles for later viewing like folded notes stuck inside the pages of a King James Bible. Except these are more than blissful recollections, uh-uh, these are nightmares.

Tom read down into a South Carolina front page story, but found his eyes kept leaping back to the headlines:

KRIS KRINGLE MURDERED
FBI Suspect a Serial Killer

"Tommy!" Murray screamed into the depths. "Let me know you're breathing down there!"

"Yeah, we're okay," Tom replied while scanning the newspaper articles. "Get homicide on the horn, Murray! We have a huge graveyard down here!"

"That's putting it lightly," the cop added. "What we have is a *boneyard basement*… a collection of human remnants that once walked, laughed and cried."

"And they screamed," Tom added, nodding from the staircase back to the graves. "I bet they begged and shook in fear as the slaughterer dragged them down those creaking wooden stairs and pushed their bodies into these shallow graves."

"After being beaten," the cop threw in, "choked, tied, and who knows what else, bloody and howling, thrust into the hereafter."

That was a long time ago by the look of things.

These bones had been lying in wait of discovery for decades. Now, only apparitions loomed, perhaps watching from the ghostly realm.

"How many are there, Tommy?"

He didn't answer. Distracted by a word written on the wall, he barely heard Kathleen's voice.

R E D R U M

It was written in blood, from ceiling to floor.

"Redrum, Redrum, Redrum," Tom mumbled. "Why does that seem so familiar?"

"It's the King of Horror," the cop answered. "We have ourselves a fan of the scariest novelist who ever lived!"

"Huh? What are you talking about?"

"The Shining… Stephen King, remember? The Overlook Hotel, that kid who writes REDRUM on a door with lipstick and the mother wakes up and stares at the reflected word on the mirror."

"Get to the point, please?"

"What the mother saw spelled out was murder."

"I remember now," Tom nodded.

"Exactly, and look over there on that wall," the young buck pointed out. "Live spelled backwards is *evil*."

"He's toying with us." Tom murmured and briefly lost his equilibrium. Stumbling, he stepped on a skeleton lying in the grave and broke its femur bone.

A noise from behind snapped his attention to Kathleen and Murray shielding their eyes at the bottom of a ladder.

"Are those corpses in Santa suits, Tom?" Murray queried staring at the numerous graves.

"Skeletons," Tom nodded. "Only their ghosts remain."

Chapter 43

Meet the Press

THE AMERICAN Broadcasting Company took up an entire block on the Upper West Side.

It employed eight-hundred people throughout thirteen floors and boasted one of the most technologically advanced monitoring stations in Network News.

Anything that happened globally in ABC News filtered through the *Digital Media Center*. With over ten-million-feet of cable, five-hundred LCD screens and two-hundred people working around the clock, this place monitored every affiliate.

"So, explain this all to me again," Rico probed Timothy Smith. "Tell me like I'm a three-year-old learning my ABC's."

"That's funny," Murphy retorted.

"What's that, partner?"

"We're in ABC and you're learning *your* ABC's."

Rico shook his head. "Ignore my partner, Tim, and let's get back to the business at hand.

Tim smiled. "Nothing happens around the world," he explained pointing at the monitors, "without ABC Headquarters knowing about it here in the center, whether it occurs in New York, or anywhere in the world."

"And why is that important to the dead girl upstairs? You're not going to show viewers her beheading, I hope?"

"No, but we did get that on digital." Tim stated cueing a reel he'd prepared a few minutes earlier. "However, that's not what I wanted to show you."

"You know," Rico offered, watching a screen of Egypt erupting in violence. "Nobody really gives two shits about what happens in Islamabad or Egypt. Or, how many Afghan heads get cut off by Taliban extremists because of dancing and singing. What New Yorkers want to know is how to feed their families."

"They care, all right," Tim responded, "especially what happened in Pakistan when Seal Team Six took out that coward, Osama Bin Laden."

"Okay, point taken. That was one hell of a night for America and New York."

"It was! Thank God for those guys! I was working the day the Twin Towers fell and let me tell you, it was like I got *punched* in the stomach."

"Bastards. We should turn that region into green glass."

"What are you talking about, Detective?" Dianne Sanders asked moseying into the conversation.

"Payback," Murphy advised.

"And this," Tim said pressing a button on a video player where clips from Miami, Key West, Charleston, and DC began to play. The reel was a collection of news stories covering murdered Santas that occurred over a period of fifteen years. "I first noticed the pattern, when a wire came across my desk from WPTS channel ten, our Miami affiliate, and then a few weeks later at WSB-TV channel two in Atlanta, and so forth, and so on."

"The pattern matched what is happening here?"

"Yeah," Tim said, "Not long after Atlanta, I started seeing a pattern that someone was killing Santas along the I-95 corridor. But, what really floated my boat was the day I covered a court case involving the young boy who threw the bottle at Santa in the Macy's Thanksgiving Parade."

"What about it?" Rico probed. "The case was dismissed; the victim didn't press charges."

"Nevertheless, I think the killer showed his face. My cameraman happened to be shooting a group of Santas, and look what we found."

On the monitor, Mr. Berrymoore jumped to his feet in protest of releasing Stefan from custody.

"Look closely," Tim continued, reducing the playback speed to slow motion, "at the Santa standing right behind Berrymoore in the courtroom. He stares into the camera and runs his finger across his throat. Then he laughs and shuffles out behind the other Santas."

"One of which ends up deceased the next day in Herald Square Park," Rico added. "Then the Judge and later the black kid who cheered his friend's release."

"All three of whom are in this courtroom," Murphy added staring at the footage.

"And this note dropped outside the elevator upstairs," Rico said, pulling a photocopy from his notebook, "it reads like a murder list.

Santa's Naughty List

1) Put the big mouth Santa on a park bench!

2) Kill the judge who lady justice doesn't see!

3) Behead a thug and scoop out his eyes!

4) Dig up the Ghosts of Christmas Past!

5) Stalk the lady who sent me to a shrink!

6) Kill the Puerto Rican who beat me!

7) Slay the Santa Convention posers!

8) Remove the lawyer's fibbing head!

9) Strangle the boy who ruined my life!

Murphy ran his fingers through his hair. "I'd say we have ourselves one hell of a Christmas hit list."

"FBI Serial Killer Task Force case," Captain McKenzie announced walking into the media center.

"You know we have to release this to the public," Tim stated. "It's too big to keep quiet."

The captain shook his head. "If we do that, before bringing in the FBI, the butcher could see the news report and vanish in the dead of night."

"He won't stop killing," Murphy stated. "These guys get a taste for blood and keep at it until they're either caught or gunned down like dogs."

"You think?" Tim asked. "Why wouldn't he just stop killing before we find him?"

"Because the madman came to your newsroom for publicity, wants his fifteen minutes, and will probably come after you next to ensure he gets his shot at fame."

"Seriously? He got it then, we went live with it."

Rico's phone rang. Grabbing it from his coat pocket, he accepted the call and mumbled a reply while glancing to his commander. "Okay, I'll tell him right now."

"What is it, Rico?"

"Brooklyn P.D. just found twelve skeletons half buried in the basement of a house. The bones have on Santa suits."

"What?" Murphy sighed. "Guess the Brooklyn squad just found the dig mentioned on our Naughty List!"

"Yup, ghosts of Christmas past, all dug up! Deputy Inspector Morrison was trying to convince me this case was overblown. Yet I knew this was big. I want my best guys from the Homicide Task Force on this excavation in Brooklyn. Want to guess who those lucky bastards are?"

"Damn it, Sir," Rico mumbled. "I can't take this on; I retire the first of the year."

"Tough shit. You and Murphy lock down this scene and then get rolling to that shithole in Brooklyn."

"Aw, come on, Anton!" Rico complained. "Let someone else run this one!"

"I'll call the New York Field Office at Federal Plaza," McKenzie said, ignoring the whining. "They'll activate Special Agent Ling at the Serial Killer Task Force."

"This isn't right, Commander," Rico grumbled. "I have a wife at home who won't be happy!"

"Get her flowers. That'll calm her down."

"Fuck me," Rico griped. "First the train show and now this; I'm supposed to take her to Rockefeller Center tomorrow night."

"Ice skating?" McKenzie chuckled. "You gotta be kidding me." Sometimes, even the most hardnosed cops surprised him. "Get moving, guys, time is wasting away."

Murphy snorted. "Well, partner, you better buy floral stocks in 1-800-Flowers. At least you'll have dividends after the roses wilt and she files for divorce."

"You're an ass," Rico complained. "Ashes to ashes, dust to dust, we all fall down."

"That's the job," Murphy agreed.

"God, I can't wait for Miami Beach!"

Chapter 44

The Greatest Crooner

YOU'RE GONNA BE A STAR! Daddy shrieked within the complexities of Richard's thoughts.

It's all happening! Mammy assured, *just like in the movies!*

That's when Frank Sinatra started snapping his fingers and crooning. He wasn't muttering gently like the other voices, but rather, he belted out his signature tune like a tambourine!

Frank could always hold a note, Richard thought.

Well, dip me in shit, Daddy chuckled, *my son has an opinion!*

Oh, shut up and let's hear him sing, Mammy muttered. *Go ahead, Sonny, let it rip!*

So, the killer shrugged away the commentaries and whistled to the tune playing in his head. The meat wagon's radio hadn't worked since the CD player stopped spinning a year ago, but that didn't matter since Frankie belted out his jingles in Richard's mind.

But his voice sounded different, didn't it? Richard thought, transitioning from whistling to humming with the best crooner who ever lived. When the intro ended, the lyrics came to mind and he butchered the first verse of *spreading the news.*

"I'm gonna make a brand new start of it in old New York," he sung. Had anyone glanced at the loony-tune behind the wheel they might've considered calling the cops. On his face was a smile that could sell an aluminum siding shed to an Eskimo, or an Igloo, or perhaps both.

Not because they needed it, but just to get the mental case as far away as possible. And fast!

Either way…

You could tell this fella was downright wacky.

However, nobody saw the singing *freak-show* as he drove along Flatbush Avenue because sane folks huddled around their fireplaces safe and sound inside.

Or, perhaps they were doing other things, Richard considered, *like fucking their wives while fantasizing of their sidebar girlfriends.*

"Then again, they're probably just glad to be in a house and not trembling in some cardboard box with newspapers for blankets like the homeless down in the Bowery."

They called 'em bums when I was coming up, Daddy whispered. *Hobos, Waifs, Ass-outs!*

Nowadays they call them displaced persons, Mammy whispered.

Ha! Daddy laughed. *Tell that one to Mr. Forty-Seven Percent, and see how well that sells to his crowd!*

That comment brought a laugh from everyone in Richard's head… that is, until the mental case continued his singing.

And, brother, singing wasn't his strong point.

Anyone who might've overheard the executioner doing a hatchet job on the classic Sinatra song would have done one of two things.

First, they would have asked him nicely–in a New Yorker friendly sort of way–to shut the fuck up.

Not *shut the front door…* or *please be quiet.*

Politeness was for the retirement crowd down in Florida, or out west in California, maybe.

This was Brooklyn, after all, and shut-the-fuck-up meant just that.

Second, and *most probably*–this would have been the prize behind door number TWO.

When Richard didn't shut up... the shit would hit the fan. We're not talking pushing and shoving, or knock *such and such* off my shoulder.

What we're talking about here are 9mm bullet holes between the eyes. Maybe he'd get shot in the leg or arm–if the shooter thought he wouldn't snitch–that's how they rolled on Flatbush Avenue.

But, therein waits another story, and another $9.99 or whatever they charge for things like that at Barnes & Noble if their stores stop closing. Nowadays, stories lived in E-pub or MOBI files... everybody wanted a *Kindle or Nook*.

Hoo! Hoo! Hoo! Isn't that special... save the trees, care for the planet, and screw the authors!

The point is... *nobody heard a peep*... so the killer sang on and the roaches in the van leapt from the vehicle into the falling snow. Because even they knew, Terminix, Orkin, or those little yellow mouse cars didn't venture out in snowstorms. So, the pests would do just fine until the spring thaw. Lucky for those who survived the escape, because when Richard let the next verse rip, the windows shuddered and, for a fleeting second, the voices who rented space in his head imagined the glass might shatter like in the Sunday morning cartoons.

It was bad. Because, after Santa sang the *New York, New York* verse, the dumbass had no clue what came next.

So, he did like all mumbling song murderers did; he *hemmed* and *hawed*, right back where he started off *whistling*.

A mumbling, humming, whistling jackass! Mammy whispered. *Can't even remember your hometown Sinatra song, how pitiful is that?*

Just as the jingle wrapped up, he turned the van onto Eighty-Eighth Street where sanity reared its head for the first time in years.

"Maybe, possibly," he muttered staring out the windshield, "the jig might be up."

For through the snowfall he glimpsed an army of cops surrounding his childhood home!

It's Showtime! Daddy cheered.

Chapter 45

Just the Facts

THE BUILDING was searched and four hundred ABC employees were shuffled onto the street.

Where they went from there was anyone's guess.

The show went on; the network's transmitter atop the Empire State Building continued sending out broadcasts of the derelict Santa Claus, now New York's Most Wanted fugitive.

Here on the street, yellow crime scene tape cordoned off the entrance as the intern's body was loaded into the Medical Examiner's van. The autopsy was required by law since death occurred due to criminal violence.

In ABCs lobby, Detective Romero was perplexed at how the killer slipped away.

"There's no sign of him, Commander. The guys have rifled through all the floors and there's no Santa Claus anywhere!"

He and Arias were ordered to direct the search tying up hundreds of officers going floor-to-floor, office-to-office, searching every nook and cranny.

"Nothing, nobody has seen him. I don't know where else to look."

"What are you saying?" McKenzie snapped. "That Santa pulled a David Blaine? He just disappeared?"

Romero shrugged. "We know he got on the elevator at the fifth floor, and when it reached the lobby the guard was laid-up waiting. He told us an ABC executive was the only one inside, no Santa Claus."

"Which tells me fatso got off on another floor," McKenzie growled.

The problem was... none of the employees could confirm observing a Kris Kringle look alike waltzing through their offices.

"I know. It doesn't make any sense," Romero stated. "Nobody just disappears."

Actually, McKenzie thought, *people disappear every day. There was a mass exodus of folks who did vanish in Manhattan.* He'd seen the reports. Missing individuals had increased six-fold in the United States during the past twenty-five years. "Twenty-three hundred Americans are reported missing every day. Every year in New York City alone, four-thousand commuters climb down the subway stairs and are never seen again."

And, that meant something peculiar was going on down in the dark, damp, subway tunnels beneath the city streets.

There really are body snatchers down there, McKenzie thought, *waiting for fresh meat to stumble into their grasp.*

"So, what are you telling us, Commander?" Romero chuckled. "Santa Claus went up to the roof, climbed onto a sleigh and took off for the North Pole?"

Smart-ass... I should bust him back to vice like Rico wants. But he couldn't have detectives riding desks at a moment like this. Therefore, instead of repeating those thoughts, he said: "I'll forget you supposed that, Bobby. But, next time, I'll have you brought up on insubordination charges."

"Sorry, Chief. I meant he has to be here somewhere."

"Or, Santa escaped from another door," Arias suggested.

"Captain?" a K-9 Officer called standing beside the elevator where a German Shepard crouched staring at the hatch of the winch. "I think Gonzo is hitting on something up there." The dog was part of the NYPD K-9 Unit, a sub-unit of the *NYPD Emergency Service,* which consisted of thirty more German Shepherds, cross-trained patrol canines and three Bloodhounds specifically trained to track criminal suspects. In New York County, and most of

America, the dogs were considered sworn officers who wore police badges and ballistic vests. During swearing-in ceremonies, the department required them to bark. And, if killed in the line of duty, the manhunters were often given full police funerals.

That was American tax dollars at work.

McKenzie hurried to the elevator and stood beside Romero. "Reach up there, Bobby, and open that hatch!"

Drawing his weapon, Romero grasped the trap door and jerked it open.

To everyone's surprise a blood soaked Santa suit fell through the opening and landed in a heap on the floor.

"We got his Santa suit," Romero shouted, "but where is the suspect who should be wearing it?"

"Get Murphy and Rico on the horn," the commander barked. "Tell 'em we need a picture of the Brooklyn basement killer."

"You want us to show the photo to the guard who eyeballed the fella walking out of the elevator? See if he can I.D. him as our suspect?"

"Precisely, I'd bet a c-note the killer changed out of that Santa outfit in the elevator and walked past the guard."

"Subsequently, we're looking for a man in a business suit?" Romero chuckled. "Here on Sixty-Sixth Street? That's like finding a needle in a haystack."

"So be a magnet!" McKenzie barked. "Find the needle!"

Chapter 46

The Cat's Meow

HAMILTON FISH was Brooklyn's first serial killer.

Called lots of things by many people, he liked *Boogeyman* best. A suspect in five murders, he confessed to three bodies and was sent along his way to the electric chair at Sing-Sing. Some said the warden smiled when guards juiced the power.

Nice toasty ending.

They dubbed him the Gray Man, The Boogeyman, and, The Moon Maniac.

Holy Freaking crap, Batman! Daddy hooted, *what the hell is a Moon Maniac?*

Santa sniggered; that's the kind of notoriety he craved. To be feared, reviled, and gossiped about for as long as memory served humanity. *I'm about to be way bigger than the Brooklyn Vampire ever was!*

Three murders is chump change, Daddy guaranteed. *Compared to what's in our basement!*

Santa romanced the idea of getting gone; just vanishing into oblivion. If he could somehow step into the shadows, people would always speculate if the hatchet wielding Gift Giver would reappear next Christmas. He wanted to place fear into folks, like the *Cannibal Cop Killer* had recently done. The NYPD officer was arrested by the FBI for conspiracy to kidnap, torture, cook–*at low heat*–and *eat* women. But the best part for Richard was this: the judge handling the case threatened if the Cannibal Cop was convicted, he'd be sentenced to life in prison and ordered to pay a *$250,000.00* fine.

"Imagine that!" Santa laughed. "A destitute, convicted killer sitting in a protective custody cell in Attica being ordered to pay a quarter million dollars."

It would never happen.

The Giver of Gifts grunted and pulled into an empty parking space beside a depressed two-story brick apartment building at 920 East 88th Street. He recalled a childhood friend once resided here in a room just beside the black fire escape clinging to the chipped bricks above the weathered archway.

"Those were the days, when the community was safe!"

Well, Mr. Boogeyman, Mammy snickered, *you've got some balls to say that. This street will go down in history as exceptionally traitorous, thanks to you!*

It could have been Anyplace USA:

Miami, Charleston, Washington D.C...

Neighborhoods like this one all looked alike. A quiet, lazy, side street by day, but nightfall brought in the twenty-dollar drug trade. Those crowds of *pimps* and *hookers* dodged into the alleyways to circumvent the spotlight of a passing *One-Adam-Twelve's, PO-PO's, Five-0's* cruiser, or whatever other *police slang* they hollered when the law came probing the darkness.

Santa shook his head and chuckled while staring down the street where police rushed into his house. The road was packed with people jockeying for a look at the commotion. Briefly, he considered hopping from the meat wagon and ripping off their skulls.

"Let them get a touch of the real thing, see how they feel about homicide, up close and personal!"

There was something about manslaughter that made people sit up and pay attention. They slammed down millions of dollars at movie theaters to experience bloodletting from the coziness of their seats. The Hollywood serial killer franchise *"SAW"* was Richard's favorite. It presented a merciless fictitious killer toying with captives before massacring them, one by one.

However, real MURDER was *another machine*, a commonplace occurrence where nobody batted an eye so long as the lifeless victim was a stranger.

It wasn't long ago, Richard reminisced, *when Brooklyn cops arrested a man for killing and dismembering his roommate inside an apartment on Nostrand Avenue.*

It was gargantuan news, bringing out all the networks, and it did something else... the murder introduced Timothy Smith to Richard. Tim's newscast outlined the discovery of human body parts–*legs and arms*–butchered along with a set of ribs that cooled in a refrigerator.

It was reported there was so much flesh inside that icebox that an egg wouldn't fit inside.

Wait 'til they see my basement, they're going to need CSI New York! Just as he thought this, a cat's meow infiltrated his head with a long sustained cry.

Meooowww, it screamed, *Meeeoooowww!*

Richard shuddered and tendrils of anxiety caused his skin to crawl with terror as he gazed towards the building where a Siamese cat crouched watching from the windowsill.

Riiiiiieeehaaaaard! It called to him, *Oh, Mr. Santa Claus; it's time to go to work!* Its face, tail, and feet were black as death, the white body crouched, ready to spring through the glass. And then, the devilish thing did something odd.

Son of a bitch! It smiled.

Not a friendly grin either... Santa thought. *This is no Garfield or Tom & Jerry joke-a-thon... no cute little Talking Tom Cat iPhone app–this was a SNEER!*

It was the devil himself presenting thirty white fangs to bite into flesh with multiple scissor-like chomps.

It's time to drink the catnip, Richie Boy.

Santa knew kittens meowed when hungry, cold, or scared. But, once they got older, they used other vocalizations... like *yowling*, *hissing*, and *growling*, to communicate with each other.

As adults, they meowed for only *one* reason: to communicate with people! But their real intention is to steal my breath and take my life.

"What is it?" he begged the blue eyed monster in the window. "What do you want from me?"

I see you, Richie; I know what you're thinking.

At that moment, just as he was about to navigate the van back into the street and high-tail it as far away as he could, the cat raised its paw and pointed down the street... just like a kid might do when something shocking occurred.

In the distance, Kathleen stood vomiting on his lawn.

It's time to get the woman; she's on our Naughty List!

Richard was spellbound.

His gaze was caught in the captivating brilliance of the Siamese's eyeballs. Somehow, the blue irises made him want to scramble into mommy's womb and slurp on his thumb.

♫♪♫ *Rock-a-bye Santa, on the roof top,*
When the night comes...
Murder will knock! ♫♪♫

Santa glanced away in shame, embarrassed he still mumbled nursery rhymes. "Mammy, please make it go away!" He felt sick to his stomach, like the surge one experienced when grasping the rails of a theme park rollercoaster as it vaulted down the tracks towards Earth.

Snap out of it! Mammy shrieked. *And follow Mr. Siamese's instructions!*

He reluctantly glanced back to the windowsill and trembled in fear as the Siamese blinked one eye–*and that was strange, because cat's rarely blinked at all*–and then it turned from the window and leapt from view into the recess of the apartment.

Follow her home you no good bastard! And bring me her eyes to roll across the floor!

That's the cat's meow, Daddy whispered. *I'd say those tabbies have your number!*

So, Santa looked back down the street and knew immediately he had to follow instructions.

"I'll kill her, Daddy; and gouge out the eyes for the Siamese."

Chapter 47

Boneyard Basement

MURDERERS ROW was a term assigned to the first six sluggers of the 1927 New York Yankees line-up.

The term was commonly recycled to depict a force that contained intimidating ability.

"Get your game face on," Lieutenant Rico Martinez barked to Murphy as they climbed down an aluminum ladder leading to the boneyard basement. "This is the real *Murderers Row*."

It was true, Murphy realized, stepping off the bottom rung and examining the dimly illuminated subterranean tunnel. "Look at this bundle of pain and sorrow," he pointed in stunned surprise. Laid out before them were the ghastly remains of exhumed skeletons surrounded by assistants from the Medical Examiner's Office. Murphy was captivated by the bloody R E D R U M. "Good God," he stated pointing his flashlight from the word and towards the newspaper articles lining the wall. "Take a look at these interstate cases."

"Lieutenant Martinez!" Chief Medical Examiner Dr. Heung called out. "Sergeant Murphy! Welcome to our little section of perdition."

Rico shook the coroner's hand and scanned the dank, spine-chilling crypt. "Have you ever seen anything like this before, Doc?"

"Actually, yes, in 1998 a colleague asked for my humble assistance excavating skeletons from Benjamin Franklin's basement in London."

Murphy forced himself to glance away from the articles. He'd never heard of such a thing. "Ben Franklin, our founding father who invented electricity and eye glasses?"

"He invented bifocals." Dr. Heung corrected. "The first eyeglasses were invented by Giordano da Pisa of Italy in 1286."

"I'm having a problem digesting the fact bones were found in his basement."

"It's true," the coroner confirmed. "Over twelve hundred human bones from ten different bodies were buried in his basement during the time he lived there."

"Get outta here!" Rico dismissed. "Are you pulling my chain here?"

"No, it's true! Of course, nobody believes the bones were the result of homicide. Ben Franklin didn't participate in a murder spree between flying kites and designing bifocals, but it's still a great story; the bones were severed and had scalpel marks leading many to suppose they were used for research by Franklin's friend who'd set up a lab in the basement for anatomical studies."

Then again, the M.E. thought, *speculation was just that. Nobody really knew the truth.*

"Wouldn't that be something if *Old Ben* had a skeleton in his closet," Rico snorted while counting black body bags lying on the dirt floor. "Walk me through what we have here. I see twelve bags."

They were lined up one after another awaiting removal by the coroner's office.

It jogged his memory of a recent stunt where body bags containing fake bodies were laid before the United Nations building to represent fifteen hundred people who died daily around the world from armed violence.

Except in these bags were real skeletons of people who'd lost their life to a murdering sociopath.

The Medical Examiner walked the detectives through the scene and over to a damp wall where crusty, bloody, words were etched on the back wall.

TO LIVE IS EVIL

"We've confirmed a few things right off the bat," Heung stated. "The handwriting is by the same hand as the notes discovered in the former homicides."

"It looks like blood," Murphy said.

"It is. Brooklyn CSI tested it with Luminol and it's positive. It glowed for thirty seconds before fading which allowed them time to take photographs for you guys."

"Rico, my friend," Warrants Division Murray Matthews shouted from the ladder. "Good to see you again!"

He stepped gingerly around the shallow graves and frowned at his long-time colleague.

"Are you getting a load of all this, buddy?"

"We're up to our neck in it, Murray," Rico responded. "Were you serving the warrant?"

"Yeah, along with Probation and Parole."

"What do we know?" Murphy asked.

"Not a whole hell of a lot, Mike. Our suspect wasn't here and we landed in a lonely graveyard jam-packed with John Does."

"Actually," the coroner interrupted handing over a paper bag, "we just found this sack of identification cards."

Rico pulled on a pair of latex gloves and poked through the bag's contents of drivers' licenses, social security cards, and employment I.D. badges.

"They date back fifteen years. Looks like your John Does just spoke to us from their graves."

Chapter 48

Ðǫad Ǫndǫr

ℬROADWAY LIQUORS sat in darkness.

It did a brisk business in Washington Heights tending to the shattered, intoxicated patrons who'd long ago traded in hopes and dreams for the bottom of a bottle.

Stefan supposed there wasn't anything wrong with wishing and hoping, so long as you understood one little thing. Once the buzz wore off, hopelessness returned.

Yet, as Marco and he hiked through its grimy entrance, the only thing they wished for was a bag full of money; nothing else counted.

It was a robbery, plain and simple, a means to an end in order to eat and survive.

That's the lie they told one another.

What it really was–*the motive for robbing this store*– was payback for a year-old shoplifting arrest the fat Columbian owner had leveled against Marco.

"Three days in jail!" Marco grumbled earlier that day, "all for a lousy Three Musketeer bar and a Miller Lite!"

"It's a convenient excuse to fill our pockets with cash we haven't earned." Stefan insincerely protested.

"Either you're with me or you can go home to Mirabel," Marco threatened. "There isn't anything in between!"

That made things interesting; a choice between keeping the only pal he'd ever known or shuffling to a mommy wannabe; that's how it was.

So, Stefan made his choice and here he stood with Marco pointing his revolver at the fat man's head.

¿Qué pasa gordo?" Marco asked. "You see my face?"

The man didn't quiver.

"No, no veo nada, papo."

He knew all too well, the best way to handle hoodlums with guns–*especially the young ones*–was to give them what they wanted and continue living another day.

"Mighty Whitey," Marco nodded. "Open the register and see what fat boy has in the cash drawer!"

Stefan darted behind the counter, packed his pockets with cash, and stuffed cartons of cigarettes into his backpack. "I got it all," he confirmed running through the door and hitting the sidewalk just as an alarm shrieked.

"That Chico tripped an alarm," Marco bellowed, running into the dark street and almost getting clipped by a car.

"Hey!" a man yelled from its window, "watch where the hell you're running!"

Suddenly, gunshots echoed from the storefront and bullets punched through the thin metal.

The sound reminded Stefan of a childhood memory shooting pellets at hubcaps. But, these gunshots were much louder and Stefan knew he was a long way from those innocent memories of shooting air guns. Diving for cover, he glanced at the driver and noticed a gaping hole in his head, a blank stare in the eyes and brains splattered across the dashboard.

"Maricón!" the fat man shrieked firing at the car where a bullet whizzed past Marco's head.

"Sucker!" Marco shouted in wounded agony when glass carved out a section of his cheek. "I'm hit, the bastard shot me in the face!"

"Ayuda, Ayuda!" Gordo shrieked, "me están robando!" He scanned the abandoned dark street for assistance just as Marco pushed the revolver over the hood and let loose three loud rounds.

The store's plate glass window exploded in a spray of glass, hitting Gordo and sending him to the ground screaming in pain.

"Oh, Jesus, me dispararon, por favor ayúdame!"

"What the fuck's he saying?" Stefan shouted peeking over the car's roof.

Marco snorted, "He's telling the Lord he needs help and that he's been shot!"

At this instant, the boys saw their chance for escape and sprinted down the shadowy street, through a long forgotten abandoned lot and into the relative comfort of Bennet Park.

By the time they entered the safety of the apartment, they were drenched with sweat and out of breath from the near death experience.

"He tried to kill us!" Marco gasped pulling off his New York Knicks sweatshirt and noticing a bullet hole in his chest. "Aw, shit, Stefan, I'm shot!"

"Oh, man!" Stefan whimpered, rushing to his friend who abruptly collapsed onto the couch, blood seeping from the wound. "Marco, we have to get you to the hospital!"

"That fucker," Marco coughed, blood bubbling through his lips, "I sh-sh-should have p-put more holes in his ass!"

"It's going to be all right, buddy," Stefan lied.

Marco looked bad; his body had begun to shudder from death's frosty arrival.

"Marco, please, Marco, please don't die."

"Stefan," Marco's lips trembled, "you... ha-ha-have to... make me... *one*... promise." He knew there were just instants before the finish line of life approached. Then, the reaper would appear and he'd be ferried to purgatory for judgment of his sins. *That's how it goes,* he thought struggling for breath, recalling nights long ago when his mother sat on his bed and read the King James Bible. He felt himself drifting away now; lightness came over his body and for a moment, he believed he saw dark shadows surrounding him, welcoming his arrival to hell.

"Marco! What is the promise? I swear, just name it!"

The tough Puerto Rican glanced at his friend and noticed his vision fading, *dimming*, like a fog had moved into the room making things hard to see.

"Find... *hap... hap... happiness*," he stuttered.

And then, the boy gasped a final breath and his body froze as the hushes of eternity extracted his spirit from the now lifeless body.

"No! Please, Marco, noooooooooo!"

But, silently, he knew, the reaper did what it wanted.

Death had arrived.

Chapter 49

Sugar Plum Fairies

GOLDIE WAS NESTLED snug in her bed as visions of fairies danced in her head.

The slumbering little princesses flickering dreams complemented harpsichord notes from: *The Dance of the Sugar Plum Fairy*. It was a remnant memory of a YouTube's Fantasia video she'd viewed before slipping between the sheets. In the dream, a pirouetting fairy dashed pixie dust amongst teeming flowers. And then... flocks of whirling nymphs illuminated a wondrous silk spider web.

Her fluttering mind skipped and giggled amongst all things enchanted and beautiful... *until it faded to shadows...* as the orchestra gave way to a weak tapping sound, like a toy hammer striking a nail.

Her nine-year-old green eyes snapped awake and the princess squinted about her room. Here, bears didn't fight for bed space, fairies failed to zigzag through the air and nothing seemed out of place.

The fairytale was *just a dream.*

Then again, something WAS out of place, Goldie knew, glancing at the Princess Doll in her grasp. She recalled combing its hair just before her eyelids fluttered into *Never-Never Land.*

The air was heavy with a sense something wasn't right.

She had a feeling, the kind kids could tune into. They were like an antenna receiving unseen signals from the Wizard of Childhood... indications that were outside the gateways of adult comprehension. The sensation was like a hand of destiny –*cautioning her*– awakening the princess from her glittering sleep.

"Is that you, Peter Pan?" she whispered. "Have you knocked something over, Tinker Bell?" Goosebumps raised themselves along her skin, causing her to tremble... as if a cool breeze had passed through the room.

"I know you're out there," she whispered slipping from the covers. Stepping into her slippers, she tiptoed across the room to the window. "Come out; come out, wherever you are."

Giggling, she pulled aside the curtains and pushed onto her tippy-toes to peer through the foggy window. Running her hand across the chilly glass, she glared into the darkness at the neighbors' houses.

All is silent, she thought, *not a creature is stirring. Not even a mouse!* "I know you're out there, Mr. Peter Pan," she muttered–as if holding a clandestine knowledge reserved for invisible friends–before she released the drapes and pushed back to her bed.

Then, a thump came from somewhere directly beneath her bedroom.

She stared at Justin Bieber's, *Never Say Never,* movie poster taped to the back of her door.

"Hello?" she whispered, reaching for the handle. "Mommy, is that you?" *Might have just been a mouse, if my ears didn't fool me. I could have sworn there were footsteps with that bumpy-thumpy noise.*

Again the noise erupted.

It wasn't a deliberate thud she overheard... but rather a soft transitory encounter with something. Like when someone creeps through a dark room and collides with a table... *by accident.* And then, shuffles across the floor to *hide* in a corner.

"Mommy," she called turning the doorknob, "Mommy, is that you?" The latch clicked loudly in her ears as she pulled open the door, craned her neck around its frame, and squinted down the second story staircase.

The stairwell was lit by faint baseboard lights displaying a path for bathroom seekers misplaced to bursting bladders in the dead of night.

Shuffle! Shuffle! Shuffle!

There it is again!

The urgency in the scampering paces was akin to a fretful dog's nails gliding over a wooden floor. Either happy it had a playmate... or angry enough to take a chunk!

Goldie crept to the staircase and flipped on the lights. "Hello?" she called into the fading light descending into the dark living room. "Is anyone there?"

She wondered why her mom didn't answer.

Maybe she's fallen down and can't get up!

With apprehension, she hurried down the staircase and flipped on the light at the bottom stair landing.

"Mommy..." she called into the empty room, just milliseconds before Santa Claus sprung from behind the Christmas tree and began to sing a nursery rhyme.

♫ Hush up, bratty baby, don't you cry! Momma loves you... And so do I. ♫

Dumbass, Mammy whispered in Santa's head. *That's not how the rhyme goes!*

Yet... the giver of gifts was not the least bit interested in what his blathering deadbeat mother had to say. What held his attention, *the thing which made his blood boil...* was the petite, smiling angel who stood before his eyes!

Now what are you going to do? Daddy growled. *You're not going to kill her, too... are you?*

"She does have bright green eyes!" Santa mumbled, creeping towards the blonde haired child.

Chapter 50

The Task At Hand

THE JACOB K. JAVITZ Federal Building sat at 26 Federal Plaza and was the tallest federal skyscraper in the United States.

Hosting countless federal agencies over forty-one floors, the boys with the biggest sticks were the Department of Homeland Security and the New York Field Office of the FBI.

The Bureau employed over two thousand agents, staff members, and task force officials all under the jurisdiction of the United States Federal Protective Service for law enforcement and security matters.

The Serial Killer Task Force was now in session.

"I'm not buying Blake is the I-95 Corridor Killer," NYPD Deputy Inspector Morrison stated. "And I'm having a hard time believing he's *The Santa Claus Killer*."

"It seems like the evidence is against you on that, Sir." Special Agent Mei Ling argued.

It was close to midnight on the twenty-third floor of a cramped conference room and she was tired.

Studying Morrison, Agent Ling knew the deputy inspector was a twenty-five-year veteran with a cutthroat politician's tongue. Staring at his stiff white command shirt decorated with an oak leaf insignia on the shoulder, Mei's eyes moved to the silver and gold badge.

"This seems like a witch hunt," the inspector said springing from his chair and moving to a high definition flat screen displaying images of the boneyard basement.

Captain Anton McKenzie stood sentinel beside Rico and Murphy along the back wall. Not because they were lowly street homicide investigators, but simply due to the lack of space in the standing room only meeting.

"The NYPD thanks our partners here at the Bureau," Morrison continued with clipped words. "And although I have reservations about Blake as the suspect, my Deputy Chief and Inspector assure the FBI our full resources on this case."

He pointed to Kathleen Royce.

"I'd like the suspect's probation officer to give us background data on Blake and then we'll hear from our lead investigators."

Kathleen straightened her Liz Claiborne New York Sweater Tunic, grabbed a manila file folder, and hurried to the front of the room.

"Just give the task force a quick overview of his history," Morrison instructed stepping aside and buttoning up his frame. "After you are done we will decide the course of action that lies ahead."

Control freak, Kathleen thought nodding politely and pulling a fact sheet from the folder. Her bosses had spent hours preparing her for this meeting, warning of the aggravation Morrison would present and instructing her to *'just smile and take it.'*

Nobody in law enforcement wanted to be unprepared when called down to the federal building, and Kathleen was no exception.

"Good evening. I was the case officer assigned to supervise the release conditions and probation fulfillment terms for Richard Blake."

"Good morning, Kathy," Agent Ling smiled. "No need to be nervous, we're all on *offense* here."

Kathleen nodded her appreciation and glanced to her watch. It was 12:13 a.m. and she'd just arrived at the briefing after running home from the boneyard basement to tuck her daughter into bed.

She had allowed the baby sitter to go home moments before her pager instructed her to high-tail it down to the Federal Building. Having no choice, she left her sleeping daughter home alone, and that bothered her now.

"Richard Blake was convicted of twenty-seven counts of cruelty to animals," she continued. "Dubbed the *Cat Man of Brooklyn* by the New York media, he was sent to a facility for supposed schizophrenia. Released to our supervision after three years of treatment, he maintained regular appointments with an assigned psychiatrist and was being medicated with the anti-psychotic drug, Haloperidol. However, earlier this week, he disappeared and a warrant was issued for his arrest."

"Why was he released from the hospital to begin with?" Agent Ling asked. "How did that happen without a court order?"

"We aren't clear on that."

"Let's not get caught up on how or why Blake was released," Deputy Inspector Morrison stated. "Let's focus on what we do know... detectives?"

"The shrink has come up missing," Detective John Arias stated from the back of the room. "His mother and father have also gone missing."

"Thank you," the deputy inspector nodded. "Is there anything else for the FBI to know?"

Captain McKenzie stepped to the front of the room. "The first local case was investigated by Manhattan South Homicide and for that I'll ask my guys to give their overview of what's transpired to date."

Murphy stepped forward.

"I'm Sergeant Mike Murphy of Manhattan South," he introduced. "I'm also the lead detective on the Santa case."

"How many are on your team?" Agent Ling asked.

"There are four of us. My supervisor, as many of you know, is Lieutenant Rico Martinez, who oversees Manhattan South homicide investigations."

Rico nodded to the group.

"Yeah," Agent Ling snickered, "we know the head burrito. He's a regular *Lone Ranger*."

Everyone chuckled, in spite of twelve hours of intense briefings like this one.

When the sniggers died down Murphy continued.

"However, Rico is hanging up the badge at year's end, so you guys are stuck with me unless we nab this monster in the next couple of weeks."

"You said there were four?" Mei probed. "Who are the other two detectives?"

Murphy pointed to the rear of the room where Romero and Arias stood whispering into one another's ears. "Both those guys are crackerjack, first rate investigators with good experience in digging deep."

"Okay," Agent Ling smiled, "pull it all in for us, will you, Mike?"

Picking up a remote control, he pointed it at the flat screen, and reached into his mental file cabinet. "The first body was found on a Herald Square Park bench just a week after Thanksgiving."

On the flat screen, the corpse of Mr. Berrymoore was sprawled on the park bench.

"It was the first time we had seen anything quite like this, eyes missing, head bashed in and dressed, as you can see, in a Santa suit."

A grunt went up from the room, like something familiar had just occurred and connected the dots.

"Just like Charleston, South Carolina," Mei offered.

"And Bangor, Maine," another agent added. "Hackensack, New Jersey, Miami Beach and Atlanta, just to name a few."

"How many of these pattern killings have you got?" Agent Ling asked.

Murphy went through the images on the monitor. "To date we have three fresh bodies, the park bench Santa

Claus, a Manhattan Criminal Court Judge and a black homeless kid…. and the twelve skeletons in the basement."

"And the recent connection is these three new cases," Mei said, "along with the similar case traits of missing eyes and hand written notes?"

"Etched by the same hand," Rico pitched in, "according to the New York County Chief Medical Examiner."

Mei stood from her seat and walked to the front of the room. "I'm Special Agent Mei Ling of the Serial Killer Task Force, and I've been working *patterns* and *serials* for the last twelve years. I have a team of profilers and forensic psychiatrists on the squad as well."

She indicated for Murphy to hand her the remote, and when he did, Mei brought horror to the screen behind her.

"The killer stalking New York City is one and the same we've been hunting for years. He's laid a graveyard of bodies from Key West to Maine."

A knock at the door brought everyone's attention to Special Agent in Charge, Larry Magley, who marched into the room with a nerdish agent following close behind.

"Folks," Magley nodded towards the man beside him. "Agent Blau here, from ViCAP, just notified me of a disturbing connection to the corpses found in your basement."

The Violent Criminal Apprehension Program maintained the largest analytical storehouse of major violent crime cases in America. It collected and analyzed data of homicides, sexual assaults, missing persons and other violent criminalities involving unidentified human remains.

All eyes were on the head of the New York office as he pointed to the analytical agent flipping through electronic pages of data on his iPad.

"Tell them what you found," Magley ordered, "and don't sugarcoat it."

Agent Blau plugged his tablet into the flat screen and sent a stream of electronic documents to the display.

"What you're observing are the names of the twelve skeletons found in the Brooklyn basement."

"The problematic issue," Magley advised, "is they all went missing in one place and one event over a period of twelve years."

"The New York City SantaCon event," Agent Blau mumbled. "Every year since 1997, one of the recovered skeletons went missing there except for a three year period."

"What period is that?" Murphy questioned.

"When Blake was in the hospital."

"Holy Christ," Deputy Inspector Morrison regretfully groaned. "Hundreds of thousands of people dressed as Santa Claus fill Manhattan streets for this event every year; it could have been any of them who did the killings."

"Sure, but you have to admit, Harold," Mei said, "It looks like Blake stalks the venue, especially since the killing stopped when he was in the hospital. This year's SantaCon is scheduled to take place throughout Manhattan in dozens of events all the way through Christmas Eve."

"And he'll be looking to compliment his personal collection of bodies," Murphy supposed. "That means more corpses lined up throughout the city."

"With more dead Santas," Mei agreed.

"Saddle up, everybody!" Magley ordered. "And get over to his butcher shop to see if we can track down this madman before he kills again!"

"I'm still not buying Blake as the killer," Morrison huffed. "I think the Bureau is jumping to some pretty big conclusions here."

SAC Magley turned on the inspector. "Do we have your cooperation on this one, Harold?"

"Of course, Larry, I just want to explore every possible suspect and not get bogged down on this one guy."

"This is *the* guy," the agent stated. "I'd bet my ass on it…and so should you."

Chapter 51

Nowhere to Run

TRISHA PUSHED into the filthy apartment building.

She scanned the filthy, crumbling drywall fragmenting its way to extinction. Graffiti wound its way across the walls weaving a story of artistic hope, dreams, and agony.

These were messages painted by poor kids who once stood before the white paint and had their say on life and anger.

Staring down the long hallway, Trisha hurried over a sullied, worn carpet.

"Nasty slum," she murmured, stepping into a dank stairway. The weight of her figure caused the failing wooden planks to creak while stepping up the stairs.

"Stefan?" she hollered into the echoing stairwell, "baby-boy, are you home?"

The sound of her voice echoed through the stairway.

"Hello!" she screamed, grabbing hold of a weak oak bannister and peering up into the darkness.

"Is anyone up there?"

Up-therrrrre... the echo vibrated through the shaft.

There-there-there-therrrre... –

The echo pushed forth memories of the State Fair–the fun house in particular–but *fun* was not the portrayal this place merited. Filthy, stinky, disgustingly damp... Any of those worked just fine. Or mildewed, moldy... Asbestos filled and rat infested.

Stopping to catch her breath at the top floor landing, she leaned against the frigid wall, grasped the doorknob, and marched into a blustery passageway that once welcomed skipping, laughing, children who'd played hopscotch or tag.

Nowadays, growing-up was a Facebook update.

Sometimes her phone sounded like a bird chirping constant notifications from friends about celebrities' lives and their favorite movies or music.

Then… a muffled cry brought her attention back to the loneliness of the rundown hallway.

"Trishaaaaaa!" Stefan's voice cut through the passageway. "Trisha… is that you?"

She sensed agony in the voice, a *squeal* right at the end. It reminded her of that boyish country singer from American Idol, Scott "Scotty" McCrery, who hit her sweet spot with his deep crying notes.

However, Stefan's scream carried a tremor.

"Baaaaaaaby," he called a moment before she stormed through the doorway and into the apartment.

She hadn't run like that since her little sister went to the emergency room with a broken leg.

That kind of running was reserved for panic.

That's what she felt now staring at her lover.

"Oh, no…" she gulped, her palms slapping the sides of her cheeks in disbelief at the horror before her.

Stefan was hunched on the floor in a pool of desiccating, black blood. In his arms stretched the lifeless body of Marco, his eyes entombed in the sightless stare of death.

"Baaaaby," Stefan sobbed, his tears rolling down red cheeks. "He's dead, Trisha. My best friend is gone!"

She knelt in the blood and stared into Stefan's blue eyes. "It's going to be all right." she hopelessly offered.

That's when she saw the bullet hole in Marco's chest.

His body was white as a sheet, as if every ounce of blood had been siphoned from his veins, leaving an empty shell in place of the once playful boy she'd come to know.

That was yesterday; a nevermore.

Right now is what counted.

And that meant getting Stefan out of there no matter the consequences.

And there would be consequences, her thoughts damned. "Stefan. We have to get you out of here right now!"

Yet, it was almost as if her words fluttered around his ears and drifted, unheeded, into the space of unknown considerations. He appeared detached, misplaced in the desolation of his thoughts, rocking back and forth grasping his departed friend in his embrace.

"Marco," he sobbed, "Marco!"

It was then she glanced to the coffee table and saw the revolver sitting on the cracked glass.

"Stefan," she pointed. "Did you shoot him?"

He glanced at her, his stare rebounding from the valley of death. But, he didn't recognize the accusation.

What he did hear... down in the pits of despair was mumbo jumbo nonsense, *Diib bu choot hihm?* Blinking back the senselessness he glared into her eyes.

What burned there was anger.

"Huh?"

"Did you shoot him?" she demanded backing away from Marco's lifeless body.

Now, Stefan understood. Her condemnation rang louder than a ringing bell on Sunday morning.

She thinks I killed him.

He shook his head and stared into Marco's empty gaze.

She is accusing me of killing my best friend!

But, as far as Trisha was concerned, the evidence before her pointed to the killer sitting on the bloody floor with fake tears and an Academy Award performance.

So, she ran out the door, down the creaking stairs and departed the abandoned building as fast as her legs could move, to a place as distant as she could stretch.

"Trisha! Come baaaaaaaack!"

But she didn't go back.

What she did was run into the darkness... where her silhouette disappeared into the shadows of uncertainty.

Chapter 52

Daddy Christmas

PRINCESS GOLDIE pointed her little finger in excitement–*and then confusion*–at Santa Claus.

"You're not supposed to be here until Christmas Eve!"

The murderer stood dazed as a reindeer transfixed by the glare of an 18-wheeler's headlights. He didn't expect to find a little girl standing in the living room.

You didn't expect it? Mammy whispered. *You're Daddy Christmas who promises to slide down the chimney and shuffle around the Christmas tree.*

It's two weeks before Christmas, Daddy mumbled. *He can't do anything correctly.*

Santa was speechless.

He'd followed Kathleen home, observed her climb from the car and pace through the slush filled street before pushing into the house in Queens.

And yet, only this angel stood at his feet.

She's beautiful, just perfect!

"I'm looking for your mommy."

"What were you doing behind the Christmas tree? And where are your reindeer?"

"They're on the roof," Santa grinned with a wink, "waiting to take me back to the North Pole." Glancing at the Colorado blue spruce, he saw it was draped with strings of blinking lights. The branches drooped with silvery icicles, large red bulbs, and candy canes. At its apex sat a heavenly angel about to finger a plastic harp. That's when it morphed into a flesh and blood entity and began plucking the harp's strings.

Notes of *The Christmas Song* filled his head and it reminded him of a YouTube video of harpist Michelle Whitson.

Then, a voice in his head rang like thunder.

The spruce angel stared at him, its eyes ablaze with piercing condemnation.

Pain shot through Santa's cranium and for an instant, he blinked back the torment.

She's not on your naughty list, the angel spoke. *You better watch out, don't make her cry and I'll tell you why... I'll rip your soul to shreds the second you die!*

Flinching in fear at the grinning emissary, he watched as it ended its recital and changed back to the land of Ornamentville.

Turning to the girl he winced, "you're not naughty!"

Goldie lumbered across the shagged-rug, grabbed Santa's hand, and peered hopefully into his glare.

"Of course I'm not, silly. I've been a good girl!"

She led him to the kitchen and pointed towards paneled cabinets over her head. "I can give you cookies and milk if you grab two glasses from up there."

Santa was shaken, lost within her burning stare. "I'd love some milk and a cookie or two," he muttered grabbing two cheap glasses.

"Not two percent milk," Goldie giggled as he picked up the wrong container, "that's for Mommy and her boyfriend. I have to drink whole milk. She says vitamin-D will make my bones stronger."

Santa pushed aside a pan of lasagna and grabbed a gallon of *Organic Valley* milk before pushing the fridge door closed and shuffling over to the little girl.

"You lost weight, Santa. On TV they show you as a big old fat man!"

He grunted, scrutinized his body, and readjusted his huge black belt. It was true; he hadn't the opportunity to pack this new suit with padding to give the appearance of plumpness.

"Does Mrs. Claus have you on a diet?" she asked, placing a cookie on a plate and pushing it across the table.

You know you have to kill her, Mammy suggested. *She has to go bye-bye! Maybe put her in a box and throw her under the tree. Merry Christmas and Happy New Year!*

No, you will not, another voice interrupted. *Killing the child is a sin!*

Santa glanced to a picture of the Virgin Mary that came alive and waved a finger at him.

Ah-ah-ah, it warned, *No, you won't!*

Richard watched the apparition moving inside the picture frame. It sprung to life by his mental illness and the dim capabilities of an unmedicated mind.

But to him, this was as real as it got.

There was no convincing *the poser* the Holy Mother in the picture wasn't alive and well… and certainly muttering her two cents.

Leave this child alone, and flee from her at once!

Santa gasped, leapt from the chair, and fell to his knees in prayer. "Hail Mary, full of grace, the Lord is with thee; blessed art thou among women … blessed is the fruit of thy womb, Lord Jesus. Amen."

Princess Goldie was stunned to silence and frightfully hurried to the corner staring at the lunatic Santa mumbling his prayer.

"What are you doing, Santa?"

Then, a car door slammed out in the driveway and footsteps shuffled towards the house. The sound of keys jingled, and then a squall of cold air swept through the kitchen.

"Goldie," Kathleen called, "why are all the lights on?"

The little girl watched Santa place a finger to his lips.

"Shhhhhhhhh… or I'll put you on my naughty list!"

"Mommy, I'm scared!"

Santa threw his glass against the wall, jumped onto the counter and leapt through the glass kitchen window and out into the wintry night.

"Oh, my God!" Kathleen screamed hurrying into the kitchen and over to her daughter. Lifting her into her arms, she stared out the window.

"What is it, Sweetie, what happened to the window?"

"It was Santa, Momma. He came looking for you."

Chapter 53

Childhood Memories

GRAND CENTRAL STATION loomed at the corner of 42nd and Park Avenue in Midtown.

It was the most magnificent train terminal in the world hosting forty-four platforms along sixty-seven tracks on two levels.

These tracks served as an escape route to the suburbs and up into Connecticut. But hunting down anyone who'd admit to that was comparable to wrenching teeth from a ravenous black bear caged at the Bronx Zoo.

Of the twenty-one-million annual passengers who walked across the station's Tennessee marbled main concourse, Stefan was a mere spec in the vessel of humanity.

"I'm gonna miss you, bro," he whispered while pushing a photo of Marco into his jeans and shuffling across the smooth floor. Glancing at the Grand Clock situated in the middle of the concourse, he saw it was 1:15 a.m. Pulling his iPhone from a pocket, he pushed the white buds into his ears and removed the wad of stolen liquor store money from his jeans.

Selecting a twenty-dollar bill he pushed it into the ticket machine and ordered a round trip voucher to Peekskill.

He'd decided to venture back to where it all began, in exploration of his past, to discover where he'd come from and why he'd been abandoned.

Flipping through the iPhone's digital music tracks, he selected one of his favorites and pressed the play button.

The *Hudson River Line* ticket slid from the vending machine just as Michael Jackson's *Childhood* lyrics filled his ears. He mumbled along to the lullabied melody and thought about what he'd been through, where he'd been… and what he wanted to discover.

When Stefan was younger, right after his mom had died, he was placed into a boy's home in New Windsor, New York, where he rebelled, fought, and struggled to cope.

The *McQuade Foundation for Boys* was one of those lonely backwoods organizations where dispossessed and neglected kids were sent for residential attention.

"Lame asses," he grumbled staring at passengers shuffling along the platform.

He would take the train close to the Bear Mountain Bridge before catching a short ride to New Windsor.

And, hopefully, I'll find some answers.

What he would do when he got there was another story.

He hadn't a clue other than to talk to his one-time cottage father, Clifford Webb.

Just walk right up to the door, knock on it, and hug him.

Clifford had been the glue that held the boys together when he was a resident at McQuade. The houseparent gave the boys hope that tomorrow wasn't a phony con job where paper pushers determined their futures.

"You can be anything you want," Clifford had encouraged them, "you just have to want it!"

"And look at me now," he whispered taking a seat on a bench along the deserted platform. "I sure messed-up everything."

Clifford would have said he was on a journey of discovery. And maybe that was true.

I'd have been graduating from McQuade if I didn't break Marc Jacobsen's jaw.

Marc had killed Stefan's friend in the swimming pool one windy summer afternoon.

"Go, Stefan!" his best friend, Anson, yelled back in his childhood memory. "Kick their skinny rumps!"

Stefan was leading the race on the third lap, when only he and Marc were left to battle it out for the win, *side by side* and *shoulder to shoulder*, the blood pumped through their veins as if Olympic Gold Medalist, Michael Phelps stroked at their side.

"Lap number four," Tito the coach yelled.

That's when *Marc the Shark* pulled Stefan's leg to fudge the outcome. *Cheater!*

Stefan kicked out Mark's front teeth and swam another four laps. Not only beating the school's bully in charge–but setting an all-time record for endurance.

The boys *cheered, hollered,* and *pulled* their hero from the pool with excited slaps on his back.

"Goddamn right!" Anson squealed hugging his pal and shooting *the finger* at Marc the *toothless* Shark.

"Who's your daddy now, bitch?"

That brought the brute charging and swinging a pool skimmer that hit Anson in the head, sending him flying into the pool where he convulsed and later died of head trauma.

That night, as silence hung over the school from word of the death, Stefan crept into Mark's room in Windsor Cottage, and beat him unconscious with a shower rod.

Game... Set... Match.

He was expelled and sent to Spofford Detention where he was charged with 2nd Degree Assault.

Weeks later, he stumbled into Marc the Shark and beat his pussy-ass every day while awaiting his trial.

Sometimes life threw a curveball, and that squared things up. And sometimes it didn't.

Chapter 54

Cat Man of Queens

$\mathcal{B}$RIARWOOD WAS the hidden gem of Queens.

But, when a serial killer stalked the shadows, 911 calls brought the cops, FEDS, and blood sucking reporters.

"We are live in the hometown of Governor Andrew Cuomo and CSI Miami star, David Caruso," Reporter Tim Smith said staring into the news camera. "Tonight, this quiet community is the backdrop for a massive manhunt seeking The Santa Claus Killer."

The town was now a dreadful headline.

Security was so tight that if Goldie's real-life *American Idol* showed up, *The Biebs* himself wouldn't get through the crime scene perimeter. In fact, there was a better chance of a grey alien landing and belting out its own rendition of Baby, baby, baby.

"There she is!" a reporter shouted, pointing toward Kathleen carrying Goldie to an unmarked Dodge Charger where burly FBI Agents stood guard.

"Come on, people," an FBI escort barked. "Make way for the lady, will ya?"

"Momma, will Santa Claus get in trouble?"

"No, kitten," Kathleen answered, catching the horrid irony. "He'll still deliver presents on Christmas Eve."

After what they found behind our tree, I won't be calling my baby girl a little purrball ever again!

"Ma`am," another FBI Agent nodded opening the Charger's rear door, "I'll take you to the hotel."

"Thank you so much," Kathleen mumbled, offering a faint smile and guiding Goldie into the backseat.

"Kathleen!" Murphy shouted rushing from the house, sprinting down the porch stairs and dashing through the snow. "Can I have a minute before you leave?"

"Sure, Fighting Irish."

"Did Goldie tell you anything the killer said?"

She leaned into the car. "Bunny, did Santa say anything to you in the kitchen?"

"He said I wasn't on his naughty list, Momma."

Kathleen turned to Murphy and saw recognition in his stare. "What's up, Mike? I can tell a freight train just hit you in the gut."

He pulled out the naughty list. "I think he's after you, Kathy, if you are the one who sent him for loony-tune hour with the headshrinker."

"What makes you say that? I was good to him."

Murphy unfolded the note and showed her the fifth entry written on the message.

5) Slaughter the lady who sent me to a shrink!

She gasped. "How long have you known?"

Murphy shook his head, "Agent Ling just figured it out up in the house. We were questioning his motive for coming to your house, not injuring your daughter, and jumping through the kitchen window."

"Instead of killing her, you mean?"

"Yeah, but it makes sense. In his mind, your daughter wasn't on the list so he didn't hurt her."

"But I'm on it? He wants me dead next?"

"It's possible you might have been killed if Goldie didn't scream."

She pulled aside her jacket and showed the Sig Sauer P-229. "He would've had slugs in his head."

"It's going to be okay, Kathy," Murphy assured. "We're going to get this guy!"

She nodded. "Keep me in the loop, Murphy," she ordered before sliding into the backseat, "and notify me if you find Blake at the butcher shop."

"We're going to hit it at first light. In the meantime, we have unmarked units at the front and rear entrances just in case he shows up."

"Thanks, Irish. See you at the Task Force Meeting."

"We're not going to have you involved in this, Kathy. You're too close to it now." Knowing a protest would come he hurried to the house where Mei stood waiting.

"What did she say?"

"It's like you thought," Murphy answered. "Kris Kringle told the kid she wasn't on his Naughty List so he left her alone."

Walking into the house, they watched a forensic technician place shattered pieces of Santa's glass and half-eaten cookie into plastic evidence bags. They'd be taken to the FBI crime lab and checked for prints and DNA.

Hiking to the Christmas tree, Murphy stared at the eyeless Bengal cat that was nailed to the drywall. They had almost missed the slaughter because it was hidden by the spruce. Three-inch nails were driven through each paw; just like Jesus nailed to his cross at Calvary. The cat's eye sockets were empty and the tongue was carved from its mouth.

"This feline won't get another life," Murphy snorted. "There will be no more catnip or scratches behind its ears."

"Wow," Mei stared, "the bureau hasn't seen this kind of cat mutilation since Jeffrey Dahmer impaled frog, cat, and dog heads on sticks."

Above the cat, this was written in blood:

DOG TAC

"What's up with this guy? Why write bloody messages on walls at the scenes?"

"He wants our attention," Mei supposed glancing to her partner. "This is one of the sickest things I've ever seen."

"Well, if nothing else, he has that!" Murphy huffed pulling a notepad from his pocket and unscrambling the letters. When finished, he showed the pad to Mei.

"Son of a bitch... another secret message."

"*Dogtac* spelled backwards is *Cat God*," Murphy snickered, "what a psychopath, huh? It looks like we've got a modern day Son of Sam." Between 1976 and '77 the city was living on a razor's edge as the serial killer slaughtered six people. Later claiming his black Labrador, Harvey, was possessed by a demon, he told police the canine ordered him to kill people. Trying to execute the mongrel, he failed because of imagined supernatural interference.

"Jesus," Murphy muttered. "I remember dad saying the Son of Sam wrote a note to the newspaper stating he was a monster." Staring at the feline secured to the wall, he couldn't help but wonder what other presents Santa carried in his little red sack.

"Crazy is as crazy does," Mei joked.

Goddamn, wasn't that the truth.

Chapter 55

ᗅll Worked Up

IF TEMPER TANTRUMS were an art form:

This was the Picasso of Rage.

Santa was furious he'd been cheated.

He had wanted to collect Kathleen's eyes, and now… somebody had to pay!

Give them an inch and they take a mile!

His face was streaked with dried blood. Deep lacerations crisscrossed his angry face and jagged shards of glass protruded from red cheeks. The kitchen window had done a number on the Red Suited Fool.

"Kathy, Kathy, Kathy! You lousy father humper! No good Pinocchio-nosed, probation scum sucking witch!"

He wanted to cut off her nose, to *SPEIGHT* her face.

And that's not the half of it, Mammy's ghost shrieked.

Santa trembled in anger while staring at Marco's corpse lying on the apartment sofa. His fist was clenched tightly around the hatchet, the muscles bulging from his forearm.

He was ready to strike anything that moved.

Everyone felt that sort of rage at least once in life.

But they don't chop up bodies, Daddy snickered. *What are you going to do now? Lie in the corner and suck your immature thumb?*

Aw! Mammy cackled. *You got his number, Mr. Thought Snooper… yes, you do!*

"Shut up!" Santa screamed. "Just leave me alone!"

He stomped across the creaking wooden floor like a lunatic off his meds, sealed in an asylum's padded room.

"What am I going to do? What the fuck to do? This jumbles the order of my list!"

The Naughty List was all he had in life.

It was his to do list of people to see and things to collect. Thinking about it now, he considered the mental checklist comparable to etching a grocery list and heading off to market to round things up.

Sometimes stampedes occur when shoppers find items out of stock.

"I want my stuff!" he growled, turning to the corpse and falling to the floor beside it. "I just wanted to take you home. We could have had *such fun* together... just the *two* of us." Dropping the hatchet, he ran his hand through the corpse's thick black hair and along a cool clammy cheek.

"Time to get down to business, collect what I can and move on to my next errand."

You're such a sucker for the pretty ones, Daddy spat in disgust. *Always did like those dark skinned boys.*

"You ruined everything!" Santa shrieked to the body, anger rising in his tone. "But we'll make things right; pieces of you are just as good as the whole!"

Pulling an icepick from a sack, he peeled back Marco's eyelid and thrust the iron into a socket, gouging out the deflated membrane.

That brought on the singing.

Deflating the second eye, he cut the optic nerve, placed the membrane into his sack, and crooned a parody of the Twelve Days of Christmas.

♫ On the twelfth day of Christmas, my true love gave to me, twelve buried skeletons, eleven cats-a-hanging, ten frozen eyeballs, and *a* dead Puerto Rican, all for free! ♫

This is where he picked up the hatchet, raised it over his head... and went to work on the body.

First, he chopped off the legs, removed by two swift plunging strikes to the sound of bones crunching.

A thump occurred when he tossed the first leg into his bag and the floor caught its weight. It was a dull, momentary thud... if you didn't know what to listen for, you'd have missed the finality of the racket. It was similar to what a hand might sound like slapping a surface.

Smiling, he picked up the second amputated leg and dropped it into the bloody sack. It was almost like the thighbone hit first and then the ankle followed.

Santa chuckled at the sightless skull. "You've got some muscle tone there, don't you, Mr. Black Beans and Rice?"

The mention of food caused his stomach to growl, and suddenly, he realized he hadn't eaten all day.

What I would give for some Frijoles Negros y Arroz!

He recalled a recent jaunt to Miami's Versailles Restaurant on SW 8th Street in Little Havana. The eatery was the World's Most Famous Cuban Restaurant, or so they claimed.

Who the fuck are you, Mammy said. *You don't know jack shit about the struggle of the Cuban people.*

That was true.

All Santa knew was Versailles cooked up some tasty food... and it had quickly become his favorite place in South Florida for Cuban fare.

"They call the street, Calle Ocho," he mumbled to the body. "It's home to Cuban immigrants and people from Central and South America. I don't suppose you've ever been that far south, huh?"

Only the silence of death answered.

"Oh, well, I can't expect you to answer. After all, you are break dancing with the devil right now."

Chopping up Marco, the fiend thought about a plate of Picadillo a La Cubana. Made from ground beef, cooked with onions, bell peppers, raisins, olives, wine and a light tomato sauce, it was usually served with white rice, black beans, and sweet plantains.

"Scrumptious," he muttered while butchering the body. Piece by piece, he tossed the parts into his red satchel.

Then, the unexpected occurred.

A police siren shrieked out on the street.

Richard froze. *It can't be! They have no idea where I am hiding out or where I am headed!*

Hurrying to the window he glared towards an NYPD car that was pulling up to the entrance of the building.

Ya better get a move on, Son! Daddy prodded. *Pick up your bag of goodies and haul ass!*

Santa grasped the bloody sack and threw it over his shoulder. Should anyone have taken his picture at this precise moment, the image could have later been sold on eBay where true crime murderabilia was sold to macabre seekers. He thought John Edward Robinson was his idol as far as serial killers went; but Richard didn't want to end up in a prison cell waiting for a needle prick in the death house at Terre Haut, Indiana. That's where the feds marched Timothy McVeigh and would certainly drag Santa's sorry-ass to death if convicted of a national killing spree.

Strap him down real tight, partner, Santa imagined the warden saying. *Let's get a good fat vein for the needle!*

Thinking this, he peered back through the cracked window and watched the cop car disappear from view. When gone, he climbed onto the fire escape, scrambled down its steps, and made a rapid escape from the snooping, wandering eyes of the law.

In the bloody sack bounced the body of his sixth entry on the Naughty List.

6) Kill the Puerto Rican who beat me!

Although Santa didn't have the pleasure of killing the boy, he smiled at the thought of his next target.

Soon, he'd have the pleasure of slaughtering the attorney who got the punk out of jail!

And then, justice would be served.

Chapter 56

Night Train to Dreamland

*A*NY CHILD WOULD agree…

A train goes:

🔊 *Choo – chooooooooo!*
Chug –uh – chug – uh…
Choo – chooooooooo!

But electric railroad engines didn't make that sound.

Stefan slept in such a train. His body was oblivious to the intermittent pitches and *clickety–clack* of its wheels rolling over the steel rails.

However, deep within the sinister caverns of his mind, visions tormented and nudged his dreams, warning of something bordering a Nostradamus prophesy.

> "Next stop is Croton-on-Hudson. Please exit here for Amtrak connections up to the Adirondacks, Empire Service, Ethan Allen Express, Lake Shore Limited and Maple Leaf."

That little announcement would've normally fetched stampeding tourists had it been Saturday morning. But now, at 2:55 in the morning, the Pullman was a lonely graveyard of red-eyed desperados.

"M-m-m-Mirabel," Stefan mumbled, "he's going to hurt you!" He was envisioning her through the piercing yellow eyes of a regal Snowy Owl circling above Rockefeller Center's seventy foot Norway spruce.

Beside her skated the love of her life, their hands clasped lovingly together while gliding around the rink. Encircled by sparkling lights and joyful folks, it was clear they were relishing the cold winter evening.

That's when Stefan glimpsed the Santa Claus.

"G-g-g-get away fr-fr-from them," Stefan moaned, his brain fighting the demons of a terrible nightmare. "Ja-ja-ja-just leave them be!"

But nobody could hear him, and everyone in the dream continued skating past the bronze statue of Prometheus standing guard beside the rink. It was one of the most famous statues in the world. After the Statue of Liberty, Prometheus remained the most well-known piece of artwork in the United States and was believed to be the most photographed in Manhattan.

Sitting horizontal, the bronze depiction had brought fire to man, and was featured prominently in the sunken rink.

An inscription on its granite read:

"Prometheus,
Teacher in every art brought the fire
that hath proved to mortals a means to
mighty ends."

"Hoooooot! Hoooooot!" the Snowy Owl crooned.

Terry heard it, peered overhead, and pointed to the *bird of prey* moments before it swooped over the skater's heads.

"Oh, Terry!" Mirabel squealed. "Look how big he is! He must be two or three feet tall from talons to skull!"

Every year the majestic Snowy Owls of the Arctic Tundra invaded the northern United States.

This was the first to arrive in the city.

As they watched in awe, the bird ascended in a circling pattern and disappeared from sight into the dark sky.

What Stefan saw in the dream was in reverse; the diminishing outline of Mirabel and Terry looming below, as the owl slipped into the clouds and lost sight of the ground.

"Ooh, no! Go baaaaaack!"

That's when a high pitched chortle snapped him awake.

Jumping to his feet, the train jilted his equilibrium and sent him to the floor.

"Hackigi-gi-gi-gi," an old black man snickered slapping the side of his knee. His bony face twisted in amusement just before he started whistling *Rudolph the Red Nosed Reindeer*. "Boy, you've got to watch them-there dreams."

"Go away, old man, have a Merry Christmas."

The old guy winked, grinned, and walked through the train laughing, "ha-ha-ha-HA-ha… a Merry Christmas!"

And then, the giggles faded as he disappeared.

"Crazy old loon," Stefan muttered pulling himself from the floor and glancing at advertisements above his head.

On almost every train in New York a commuter saw a poster which read:

IF YOU SEE SOMETHING, SAY SOMETHING
(888) NYC-SAFE

This sent Stefan into a fit of laughter as the train pulled into the Croton-on-Hudson Station at 3 a.m.

"Isn't that some shit," he mumbled catching his breath. He thought it insane the SNITCH-LINE was written out with letters instead of numbers. Who would know how to call NYC-SAFE while watching a robbery, assault, or worse. Why not put the *number* up there, nice and simple? No figuring out what numbers correspond to letters of the goddamn alphabet. Government, they never consider practicality.

Walking off the train, he boarded a connecting locomotive waiting at the platform.

This electrified-rail ended here and passengers were forced to change to a diesel engine headed for the mountains. Anything north of Croton was the boonies, the middle of nowhere... boredom-town.

Bounding through the train, Stefan halted at the sight of an obese man wearing a Santa outfit.

"Hello, young man. Where you headed?"

"To the past, old man... back to the beginning."

Chapter 57

Breaching Madness

THE FEDS didn't want to sit on fresh intelligence.

Waiting and hoping always led to tragedy.

This morning was no different.

Special Agent in Charge Larry Magley had spent the last two hours before sunrise working with the Bureau's Crisis Management Unit, Special Weapons and Tactics (SWAT) and the NYPD Deputy Inspector's Office. The no-knock search warrant was now a joint operation of the Federal Government and the New York Police Department.

"Hell on Earth has arrived to Manhattan's Best Meat Market," Magley grunted to Mei's image upon a computer screen. He was coordinating the operation from the New York Field Office while everyone else huddled inside the Mobile Command Post in Columbus Park.

It resembled a fire truck outfitted with satellite and communication capabilities, and boasted a half-dozen computer systems which did everything but serve coffee.

The donuts were sitting atop the computers.

"Nothing is going to move in Wonton soup town," Mei assured the SAC, "unless you give the *all clear*. The NYPD is surrounding Mott, Baxter, Baynard, and Canal Streets."

"So, you're all set, then?" Magley asked.

"We've got this buttoned up," she affirmed while surrounded by the SWAT team who were busily eyeing a 3D animation of the building.

"Sir, we are GO for Operation Mistletoe!"

At that juncture, Deputy Morrison's voice came over an open radio channel. "Agent Ling, my *boys in blue* are authorized for entry when you give the go ahead."

He was huddled at One Police Plaza coordinating his own commanders.

"We're sealed up tighter than a virgin's twat," Lieutenant Rico Martinez stated stepping into the MCP.

"Who said that?" the SAC barked over the video link.

Rico leaned in. "Hello, Larry, its Martinez. I just got off the horn with the Department of Environmental Protection's Bureau of Water and Sewer Operations. They've assured me the sewers are secured."

"Lieutenant Martinez," Magley chuckled. "Looks like we're finally going to catch this guy; these serials usually don't get caught, not this easy, anyway."

"Not usually," Rico agreed. "But we've got a good team, and Mei, of course, is leading the Bureau's charge here at ground-zero."

Privately, Mei understood why serial killers DID get caught; they simply made a mistake of arrogance.

Like Ted Bundy, approaching women in broad daylight.

"Hi, my name is Ted... can you help me out?"

Mei shook her head in disgust of the recollection.

Bundy's women never got out alive.

She recalled a training video where the Bureau had distributed a composite of the killer and underneath it was written: *A guy named Ted driving a gold Volkswagen.*

What an idiot, she thought.

After ten years of appeals, Ted Bundy was finally executed in February 1989. During his last conversation, he confessed to a total of twenty-eight heinous slayings.

"She's our bright light on the ground," Magley agreed, snapping Mei back from her thoughts.

"What's that, boss?"

Chuckling, the SAC let her off the hook. "You really need to get more sleep, take a few days off, maybe when this is over, and forget about bodies and death."

"Just doing my job, boss," she said brushing aside the comment. "I've got the guys all set to go! SWAT has been studying the animation of the interior and they're ready to make entry on your order."

There was a moment of silence as Magley thought through his options. "It's your call, Mei."

Mei nodded to SWAT. "You guys are good to go!"

"Roger that!" the SWAT leader grunted. "Let's hit it; time to rumble!" Bursting from the Mobile Command Post, they spread out across the street taking up pre-planned positions around the butcher shop. The team was a heavily armed tactical intrusion squadron with advanced expertise in weaponry, pistols, assault and sniper rifles, and, of course, shotguns. And just in case the suspect held hostages, a *Hostage Rescue Team* staged at the rear.

"We are moving!" Mei turned to Murphy and Rico. "I've got TAC and SWAT locked-in, the US Marshalls have the loading dock, ATF is peppering the rooftops and your department is lining the perimeter."

"We're clear to engage," Murphy confirmed.

Mei raised her finger in the air, completed a circling motion, and then pointed towards the front door.

"Go! Go! Go!" the tactical squad urged storming the entrance, crashing a ramming pole into the door, and hurling flash grenades through the windows.

There was a huge blast of light when the grenades detonated and blew the door off its hinges.

"FBI! SWAT!" the agents shouted. "Federal warrant!"

"Lemme see your hands!" another yelled.

"Hands! Hands! Hands!"

However, there was nobody inside.

"Negative," a radio squawked. "We have zero contacts. There are three deceased in a walk-in freezer, over!"

Mei placed the radio to her lips. "Repeat, no suspect is present?"

"Negative! We are clear, over!"

"All right, everybody!" Mei waved. "Let's get in there and collect evidence!"

"Damn it!" Murphy grunted. "That idiot is still out here on the streets!

"We'll get his ass," Mei assured staring into the dark sky. "He can't run forever."

"Or fly without reindeer," Rico snickered.

Chapter 58

Jolly Fat Man

STEFAN STARED at the Jolly Fat Man.

He wasn't Santa's biggest fan.

In fact, he wanted to leap from his seat and beat the lights outta him.

Yet, deep down, he knew *this man* wasn't the enemy.

"Christmas is the gift that keeps on giving," he muttered glancing out the frosted window at a string of navigation lights aboard a ship moving through the icy Hudson River.

"What's that you said?" Santa asked, a kind smile stretching out his face. "That comment about a gift that keeps on giving?"

Glancing to the man, the boy knew the Santa wannabe was the kind of fellow most people wanted to turn away from. Everyone, at some point in life, got trapped sitting beside someone like this. They were the *friendlies* who shoved their noses into things not concerning them and usually appeared on airplanes, automobiles and, *apparently,* trains. These places were full of nosy chatterboxes who blathered on about everything boring and insignificant.

Even on a deserted locomotive headed into the isolated mountains, they sought you out... *the friendlies of Boredomville.*

"Just my luck," Stefan whispered.

"You know," Mr. Friendly went on, "I keep thinking about that phrase you mentioned."

Stefan squinted at Santa, not because he was interested or sought to converse with the guy. It was a sideways, cross-eyed glance–the type presented when someone was annoying–and you hoped they'd get the hint.

"The gift that keeps on giving," fatso went on. "That's an old ad-slogan that's been used for various products since the early nineteen-hundred's. One of its first uses was by the Victor Talking Machine Company to promote phonographs. But, I suppose, you're too young to remember any of that."

Stefan nodded, rolled his eyes, and pushed the iPhone earbuds into his ears. A tactic kids used to tune out.

"Oh, is that an iPhone?" Mr. Aggravation pointed. "I have a *Samsung Galaxy S*, but those Apple products are pretty slick little gadgets!"

And then, Santa did the unthinkable. He rose from his seat, stepped across the aisle and plopped beside Stefan before he could disappear into the iTunes store.

Are you kidding me right now?

"Can I look at it?" Santa asked. "Looks like the Verizon wireless 4G network. I read in the *Wall Street Journal* the new iPhone includes the best music player of all previous versions and has noise canceling earbuds."

But that doesn't mean squat, if people prevent me from pressing play.

Deciding to be nice, he pulled the buds from his auricles and handed over the aluminum and glass device.

"What's your name, kid?"

"They call me Mighty Whitey, or they used to, when I had friends and thought I knew who I'd spend Christmas with."

The man was blown away by the lonely statement... *sent speechless...* and seemingly cured of all friendly tidings with that one little answer.

"Well... that's so sad..."

"It's all right, mister," Stefan muttered staring out the window. "Just forget I said anything."

His mind wandered back to the rooftop conversations with Marco and the Manhattan skyline.

It wasn't the best existence, but it was my life. Now it's all just a memory.

The fat man handed back the phone. "You know, I had a family once, two boys, just about your age, fifteen, and sixteen. I loved watching them on Christmas morning; the silent understanding that I was their private Santa Claus."

Stefan peered at the man. His face was lined with regret and bygone happiness left to the damnation of memory.

"What happened to them?" he asked, pushing the phone back into his sweatshirt.

Santa smiled awkwardly, glanced to the boy, and groaned in despair. It was one of those long exaggerated huffs that spoke volumes of why me, how come, and wish I could change it. Yet, nothing could change the past.

History stuck to you like a piece of gum that latched onto the bottom of a shoe and followed you home.

"I lost them in an accident a few years back, a drunk driver on the *Bear Mountain Goat Trail* broad-sided my wife's car as she was headed home from the ski lodge."

The goat trail started northwest of Peekskill and ended at the Bear Mountain Bridge that joined Westchester to southeast Orange County. Carved into the mountain face it was known as *Anthony's Nose*, a steep, crooked road that sent many to their deaths, 400-feet below, and into the river with one wrong turn of the wheel.

"Sorry," Stefan genuinely mumbled. "I know that sucks, to say sorry, but I really am. I also lost my only two friends recently."

The man glanced at Stefan, saw the pain reflected in his gaze and nodded. Christmas reminded everyone of the good times they'd shared... but the holiday also carried with it horrid and gut wrenching moments that encircled the season like Indians on the verge of killing women and children who trembled in their wagons.

"What happened to your friends?"

Stefan shook his head, peered at the fat man and whistled. "Life happened, man, you wouldn't believe the story if I told you."

"Try me; I'm a sucker for a good story."

But then, just before the boy answered, the intercom chimed and a pre-recorded announcement filled their ears.

"Next stop... Peekskill."

"That's where I get off this bullet," the man said. "What about you? Where you headed?"

"New Windsor, it's just across the river, to a boy's home where I grew up."

Santa wondered how he'd get to his final destination. "You have a car at the station? It's pretty cold out there at this time of the morning."

Yet, he knew the boy was a wanderer, *maybe a runaway*, and that, *perhaps*, during this holiday season, he could help someone less fortunate than himself–and, maybe, in the process–heal his own wounds, which refused to scab over.

And besides, it would be like helping one of my sons who I never got to say goodbye to.

"How about I give you a lift; it would be my pleasure."

Stefan nodded his appreciation and held out a hand, "I think I'd like that. My name is Stefan."

"Bob Ferris," the man smiled, "part-time Santa Claus, red eyed desperado, and full-time insurance salesman."

It made perfect sense.

The one thing Stefan knew for sure was insurance salesmen were notorious for being boring.

"Well, Bob, as long as you don't try to sell me a load of shit, I think we're going to get along just fine."

"I sell lots of shit," Bob chuckled. "I, however, am fresh out of turds on this night."

When the train door slid open, the two lonely souls hunched their frames against the abrupt frozen breeze and hurried onto the dark platform.

Danger always lurked just around the corner.

But sometimes, *stranger* didn't have to *mean* danger.

Chapter 59

Pound of Flesh

"HAIL, HAIL, the gang's all here!" Captain McKenzie greeted his subordinate, Lieutenant Rico Martinez.

"What's that," Rico asked, "an Ed McBain novel?"

"Yeah, it's one of the *Eighty-Seventh Precinct* series," McKenzie nodded. "Are you a fan?"

"I read *Cop Hater* in college. But, now that I run the Task Force, what's the point?"

They were plodding through the butcher shop's commercial walk-in freezer and observing Murphy who busily examined corpses suspended by meat hooks.

"What've we got, Murphy?" Rico inquired.

Pulling himself from the gore of flesh, Mike glanced at his retiring comrade and sauntered across the steel floor.

"Three dee-bees," he answered pointing at the trifecta of bodies sagging on steel hangers. "Two male white, one female ... we think two are the parents."

"And the other dead body, you figure him for the Head Shrinker, right?"

Murphy nodded.

"He's not trying to cover tracks," Mei recognized, pushing up beside them. "The evidence is everywhere, almost as if he believes he'll never be apprehended."

They had been on scene for hours now, photographing every crawl space and cataloging pieces of evidence.

"Let me show you something," Murphy gestured, walking back to the suspended bodies.

It was a scene right out of a horror movie.

Body parts lined shelves arranged by size and color.

On the left side of the freezer sat eyeless human heads, which had been chopped from their shoulders.

On the right were arms and legs, stacked vertical and resembling crab legs in a local buffet.

But all the way in the back was a steel counter with human bones that were stripped of their flesh. Beside these, piled a foot tall, sat the flesh and veins that had been scraped from the carcasses.

"Damn it!" McKenzie mumbled. "What the hell?"

Mei progressed to the table, pulled on a new pair of latex gloves, and picked up one of a dozen human livers.

"I don't want to be the one who tells the media, but I think Mr. Hannibal Lecter was hawking human meat to his customers."

Murphy moved beside her, "I'd say Hannibal can't hold a candlestick to our murderous Santa Claus. Hollywood will be lining up to make a modern day *Silence of the Lambs* featuring our fiendish little butcher."

"That was one sick bastard," Mei chuckled.

"Clarice, can you hear the lambs?" Murphy creepily muttered, imitating the cannibalistic killer, Dr. Lecter.

Mei smiled while recalling the 1991 motion picture based on Thomas Harris' novel. She adored its star, Jodie Foster, and often believed herself to be the real life version of the female FBI Agent character.

"The lambs are calling," Murphy grumbled. "Those little wooly sheep, can you hear them?"

"For heaven's sake, Murphy," McKenzie complained. "Come back to reality, will ya?"

Everyone snickered.

A homicide detective grew into murder–*like slipping on a new pair of shoes*–at first, the leather was tight and impractical, and the feet loathed the pressure and cramping.

Wearing shoes–like murder–was unnatural.

But… after a couple weeks, and a few mutilated bodies, the job of homicide hunting broke people in, stretched out their tight fitting skin ... *and after a while...* massacre became *comfortable*, the brain's grey matter adapted and grew accustomed to the carnage of death.

"Why is this guy cutting up bodies?" McKenzie asked while inspecting the body-parts. "And what's the correlation to abuse and the killing of cats?"

Mei replaced the liver and pulled off the gloves. "Serial killers begin their homicidal callings by refining their abilities on animals long before progressing to humans."

"Where does this come from?"

"All serials have one thing in common. They start by torturing and killing animals... which has been linked to *child abuse, domestic violence, serial killings,* and *murders* by school age children. But serials usually torture animals purely for their own enjoyment. Animal abuse is psychological in nature. When children hurt animals, it's a red flag."

"So, the one constant serials share is animal abuse?"

"Absolutely, and what we have in Mr. Blake is someone who has been killing for a very long time, possibly more than twenty years, perhaps his whole life. He gets off on it, the thrill drives him, and his rush of anger is a high; addictive, compelling and ongoing."

"Excuse me, detectives?" Chief Medical Examiner Heung interrupted. "I think you need to see this."

"What's up, Dr. H?" Rico asked.

"I found a display case full of human flesh!"

All heads turned to him, eyes wide, faces stern, as they hurried from the freezer and approached a refrigerated meat display case. Behind the glass–the type one might find in the local meat section of the supermarket–was arranged in what appeared to be Rib Eye and Porterhouse steaks. Not your average run of the mill lean cuts, these were *enormous slabs* of mouthwatering flanks of *beef* that were prepared for purchase.

"Medium rare or well done," Murphy whispered, "human flesh is the new white meat."

"I've checked it twice and it's definitely tissue from a human buttock," the M.E. confirmed pointing to brown packaging paper. "Blake was wrapping the flesh and selling it to the public."

"Like the way they wrap ground beef at Walmart," Murphy grunted. "But this is a delicacy all his own."

"And then, there's this I discovered," the corpse examiner whispered opening the lid of a freezer just behind the counter. "It contains the dismembered remains of a teenage Latino boy."

Rico stared at the sight, recalling his dealings with the boy who'd once sat inside Manhattan South Homicide.

"Jesus, that's the Spanish kid we questioned about the judge's murder."

"Marco Alvarez," Murphy stated. "Santa is taking them out one at a time, something pissed this guy off in the courtroom that day, and he's taking his revenge."

"The question is," Captain McKenzie asked, "where is our lunatic hiding right now?"

"And who is he eating?' Murphy asked.

Chapter 60

Clean Getaway

THE ANSWER to McKenzie's question was simple.

Santa was hiding in plain sight.

Steering the meat wagon out of Saint John's Park, he circled the loop and headed west on Canal. There was no question in Richard's mind that the police would come one day. He'd anticipated it years earlier... and, thus, had long ago installed reconnaissance cameras at every entrance.

The cameras offered *Remote Access* and permitted observation of the meat market from an Android phone.

So, the killer wasn't surprised when a monitor displayed cops staring through the windows.

Minutes before he saw them, he'd changed into a fresh Santa suit, packed his bags and escaped through a hidden trap door.

Now, driving into the night, he chuckled.

"Sneaky little bastards thought I was surrounded!" Whacking his palm against the dashboard, he pulled to the side of the empty road. "Wait 'til America's Most Wanted gets a load of me!"

Bad boy, bad boy, Daddy rhymed. *What ya gonna do when they come for you!*

That's his tune! Mammy shrieked. *The jingle for COPS!*

Santa smiled, recollecting another hit series he loved watching. *The Sopranos* had kept him glued to the couch.

"Mother, your attitude puts Livia Soprano's lack of respect to shame!" That meant something, because Livia was the Angel of Death, the Matriarch of Damnation.

No contest, hands down!

Oh, go on! Mammy snorted in mocked imitation of Livia. *At least Tony didn't kill his mother!*

"But he wanted to," Richard argued. "Especially after she and Junior tried to have Tony knocked off and maybe... just maybe... they would have thrown him into the ocean a few miles off the Jersey Shore with *Big Pussy* Bonpensiero who slept with the fishes."

He was referring to an episode in season one, where Livia had manipulated her brother-in-law, Junior, to put a hit out on Tony after he'd tried to place her in the old folks home.

I wish the lord Jesus would take you right now.

"I'm going to live a nice long happy life, Ma!" Richard assured. "Which is more than I can say for you, right?"

She didn't have a comeback for that one.

"HA! HA! HA!" the fiend cackled. "Just when you thought I was out, they pulled me back in!"

It was a line from the show.

Richard adored the way Soprano mobster, *Silvio, Sil Dante,* uttered the line. There was heart to it–*swagger* of a street level mobster standing with his soldiers acting out the scene–gesturing with his hands a section from the preeminent mafia movie of all time.

"Steven Van Zandt knew how to pull off a line like that," Santa glanced to the empty passenger seat. "You know, being a consigliore to Tony Soprano in his crime family meant you had to be all in!"

Suddenly, he realized the recriminations of Mammy had stopped. Only stillness filled the lonesome meat wagon.

"Right, Mommy Dearest? Don't you want to contribute two cents?"

They're leaving, Richard, his mind whispered. *They won't be talking to you for a while.*

"Mommy, talk to me, damn it!"

Nevertheless, the malicious commentaries didn't plug his thoughts. Gone were the scornful mutterings and snickering, head shaking abuses.

We're leaving now, Son, Daddy gratefully stated. *We're going into the light.*

So long, you murdering little prick, Mammy snipped, *farewell... and good riddance!*

Panic set into Richard's eyes and they flew wide with terror, his cheeks enflamed with rosy splotches and perspiration beaded across his brow.

The cops found us, boy, Daddy offered, *hanging on the hooks. We're going onto the Promised Land...*

"Talk to me, Mother! You're not allowed to leave!"

They were *gone*.

Richard could truly sense the *emptiness*... like a balloon as it collapsed from lack of air.

"Mother, Daddy, talk to me right this instant!"

Had a dime dropped, the good people of New York City might've overheard it hitting the rug. That was... until Santa saw a man exiting a nightclub wearing a Santa hat.

"Hey, buddy," *The Santa Claus Killer* hollered through the window, his hand wrapping around his hatchet. "Do you happen to have the time?"

It's time to kill! The purring voice of a cat ordered.

And that's what Santa planned on doing, right through Christmas day, on the streets of Manhattan.

Chapter 61

Memory Lane

BLOOMING GROVE TURNPIKE was the road that ferried Stefan home.

The boy's institution sat in darkness back off the freshly plowed roadway. It was lost in a labyrinth of hidden shadows and long-suffering recollections.

Stepping through the crusted snow, Stefan tramped beneath a swath of Weeping Willow branches weighted with ice tentacles. Graceful and refined, their mushroom shaped crowns usually dotted the landscape like ornaments waiting strings of decorations. But in the dead of winter only frozen bark held back the wind swept landscape.

"Wowser," the boy whispered at the sight of the uninhabited compound. The portrait seemed unlike his memories and wistful expectations of his trip down memory lane. Cupping his hands around his mouth, he shouted into the sallowness. "Hello... anybody out there?"

To the right stood a *McQuade Children's Services* rotting sign that once welcomed his ten-year-old vision. Attached to the memory was a State Child Protective Services *nine-to-fiver* pulling him from the car and into the administration building. Shaking off the memory, he peered back into the present.

If I could just reach back in time and talk to that screaming kid I once was... things might have been much different right now.

Yet, glaring across the windblown scene there was one thing he knew for sure, during the journey of life there were no do-overs! No second chances, only the narrow arrow ahead.

Left! Right! Maaaaaaarch!

"Is anybody out there?" he called into a freezing squall whipping through the woodland.

Crap, looks like it's just me out here!

He'd traveled too far to just turn around, mutter excuses of *should have* or *would have,* and then creep back to the city without answers to his questions. "Screw it," he mumbled plowing through the hillocks of snow and into the only home he'd ever known.

Founded in 1862, the *Home for the Friendless* was created by the Newburgh Union Female Guardian Society to aid abused and abandoned children. Enter Dr. Milton Ash McQuade… a Canadian born doctor who bequeathed $200-grand to the boy's home in 1945. The home was renamed to *The McQuade Foundation for Boys* in Milton's memory.

It was a jolly good story, a fairytale of hope and triumph! Yet, of the thousands of youngsters who rotated through McQuade's residential cottages, few ever heard of the hero who saved their asses. It was a crying shame, because the legend of Dr. McQuade and what his money ensured for homeless kids was big stuff. *He was a hero!*

Marching through the abandoned compound, Stefan couldn't believe it was all gone! It was all wiped away with the howling wind as if none of it had ever happened!

"It's not fair," he mumbled pushing through the compound. Memories were just that–wisps of past images to regret or savor–often the reality they were constructed from wasn't that great to begin with.

Continuing through the snow, he realized the abandoned facility would now be joining a long list of romanticized *what ifs*. Before him was a fork in the woods; similar to the proverbial road of life, the one where old timers warned one direction led to success, and the other went straight to hell.

Stefan had traveled down either road at one time or another and couldn't help but chuckle in the understanding that neither headed to a pot of gold at the end of a rainbow or a pointy headed devil.

Rainbows and brimstone were a rarity, especially in the dead of winter.

But here, in the middle of nowhere, with glacial squalls biting at his earlobes, there was another choice.

To the right stood a weathered, two-story white oak mansion once serving as the administration building. What they administered there, and who it helped, was another story. Back then, however, all the boys would gather 'round the campfire on a mid-summer eve, tell their ghost stories and suppose *Mountain Monsters* lurked out in the woods.

Deciding to dismiss the fork, he glanced to Windsor Cottage and an abandoned box of memories held prisoner in its attic. Stepping through the snow, he arrived at the old timber cottage he once called home.

It was here where he learned how to survive.

However... he also discovered compassion and love, in the form of Clifford Webb... the cottage father who took him beneath his wing and tried to save his childhood.

Kids have heroes. Huge, gigantic ideals of what might be and how to get there... and every once in a while people stumbled into the path to show the way to safety.

That's who Clifford was; a light which stomped despair from his thoughts and made him believe in something better.

Now, walking through the doorway, he caught his breath. The cottage was empty. Gone were the haphazardly scattered furnishings that once lined the day room; the ceiling, once painted with stars and planets, had long ago crumbled to the ground.

"Damn, there's nothing left to hold on to."

Walking into a bedroom, the teenager recalled his long hours spent gazing through its windows where tall pine trees cast shadows that looked like fingers reaching for his flesh.

It was the stuff of childhood freak-outs.

Monsters, everyone at McQuade knew, lurked behind every door, back behind the Sunday dress shirts hanging in the closet. It was there, in the darkness of the closet, where *shadow people, gremlins* and *ghosts* pushed aside the hangers and crept through the dimness.

Back then, the kids believed monsters crawled from a secret door nobody could ever find.

Stefan recalled curling up next to a transistor radio late at night and listening to the radio talk show, Coast to Coast, dealing with secret things like aliens and government conspiracies.

He smiled at the memory, shook his head, and turned back to the hallway and a trapdoor above his head. Reaching to the latch, he pulled it open, climbed up the ladder and crawled through the fiberglass.

"I know it's got to still be here," he mumbled, pulling away insulation and staring in surprise at the old *Pro Keds* box. Excitedly, he pulled open its lid and stared at the long forgotten snapshots of his mother, father, and the life they once shared. Sobbing softly, he flipped through them... one at a time; knowing that no matter how badly he wanted things to be different ...nothing from the past could ever be brought back. Except for the little brown box and the family fantasies he had once.

Kids dream of being adults, but once they get there... they find a horde of grownups who dream of reliving childhood.

Everybody wanted what they couldn't have.

Chapter 62

The Secret Passage

THE GIVER OF GIFTS could be anywhere.

"We need to track him down!" Agent Mei Ling stated. "Preferably before he swings that hatchet and steals another life."

Before her, the Medical Examiner knelt on a thick rubber mat bagging human ham hocks. Of course, the meat wasn't truly the lower hind legs of hogs.

They weren't smoked hams cured and salted down to flavor preferences. These pink, fatty slabs were human rump and thigh, with a slathering of *Sazon Seasoned Salt* massaged into the flesh with care.

Just like grandma used to make on Thanksgiving Day before sliding the turkey into the oven at 350 degrees.

"Can somebody hand me a bottle of water?" the M.E. asked, wiping a bead of perspiration from his forehead. "I'm feeling sick to my stomach just looking at this."

Snatching a bottle from the cooler, Murphy handed it over and watched the coroner toss back a swallow before placing it on the mat beside him.

"Thanks, Murphy. I haven't felt this woozy in a long time."

It took a hit parade of insanity to shake the coroner.

This was *Dr. Death* himself, the man who dabbled in the garden of evil. He was the guy who wrestled bodies onto stainless steel slabs, cut them to pieces, and pushed them into refrigerated drawers.

Day… *after day*… after day!

The only person who saw more bodies than a County Medical Examiner was Saint Peter when he welcomed departed souls at the pearly gates. Of course, there's no guarantee that's where the dead ended up. Hell waited, too, and a little red devil holding his pitchfork to stab into the heart.

But who really knew... there was a story for everything and everyone had a tale.

Here, in the butcher shop, Captain McKenzie and Lieutenant Martinez had just returned from inspecting the bodies hanging on the meat hooks in the freezer.

"How many stiffs," Rico gestured to the display case, "do you think are in there?"

"Hard to tell," Dr. Heung answered reaching for his water. "We've bagged over three hundred pounds of flesh so far."

This is when something unusual happened... not the fact the water bottle fell over all by itself, or the rumble felt beneath their feet... but that everyone saw it happen in slow motion.

"What the fuck caused that?" Murphy stared at the bottle sitting on the mat, the water trembling within the plastic.

On solid ground!

One thing was sure, amongst the hardnosed cops, nobody considered the possibility of a ghost.

"Pull up that rubber pad!" Murphy grunted.

Rico lifted the heavy, filthy, stench encrusted rubber and stared in disbelief at what lay beneath.

"Son-of-a-gun! Are you kidding me?" Peering at a corroded steel trapdoor, he watched it rattle in the frame. Beside it, bloodstained boot prints vanished into the door where a subway thundered from somewhere down below.

Murphy yanked the heavy screeching door and pointed his flashlight into the darkness. The hole resembled a public works tunnel that employees disappeared into on every street, USA.

But this one... *the hole at their feet...* was something entirely different.

"It's his getaway route," Murphy mumbled.

"You think it leads to hell?" Rico clowned.

Murphy glanced at his partner, nodded and pulled out his gun. "Or worse… are you behind me, Partner?"

There was a moment of silence; a momentary heartbeat as everyone peered at the lieutenant with a hushed understanding. He was weeks from hanging up the badge, moving to paradise, and pushing paper for a younger force.

Rico could have said, *too bad, so sad, and no thanks.*

But that wasn't his style.

Everybody knew it.

He would die on the job rather than deny his duty.

"You bet your ass I'm behind you," he replied. "I wouldn't miss this rodeo even if it took place at Angola."

It was a sarcastic reference to Murphy's infatuation with *Angola's Prison Rodeo*, staged at the Louisiana State Penitentiary. *The Farm*, as it was lovingly coined, confined the state's worst monsters after they received life sentences.

Murphy had been invited every October by the warden, Burl Cain, and the two had become good friends.

Cain was a *good Christian man* and believed *redemption* and *rehabilitation* were possible for any human being, so long as they were given the right *guidance, teaching,* and *incentive.*

Thus, the rodeo offered hope.

Rico thought the entire thing was a moneymaking machine and PR stunt to harvest sympathy for killers.

"Let's do it, people!" Captain McKenzie yelled. "Get down into the hole and search for our madman!"

Murphy stepped onto square iron bars embedded in the concrete walls. Step by step, he paced into the dark.

Behind him were Rico, Mei… and a long line of cops.

"Keep your wits about you," the commander yelled taking up the rear. "You never know what lurks beneath the surface!"

It was said that when a man scrambled into the trenches of humanity he often found his soul.

Rico just wanted to make it out alive.

Chapter 63

Live from New York

TIMOTHY SMITH stared into the HD camera.

"We're up next," Ahmed stated framing his close shot. "We're just on the other side of a commercial."

"Do you have the chaos behind me squared up? Getting the body bags coming out of the entrance?"

"You better believe it, Tim!" Ahmed excitedly pointed into the sky. "We're in a ratings war and the competition on this story is huge."

It was pandemonium at Manhattan's Best Meat Market.

Every network in New York had their chopper blades cutting the air above the murder zone. The choppers reminded Tim of *Apocalypse Now* and the Marine Corps Huey's rumbling through an auburn Vietnam sky as sunrise peeked over the mountains.

The only thing missing here is the aroma of napalm and a US Military Bugle Charge call.

Ahmed snapped his fingers, pointed at the reporter and counted down, "three, two, and your live!"

Detectives Arias and Romero leapt from an unmarked Dodge Charger and advanced on the butcher shop entrance.

"The scene behind me is one of intensity and gloominess," Tim stated into the camera. "Here, in Chinatown, detectives from Manhattan South Homicide and agents of the FBI Serial Killer Task Force are hunting a vicious killer described as a modern day Hannibal Lecter."

"Who told you that?" Romero interrupted. "Nobody released that information!" A push of reporters pushed into the detective.

"Detective!" Tim shouted. "Can you tell our viewers what they can do to protect themselves?"

Before Arias could advise his apprentice to state 'no comment', the young-buck leaned over, smiled into the camera, and boldly went where no cop would dare.

"They need to get the hell out of the city before the killer hacks off the heads of every Santa on the streets."

"Is the department finally confirming that a murderer is stalking people dressed as Santa Claus?"

"Damn it!" Arias shuddered. "That's not what my partner meant to say."

"But he did say that. Didn't he?"

"Are you saying residents are in danger?" a *Daily News* Reporter inquired while shoving a digital recorder towards the detective.

"Of course, they're in danger! The killer is wandering the streets chopping people to pieces."

"Is that on the record, detective? And how do you spell your name for the story, please?

"R-O-M-E-R-O. We're dealing with a creature here, not a human being!"

Detective Arias was beside himself, flabbergasted by the unanticipated mouth diarrhea bucketing from his idiot partner. "That's all," he stated to the burgeoning crowd, "no more questions!"

"But, detective," Tim Smith pressed, shoving his *Channel-7* microphone into the face of the beleaguered investigator. "How do you know all this?"

"Just... *shut up*, Bobby!" Arias ordered. "No more interpretations, let's just get inside!"

Romero was sick of the secrecy and afraid for the people who didn't know any better. So, he shook his head, brushed off his senior partner, and answered the question.

"I saw the bodies, with their eyes torn from their sockets and evil words written in blood at the scenes!"

There was a hiatus of questioning as the reporters absorbed the unprecedented release of morbid details of an ongoing investigation. It was almost as if the press knew, right then and there, the glimmering career of a detective had flickered out.

Suddenly, police radios cracked to life.

"Attention… all units! Attention… all units!" the voice of Captain McKenzie blurted. "The suspect is on the loose below the streets in the sewer system, over!"

"Did you guys hear that!" a *New York Post* journalist screamed. "The killer is in the sewer!"

"He's in the cesspit!" an NBC Reporter repeated dragging out his cellphone.

Turning back to his camera, Tim urgently gave his viewers this: "You heard it here, according to NYPD Homicide Detective Romero; New York City is under attack tonight by a diabolical murderer…"

"I didn't say that!"

"May the Lord have mercy, Bobby," Arias said. "You'll be lucky to be riding a desk in Animal Control if you're not fired."

Chapter 64

The Morning Joe

THE SWANK Fifth Avenue penthouse offered spectacular 360-degree views of Manhattan.

Mirabel had completely renovated the entire apartment since a conservative talk show host had sold her the castle in the sky following a state proposed tax increase for the wealthy.

The rich didn't believe in paying taxes, so he sold off his New York assets and hauled ass to Palm Beach.

It reminded Mirabel of a recent conversation she'd had with a community organizer of the *Obama for America* Presidential Campaign. They were chatting of recent revelations regarding a certain presidential candidate's refusal to hand over his tax returns.

The organizer said:

> "A priest, politician and a millionaire are playing through eighteen holes and attempting to agree on how much cash to donate to the poor."

The priest suggests:

> "Draw a chalk circle on the ground, throw our money into the air and whatever lands inside the loop, we'll give to charity."

The politician disagrees:

> "No way! Draw the circle; toss the currency and what lands *outside* the circle we'll contribute to the charity."

The millionaire laughs:

"You guys have been drinking way too much church wine! I toss up my money and whatever God wants... he takes while it falls to the ground... whatever dough hits the ground goes into my pocket!"

The Organizer laughs. "You just can't make up stuff like that. They really are cheap little fuckers!"

Mirabel giggled "Idiots," she mumbled, "forty-seven percent China trading dopes." Walking through the new French doors she had installed to provide generous access to the wrap-around terrace, she knew Terry would one day write his great American novel here.

She always believed he could replace John Grisham on the New York Times bestseller list. And maybe even a few other authors who she'd not bother naming.

Sipping a freshly brewed cup of Columbian Morning Joe, she glanced at the television and found the smile of the African American President.

Being a top tier donor, she attended the Democratic National Convention in South Carolina and was a personal friend of the First Lady.

"Good morning, honey bun." Terry mumbled stepping through the garden dressed in his pressed trial suit. "Did you sleep well?"

"Not bad, but I'm worried about Stefan and why he's not answering his phone."

"Ah, he's okay, I am sure." he responded grabbing the *Wall Street Journal* and scanning the front page. "He is probably out chasing that girl of his,"

Mirabel frowned. "There's something I dislike about that young lady." Though, privately, she was unable to place a finger on what exactly that was.

"Like what?" Terry asked flipping the front page.

"Why doesn't he bring her over to the house? What's the big secret with this girl and her motives?"

So, that's the deal, Terry thought throwing down the paper. *She wants to inspect the girl.* "I see you're watching Mr. Hope and Change," he shifted the subject picking up his coffee. "Still going down to Washington in January?"

She sighed, glanced at the television, and squinted with interest when the regularly scheduled interview was interrupted by breaking news.

> "We interrupt this broadcast to report on a serious situation unfolding in lower Manhattan," a WABC newscaster stated. "For that story, we take you live to Timothy Smith standing outside a Chinatown butcher shop where police say a murderer is on the loose. Is that right, Tim?"

On the TV, the reporter pointed to the entrance of a butcher shop where throngs of police and FBI Agents hurried through the scene.

> "That's correct, Sheila. As you can see behind me, hundreds of City, State and Federal law enforcement agencies are, at this moment, engaged in a manhunt for a serial killer."

Body bags were being removed on morgue stretchers; the finality of their gloom draped ominously with red and black felt coverings.

> "Here's the latest information," the reporter went on. "Manhattan South Homicide is searching through the sewer system directly beneath our feet and chasing the FBI's Most Wanted mass murderer, The Santa Claus Killer."

"Oh, no!" Mirabel feared, placing her trembling hands to her face. "Isn't this the same killer Murphy and Rico are looking for, the guy who killed Stefan's friend, Darius?"

Terry placed his coffee cup on the table, hurried to his wife, and grabbed her hand as a phone rang on his hip. "It's okay, Sweetie, I'm sure they'll catch him."

"But what if they don't, Terry? What if he goes after Marco and Stefan?"

"He won't," Terry hoped answering the phone, "Hello?"

"Terry!" McKenzie's voice shouted through the phone.

In the background, Terry heard the cacophony of sirens and police officers yelling.

"Where is that kid of yours?"

"Which kid is that?" Terry mumbled peeking at the TV. *This can't be one of those good calls,* he thought, creeping away from the spying ears of his wife who sat tuned-in like a heat seeking missile.

"Who is it, Terry?" Mirabel asked, following close on his heels. "It's about Stefan, isn't it?"

Terry covered the mouthpiece with his palm, "Let's not jump to conclusions, darling."

But, silently, in the place where horror tore at the corners of his mind, he knew the call was about to shake her to the core.

"Where is Stefan?" the commander repeated. "Now is no time for games. We just found his Puerto Rican friend relieved of his head. Is *your* boy alive?"

Terry ripped his eyes from Mirabel and nervously sauntered across the terrace.

On the horizon, helicopters hovered above the skyscrapers.

"I don't know where he is, Captain, but I can raise him on his cell if you'd like."

The commanding officer growled, "I don't just like that, I love it so much I'm pissing my pants waiting for you to finger your phone!"

"Okay–*all right*–give me a second," Terry retorted while toggling between screens and clicking the *ADD CALL* button. Touching a contact photo of Stefan, he realized it was the only image he owned of the boy outwardly comfortable in his own skin.

As Stefan's handset began to ring somewhere down in the valley of death and destruction, the lawyer prayed.

"Come on, kid, answer!"

When Eminem's ringback tone, *I'm Not Afraid,* assaulted Terry's eardrums, he questioned if perhaps time had run out on his promise to Stefan's crack-head mother.

Maybe, the kid lay murdered in a gutter.

Chapter 65

Go Greyhound!

$\mathcal{S}$TEFAN FELT the phone vibrating in his pocket and considered letting it go to voicemail.

You know what to do, so get busy chatting!

That's what his greeting blurted after rapper superstar Eminem dropped his pearls of wisdom of standing up, walking hand-in-hand through storms and not being afraid!

Maybe people could learn from the Master of Rap, the King of Spitting. That was the purpose of Slim Shady, after all… telling his fans they weren't alone, that they'd been down the same lonely road.

Stefan felt alone–lost in the wasteland of a world that chiseled away the good stuff, revealing battle scabs and the carnage of childhood.

It doesn't take a rapper to tell me about hell. I'm living it. Sliding the cellphone from his jeans, he saw Terry's photo and pressed the accept call button.

"Hello? What's up, Mr. Public Pretender?"

"Stefan, kiddo… where the heck are you?"

"I'm on Greyhound's Hudson River Line, pushed against a window above the rier."

"Sounds romantic," the lawyer supposed recognizing the route thanks to Billy Joel's smash-hit–*New York State of Mind*–which the singer wrote on a Greyhound bus.

Of course, Joel didn't take buses any more.

"What are you doing upstate?" Terry quizzed. "Mirabel and I are worried sick about you!"

Stefan groaned. It bothered him Mirabel fretted over his well-being, especially since she cared whether he lived or died.

"Can I talk to her? Let her know I'm coming to the house, and want you guys to be my parents, that I love her and you Terry very much!"

There was silence on the other end, and a sigh as the words settled into Terry's thoughts.

"Gosh, Stefan, she's been waiting forever to hear that."

"What about you, huh?" Stefan asked gazing across the Hudson River, Manhattan's skyline looming at the outward boundaries of vision.

"I'd be honored to show you what life is about," Terry mumbled. "To be a father figure and share summer afternoons at Yankee Stadium, enroll you in the best schools, steward your young life to something better than you've received so far. That would be my justice, to have you look to me for guidance on how to be a man."

Stefan sat stunned. Tears trolled from his eyes, straggled down his blushed cheeks, and then... the droplets fell from his chin where they plopped onto his lap.

"Really? We could do that, like a real family?"

"We *would* be a family, that's what Mirabel and I want for you... *for us.* It's what I promised your mother years ago."

Stefan barely recalled his mother.

The years had been long and his remembrances were well worn–like the yellowing edges of the pictures in his shoebox–everything washed out with time, withering his hopes and dreams like the dwindling images dragging themselves from his mind.

"I'd like that," he slurred into the phone, wiping his face, stiffening his upper lip, like his idol Eminem had sung about. "I needed to hear that."

"I know, kid," Terry admitted. "I've known that for a very long time."

Opening his sneaker box, the boy plunged through the photos of his mom and dad, locked eternally in comedic poses from another time. There were seven pictures in all, taken right around Christmas time. His mother smiled up at him, her memory burning into an unknown future. And then, right beside her, the annoyed grin of his father holding a can of *Pabst Blue Ribbon*.

It was one of the cheapest beers on the market, costing about $4.00 a six-pack.

His dad could drink a case in one day.

"Stefan," Terry sniffled, fighting back his own emotions. "Mirabel is here; she'd like to talk with you."

"Okay," he said, gazing at another image of dad, dressed as Santa Claus and handing over a wrapped present to his six-year-old son. Mighty Whitey recalled that present, and it made him angry now, recalling having ripped open the gift, only to find a new starched white apron.

His father laughed so hard he almost passed out in an alcoholic fit. *"What did you think, Son? You thought there was a toy in there? Is that it?"*

He remembered springing to his feet, running to the bedroom and crying into his lumpy pillow.

Every year his father would purchase a lamb... *a little cute wooly love stack* ... and Stefan would take care of it out in the barn. Until Easter rolled around and Daddy would creep out to the slaughterhouse and massacre the animal for Easter dinner.

It ripped Stefan's heart out.

He gasped at the memory, dropped the photo, and closed the lid of the shoebox. "You ruined my life."

"Stefan, sweetheart, are you okay?" Mirabel whispered through the phone. "I want you to come live with us; this is your home, not out on the street."

He knew they loved him like a lost puppy that wandered up to the front door and let the homeowner know it sucked being alone. And so... most decent folks let the stray bounce into their family and from there on out it was a friendship of unconditional love. There would be endless hours of emotional moments as the puppy snuggled in bed, gazed into human eyes, and fell asleep knowing it was safe from the treachery of the wilderness.

"Will you come home to us?" Mirabel asked.

"Yes, Ma'am, I would really like to call you my Mom."

"That's not a bad thing, you know."

"I know." he mumbled into the phone.

But there was something else he knew then, too.

There was someone else out there at the edge of darkness who wanted his head. Maybe there was something he could do about that. Or maybe, he'd end up a Dead Ender like all the others who disappeared in the subway.

New York City was built on blood.

Chapter 66

Clean Get-a-Way

BIRTH AND DEATH silence us all in the end.

It was one of Santa's favorite quotes.

AND it drove him bonkers not remembering the author's name.

"Rumphole! Dumphole!" he muttered, "imagine growing up with that name in middle school!"

The silence was driving him over the edge of psychosis, down the steep slope of deafening nothingness, where his thoughts begged the return of the voices.

"Hey, Rumphole!" he shouted out the van's window to a passing motorist. "How'd you like me to rump your pink little hole!"

Driving beside him was a student in a shiny new Smart Car, one of those miniature antlike vehicles that everyone knew would fetch death... if ever involved in a serious accident. He'd viewed the manufacturer's website and laughed loudly when he read the claims of "safety first" and "strong like a bull." A quick Google search of "smart car deaths" proved just how lethal the mini was when it crossed paths with its superior road cousins.

"Ha!" Santa grunted at his thoughts before looking to the driver. "You're dead boy, and you don't even know it!"

Unknown to the madman–at that exact moment, as he watched the youngster texting behind the wheel–Stefan was heading in the opposite direction onboard the Greyhound.

"Stupid kids!" Santa mumbled, reaching over to a JVC portable radio he'd bought at a Walgreens drug store. "They're killing themselves while texting on the road!"

Glancing at his new TRAC Phone sitting on the seat beside him, he considered calling the State Copperheads to report the law-breaking brat.

After all, texting and driving in New York is illegal.

The State Police loved giving out tickets around Christmas time.

"Fuck it. The dumbass will probably crash anyway!"

He flipped on the radio and turned it to: *1010 WINS – All News All the Time.* It was the longest running news station in the nation. For more than forty-six years, it had been famous around the world for its slogan:

> 'You give *us* 22-minutes…
> We'll give *you* the world!'

Richard was a follower.

Not on Twitter or anything like that, he could care less about social media. But, he wouldn't think of listening to any other station, especially since he *was* the breaking news!

Suddenly, through the rearview mirror he saw the Smart Car swerving, rolling, and crashing into the guardrail. Then, an enormous explosion rocked the roadway when an oil truck plowed into the pile-up.

"So much for the data plan, that'll slow things down for the sloggers of Manhattan."

After a few minutes, he raised the volume of the radio, and settled in on the station.

> "Good morning, it is twenty-nine degrees and this is Pete Torrey," the reporter's voice blurted from the radio. "W-I-N-S news time is nine fifty-five a.m. and it's a morning drive in slow-mo! We're monitoring accidents on the Garden State, Northern State Parkway and a report just came in of a rollover explosion on the George

Washington westbound involving multiple
cars and a gas truck."

The killer crossed the bridge and steered the meat wagon
along the Palisades Interstate Parkway. It would take him to
the safety of the family farm in Spring Valley.

"Maybe, I'll find a soul to harvest along the way."

> "W-I-N-S news time is ten fifteen a.m.," the
> reporter continued. "The New York Field
> Office of the FBI is on a manhunt this
> morning with the NYPD Homicide Squad
> searching a lower Manhattan butcher shop
> and the sewer system for murderer Richard
> Blake."

"Well, I'll be damned!" Santa cackled. "I'm a regular
celebrity!" Pulling to the curb, he turned up the volume and
stared at the digital dial as if watching a television show.

> "Accused of more than three dozen slayings
> along the east coast of the United States, the
> Mayor of New York is expected to give a
> joint news conference regarding the case.
> Ten-ten W-I-N-S news time is now, ten
> eighteen a.m."

The station went to a commercial then and the killer
turned off the radio. He was bursting with enthusiasm. Not
the variety that occupied the heart and triggered people to
break out in song… this was more comparable to a
sensation of pride of making it to the top of his game.

"Number one, the big dog, king of the hill; perchance
Daddy was correct when he whispered I'd be a star."

He could already see himself outwitting the snooping
eyes of *Mr. John Walsh* with his macho leather jacket,
pointing his finger into the camera with police car lights
flashing behind him on the set of *The Hunt*.

"Boo-hoo-hoo, little crime fighter might have met his match this time."

Walsh was the host of AMW and it had been the longest-running program of any kind in the history of the Fox Television Network until it was announced in 2011 that the series was being canceled after twenty-three years.

Not long after, FOX offered the manhunter his own show in The Hunt with John Walsh.

But Santa was a bit behind on that news.

Richard was a really big fan of the show, and examined their website twice a day, trusting that one day, he'd click the *'Fugitives'* tab and then and stumble across his name on the *'FBI Most Wanted'* page.

Most Wanted... that's the spot he craved.

"Nobody remembers second place," he grumbled staring into the rearview. "Second place is for losers!"

Steering back onto the roadway, he grinned and wondered where he'd find a little something for his collection back at the farm.

That's when he decided to make the detour... a special pit-stop for a hot apple cider.

They'd be dying to see Santa climb from his van, hatchet hand, stalking the cider store with cruel intentions tumbling through his mind.

"I'm going to bring them the Christmas spirit"

Knock, Knock! Who's there?
SANTA CLAUS... off with your head!

Chapter 67

Stalking the Shadows

THE STENCH OF DECAY attacked Murphy's senses as he descended the iron handholds.

The concrete walls were damp with putrid goop. Brown pigments marbled the disintegrating stone and it didn't take a rocket scientist to guesstimate what adhered to the surface just inches in front of his face.

An enormous disgusting turd!

Packed tight by hundreds of thousands of toilets that had flushed their waste into the shaft.

"What the hell died down here?" Rico complained. "It smells like the elevator shaft at the county morgue."

It had been less than two months since the worst storm in the New York City subway system's 108-year history had hit. Seven tunnels beneath the East River were flooded.

Entire platforms were still submerged.

Underground equipment, some of it decades old, was ruined. Superstorm Sandy had really done a number on Lower Manhattan and there were still sewers filled with water.

Murphy coughed continuously. He suffered from asthma, a chronic inflammatory ailment of the bronchial airways causing reversible airflow obstruction and bronchospasms. Anyone who suffered a lung infection or panic attack knew what it felt like when the lungs fought for oxygen. His disease was thought to have been caused by genetic and environmental factors. Some blamed the dust clouds of September 11, 2001 which had formed after the towers collapsed and Lower Manhattan became shrouded in heavy white and grey powder.

"You all right, Murphy?" Rico called.

"Yeah, yeah, keep stepping, I'll be fine!"

The Serial Killer Task Force had scrambled down a hundred or so rungs. Hundreds of feet below the surface sat the MTA subway system... the most extensive public transportation system in the world which contained more than eight-hundred miles of track that delivered over one billion rides a year.

The killer could be anywhere, Murphy supposed hopping from the bottom rung and swinging his flashlight through the darkness. On the cement floor tracked hundreds of bloodstained bootprints leading into the tunnel.

"Look at this," he said shining the light along the tracks. "Blake left us a trail, maybe setting us up for an ambush."

Rico stared at the bloody prints. "They're just a few minutes old; get your weapons ready, this psychopath could be anywhere down here."

The click and clack of automatic weapons echoed through the tunnel as dozens of cops panned-out, cautiously stepping through the abandoned brick channel.

"Somebody get more light down here!" Captain McKenzie ordered.

Uniformed cops lumbered to the front of the procession and were now leading the Task.

Murphy heaved into another coughing frenzy. "Give me a second, fellas, let me catch my breath." Pulling the inhaler out once more, he sucked in the medicine's mist and brought his breathing back under control.

The cops moved on, plodding deeper into the channel, their guns at the ready, until finally, the cavernous passageway ended at a red-bricked sewer line. Running down its center was a stream of feces infested sludge.

Glancing down to it, Murphy saw rats swimming in the toxic waste, their craniums plopping beneath the water when his flashlight beam scanned the surface.

"For heaven sake!" he groaned, pushing a fist against his nose, "the stench is unbearable!"

Beside him, Mei vomited near a putrid wall.

"Are you going to be all right, partner?" Rico probed, rubbing the palm of his hand on her back. "You can go back up to the surface if it's too much!"

Mei ran her fingers across her lips, shook her head, and shone her flashlight laterally and into the culvert. Moving through the nastiness, she followed the bootprints following the sewer. Moving on, she knew each step brought her closer to the unknown, until the end of the passageway dropped into a pipe that disappeared into the depths.

Then, just above their heads, through a hollowed out wall, they first heard... and then saw, a passing subway car.

That's where they headed, climbing through the channeled out rock and into a subway tube.

"Shut this line down!" McKenzie barked to a Transit Authority cop standing beside him. "What line is this?"

The MTA cop glanced at markings painted along the fortification and turned back to his commander. "The number one, two, and three trains, sir, this is the red line!"

"Dammit," McKenzie muttered, "the Seventh Avenue Express? Son, order this line closed to traffic, do we understand one another?"

"Sir, yes, Sir!"

The Seventh Avenue Express was the rapid transit service of the New York City Subway system. The busiest north-south track of the system, riders recognized the route by its tomato-red colored station indicators and the official subway map signs. Since this track used the IRT Broadway–the Seventh Avenue Line ran through most of Manhattan. Any time of day, there were people on these trains.

McKenzie made his decision. "Make the call to Port Authority and inform command we've got a priority one eighty seven manhunt down here."

"Transit eight-seven-two," the officer called into his radio. "Notify Command Center that Manhattan South and the New York Field Office of the FBI is tracking a suspect through the tomato, over?"

"Roger that, eight-seven-two," a dispatcher responded over the radio, "Give us five minutes to halt traffic, over!"

Murphy directed his light back to the bloody bootprints and continued trailing them along the damp, dark tunnel.

"That son-of-a-bitch has to be down here," McKenzie barked. "I can smell the scent of death in the air."

The stench of death was overwhelming.

"We better get this perp," Rico urged his men. "This guy is a rattle snake with a toothache, and if we don't watch our backs, this psycho will strike us from the shadows."

"Fan out, men," the agent in charge ordered.

"But Agent Ling," one of the patrolmen argued. "This isn't an exercise; this murdering madman will take us out at his first opportunity."

Nodding her understanding, Mei knew he was correct. But despite the sense of danger, she assumed the risks were well worth it. These cops had all been hand selected for the fatal mission precisely due to their propensity for viciousness. Individually, they'd all been targets of Internal Affairs investigations for alleged misconduct and violating civil rights of detainee

"You're all better off down here, defending the innocent citizens who are walking the streets above. Trust me when I say, NYPD command and the FBI Feld Office will certainly put you in front of TV cameras and strong-arm the department to drop their frivolous witch hunts,"

"Okay," Rico said staring into the men's eyes. "We're just hunting

Chapter 68

Eyeball Witness

$\mathcal{D}$ETECTIVE ARIAS stood over the corpse.

"You must have a shamrock shoved up your ass," he chuckled at Romero. "If Morrison wasn't beaten down with this manhunt, you'd be handing out jaywalking tickets in Harlem."

As luck would have it, just as the D.I. was chewing Romero's ass for talking to the media, Detective Operations jingled up his number for this homicide in Chinatown.

The neighborhood was home to the largest enclave of Chinese folks in the Western Hemisphere. It bordered the Lower East Side and Little Italy. With a population of 100,000 residents, the district was the oldest ethnic Chinese territory outside of Asia. They spoke Cantonese and came from several regions of China in Guangdong, Hong Kong, and Fujian Provinces.

Nonetheless, this was the first time someone wearing a Santa hat had found their cranium split in two.

"Right down the middle, Johnnie," Arias whispered arching over the body where grey brain splatter speckled the sidewalk. "The head resembles a cantaloupe chopped in half."

"Throw on a little mozzarella," Romero mumbled, "and the blood would resemble a twelve-inch pie from New York Pizzeria!"

"Jesus, Bobby, who thinks about crap like that, huh?"

At that moment, an old Asian woman hobbled over leaning on a handmade bamboo cane, her sagging facial skin covered entirely with hand drawn tattoos.

我看到了
个圣诞老人的飞跃，从
辆面包车，并杀死洪先生

That's what the old timer screamed, her eyes squinting to a thin line, pointing down Canal Street.

"What the hell did she say?" Romero asked.

They could use a *Google translator* out there!

"Who knows," Arias responded.

As far as they were concerned, it sounded like a lunchtime order of sweet and sour pork and fried rice. Neither understood linguistics, so they gawked at the ancient woman with her ink-drawn face.

"The facial tattoos," Arias said, "are part of the Dulong people's culture. Known as the *Facial Tattoo Tribe*, they are an ethnic minority who survived along the River Valley in China's southwestern Yunnan Province."

"Why?" Romero chuckled.

"Whaddaya mean, kid?"

Romero nodded at the tattoos. "Why do they go and put that shit all over their faces?"

Arias shrugged. "I read about it in Time Magazine. In ancient times, young girls were forced to get their faces tattooed with indigo ink by sharpened bamboo needles or thorns at puberty to show they'd come of age. The ink design differed between tribes, but butterflies are the most common because they believe the souls of the departed morph into the flying insects."

"Freaking serious?"

"It's true," Arias nodded approaching the old woman. "The origins of facemask tattoos occurred when Tibetan tribal leaders enslaved the Dulong and abducted their women. Their faces were tattooed to brand them unappealing to bandits."

Some said they warded off evil spirits.

Either way, Arias thought, *it was downright freaky.*

Another Chinese shopkeeper emerged from a knockoff purse storefront, walked to the old woman, and started speaking in the native language.

"What the hell are they saying?" Romero shrugged turning to his partner. "We're going to need an interpreter down here."

The Chinaman turned back to Romero.

"You know, not all Asian people learn how to speak your stupid American language. This old woman says she saw a Santa Claus leap from a van and kill Mr. Hong! And then he got into his vehicle and sped down the street!"

"Down Canal Street? Is she sure?"

"Yes, very sure. She says the man often climbed out of the manhole cover in Saint John's Park and got into a van he keeps parked there."

"You know what I'm thinking?" Arias whispered.

"We just found the killer's escape route," Romero nodded. "The one Murphy and Rico are looking for down in the tunnels!"

"How did he kill Mr. Hong?" Arias asked.

The Asian shopkeeper turned to the old tattooed woman and asked the question. As he listened to her response, his face took on a grave scowl.

Turning back, he sadly told them what she had said.

"She says the executioner pulled out a tomahawk and slammed it into Mr. Hong's head. Then... he walked back to his van like nothing happened."

Suddenly, just across the roadway, a slew of Transit Cops stormed from the park and glanced along the street.

"Hey, Arias!" one of them yelled, sprinting across the road and shaking his hand, "What the hell are you guys doing here?"

"Another one eighty-seven," Romero answered pointing to the corpse on the pavement. "And we found an eyeball witness!"

"Is that right? We just spent an hour walking through turds and piss in a tunnel that led us to the parking lot over in the Saint John's Park."

"You guys find anything?"

"Not yet, but the search continues."

At that moment, unknown to the cop, the Task Force did find something...

Deadly things that had no business living.

Chapter 69

Junkies & Sex Slaves

Manhattan's PORT AUTHORITY bus terminal was a central gateway for public transportation, junkies, sex slaves, and perverts.

No matter the desire, several *personal* connections were available for the right price.

Owned and operated by the Port Authority of New York and New Jersey, the station sat off Eighth Avenue, a hop and a skip east of the Lincoln Tunnel and a couple blocks west of Times Square.

"Does anybody want a date?" an exotic brown sugar prostitute purred to uninterested Greyhound passengers exiting the coaches. "Twenty bucks for lips… forty-five for hips!"

"Oh, yeah, baby girl!" Stefan snarled as he stepped to the asphalt, "you look good as hell, with those thunder thighs!"

She is thick in all the right places.

Her ass bounced as she sashayed along the platform, a hand on her hip, her bright red lips puckered in welcoming promises.

It had been weeks since Stefan had gotten his rocks off, kicking back with Trisha who rode atop his trembling frame. Of course, she'd made him cuddle with her for hours afterwards.

He thought back to that now and wondered… *what the hell was so great about cuddling? When guys had sex, they just wanted to do it and get the hell away.*

He chuckled at his cogitation and imagined the sexual healer standing before him. She looked like she could suck a golf ball through a garden hose if she set her mind to it.

"Are you looking for some jungle love?" she asked moseying close and blowing a bursting kiss at his fantasies. "Want some hot chocolate for your fluffy marshmallows?"

He felt himself getting hard.

What the hell, twenty bucks is a steal, as long as I don't catch crabs!

However, there were much worse infections out there waiting to find a way into young blood. Hepatitis, gonorrhea, and the *king of death* and destruction: AIDS.

But to a seventeen-year-old street kid, death by bullets and knives seemed more realistic.

So, he winked at the GIRL, clutched HER hand, and permitted the goddess to lead him to the *ladies* restroom where they found an empty booth and locked the door.

"Whatcha want, sexy white boy?" she whispered into his ear, nibbling his lobes, and sucking his pale white neck.

"Just blow me, girl."

Bending to a knee, she pulled his pants down around his ankles, and grasped his buttocks.

Feeling the orgasm rising... Stefan slammed his eyes shut and exploded.

"Oh, baby! Arghhhhhh yeah!" Then, he glanced at the sexpot and almost lost his lunch.

His Oscar Meyer Weiner lay in ITS mouth, AND in the Amazon's hand was a huge black python.

"What the fuck?" Stefan shrieked, securing his zipper and vomiting on the floor.

On *HIS* knees, the female impersonator finished his deed, grinned at Stefan, and blew another kiss towards his perturbed expression.

"What's the matter, chicken wing?" the drag queen challenged. "You've never gotten head from a *polefessional* before, huh?"

"You bitch!" Stefan howled. "You double dealing nasty whore!" He shoved the impersonator to the floor, grabbed his shoebox of memories, and sprinted for sanity.

Pushing into the terminal, his pants fell to his knees and he stumbled to the concrete. There, he fluttered off to Sand Man Land, lost to his subconscious and the monstrosity that just occurred.

Little sissy boy, the voice in his head returned. *Letting another MAN slurp your junk!*

"Somebody, get him an ambulance!" a woman screamed. "This boy has had a stroke!"

"It's a seizure!" another shouted, bending beside the trembling boy. "I'm a doctor, give me some space!"

A crowd surrounded Stefan as his body shook in a Grand Mal epileptic fit. But inside his mind, down where the brain analyzed things, he was warm and fuzzy floating inside a dream.

The OWL was circling high above Rockefeller Plaza, its eyes burning into his gaze.

"Hoot! Hoot!" It called, "Hoot! Hoot!"

Watch out for the boogeyman!

In the dream, Stefan ripped his eyes from the owl swooping above the skaters. That's when his mind's eye saw the madman smiling in his direction.

I'm coming... for them... The Santa Claus Killer whispered, and *for you... ya little fucker. My whip isn't just for the reindeer! Daddy Christmas is on his way!*

You're not my daddy!

And just as quick as he had passed out, Stefan snapped from the dream, leapt to his feet and bounded through the terminal in search of his sanity.

Little did he know: dreams were visions of the future.

Chapter 70

Cry of the Cats

MURPHY HEARD THE SCREAMS.

Then he saw the bodies.

He'd been leading the task force along the path of bloody boot prints beside the tracks, twisting and turning into a maze of misdirection.

"Aaaaooooowwwwwwwwwrrrrrrr!"

The cries boomed through the tunnel, bouncing along the bulwarks, echoing into the dark far beyond the police flashlight beams. The cries were *horrifying*, painful, *echoing* squeals slamming into his ears, like a bawling infant ceaselessly hammering its high notes on an airplane.

Murphy recalled just such an incident.

He was on a 747, the passengers *groaning, nodding,* and *sneering* at the baby's mother.

Shut it up, right this instant!

Up in First Class, a Fortune-500 executive pushed aside his roast duck, scrambled from an oversized seat, and stomped back to the *cheap seats.* He was irate and unstable from gallons of coffee swallowed during a corporate shareholders conference.

"I'll snap that little brat's neck if you don't shut it up!"

The veins in his neck bulged with rage and Murphy had to wrestle *the elitist* to the floor, snap bracelets on his wrists, and turn him over to Feds.

Now, *that* was one hell of a return on investment.

"Mrrroooooowww!"

"Jesus, that sounds like bloody murder."

"Where is it coming from?" Special Agent Mei Ling complained walking into a cavern.

"Cats!" Murphy replied, scrutinizing a cage crowded with feline carcasses; their fur gnawed from their skeletons, the bones chomped through; comparable to what a ravenous dog might've left behind had it gotten hold of the gristle, detained a cat in its paws, and crunched away.

"Look at this!" Rico bellowed pacing the enclosure. "They've feasted on themselves." Counting the skulls of dead cats, he saw there were eighteen in all; each pushed to the perimeter of the cage, their flesh picked clean by a hungry aggressor. At the center of the cat penitentiary crouched a gigantic plump tomcat, eating a smaller, starved kitten that screamed for its life.

"Mrrrrrroooooooowwwwww!"

"He's about thirty pounds!" the commander noticed, watching the tomcat as it ripped the intestines from the dying kitten's body.

"Looks like it consumed the weak." Mei suggested. "He was so hungry the smaller kittens became a meal."

"Jesus Christ!" Rico pointed to the fat cat. "So he's the winner of the day, huh?"

Murphy was disgusted. Motioning for a transit cop to open the cage, he pointed at the tomcat. "Put that poor bastard out of its misery, will ya?"

The cop pulled open the cage, shoved his nightstick into the pen, and cracked the wooden stick over tomcat's head.

The bone shattered as the club smashed the animal's skull. "Night, night," the cop whispered as the meat-eater fell dead with the lifeless kitten still in its jaws.

Rico winced. "Sleep well, Mr. Carnivore!"

Turning back to the assassin's lair, his flashlight tumbled over the dingy walls and illuminated the rusty chains dangling from the ceiling. At the end of those iron links swung decomposing human bodies sagging on heavy steel hooks.

"I've got three bodies suspended from chains," he counted. "Meat hooks are attached to their collarbones!"

Mei rushed to the scene and stared at the hooks supporting unrecognizable flesh rotting from the skeletons.

"Hey, Commander!" an NYPD cop called from across the cavern. "Get a load of this!"

Taped to the walls were newspaper stories from Miami, Washington, D.C., and Charleston.

And, right beside them, were new articles.

HANGING JUDGE FOUND MURDERED
Manhattan South Homicide on the Case

The next was a *Daily News* front page with black marker handwriting across the yellowing paper:

For Timothy Smith!

ABC INTERN BEHEADED
'Just working her way through college,' says Mother.

And then this:

NOT A SILENT NIGHT IN QUEENS
Probation Officer's Daughter Accosted by Santa Claus

McKenzie shone his flashlight across the headlines, grunted in disgust, and turned to Murphy.

"This guy has to be put down!"

Murphy was spellbound. "I suspect we haven't seen anything, yet." He'd seen his share of murder scenes over the years, but nothing reeked of sadistic elements like this.

It reminded of scenes from the Brad Pitt thriller movie, *Se7en*. In the film, Pitt played a newly transferred detective, David Mills, who became entangled in the case of a merciless serial killer who methodically planned homicides corresponding to the seven deadly sins: Gluttony, Greed, Sloth, Wrath, Pride, Lust, and, Envy.

Scanning the cave, Murphy noticed mounds of cat bodies that once hung on the meat hooks. Now, they were mere skeletons. Their flesh consumed by flies and bluebottles whose larvae fed on the meat of departed creatures. And written in blood on the broken mirror across from the hanging bodies was this:

L I V E D S D O G M A I

"What the hell does *that* mean, Murphy?" Commander McKenzie grunted. "The letters don't make sense."

Murphy pulled out his notepad, rearranged the letters, and presented the decoded message to the captain.

"I AM GODS DEVIL," McKenzie read the scratched out declaration. "Well, isn't that wonderful?"

"At least he knows what he is," Mei offered walking through the torture chamber.

Then, somewhere in the darkness, Rico shouted.

"You sick murdering prick!"

Murphy trailed Mei as they rushed into the back cavern where their lights revealed a naked man being eaten alive by rats. He was chained to a stone wall like the British had once done to patriots imprisoned in dungeon stockades to die of disease, injury, parasites and the nibbles of rats.

"Help me," the man whispered. "Please!"

"Jeez!" McKenzie shrieked at the spectacle of the half-eaten man. "Somebody get EMS on the radio and get this guy out of those chains."

A swat member rushed forward with bolt cutters, snapped the cuffs from the dehydrated man's wrists, and watched in horror as detectives laid the man onto the filthy ground.

"Stay with us!" Murphy begged gazing at the masticated chest cavity where the heart weakly beat for all to see.

"It was the guy from the newspapers," the victim weakly alleged coughing up dark red blood. "*The Santa Claus Killer*, he watched as the rats chewed away my ribs!"

Mei glanced at Murphy.

It was not going to be a Silent Night in Manhattan.

Chapter 71

No Place Like Home

THE BENTLEY LIMO hummed at the curb.

Heads *turned,* eyes *glanced,* and minds *wished*–that someday–destiny would shine on their misery and lady luck would send the Mega Millions jackpot their way.

Suckers!

All would give *some* and most would give *all,* just for a chance to ride in the swanky chromed elegance that screamed its owner had been *there,* done *that,* and was certainly NOT over it. In fact, being over it... wasn't even a possibility. The billionaires who had that kind of scratch, the upper echelons, the nose lifters, the filthy rich didn't trouble themselves with price tags or invoices. As long as Brinks trucks continued dumping cash into their offshore accounts... nothing else mattered.

But Mirabel was a tad on the liberal side.

She knew what it was like to be poor; she'd once saved supermarket coupons of *BUY ONE-GET ONE* free.

So, as she stood alongside the spotless moneyed limo, its door held ajar by an aging, balding, loyal driver, she couldn't help resist recalling those humble beginnings.

That was a long time ago; things sure have changed.

What didn't change was the offensiveness of the streets, the downright nastiness of the piled-up trash along its sidewalks, lost within a sea of fast food wrappers and snuffed out cigarette butts.

She shook her head at the sight and thought that perhaps the *Department of Health* should paint their forewarnings on curbs as well as cigarette packages.

<u>SURGEON GENERAL'S WARNING</u>

Walking in Manhattan Causes
Death
Heartache
Emphysema
And May Cause Foot Pain...

And will definitely muck up the soles of my shoes!
Bending her ankle, she grinned with gratitude that black cigarette ashes hadn't stained her Kate Spade New York Karolina Pumps.

"Where the hell is this boy, James?"

A response wasn't expected; her utterance was an off-handed murmur of boredom.

"I swear he's like a caffeinated gerbil!"

"He *jus'* keeps on movin', *Missa* Woodward," the African American butler answered. "This here station ain't *mo-better* since I was a *shoat* rug-rat, Mmm-hmm."

She glanced at her trusted manservant. He had been through hell and high water over the years.

"I suppose you're right, James. The only thing that's changed in Times Square is the absence of triple-x stores on every single corner."

"*Yessum*, the Square is *jus'* like that old watch; it takes a lickin' and keeps right on tickin'."

"We've been through a lot, huh?" Mirabel smiled, "you, Terry and I?"

"Fifteen calendars and memories long lost to senility. That's a whole *buncha* recollections faded into God's good earth, Mmm-hmm."

It is reality spoken from wisdom, Mirabel supposed.

James had been part of Mirabel's extended family since she hired him on. Originally from Savannah, Georgia, he possessed that down south, lazy, sunny afternoon manner.

His tongue pronounced words parodied on shows like *The Beverly Hillbillies* and *Here Comes Honey Boo-Boo.*

Damn nonsense, she thought.

Nevertheless, there wasn't anything humorous about James. He was a kind old-soul of southern hospitality born of a humbler period. Back when *Hope & Change* meant school grades had better improve or else the paddle came!

Glancing across 9th Avenue, Mirabel noticed a crowd exiting the stainless steel doors of the Port Authority terminal. Instantly, the street became a mass exodus of colors rushing past, disbursing like ants into the security of waiting yellow cabs and city busses.

"Mirabel!" Stefan yelled pushing through the horde, sprinting across the street and into her waiting embrace.

"Boy!" James drawled, "you done gone and gave Ms. Mirabel a worrisome mind, Mmmm-hmm!"

Stefan smiled, rocking back and forth in the hug of all hugs. "Hey, James, are you taking good care of her?"

"I sho-nuff is!" he replied, tapping bony fingers on his chest, "keeps my worn down ticker drumming' along *jus'* fine, yes it does."

That brought a chuckle from Stefan as Mirabel pushed him to arm's length and eyeballed his frazzled blonde hair, thin worn face and soiled clothing.

"I've missed you so much!" she said, clutching Stefan's slender frame securely, petrified to let go for fright of losing him to the streets. "What have you gotten yourself into? You smell like the bathroom at Kennedy Airport!"

"How would you know what that smells like?"

"Don't you be *sassin'* any grown people," James muttered. "You ain't too grown to chew a bar of Ivory soap to clean out that raggedy mouth!"

Stefan smiled–*a big titanic smirk*–an expression that indicated everything was *gravy* so long as that instant… and the following one… continued.

"I missed you guys so much," he assured them, releasing his grip on the only woman who dared to envision something better for his life.

But destiny and fate were odd twins, they fought and scratched and sometimes, when people least expected it, the rain exploded onto the parade.

The parade leader of freaks now headed their way.

"Hey, white boy!" the drag queen from the restroom screamed, *his* lipstick smeared across his cheeks, the *now apparent* wig skewed atop *he-she's* head.

"Where's my money, cotton candy ass?"

For a split second, had the Earth stopped rotating and the universe ceased expanding, there might have been a millisecond where a movie producer avatar leapt onto this page and yelled: Cut! Take two! Quiet on the set!

But the planet still whirled, the deep echo of space further expanded and Hollywood producers were busy figuring out how to *re-do* a *re-make* and call it an *original*.

So, there you are, dear reader, scrutinizing the make-believe female charging across the roadway, his teeth bared, a snarl growling from deep within its throat–*what's been down there is anyone's guess*–and demanding a fair shake on a fraudulent deal.

"I want my sexy back," the fire-eyed transvestite yelled, "you pussy-ass white boy!"

Stefan charged into the street, pulled out Marco's gun hidden in his jeans and pointed its barrel straight for the drag queen's horse-haired wig.

"I've got a head job for you, right here!"

That's when the drama started, because just then, the female impersonator lost all brainwaves and fainted into *Sissyville*.

"Stefan!" Mirabel yelled. "Give me that lousy weapon and get your raggedy behind in the car, right now!"

Beside the Bentley, James slapped his thigh and hooted in amusement. "Boy, oh, boy! Bend a wandering eye at that thing!"

Nobody knew if he was chattering of the gun, the woman wannabe, or the thick stallion mane wig lying on the asphalt beside the passed out *fudge-packer*.

One thing was for sure, it was on and popping in the *Orville Redenbacher Lounge* as folks clogged the thoroughfare pointing at the spectacle before them.

Things like this could only happen in New York.

And man, wasn't it all such fun!

Chapter 72

Ɖҽtour to Ĉiɖҽrvillҽ

Ɖʀ. DAVIES FARM in Congers, New York, was built in 1836 and boasted four hundred and fifty acres along the Hudson River.

With over four-thousand apple trees, the family-owned orchard operated a roadside hot cider stand where they pressed apples several times a week.

It was the most famed apple farm along the river and had been the site of innumerable *Saturday Night Live* spoofs, TV commercials, and major motion pictures.

But that's not why Santa pulled his meat wagon up to the snow-covered red barn. During his escape from Manhattan, he recalled childhood memories of harvesting apples and downing hot cider with Daddy and Mammy.

"Those were the days," he mumbled, "a time when Mammy looked upon me with love and dedication."

That was, until the cats started showing up on the farm.

First, there was just a single female, and then came its mate, which soon produced multiple litters that gave birth to *The Chatterer* that began whispering its demands.

Richard! Oh, Richard... Chatterbox Charlie had purred outside his bedroom window–*every night, all night*–until Richard gathered the nerve to step from his bed, frightfully stride across the hardwood floor, and peep through the frosted window.

Want to come out and play, Richard? The Chatterer inquired each night... until Richie Rich wandered into the moonlight to stroke its belly and listen to the feline's murderous propositions.

We have things to do, Richie! Lots of work to accomplish!

Santa pushed aside the memory of the white Persian and glared through the windshield to a fading wooden sign.

DR. DAVIES
FARMSTAND
Pick Your Own APPLES

The words were sketched out in white paint upon a chocolate skirt of scrap wood. It hung from a miniature pole haphazardly attached to a wooden arrow. Below hung a closed sign with bright red lettering that swayed on a wintry gust to the faint squeaking carrying on the breeze.

Santa stared at the hooks, recalling the work he'd left behind. The fleshy things abandoned on their own sort of meat hooks in the Canal Street lair. Glancing at the entrance of the fruit stand, he noticed another sign:

Hours of Operation

Rt. 9W stand-9:00-5:30 July thru November
Rt. 304 stand-9:00-5:30 July thru November

* Cash Only - No Credit cards accepted *

Santa made his decision then.

Climbing from the vehicle, he tracked through the snow blown orchard and wandered up to the huge white house.

Somebody has to give me cider. I didn't come here for nothing.

The house was surrounded on either side by barren trees.

Moving towards the entrance, Santa lifted the Condor Greenland Hatchet and knocked on the door with its blunt edge. On the other side of this door, an aging matriarch curiously brought her frail frame to the entrance, swung open the door and gasped at the sight before her.

"May I help you?"

Santa smiled. "Here comes Santa Claus!"

Pushing the door open, he raised the hatchet and watched as granny stumbled into the foyer.

"What do you want?"

Santa swung the hatchet through the warm interior air.

It felt *good in* his hand, like a form fitting leather glove. Offering a sense that the hardwood, non-slip handle belonged in his clutch.

The old woman fell to the floor.

"Please, just take what you want and leave us alone!"

It occurred to Santa, that they weren't alone. Sensing the manifestation of something behind him, he swung around to face a frightened schoolboy gawking at the scene of his grandmother bawling on the floor of her lifelong home.

"Hey, buddy," Santa smiled, pushing the hatchet behind his back. Then, movement in the corner drew his attention.

Richard Blake! A tiger-striped cat screeched in his head.

Oh, Richie Boy! Its fangs were bared; the green eyes were angry and demanding.

It sprung atop a couch.

"Get away from me!"

Get out of this house; you will NOT kill! The hissing feline growled; its spine arched in rage.

The Santa Claus Killer was stunned, his body quaked in panic, and droplets of perspiration broke out on his forehead as he crept back to the foyer.

The boy ran to his grandmother, hugged her tight, and screamed at Santa. "I don't like you anymore!"

Santa scanned the room, keeping an uneasy eye on the mouse-eater that seemed prepared to leap for his face.

Then, he turned, hurried out the door, and began to sing.

♫♪♫ Grandma was run over by a reindeer,
    Sitting in her house this winter's eve…
Kids can say there's no such thing as Santa,

But as for frightened Grandma, she believes! ♫♪♫

Scurrying across the driveway, he hopped into the wagon and sped down the road. Behind the wheel of the death wagon, he couldn't help but wonder why the cats had turned on him.

It was the first time he'd been told NOT to kill.

Chapter 73

Feeding the Wolves

ONE POLICE PLAZA was headquarters of the NYPD.

Located on Park Row in downtown Manhattan, it neighbored City Hall and the Brooklyn Bridge.

On the eighth was the Real Time Crime Center, a computer network exploration machine operated by law enforcement personnel to support field officers' active investigations.

But outside, on the square, that's where the meat and potatoes were fed to the unforgiving wolves of Network News.

Today, a cheap aluminum podium was erected on the plaza steps where an energetic news conference was about to begin. The seal of the New York City Mayor's Office was attached to the pedestal by an overworked and underpaid staffer who held up his hands when the lions shouted their questions.

"The mayor will be making a statement shortly."

"Is the killer still loose in the sewer?" NBC reporter, Les Bolt yelled above the chaos.

"What about public safety?"

Timothy Smith waited to ask his questions of the mayor. Glancing at the correspondents, they reminded him of the Bronx Zoo. A man riding the monorail had recently jumped from his seat and into the tiger den as the railcar passed over the habitat. Dismayed zoo patrons reported staring in astonishment as the fellow landed in the den, was attacked by the tigers, and ended up with a punctured lung and gnawed away foot.

Tim envisioned the expression on the onlooker's faces and imagined it wasn't much different than this scene of vultures around him.

Press conferences matched the entertainment factor of Ringling Bros. and Barnum & Bailey Circus.

He recalled attending *The Greatest Show on Earth* at Barclay's Center last April. His favorite acts were the clowns; they always had been, hands down. After thirty years of attending the circus, he still struggled to understand how all those little freaks fit into a Volkswagen Beetle.

In the midst of this thought, another type of clown appeared through the command center door.

The *Man with the Plan* faced the cameras with a gang of high-ranking cohorts at his right side. \

Thus the term: *Right Hand Man.*

"Good morning," the mayor began. "I'm here with Police Commissioner McReynolds, Chief of the Department, Joe Esperanza, and Deputy Inspector, Harold Morrison. The Commissioner will fill you in on more of the details, but earlier this morning, a little after 4 a.m., a task force comprised of detectives from the NYPD and the FBI made entry into a Chinatown meat market and discovered human remains of multiple victims hanging in a freezer."

He paused for effect here and nobody knew why.

But Tim supposed it was all planned out, like an actor walking on set and waiting for the ACTION cue.

"During the course of searching for a serial killer," the mayor continued, "the task force discovered a tunnel which led them into our subway system and it is there in a cavern where victims and a survivor were discovered. Make no mistake… the City of New York will spare no expense in seeking out and tracking down this man to bring him to justice before a jury of his peers."

Gathering his prepared statement, the mayor moved aside and nodded to the commissioner who wanted nothing to do with the spotlight.

In his stead, Deputy Inspector Morrison stepped to the feeding frenzy. "This is what we know so far," the twenty-five year veteran mumbled off the facts. "The suspect is well known to the department and media due to a previous high profile arrest for animal abuse. He was ordered by the criminal court system to be admitted to Bellevue and was held in the psychiatric unit for quite some time."

Timothy Smith knew all too well about Bellevue.

It opened on March 31, 1736 as the Public Workhouse and House of Correction of the City of New York, which hosted a six-bed infirmary that became America's oldest continuously operated hospital providing medical, surgical, and psychiatric services for highly complex cases.

Bellevue boasted lots of firsts in its history and the reporter recently reported on most of those accomplishments.

Tim realized something just then.

Bellevue now partook in another leading factoid.

It had unleashed *The Santa Claus Killer* on an unsuspecting city, and that was certainly a *FIRST* with which the hospital administration wanted no association.

Tim grunted and wrote a question in a notebook:

Who is H. C. M. to Richard Blake?

"A few days ago," Inspector Morrison continued, "a bench warrant was issued for Blake's arrest and during the course of serving that instrument his Brooklyn house was searched. At that time, we discovered a graveyard of skeletons. Most of the rest everybody knows as the PIO has passed out fact sheets for your media outlets. Questions?"

"Inspector!" Les Bolt shouted. "Who is the survivor found in the tunnel, and what is his condition?"

"The unnamed victim is in protective custody," the inspector responded, "at an undisclosed hospital where he is undergoing treatment for serious injuries."

A New York Daily News Reporter yelled next.

"Where is the suspect now?"

"We are running down leads as they come in. The manhunt is ongoing and we won't comment publicly on specifics."

"Deputy!" a CBS Correspondent hollered. "Is it true the skeletons found in the basement were all dressed in Santa outfits?"

The mayor elbowed his aide who leaned into the high ranking NYPD commander's ear, whispered something and then glanced towards Agent Mei Ling, Murphy, and Rico who were pulling up to the conference.

"We cannot comment on the facts relating to an ongoing investigation," the mayor stated before leading his commanders from the podium.

"Deputy Inspector!" Timothy Smith yelled. "Isn't it true you were a college acquaintance of the killer?"

"No more questions!" the aide answered ushering the shaken deputy inspector into the fold of departing officials.

"Jesus, Harold!" the mayor barked once inside the security of the structure. "I knew this was going to get out to the wolves."

"He was an upstanding doctor at one time! How the hell were we supposed to know this would happen?"

"Have your people found the pictures?" the mayor asked. "Are they in the house or in any of his family's businesses?"

Deputy Inspector Harold C. Morrison had a long history with Richard Blake. They were college roommates and best friends at New York University.

And there was something else, too.

"No, sir." the inspector responded. "They could be anywhere."

"Including," the mayor spat, "in the hands of the Daily fucking News!"

And that meant the following day was going to be rife with denials and sidestepping.

And maybe... there would be hell to pay.

Chapter 74

The Madhouse

THE OLD PSYCHIATRIC HOSPITAL was erected in the Italian Renaissance style forty years before the signing of the Declaration of Independence.

"For centuries," a tall, finely dressed Public Information Official babbled, "Bellevue functioned as an incubator of major advances in public health and defined the supreme traditions of public medicine for the city."

Agent Mei Ling stared at the ostentatious pencil pusher with the enormous white dental implants. They were captivating–their pearliness drew her attention right into his mouth–and the choppers reminded her of Vice President Joe Biden's chattering-teeth, which had captivated her during the 2012 V.P. debate she'd watched with interest.

"Of course," the Bellevue official continued, bringing Mei's attention back to the marble hallway. "Our national treasure was long ago supplanted by this state-of-the-art, sprawling, and billion dollar modern academic institute of intercontinental fame."

Mumbo jumbo wordcrafting, Murphy thought. He knew in the not so distant past, the sanatorium had developed into a dumping ground for the criminally insane and a rotating door for the homeless.

That was then, now we just throw them in prison.

"It's hard to believe this is the Bellevue I remember from childhood," he commented as they were ushered into an office and seated in leather-backed chairs. "Back then horror movies couldn't hold a candle to the lunatics locked in this madhouse."

"Madhouse?" the man grunted. "Detective Murphy, we are an institution of fine standing."

"Ah-Ha," Mei dismissed. The office was something of a futuristic take on the 1990 movie, *Total Recall,* starring Arnold Schwarzenegger. Mei had seen both versions and thought the 2012 remake was pure garbage.

Glancing around the office, she saw little furnishings before glancing out the floor-to-ceiling windows that looked out across FDR Drive.

"Do the craziest here have this kind of view?"

The insult worked its magic getting under the skin of the highly paid uppity administrator.

"We don't use words such as crazies or lunatics," the Clinical Director spun from the window. "Instead, the Behavioral Health Department considers our residents Adult Inpatients."

"Is that right?" Murphy chuckled. "Because... down at Manhattan South Homicide and in the County Courthouse they're called psychopaths."

"Yes, I'm well aware of that." the man sighed reaching across the desk. "I'm Jerrod McFarlane, Clinical Director of Adult Inpatient Services here at Bellevue. I presume this is about Dr. Blake?"

"You know exactly what this is about," Mei spat. "So, don't screw me and call it foreplay!"

The Bureau had subpoenaed Richard's records and danced the tango before a magistrate earlier that morning arguing patient rights and medical confidentiality. That dog didn't hunt when the patient in question was a murdering madman tying up hundreds of thousands of the city's dollars in manpower expenses.

So, here she sat, gawking at the keeper of the den–moving chess pieces across the bureaucracies of medical secrecy–to obtain information of the King of Christmas and his gifts of death.

"Do you have the file? I don't have time to pussyfoot around with niceties. You lost the court hearing to keep his records private."

"I don't understand," the administrator mumbled. "I already spoke to someone from your office about this."

Murphy glanced to Mei, his eyebrows raised suspiciously. "What do you mean? We didn't call you for information."

"Detective Tim Smith called about an hour ago and we gave him everything we had."

"Over the phone? You gave out our suspect's information to someone who said he was a detective?"

"You don't know Officer Smith?"

"Yeah, I know Tim Smith," Murphy sarcastically stated. "He's a reporter from Eyewitness News."

The suspender-fiddling director wrung his hands and paced the floor. "He sounded like a detective, and had the lingo of cop speak down cold!"

"Where is the file?" Mei demanded. "We need the information before you hand over the investigation to another reporter."

Reaching into his mahogany desk drawer, the director pulled out a thick manila file with CONFIDENTIAL stamped on its cover. Flipping it open, he slid a pair of Kenneth Cole eyeglasses onto his nose, scanned a document, and then passed the massive file across to Agent Ling who winced in his direction.

"Tim Smith," the director nodded, "called my assistant a few hours ago stating he was with Manhattan South's records department. Karla told him everything we know."

"Well, he got you good," Mei scolded. "You'll probably be hearing about it on the news tonight."

The clinician shrugged. "It was right after the judge issued his decision and we sought to liaise in the spirit of assistance. How could we have known?"

"I dunno," Murphy dressed the man down. "You could have called the FBI or NYPD and made sure Smith was who he claimed, maybe that would've been smart?"

Mei flipped through the worn pages of the psychiatric file. What leaped out at her was a hand written note:

> They whisper to me,
> As if locked within the recess of my thoughts,
> Bullying and threatening to devour my soul,
> Ordering me to kill complete strangers!
> They don't meow like ordinary cats...
> They communicate in words and damn me...
> For letting my wife fall into the grasp of drugs,
> And my son, lost to the endless sea of the street...

"Tell me about Blake," Murphy prodded.

"Richard was emotionally disturbed," the director answered. "We diagnosed him with schizophrenia when he experienced hallucinations and reported hearing cat voices, delusions–often bizarre or persecutory in nature–and he suffered from disorganized thinking and speech. He was constantly suffering from social withdrawal, sloppiness of dress and lack of hygiene, loss of motivation and judgment. All are common in schizophrenia, along with his feelings of paranoia and… "

"Murder," Murphy finished. "Let's not forget that one."

"It all began with the killing of animals when he was a boy," the director continued. "I recall weekly briefings with his doctor, who you found slain. He said Richard would seek out street cats at the age of ten and throw them into fire or from the rooftops of buildings."

"Jesus," Mei interrupted, handing a letter to Murphy she'd just pulled from the chart. "Take a look at this!"

"Mei, we are knee deep in a shit pile!" Staring at the letter, Murphy shook his head.

POLICE DEPARTMENT
City of New York

Jerrod McFarlane,
Clinical Director of Adult Inpatient Services
NYC HHC - Bellevue

I have known Richard Blake for much of my adult life and would like you to consider this department's request for leniency and consideration for probationary release back to the community.

Since college, he has been a staunch supporter of the NYPD, the mayor's office and the command structure for New York's finest police force.

Although I publicly supported locking him up in the MEDIA, it is my personal belief that following psychiatric care, Richard will return to his community with a renewed fervor for social acceptance and transformed mental health.

Harold C. Morrison
Deputy Inspector of Operations
NYPD

"What the hell am I reading here?" Murphy grumbled reading the letter.

The director walked to the window, stared at the river and shrugged in shame. "We released your killer to probation at the personal request of Deputy Inspector Harold Morrison."

"Christ all mighty," Mei muttered glancing at Murphy. "Why the hell would he write this letter?"

"To help out a friend," the director supposed. "At least that is what he told me."

Chapter 75

The Long Goodbye

CALVARY CEMETERY was named for *Mount Calvary.*

It's where Jesus was crucified.

The graveyard confined three-million skeletons, the largest number of interments of any necropolis in the United States.

Owned by the Roman Catholic Archdiocese of New York and managed by St. Patrick's Cathedral, it was the oldest cemetery in the country. Made famous by, *The Godfather*, the fictional burial of Don Corleone took place here overlooking Manhattan's skyline.

Cardinal Archbishop, Martin Golan, was somberly lost in prayer as a simple pearl coffin descended into a grave.

Marco Alvarez was going out in style.

"God, our Father," New York's highest ranking Catholic muttered. "Your power brings us to birth, your providence guides our lives, and by your command we return to dust."

Stefan sobbed gently alongside the casket, his hand locked tightly in Mirabel's grip.

"It's going to be all right, Stefan," Terry said. "We'll get through this tragedy together."

"Lord," the cardinal continued. "Those who die still live in your presence, their lives change but do not end. I pray, in hope for my friends here today, and for all the dead known to you alone. In company with Christ, who died and now lives, may they rejoice in your kingdom, where all our tears are wiped away. I ask you to bind Terry, Mirabel, and Stefan, in one family to sing your praise forever and ever. Amen."

The cardinal was appointed Archbishop of New York by the pope. Widely identified for his old fashioned charming media character, Golan was named in Time Magazine's list of the '100 Most Influential People in the World'.

Influence, sacrifice, and favoritisms stretched a long way in the borough of Manhattan.

The cardinal understood sacrifice. He'd given up the biggest trifecta of them all... *freewill*, *sex* and *marriage*. He also understood people like Terry had power, and the church knew how imperative his alliance was.

So, when the plea for grave space at the famed cemetery arrived at the Archdiocese, Golan knew it was the right thing to do–*but more importantly*–the request was currency of an alternative type.

It was precisely the variety of indebtedness that could be recycled for subsequent media scandals that always surprised the archdiocese.

When such circumstances arose, the cardinal's little favor for burial ground would be reimbursed in spades by the grateful attorney.

Golan knew something else, too.

Losing a gigantic case in the media meant losing the respect of your peers and the livelihood associated with it.

Losing was tantamount to career suicide.

He knew this the instant California prosecutors lost the O.J. Simpson trial. Not long after, they were thrown into the occupation suicide basket of *has-been* throwaways.

IF IT DOESN'T FIT
You MUST acquit!

The cardinal frowned in recollection of those words. Yet, he recognized OJ's eventual Las Vegas conviction and prison sentence was payback for missed opportunities in L.A. County.

That's what happens when a dream team of lawyers is not available at the right time.

So, the cardinal knew, there was something to be said for having New York's most respected criminal defense lawyer in the church's stable for just such dire occasions.

After all, receiving plot-space in Calvary Cemetery was near to impossible. Now, packed to capacity, the entombment grounds only accepted direct committals; grave plots could no longer be procured in advance of death.

That's the public line, he thought.

"Thank you so much," Terry bowed in gratitude following the service. "My wife and I appreciate the favor."

Cardinal Golan smiled. "Glad I could offer relief. Any time Saint Patrick's Cathedral, or my office, can help we'd be more than pleased."

"I'll remember this service you've done for me," Terry whispered into the consecrated man's earlobe. "Call on me when you need me the most."

Golan nodded and slapped his humble parishioner on the back. "Yes, yes, but let's not concern ourselves with that right now." Turning, he squinted at the youngster standing by the grave pitching in handfuls of dark soil. "Are you going to adopt the boy?"

Mirabel nodded, "Terry has filed the paperwork and we are trying to find him a proper school, but unfortunately with his lack of education, that may be tough."

The cardinal saw a supplementary opportunity and leapt into the fold. "Maybe I can offer my assistance with a recommendation to *Saint Agnes Boys High School* on the Upper West Side. We have just over four-hundred students during semester and the tuition is reasonable."

"It may be a bit too structured for a kid like him," Terry remarked. "Do you have any connections at a non-secular school?"

The cardinal wrestled to hide his disappointment, "Perhaps we could get him into Colombia Prep and Grammar?"

"Who runs the show over there, Cardinal?"

"Sara Kipler. I believe you helped her husband with a legal dilemma or two."

And that's how the world turns, the lawyer supposed. Everybody knew... the who, what, when, where and why of favors owed in the City of New York.

"A word from you would be appreciated," Mirabel pitched in. "We'd be in your debt."

That would be all the cardinal needed to hear, Heaven and Earth would move to find the boy a school.

And maybe a little bit of hell.

Chapter 76

Farmville Nightmares

SANTA CLAUS WANTED BLOOD.

Not fake assed vampire plasma sold at *Party City* to sucker customers or sixteen-year-old hump bunnies who sprinted through the streets on All Hallows Eve.

Ichabod Crane and the Legend of Sleepy Hollow is a goddamn fairy tale. I'd rip off his head and shit down his neck if I had the chance.

One thing about Santa: he always said what he thought, and meant what he said.

He never broke his word when it came to murder.

Not just murder…

TORTURE
MUTILATION & DISMEMBERMENT

Marching through his father's dilapidated study, he winced at the paint chipping from its walls and glanced to the ceiling that sagged from countless years of water damage.

Above the charred fireplace was a one-hundred-year-old hand carved oak mantel, which held a dozen family photos in frames.

He stared at those memories now.

"Father, I miss you," he mumbled to the long vanished caring eyes of the man who'd once directed his young path. "Where did everything go so wrong?"

Leaning on the wall, he suddenly felt dizzy. His equilibrium failing for a moment, he struggled to balance himself. The pictures morphed into a swirl of color and disfigured bodies. The room began to spin and he grasped hold of the solid bricks to hinder his fall.

As a former Emergency Medicine doctor, the killer knew the source of his lightheadedness. He'd battled a lifelong prevalence of ear-infections which caused loss of balance. Equilibrioception-*the sense of balance*-was a physical sense that prohibited falling when walking or standing. It was the result of body functions working together; the *eyes, ears,* and the body's *sense* of where it was in space.

It was also the reason humans walked the globe and didn't comprehend they weren't *really* walking vertical at all in relation to the rotation of the planet.

Nothing on Planet Earth walked upright.

If folks walked on the walls of their houses… *that* would designate how life really marched the Earth.

Sideways!

Everything slanted in relation to space, but equilibrium and gravity made things seem like *up-was-up* and *down-was-down*.

In reality there was no such thing.

The Giver of Gifts chuckled at these thoughts while staring at a photo of his father, mother, wife, and son who smiled back at him from the mantle.

"Goddamn tricks my mind plays on me!"

Glancing to a calendar, he saw it was Thursday, December 20th.

Richard! Where are you, Richie?

Santa spun in a circle, panic lining his expression. "Who the fuck is that, where are you?"

It's us, Richard! Come out to the barn and play with us!

The murderer shuffled over to the window and peered through its frosted pane. What he observed hunkered just outside the weathered barn door sent a chill up his backbone. Small piercing spikes clawed a track from his tailbone to the base of his neck. Goosebumps appeared along his arms and then a traveling chill crept along his shoulders and down his back.

"No, leave me alone, just go away!" Richard screamed at the spotted Japanese Bobtail staring from the snow-covered ground. It had an unusual *bobbed* tail resembling a rabbit. Native to Japan and Southeast Asia, it could now be found throughout the globe.

Don't make us come in there for you!

Richard was locked in fear. His eyes were held prisoner by the twenty-pound monster. Then, a movement from behind caught his attention and he glared at a litter of small kittens hissing in unison.

MEOW. Meeeeeeeeoooooooooow!

The Santa Claus Killer ran from the room, soared down two flights of stairs, and bolted from the house with his hatchet in hand.

"I'm going to seal their Meow Mix mouths once and for all! Show them who is boss!"

But that was better said than done.

Because, when the Red Suited Fool *stepped* from the farmhouse door, *trailed* through the snow, and *peeked* into the windswept barn, the tomcat was nowhere to be seen.

Beams of sunlight pierced through the warped pine boards illuminating an abandoned, corroding tractor that sat on flat, dried out tires.

Staring at a wall of stables, he took in the vision of horse skeletons laid out in locked stalls.

Beyond this, dozens of sheepskins hung from gigantic J-shaped hooks. In a corner, more than fifty withered and fleshless skulls sat piled in a small mound.

Just inside the barn door, Santa glanced toward cattle and pig skeletons, which overflowed in a huge red dumpster–the flesh long ago stripped from their skeletons and shipped off to his father's meat markets.

A rush of memories slammed into Richard then… *lambs, cows,* and *pigs* screaming for his father to stop his butchery. They would beg with horrid expressions and fright filled eyes–*their human like glares burning into his young helplessness*–as Daddy's staff hung the animals from the iron hooks, sliced open their necks and watched as bright red blood gushed onto the barn's floor.

Their hearts would cease beating and the light in their eyes faded before blinking out. Bye Bye and farewell.

"Daddy, you slave driver," Richard shrieked falling to his knees and sobbing into his hands. "I could have had a normal life!"

Meeeeeeeeooooooooooooow!

Peeking through his fingers, he watched the shrieking cats encircling him, their fangs bared, bodies tense with anger.

Yet, that wasn't the worst of it.

The wickedest was the cacophony of violent hisses pounding through his eardrums.

And then… the gang of felines parted and *the tomcat* strutted through his underlings.

Have to pay your debts, Richard! Catnip Time!

The gang sprung for Santa, their claws digging into his flesh, the choppers ripping into his red suit.

"Mommy! Get them off me!"

It was a scene right out of an unscripted horror movie, *Attack of the Cats* and maybe, possibly, it could set a new norm of animal rights.

Do unto Santa as he has done unto you.

Step right up, ladies and gentlemen; take a gander at the King of Christmas.

Chapter 77

Shamrocks & Leprechauns

PADDY RILEYS was hopping.

It was *Irish Music Dance and Cultural Night...* a popular, live entertainment, hump day hangover party held Thursdays from 10:30 p.m. to closing.

Paddy's offered live Traditional Irish music and was home to the finest *Guinness* in the city.

Some loved the music.

But everyone treasured their Guinness.

The popular Irish Dry Stout originated in the brewery of Arthur Guinness who *lived* and *died* in Dublin. The beer was considered one of the most successful brands globally selling more than 1.8 billion pints to America annually.

Detective Mike Murphy loved the burnt flavor bursting from its roasted, malted barley. And now, his frosted mug needed refreshing. "I'm going to refill this," he motioned to Mei while holding up his mug. "What about you, want another?" Staring at her short black hair, he saw the dance floor strobe lights catching her just right as she grooved to the building excitement of the tavern.

"I'd love another one, Mike!" she exclaimed guzzling the remainder of her pint. "I've never been to an Irish Pub before!"

"Really? That's a crime, you know!"

Mei thrust out her wrists. "Then take me in, officer. Throw me into your dungeon and have your way with me!"

"You like police brutality, do you?" Murphy grinned pulling out the cuffs. "Maybe S&M? Ropes and chains?"

They were taking a break from the manhunt, catching their collective breath. There wasn't another watering hole

Murphy could recommend for *disremembering* the terror of death and staving off its nightmares.

Mei kissed him on the cheek. "I've had my eye on you since the first day we met at the New York Field Office."

There it was–a deep, Eli Manning, *Hail Mary* pass into the end zone at MetLife Stadium in the Meadowlands. Just *off-handedly* pitched out there, a dispatch thrown in the airstream in hopes it would carry to the end zone.

"I kind of fancy your stare on me," Murphy chuckled.

She giggled while beaming into his gaze. "Maybe I should look at you more often."

"Maybe you should."

Murphy hadn't been in a romantic relationship in a long time. In law enforcement, relations were short lived.

Cops were well known for their crappy marriages and alcohol induced misery. Law & Order and CSI proved that storyline to the public on television.

But at this exact moment, Murphy believed again.

Staring into Mei's gaze, he winced when the lights came up and a man appeared on a small wooden stage.

"We'd like to welcome Niall O'Leary to the stage. He's an accordion, bodhran, spoons, hard shoes, and Grennan fiddle extraordinaire."

Applause went up as the three-member band began to play on the stage where Detective Mac's coffin once sat.

Behind O'Leary, on the brick wall, his shadow danced in step to his frenetic moves, the soles of his shoes knocking and pattering on the hard wood.

"Thanks for coming out tonight," the popular performer stated into his microphone.

To Mei, the *Irish Trad Session* reminded her of tap dancing on steroids. The hops and skips were quick and precise; laid forth to the sounds of Irish flutes and a banjo.

During the next thirty minutes, the beers flowed and the crowd pulsed, and before long... Mei was locked in

Murphy's embrace as the session ended and the crowd erupted in applause and cat calls.

O'Leary bowed to the patrons and stepped off the stage with a smile of satisfaction. He knew there was nothing like performing LIVE at an Irish Pub, especially when those in attendance were a bit off kilter with a pint or two coursing through their veins.

"That was outstanding!" Mei exclaimed to the passing entertainer. "You are awesome!"

Murphy was pleased she enjoyed the night out. The job wore down the spirit. The *murder, chase,* and *stress* of stomping through the shadows of death in search of a killer bore into the soul.

She turned to him, wrapped her arms around his neck, and kissed his lips.

Murphy felt the passion of it, realized the urgency in the kiss and was glad for it. It supported his feeling that they shared more than the job, maybe even having something in common beyond homicide.

"Wanna get out of here?" she asked. There was a mischievous gleam in her eye as she rubbed the small of his back.

Placing his finger under her chin, Mike lifted her lips back to his own and kissed her passionately. The moistness of the tongue was inviting and he felt her push into his embrace. The bar soon faded and he imagined they were alone in a faraway land.

It seemed an eternity before they reluctantly drew away from one another; nervously glancing to the floor and wondering, for an instant, if they should proceed along the path of broken hearts.

"Fuck it," Murphy grunted. "If this isn't right, then I don't know what's wrong."

She smiled, clutched his hand, and led him through the throngs of hangers-on who sought the solace of one more

Guinness. "I've never felt more right about anything in my life," she answered confidently.

Maybe, this is the beginning of something new and wonderful.

Murphy was thinking something as well.

This could be a train wreck.

Chapter 78

Sketchy Santa

*S*OMEONE ONCE wrote God was a Republican and Santa Claus leaned Democrat.

That made Richard think he was a Tea Party lunatic.

Those people are for the death penalty!

He stood in the living room; the deep claw gashes crisscrossed his tattered face where blood dripped onto a beige shag carpet and pooled at his feet.

Glancing into a mirror hanging on the paneled wall, he noticed the Santa suit draped from his aching back. The fabric was clawed away by the angry cats that attacked relentlessly until he left them dead in the dreadfulness of a pile of fur, bones, and blood.

"Motherfucking, catnip sucking, bastards!" he howled in agony from the stinging wounds. It felt like flames were set ablaze on his skin. Hurrying to the sofa table, he grabbed his mother's sewing kit, turned to the staircase, and started up the hardwood steps where he planned to stitch his gashes closed in the bathroom. "I'm still a good doctor. They can never take that from me."

At that moment, a stench filled his nostrils and a soft disembodied whisper occupied his ears. It reminded him of an EVP session from that television show, *Ghost Adventures*. At the start of every episode, he recalled its host stating, "I never believed in ghosts until I came face to face with one."

Wait until they come face to face with you, Mammy's cackling voice boomed through his head. Almost as if prompted, she appeared out of thin air.

Standing at the top stair, she floated down the staircase.

"Stupid little boy!" her wraithlike image groaned. "Look at what you've done!"

"Momma!" Richard blubbered, stepping to her vaporous apparition. "I miss you, Mommy!"

She cackled a piercing shriek of terror that rang through the house. "Just kill yourself, you selfish little asshole. Slice your wrists and nod off to sleepyland."

Richard slammed his eyes shut, squeezing them tightly, similar to what a child might attempt in belief that when the eyes blinked back open, whatever monster haunted them would dissolve into nothingness.

However, when he blinked open, and things came back into focus, his father's ghost had joined Mammy at the bottom of the stairs.

"Here is Johnnie!" Daddy shrieked, mimicking Ed McMahon's introduction of Johnnie Carson during a thirty year run on the Tonight Show.

"What do you want from me?" Richard screamed swinging his hatchet. Yet, striking out only made matters worse, the hatchet merely divided their ghastly images into halves, and they instantly restructured moving into his path.

"Lazy good for nothing loser!" Daddy's flickering presence growled. "Can't you *man-up* and do anything right?"

"Spare the rod and spoil the child never worked with your boy," Mammy muttered. "Jingle bells, jingle bells, jingle all the way!"

"Oh, what fun it is to ride..." Daddy joined, "in a one horse open sleigh!"

The ghosts advanced on Richard–their arms outstretched before them–like zombies stumbling after prey in *Night of The Living Dead*, their grasps reaching from beyond the grave to clutch for his throat.

"Merry Christmas, Dr. Death," Mammy cackled.

Santa stepped back in horror, slipped in a slick pool of blood and tumbled to the floor in a shout of pain.

"Go away! Just go away!"

Daddy spanked the side of his thigh–and that was the scary part–because the slap was audible, a garish reverberating whack that assaulted the stillness of the room.

"Get a clue, Son. Hell is awaiting your stinking soul!"

And, at that instant, they elevated off the ground, flew over his body and drifted across the room where they vanished into a wall mounted television. Its screen mysteriously flickered revealing Timothy Smith at a news conference outside Manhattan South Homicide.

> "Police are asking for the community's help tonight in tracking down this man," the reporter said, as an image of Richard replaced the reporter on the screen. "Dr. Richard Blake, once the attending physician at midtown's Saint Clare's Emergency Department, is now wanted in connection with multiple serial murders across the country according to NYPD Detective Mike Murphy and the FBI Serial Killer Task Force."

The Santa Claus Killer was spellbound by his picture on television. It was a photo taken by the probation office when he first reported for supervision. His hair was a mess, there were dark circles beneath his eyes from lack of sleep, and his skin was pale white.

"Get a look at yourself," he mumbled. "That photo would scare the dead back to life!"

The report ceased as suddenly as it began and was replaced by a commercial for SantaCon.

"Come on down to New York's biggest Christmas Eve event," a man stated from the TV screen. The commercial presented numerous videos from prior events.

Richard couldn't help but snicker at the prospect of another year persecuting the hordes of idiots who'd costume as Santa for a night of merrymaking.

He growled, scrambled from the floor, and picked up his hatchet, "Lousy posers! Who do they think they are impersonating me?"

At the end of the commercial, the newscaster returned with Deputy Inspector Morrison who seemed to stare right at Richard.

The stare burned into him.

"You lousy liar," Santa screamed throwing his hatchet into the television. Breaking the screen of a TV was the same as breaking a mirror.

"Fuck it! Without bad luck I'd have no luck at all!"

Chapter 79

Whoop, There It Is!

SPENDING ALL NIGHT in Paddy's wasn't a big deal.

Yet, stirring awake the following morning, Murphy found Mei curled beside him. That could start a shit storm of glitches. Especially when memory failed to recall exactly what happened the night before.

"Damn," he grumbled, reaching to a nightstand and grabbing his cell. The time on the screen showed 8:46 a.m.–an hour and forty-six minutes after the time he was supposed to punch his ticket at One Police Plaza–and yet here he lay with a pounding migraine.

Mei rolled over, folded herself into him, and smirked at his worried expression.

"Take it easy, cowboy! I don't bite, you know."

"You're not a black widow, then?"

"Nah," she purred nibbling his ear lobe. "You're no good to me dead. Besides, the only Black Widow species in which mate cannibalism is the rule, not the exception, occurs in the Southern Hemisphere. Most male Black Widows live to screw another day."

"You mean female Black Widows don't *really* kill their male sex partners?"

"Just another myth, my Irish stud."

"You always wake up like this?"

"Only when I feel like something good has happened."

Murphy stared at her smile and ran his hand through her hair. "I'm the good that happened?"

"Not bad," Mei giggled pushing him onto his back, mounting his hips and kissing his pale white neck. "Better than most, and besides, you hit my g-spot."

"I see, so I'm your sex slave, then?"

"Not a bad gig if you can get it," she assured grabbing his pulsing flesh and pushing it inside her moistness.

"I'll take it," he moaned as she moved in rhythm to his thrusting hips. The sex was tender, uncontrolled, and more thrilling than his boyhood memories of Playland.

They both exploded in shrieks, groans, and dirty talk... *and then the big finish.* A crescendo of quick grinding humps that brought on a yelp from the lovers.

"Oh, Mikey!" she sighed collapsing atop his chest. "I could get used to having you around."

He wrestled atop her. "Maybe I'd like that, being around you more often."

She kissed him–*long and deep*–one of those soaking, tongue pursuing explorations that placed one on notice LOVE might be willowing through the air.

Wouldn't that be all right? He thought, drawing back and staring into her dark brown eyes. She was beautiful... her skin was flawless, bathed in the golden rays of sunlight peeking through the curtains of the bedroom window. Her lips were pink and pouty, her body slim and muscled.

"Now, what?" she asked, her teeth nervously biting into her lower lip. "This could get serious, you know."

"It might be nice to be cared about."

Mei grinned and dimples appeared in her cheeks. "There are worse things than that, right?"

"Much worse, and this isn't bad."

"No, it's great!" she assured.

Instantly, a pager shrieked from scattered clothes on the floor.

"Is that you or me?" she asked glancing around the room. Then, another beeper shrieked and the sound was akin to twin fire alarms warning of terror headed their way.

"What the hell is it now," Murphy griped leaping from bed, rummaged through his trousers and pulling the pager from the pocket. "It's Rico on mine, what about you?"

She reached to the nightstand, grasped hers, and stared at the notification screen. "It's my SAC, Larry Magley, over at the NYFO."

"Something big is happening," he groaned, "if we're both being called in."

"Damn it. Everything was going so good this morning."

Grabbing his cell, Murphy placed it on speaker and punched in a number.

On the second ring, Rico answered. "Where are you, Mike? The captain is going crazy. We have an emerging situation over here!"

"What is it?" Mei asked.

"Who's that?" Rico blurted. "Is that Mei with you?"

"Hi, Rico," she countered before Murphy could hold up his hand. "What's going on over there this morning?"

"Well, well, well," Rico chuckled. "Isn't this an interesting development?"

"Up yours, Rico," Murphy countered. "We're just having breakfast."

"Huh, I bet you are, partner! You love bird's better get a move on and hurry downtown, pronto! We're mobilizing the Fugitive Apprehension Team and things are moving very quickly here at command."

"What's going on?" Murphy asked.

"An old woman and her grandson up in Congers were attacked by a white male dressed as Santa Claus. We've got Congers P.D. and the Rockland County Sheriff's Office gathering in ninety-minutes to brief the Task Force."

"Is it our guy?" Mei inquired throwing on her clothes. "Do we have a positive I.D. on Blake?"

"Not really sure," Rico answered. "All we know right now is that someone dressed as Kris Kringle, and wielding a hatchet, tried to sever the head of an old woman."

"We have to get this idiot off the streets!" Murphy exclaimed.

"Exactly," Rico agreed. "Now, get your naked asses out of bed and haul it down here… and fast!"

Mei strapped on her gun and watched Murphy pull on his slacks. "Don't know what you're talking about, Rico, but we're on our way."

"And, Mike," Rico shouted. "Do us a favor, huh?"

"What's that?"

"Show up in separate cars."

Mei laughed. "I like leering stares!"

Chapter 80

School of Soft Knocks

COLUMBIA PREP was the oldest secular private school in the United States.

Mirabel and Stefan were seated in Sara Kipler's office, the Prep School's Director who'd become an unusual acquaintance.

She was indebted to Terry for successfully defending her alcoholic husband who'd been *arrested, tried,* and *acquitted* of felony DUI the year before.

Not Guilty verdicts equaled favors.

"What if I didn't pass the entry exam?" Stefan worried. "Terry will be disappointed in me."

"I'm sure you did fine," Mirabel muttered. *He doesn't know how things work.* "You're a smart kid, and clever teenagers in this city attend Columbia Grammar and Prep."

Stefan's face was scrubbed, his nails manicured, and the clothes on his back sported Ralph Lauren purple labels. He'd spent hours taking tests in the admissions office and now awaited a verdict of another sort:

Acceptance or Denial.

Serving well-heeled, trust funded brats, aged six-to-eighteen, any child related to money could gain admission for $38,000 annual tuition.

The affluent didn't follow rules which applied to others, *like entrance exams.*

Those requirements were *disregarded,* test grades *abandoned* and standards *shrugged-off* when a wealthy socialite like Mirabel made her appearance.

Money talked... and BULLSHIT walked.

Scanning the office, Mirabel chuckled appreciating the antique furniture. The scent of age lingered amongst rows of dusty cherry wood shelves packed with tales by Twain, Hemingway, Whitman, and Dickens.

A sharp knock at the door brought a well-mannered woman into the room. Smiling with a smug expression, she took a seat behind a vintage English writing desk.

"Mirabel, it's good to see you again."

Fingering the keyboard of a *Dell All-In-One computer,* she pulled up Stefan's test scores.

"Oh, my, he's not at grade level in math, science, or social studies, and I'm not certain tutoring or additional courses during summer break would help him catch up."

"I'm sure Stefan will do whatever it takes," Mirabel confirmed glancing at the boy. "He'll attend winter, spring, and summer training, if needed."

Sara Kipler glanced across her desk. "Stefan, would you mind stepping outside while I speak with Mirabel?"

He stood from a hard-backed chair, kissed Mirabel on the cheek, and skulked from the office.

"Come on, Sara," Mirabel warned. "Don't play games."

"I'm not going to sugarcoat it, Darling." Sara answered. "I simply don't consider *this boy* a proper fit here. The kid barely scores mid-range eighth grade and he's seventeen years old. We, of course, could make a few calls and assist you in securing a more suitable facility, but..."

"That's simply unacceptable," Mirabel dismissed. "Stefan's been recommended by Cardinal Martin Golan at the Archdiocese."

"Yes, of course, and I'm the first to yield to the Cardinal. Unfortunately, we must maintain a higher standard than old-school intimidation."

"That seemed to help your husband just fine," Mirabel spat. She'd expected as much from the director, knew the *petty* dance, and was versed in the game of shuffleboard politics. Reaching to her Chanel Fuchsia Chevron Maxi

Flap Bag, she handed over a single sheet of paper obtained from the Massachusetts State Police.

"I'm sure your husband wasn't truly guilty of *lewd and lascivious conduct* as alleged in that arrest report from 1979. But imagine how people would perceive it?"

Sara's face drained of color. "Are you... *threatening* me, Mirabel?"

"Of course, Sara, I'm also reminding you the past is rarely forgotten."

"This allegation wasn't true. It arose from poor youthful behavior. The incident should not be remembered."

Mirabel shook her head. "Bernard Meltzer once said, *'Blessed are those who give without remembering. And blessed are those who take without forgetting.'* Since you aren't inclined to recollect the courtesy my husband showed yours in his DUI trial, I'm tasked with assisting your memory of his perversion."

Sara sighed in defeat, hung her head, and shut her eyes. *I knew his arrest would come back to bite me in the ass!* Under Massachusetts Criminal Law, behaviors sometimes concluded in criminal charges of lewd and lascivious conduct. Although defined as a misdemeanor with a sexual component, sex offenses in this day and age could reap grave consequences if not handled carefully. That was made apparent by a Penn State football coach who'd recently shamed an entire generation of alumni.

"Of course," Mirabel pointed to the arrest report, "count two of the charge-sheet accused your loving husband of *Open and Gross Lewdness* in public, meaning public masturbation, and displays of nudity were associated with his inappropriate touching and indecent assault."

Sara's face turned bright red.

"The allegation surrounded a fellow student at college, isn't that right?" Mirabel went on, shaking her head. "Shameful, really, but like the old adage states... *I.I.W.I.I.*"

"I'm sorry," Sara muttered. "What's that?"

"*It Is What It Is*, Sweetie," Mirabel smiled. "However, I'm quite certain we can work something out. That arrest report doesn't *have to* make *Page Six* of tomorrow's New York Post."

The Post highlighted dirty secrets, and just the appearance of her husband's name could end his career and ignite a police investigation at Columbia Prep.

"There will be no need for that, Mirabel," the chastened administrator muttered in defeat. "We can find a place for Stefan here. Please accept my apologies for not realizing what a great friend you and Terry have been."

Mirabel stood, beamed at the pathetic woman, and shook her hand. "Apology accepted, Sara. That's what friends are for."

"I'll have our placement aide contact you later today with Stefan's classes. He'll make a great student."

"I have no doubts about that." Then, almost off-handedly, Mirabel recalled something else. "I've heard it through the grapevine that Stefan adores playing football. Perhaps you can get him on the school's team."

"You want the boy on the football roster, without making him try out for placement?"

"Backup position at quarterback… next year, your coach *will* name Stefan starting QB."

"That's not how things work."

"Things change, Sara, and we evolve with those changes or become an irrelevant whisper of history."

"What shall I tell my administration?"

"Don't toy with me, Sara," Mirabel winked. "Terry has the ear of the mayor, governor, and every single judge, prosecutor, and politician in the state." As she pulled open the office door and stepped into the future, she realized something.

Membership did have its privilege.

Chapter 81

Special Delivery

THE HOMICIDE SQUAD was all in.

Manhattan *South* had just twelve detectives, down from twenty-six in 2001, and Manhattan *North* had another twelve for a total of twenty-four investigators.

Murphy counted fifty law enforcement officers cramming the conference room on the 23rd floor of the FBI's New York Field Office.

They were awaiting arrival of *The Brass* from multiple federal, state, and city agencies.

"The world is still here," Murphy teased Rico as they stood drinking stale coffee gazing through the windows at the city below. "It's December twenty-first, twenty-twelve, and doomsday hasn't occurred!"

"Humph," Rico mumbled. "And I thought it was all going to come to a crashing end today. Where are the global earthquakes, pole shift, and arrival of killer aliens?"

The morning airwaves were ripe with mocking sound bites regarding the absence of Armageddon and the predicted end of time as the Mayan calendar terminated its existence and predictions of judgment day vaporized with each passing second.

"Just another winter day," Murphy sniggered. "At least you didn't drink the Kool-Aid and become a *Doomsday Prepper* like those nuts on TV."

"That was one of my favorite shows on the National Geographic Channel." Rico answered with a nod. "Remember the night you came over to the house and we watched that episode of the suburban woman who handed out *pandemic kits* to her neighbors for the approaching worldwide plague?"

Murphy laughed. "Yeah, I remember *her* and how much *you* believed in all that nonsense. Everyone in the department is well aware of your fascination with the Mayan Calendar and the conspiracy theories that claimed the North and South Poles would shift and cause a global tsunami, or that a gigantic astral sphere called Planet-X would crash into Earth."

"I almost bought Liz a doomsday bunker up in the Adirondack Mountains," Rico shamefully admitted. "You should have heard Howard lambasting the end of world believers on his show this morning."

He was referring to Howard Stern–*Mr. New York himself*–an American radio personality who dubbed himself the *King of All Media* for his numerous late night television shows, pay-per-view events and home video releases.

"You still listen to Howard, really?" Murphy snorted. "He is a judge on that TV show, too, right?"

"AGT... he's extremely funny on there."

America's Got Talent was an American talent show that featured singers, dancers, magicians, comedians, and other performers of all ages who competed to win a million bucks and a farfetched promise at stardom.

Murphy thought the *talent shows* were scams to make money for production companies. Very few of the *winners* actually went on to stardom. In fifteen years on TV, only a few contestants became somebodies.

The rest faded like an old pair of jeans.

"Just another day at the office, huh?" Murphy joked. "Looks like you'll be retiring to Florida after all!"

"Listen up!" SAC Magley bellowed pushing into the room with Deputy Inspector Harold Morrison, Captain Anton McKenzie and two detectives in shabby, off the rack suits. "These detectives are from the Intelligence Unit of the Rockland County Sheriff's Office and are cross-designated US Marshals. We've aided them in countless previous operations, and this is yet another."

"Good morning," the lead investigator greeted the Task Force. "This is what we know as of five minutes ago. A guy dressed as Santa Claus approached the famed Davies Apple Grove in Congers, and threatened a seventy-year-old grandmother and her grandson with a hatchet before fleeing after a family cat appeared."

"Mrs. Davies," the second investigator pitched in, "stated when the feline appeared the suspect spoke to it."

"What did he say to the fur ball?" Murphy asked.

The investigator glanced at a notebook.

"After the cat appeared, the suspect shouted 'get away from me', backed out the door, and ran across the driveway."

"Did anyone see a car," Rico hoped. "Get a license plate, anything?"

"Mrs. Davies gave us a description of a late model white van with *Manhattan's Best Meat* painted in black along its side. A statewide BOLO has been put out. The Rockland Sheriff's Office, Troopers, and Marshall's Office are searching for the vehicle."

At that moment, a scream exploded from the exterior of the room.

"Get it away from me!" a woman yelled pointing at a package on her desk. "Federal Express just delivered that box for Agent Ling and when I opened it... that fell out!"

On the desk lay a decaying, stinking cat corpse with its eyes and tongue excised.

A bloody note was tied to its body with a ribbon.

It was the night before Christmas...
And all through the night,
The Deputy Inspector was frozen in fright...
For soon he would realize the end of his life!

All eyes turned to Harold Morrison.

"Inspector," Captain McKenzie stated pulling out the letter Murphy discovered at Bellevue Hospital. "I think it's time we had a conversation about Blake."

"What's this all about?" the SAC asked. "Is there something I should know here?"

"Let me talk to you guys in private," Morrison said. "I know this fellow and it could be a problem for our investigation."

A murmur went up amongst the investigators as Magley led the deputy inspector and captain to an office door.

"You're going to have to clue me in on this," Rico stated placing his hand on the doorknob. "It is my investigation, after all."

"Let Rico, Murphy, and Mei in here," the SAC demanded. "The time for secrets is over."

Chapter 82

On The Move

SANTA KNEW the cops would look for the wagon.

He understood Grandma Davies probably *snitched* its description to *The Oinkers*.

So, he ditched the van in exchange for Daddy's Ford Explorer and steered it along New York's Thruway.

"They're going to have to get up pretty early in the morning to fool me."

At this instant, Frankie Valli & the Four Seasons pulsed through the surround sound speakers.

"My man!" Santa shouted and turned up the volume. "Let's belt it out!"

The Giver of Gifts shouted out his re-worked lyrics. *Sherry, sherry baby...Sherry, bloody, Sherry. I'm gonna break your spine!* The Four Seasons would've beaten his worthless ass had they heard the hatchet job. Their sound was reminiscent of a 1950s doo-wop group that sold millions of records.

His parents once danced to this song, mother twisting and turning as daddy murdered the words.

"Daddy couldn't hold a tune to save his life," he chuckled glancing in the rearview mirror.

The apple didn't fall far from the tree.

"I guess you inherited my talent," Daddy muttered.

Santa saw Mammy and Daddy watching from the backseat. Their skin was rotting from death's firm clutch, the stench of decay filled the SUV, and he knew, instantly, the vision behind him was *real*.

"Surely, you didn't think we'd abandon you," Mammy smiled. Her jaw dangling from rotting muscles, the face splotched with black decay where maggots pushed through open pustules.

"Come on, Son," Daddy yelped, his eyes sunken in death's finality, the nose rotting and hair frazzling around waxy grey flesh hugging the skull.

It reminded Santa of the Crypt Keeper in *Tales from the Crypt*. He and his son would lie on their stomachs, elbows dug deep into the carpet as an episode began with a tracking shot of a crumbling mansion, creepy hallways, spooky stairs, and then... the show opening in a dark, terrifying basement.

"The Goddamn basement," Santa cackled staring at his parents in the mirror. "I can't get away from the dampness of the crypt! Jesus, Dad, you look like death himself!"

"It grows on you, Son, you'll see."

His mother glanced at her husband, leaned over, and kissed him. When she did, the grazing of their rough, dead, lips chafing against the other sounded like two sheets of sandpaper.

"Oh, that's nasty." Santa pouted. "Get a fucking crypt, will you?"

Mammy cracked up then, laughing *so hard* the bones of her neck snapped, collapsing her head onto her chest.

"Now look what you've done!" Daddy scolded. "You broke your mother's neck!"

Richard cringed at the spectacle of his father attempting to push Mammy's cranium back into place. Pulling the SUV to the side of the road, he hopped out of the Ford and stood on the shoulder bawling uncontrollably. The sound of wheels on pavement brought his attention to a Mercedes E-350 pulling in behind the Explorer. Its horn honked, and after a moment, a well off socialite stepped to the roadway.

"Is there anything I can do to help you, Santa? Has there been an accident?" he stared, reluctantly, at Santa's haphazardly hand stitched brow.

"What happened to your face? Who gave you those hideous stitches?"

Richard pointed to the SUV, "My mother broke her neck in the back of my car!"

"Oh, my lord," the fellow exclaimed dashing to the Explorer's door and yanking it open. Casting an eye over the empty interior, he seemed puzzled. "There's nobody in here. What is this, some kind of tasteless, sick, joke?"

Santa ceased his bawling then. He merely *stopped* the waterworks, ran to the vehicle, and scanned the backseat. "Mommy? Daddy? What has *he* done with you?"

The physician glared at the madman–lost in his frenzied mental breakdown–as cars whipped past on the highway.

Santa reached under the backseat and pulled a bloody hatchet into view. "What did you do with them?" he asked turning to the doctor. "It's your fault they left, sticking your fat Iranian nose where it doesn't belong!"

The doctor stepped towards the highway, cautiously placing one foot behind the other, backpedaling with one eye on the killer, and the other nervously tracking passing cars.

"What are you doing? Why me? What have I done wrong?"

But, the soon to be *Dead Ender* was well aware of his mistake. Just this morning as he snapped awake, pushed back the comforter, and placed his feet into his slippers, the doctor *knew* something wasn't quite right.

He had been plagued by nightmares.

And they weren't good.

It all made perfect sense now to his analytical mind.

This is it, the big kahuna. He wouldn't make it to his daughter's loft in SOHO to spend Christmas week. The gifts in the trunk would not be opened by his grandson; there'd be no smiles and well wishes of another prosperous year.

"Please, Sir, I have a family," *Dr. Feelgood* pleaded as the killer inched closer, the hatchet ready to strike.

Santa swung the steel and amputated the man's arm at the shoulder. As the appendage slapped onto the pavement in a bloody mess, everything slowed down, time stopped and for that one instant, everything seemed clear.

Kill the uppity healing bastard! Mammy's voice rang in Santa's head. *Goddamn Medicaid thief!*

"Pennywise, penny pinching Pollock Johnny!" Santa yelled approaching the doctor. "Who do you think you are, Jesus Christ?"

The physician screamed at the sight of his severed arm, lying on the pavement, its fingers twitching.

"My arm, you amputated my damn arm!"

"Ha, ha, ha," Santa chuckled insanely charging the man. "You should've remained in bed, Mr. Disease Healer!"

Terrified for his life, the surgeon bolted into oncoming traffic. Horns *blared*, metal *crunched,* and the *PILL PUSHER* went flying through the air to his final destination. There, Saint Peter would grasp the book of life and identify *Doc Holiday's* good deeds. Then again, the rich had nasty little skeletons in their closets... and maybe, that would purchase a trip to the flames below.

Either way, Santa couldn't be bothered with those insignificant questions. So, he scurried back to the Explorer and tracked towards his destination where people waited his thirteenth SantaCon *APPEARANCE* in the *City That Never Slept.*

In the backseat, nodding his prideful approval, Daddy desired to sing a familiar childhood Christmas song.

"This one's for you, Son*,*" Daddy offered.

"For my little Santa killer," Mammy agreed pushing her head back onto the neck bone.

Then, they sang, for their little boy.

When the vocal stopped, Santa laughed.

This was going to be a wonderful Christmas.

He might even treat himself to a hot pretzel or potato knish. The kind vendors peddled from stainless steel carts guarding street corner curbs.

Nice and hot and packed with carbohydrates!

"I'm going to need all the energy I can get." Santa winked at his parents in the mirror.

Christmas, after all, was right around the corner.

Chapter 83

The Benjamins

MAKING EXCUSES was better left to the re-election campaigns of mayors, governors, and presidents.

Cops didn't have that luxury.

"Let me get this straight, Inspector," SAC Magley grumbled. "A serial killer who's number one on the Bureau's Most Wanted List is a friend of the NYPD?"

It was an incredible revelation.

"Richard Blake isn't a friend of the department," Morrison shamefully admitted. "He was my college roommate at NYU and should be considered my problem."

Lt. McKenzie was pissed; his unit would now be placed under the microscope of improper procedure.

"That's not necessarily true, Harold."

"Especially," Rico protested, "when the *problem* is a wanted serial murderer in a city that lives and dies on twenty-four hour news cycles. Sounds like you want to cover up something. The math isn't adding up."

"It's not a cover-up," Morrison insisted. "Did I know the guy in school? Yes. Did we form a friendship over the years? Of course. However, I didn't know he'd turn out to be a killer. Besides, there are more serious incidents facing the NYPD than an inspector having once known a person who's become a demented assassin. We have cops who exchange drugs for sex, ticket fixing, excessive force, racial profiling, and the planting of drugs on innocent civilians, just to name a few."

"That's not at issue today," the SAC charged. "This is about you arranging special considerations in releasing a guy who is the worst serial killer the country has ever seen."

A knock at the door brought the mayor and his police commissioner.

"Good day, gentlemen," the mayor nodded. "I asked Commissioner McReynolds to bring me up to date on the search for our suspect and he suggested we head over to this little shindig."

"That's right," the commissioner agreed. "So, here we are. What's up with this nonsense about the department being responsible for this basket case getting out of the mental hospital?"

A moment of silence filled the room.

Nobody wanted to tell the mayor and commissioner what would appear in the *Daily News*.

The mayor glanced around the room.

"Come on, somebody speak up. Do we have a public relations problem or a criminal investigation?"

"I was just about to ask the Deputy Inspector that same question," McKenzie stated handing over Morrison's letter.

As the commissioner read the letter, he glanced at the mayor with an expression that said deniability meant everything.

The mayor headed for the door. "Well, uh, this is something that needs to be worked out internally by the NYPD. The people of New York City can't have their mayor involved in anything with the scent of impropriety."

The commissioner watched the mayor leave and turned to Morrison. "Disasters come and go, Harold, but scandals shape careers." Approaching his deputy inspector, he held up the letter. "Why did you send this official request, on NYPD letterhead, asking for Blake's release from Bellevue?"

Morrison became livid. "You write letters like that all the time, damn it! How dare you question my judgment?"

The commissioner smiled. He wasn't one to be provoked. Surviving the NYPD hierarchy meant knowing how to hold emotions in check.

"That's true, Harry. I do write these letters, but my guys don't get out of mental hospitals and kill innocent people."

"Or entomb bodies in basements," Magley added.

"I was only trying to help a friend," the inspector's voice trembled. His hand begun to shake, his eyes jumped from side-to-side, and he wasn't looking the commissioner in the eye.

Until that point, Rico stood silent in the corner of the office simply watching the body language of the inspector.

Now, something seemed off kilter.

In Rico's line of work, there were five signs of body language that indicated deceptiveness.

1) Overly talkativeness
2) A trembling voice
3) Use of contractions
4) Defensiveness

And the Mack Daddy of them all:

5) Lack of eye contact

These were all indicators of lies.

Rico saw *all five* signs now.

"You're lying, Deputy Inspector," he shouted crossing the office, pointing to the man's medaled chest and taking notice of the perspiration lining Morrison's brow. "What's the *real* deal here? What *aren't* you telling the Commissioner?"

Harold turned his back on the men, walked to the window and peered at the city. "It was Christmas in the year two-thousand, the NYPD and the United States Marine Corps joined forces for the annual Toys for Tots

Drive. I was in charge of the event, collecting new toys, wrapping and distributing them to needy children throughout the city. I organized five celebrations, one in each borough."

"Sure," Rico stated. "My wife and I are part of the annual event, bringing kids to the precinct to receive a holiday toy from the department."

"Right," Morrison acknowledged, turning back to his comrades. "Blake and his parents donated a hundred grand to the department every year until I stumbled upon something peculiar last year."

"What was that?" the commissioner inquired.

"Soon after Richard's father asked me to recommend his boy's discharge from Bellevue, I wrote the letter and he was released. Then, just after SantaCon, I began receiving bloody Santa Claus wigs in the mail."

"What's this got to do with Blake?" Rico asked.

"He admitted he'd been mailing them to me."

"Jesus!" the commissioner grumbled. "Are you telling me you suspected him of murder?"

"I had a hunch," Harold replied, "until he sent me pictures last week of dead bodies at the family farmhouse up in Spring Valley."

Chapter 84

ROC Center

NOTHING EXPRESSED Christmas like the ROC.

From the sky-high observations on *Top of the Rock* to backstage passes at NBC Studios... every tour at Rockefeller Center brought sightseers behind the scenes of Manhattan's most cherished destination.

Stefan hurried through the masses crowding the plaza carrying a cardboard cup holder with three containers of hot chocolate and whipped cream.

"Howdy, partner," a southern man drawled. "Where'd ya pony up that chocolate?"

"It's from Jacques Torres Chocolate," Stefan replied pointing towards the busy storefront on the Concourse Level, just steps from the ice rink.

Anyone who knew anything about real chocolate would attest Jacques was the perfect place to appreciate velvety sweet cocoa with freshly baked cookies.

"I can smell it in the air," the man beamed. "Nothing beats a warm cup at Christmas, huh?"

Stefan watched the hillbilly disappear into the bustling plaza packed with tourists. They'd flock here for a chance to experience what most New Yorkers took for granted, a winter wonderland of glitz and glam.

Within walking distance of Rockefeller Center, were Radio City Music Hall, The Museum of Modern Art, Saint Patrick's Cathedral, and Saks Fifth Avenue.

This was New York at its finest.

Glancing down to the ice rink, Stefan watched Terry and Mirabel gliding around the ice arena; the sparkling lights of a seventy-foot spruce glinted off the mirrored ice. As they twirled and twirled, with skaters beside them, Stefan saw the Santa Claus who'd taken Darius to his grave.

"Get away from them," he screamed, dropping the tray of hot chocolate and sprinting for the slaughterer who sneered in his direction from the far side of the plaza. "Mirabel! Hey, Terrrrrrrrrry!"

They were skating past the statue of Prometheus standing sentinel above the rink.

Then, he heard the owl's call:

Glancing into the night sky, he glimpsed the bird as clearly as in his dream.

"Oh, no," he groaned, glancing back towards the rink where Mirabel stood pointing into the heavens. "It was just a dream!"

However, deep in his mind, the boy understood reality had raised its ugly head for a gut check of astronomical proportions.

Then, he read these words on Mirabel's lips.

Oh, Terry, look how big he is!

Stefan followed her line of sight toward the owl climbing a spiraling pattern into the thick dark clouds of winter. Bringing his attention back to Santa and the outline of his escaping figure running for his life through the parting crowd, Stefan dug deep and closed in on the murdering villain sprinting past the ice rink's flagpoles that surrounded the recessed Lower Plaza.

"Somebody grab hold of that Santa Claus!" he screamed over the panicked glances of confused tourists navigating the intersection at West 49th Street and Rockefeller Plaza.

The Santa Claus Killer bounded down the street, passing the Today Show windows to the left... and to his right the studios of MSNBC.

Had anyone noticed the people staring out its windows, they might have recognized Rachel Maddow pointing towards the escaping Santa. The political pundit was in the middle of taping an episode of *The Rachel Maddow Show*.

Screams of fright erupted amongst the hordes as they stared in fear when the killer stopped, turned, and pointed a handgun at Stefan.

"He's got a gun!" a woman shouted.

Santa fired three shots into the air.

The bystanders ran for cover, their feet carrying their panicked frames into the doorways of buildings.

Stefan stood frozen, the barrel of the gun directed at his head. There were many ways to go; this was one of the worst.

"Get on the ground you lousy, no good, brat!" Santa angrily growled. His face lined with stitches; dried streaks of blood covering his brow. "If you don't, I'll blow your fucking head off your shoulders!"

Stefan raised his hands in surrender, fell to the pavement, and spread his arms and legs as if being arrested.

"Please, things don't have to end this way!"

Santa ignored the boy and pressed his knee into his back. "You're going to wish for mercy by the time I'm done with you."

In the distance police sirens wailed.

Yet, the only thing Stefan would remember was the sensation of steel smashing onto his noggin sending him to dreamland. There, amidst the lonely vacuum of murkiness, he'd dream of boyhood and a time long ago mislaid to the wasteland of memories.

And, the nightmares of his Dead End Friends…

Those visions would haunt him forever.

Chapter 85

On The Hunt

𝒜s A COLLEGE STUDENT, Mei had spent hundreds of hours studying human decomposition at Texas State University's Freeman Ranch Body Farm.

Town residents protested the farm.

San Marcos Municipal Airport claimed circling vultures were sucked into jet engines and caused airline crashes.

Mei remembered overhearing jokes that such an occurrence would add to the research.

Eventually, the corpses won their land and soon after County Road 213 northwest of San Marcos saw its dead body population increased substantially.

Some airline passengers claimed to glimpse human bodies sprawled on the Ranch during landings and takeoffs.

That's crazy, Mei recalled after the university directed her airborne in a single engine Cessna Skyhawk where she gazed through binoculars confirming the rumors false.

The way Body Farms worked was simple.

Corpses were permitted to decay outdoors so researchers could witness the effects weather, insects, birds, and animals had on dead bodies.

Five such farms existed in the United States with Freeman Ranch being the largest sitting on seven acres of rotting death.

Now, standing in the blistery cowshed of the Blake Farm, those college memories haunted Mei.

"Jesus," she said staring at hundreds of cats chopped to pieces throughout the barnyard. "We must have just missed him; this carnage is fresh!"

"He probably went out the back door," Murphy recognized, "as we came in the front."

The Serial Killer Task Force had descended on the Blake farmhouse in Spring Valley just hours following the active duty suspension of Deputy Inspector Harold Morrison. He was out, *DONE*, stripped of his badge by the mayor and sent packing by the commissioner.

In his office, the human vultures searched his files picking the bones of a dissected career.

"It's world war three in here," Mei exclaimed stalking through the barn inspecting globs of blood pooling on the ground. "A battle to the death took place!"

"However," Murphy observed staring at cat heads chopped from their bodies, the torsos ripped apart and limbs scattered throughout the barn, "cats don't use sharpened tools to cut one another in half!"

Nailed to the wall was the tomcat's eyeless skull and over it, these words were written in blood:

Baby Breath STEALERS!
Gone to Cat HEAVEN!
No More Nine LIVES!

"Take a look at that!" Murphy stared. "I'd say Richard is at war with his little furry friends."

"His rage is fighting against the psychosis," Mei observed. "If what we've learned is true about his belief cats talk to him. Then Blake is getting tired of their demands and wants free of their damnations."

"What is that, psychology mumbo jumbo?"

Mei shrugged it off. "Remember when we went to his probation officer's house in Briarwood, Queens? I told you about Berkowitz, *The Son of Sam*, who believed the dog, Sam, had talked to him?"

"Sure. He tried to kill the dog... but didn't do it."

"Exactly, the difference between Berkowitz and Blake is our suspect actually seems to be achieving it. He's assassinating the very inspiration he's garnered from the talking cats who tell him to murder."

"Sick little bastard."

"Maybe, but perhaps he's playing a part for us."

"What do you mean?" Murphy squinted.

"Dr. Richard Blake might be as sane as you and I."

"That would make me the Tooth Fairy."

"You'd look pretty funny in tights."

A Spring Valley CSI detective appeared at the barn's entrance. "Sergeant Murphy! Agent Ling! We found a video in the house that you're going to want to see!"

"What is it?" Mei asked.

"We believe it's a secretly taped conversation between the killer and someone from your department conspiring to commit murder."

"Just what we need," Murphy stated, "a big nasty scandal involving the department."

"It's worse than that, Detective," the CSI investigator sighed. "It's your Deputy Inspector."

Mei glanced at Murphy who urgently turned to the CSI investigators. "Make sure everything is cataloged out here, I don't want anything overlooked."

"And make sure there are no bodies buried in this barn," Mei added following Murphy and the investigator from the slaughterhouse, across a field and into the old house.

"You think this is where Blake's been holding up?" the investigator asked Murphy. "Hiding here just out of your reach?"

"It sure looks that way," Murphy answered stepping into the dimly lit kitchen. Walking through the timeworn, grubby room, he saw mounds of food-stained plates stacked in the sink; roaches crawled across the counter tops.

"Jeez," Mei muttered, covering her nose against the stench of rotting food.

That's when they heard the voice of Deputy Inspector Harold Morrison thundering from the adjoining room.

Entering the living room, Mei's jaw dropped when she saw his image on the television.

"We found a VHS tape with Morrison's name on it," the investigator stated. "When we pushed it into the VCR this is what we found."

The recording was old, Mei realized.

Harold Morrison's uniform was that of a precinct captain, from at least fifteen years ago, way before he rose through the ranks to command operations in the nation's largest police force.

> "I know about the murder of your wife, Richard," Morrison stated to Richard on the TV screen. "That you killed her for taking your boy away. That you made it look like a rape; you could go away for a long time."

> "I know." Richard answered. "That drug loving whore!"

They'd been seated in this very living room, Murphy realized. *It was made secretly by Blake, almost as if he wanted to preserve evidence tying the captain to crimes he'd later commit.*

> "Or, you could do something for me," Morrison urged. "For the people of New York, for City Hall, the tourists....to help us with a little problem?"

> Richard glanced up at Morrison, a sigh of hope nestled in the sudden realization he might slither off the hook of justice. "What

is it, Harold," he begged. "How can you let me get away with murdering my wife?"

On the TV, Harold Morrison rose from the couch, pushed his hands into his pockets, and paced across the floor. "Since you've shown little remorse for killing the mother of your child and you like slaughtering animals... maybe you could help me rid my precinct of another nuisance?"

Richard moved beside his co-conspirator. "Anything, just name it."

Placing his arm around Richard's shoulders, Morrison smiled. "Every Christmas the homeless dress up in Santa suits and pester the tourists for their spare change..."

The room erupted in chaos at the sudden implication.

Mei couldn't believe it. "It's not just Richard Blake," she whispered pulling out her cellphone and dialing a number. "We have ourselves a tag team killing machine."

Beside her, Murphy stood shouting into his own cellphone. "Rico, it's Deputy Inspector Morrison; he's the brains behind the Santa Claus killings!"

He could see the front pages already.

Man in Blue Kills Men in Red.

Chapter 86

The Chase

AMERICA'S MOST famous police pursuit happened on June 17, 1994. That's the date police interceptors chased a white Ford Bronco along California's 405-Interstate.

As it turned out, even Heisman winning NFL running backs couldn't outpace the law.

Lieutenant Rico Martinez had given up believing in the human condition many years before.

Like most virtuous cops, the head hunter supposed if he waited long enough, the *big surprise* would be… there were no surprises.

Man planned and God laughed.

Thus, when the AMBER ALERT came in stating a man clothed as Santa kidnapped a teenager in a Ford Explorer headed west on 49th Street… all Rico could do was shake his head and round up the cavalry.

The alert was a partnership between law enforcement, newscasters, transportation agencies, and the wireless industry to trigger critical messages during child abduction cases. The objective was simple: To rapidly inform the public a child had been kidnapped.

"What the hell is going on with Santa?" Rico huffed steering the Dodge Charger onto West 49th passing Christie's on the left and NBC to the right.

In the passenger seat, Arias activated the siren.

"Traffic is thick, and our howling sirens aren't moving the cows from the street. Their necks are stretched up to the glass skyscrapers as if they'd never seen anything like it."

Rico chuckled. "Sometimes, Liz walks the streets and points to the sky. You know how many idiots stop and stare attempting to see what she's pointing at?"

"Hundreds?"

"Try it sometime; you'll be amazed at the response. Most say they see the Virgin Mary imbedded in the white puffy clouds."

"Dumbasses," Arias chuckled.

"Ya gotta love it!"

Today the pedestrians just glared at Rico as he squeezed the car through traffic on either side of the street. One guy shot him the finger and stubbornly refused to move out of their path.

Arias showed the badge and screamed.

"Hey, asshole, you want to take a ride downtown?"

The man moved and Arias caught a glimpse of the Ford Explorer scraping past a Lincoln Stretch Limo where actor Tom Hanks stood chatting with a chauffeur.

"Look who it is," he pointed. "I read somewhere Tom has become somewhat of a philosopher wondering why bad things happen to good people and good things happen to the bad."

"It's called fate," Rico yelled to the perplexed actor before looking back to Arias. "I don't have to be the highest earning box office star to figure that one out!"

Arias grunted. "Can you believe that guy makes twenty million bucks a movie? All that cash from acting like some poor schmuck in a make believe flick!"

"You saw *Larry Crowne*, huh?" Rico laughed.

"Unbelievable! It's good to be Forrest Gump, I guess."

The traffic cleared then and the Ford Explorer sped up.

"Hold on," Rico warned putting the pedal to the metal and the Charger's grill against the bumper of the fleeing vehicle.

"Dispatch," Arias blurted into the radio. "We are in pursuit of a one eight-seven headed west on forty-ninth, requesting back-up, over."

The response was quicker than a lightning strike atop the Empire State Building. Sirens erupted from every direction as the Charger raced over Sixth Avenue.

"Jesus!" Arias shouted watching the SUV jumping the curb and hurtling along the sidewalk as pedestrians dove for safety.

"Sonuvabitch," Rico screamed. "He's going to kill somebody." Pulling the police cruiser in behind the fleeing suspect, he prayed nobody stepped from a storefront to find their path to death.

"Where the hell is he going?" Arias shouted, holding onto the dashboard with both hands.

"He's headed for the river," Rico hollered over the siren. "He's got a kid in there; let's *PIT* him at the next corner before it's too late!"

A police PIT maneuver was short for *Precision Immobilization Technique*. It was a chase technique that forced a fleeing automobile to abruptly spin out, causing the driver to lose control and bringing the chase to a safe conclusion.

"Too many people in the street for a PIT," Arias reasoned, "gotta let this play out, the road ends at the cruise terminal."

The SUV zoomed through 8th Avenue at fifty miles per hour. Horns blared, people screamed and an Eyewitness News chopper suddenly appeared overhead.

"Goddamn," Rico snarled glancing at the hovering chopper. "This isn't going to go well with a camera shoved up our ass!"

"Look!" Arias pointed.

The street ahead cleared and NYPD patrol cars blocked each intersection providing an empty road in the westbound lanes. There was nowhere else to run; the blockbusting

SUV was in a tunnel of armed police on either side with only 12th Avenue and the Hudson River ahead.

"He's going for it!" Arias shrieked into the radio. "Get water patrol over to the Hudson River Greenway, over?"

The Explorer raced across the intersection, barreled through a steel fence, and went airborne over the concrete median. There, it descended onto the cruise ship access road, landed in a spray of sparks and crunching metal, before skidding off the pier and into the icy river with a thunderous crunch of ice and water.

"Holy Mother!" Rico shrieked hitting the brakes, jerking the steering wheel and holding on for dear life as the Charger spun out of control in the middle of the roadway.

It's a good thing, too, because it would've followed the SUV into the depths, sinking rapidly one pier away from the Manhattan Cruise Terminal.

"Suspect vehicle is in the water!" Arias shrieked into his handheld, leapt from the car, and charged to the water's edge where he glared at air bubbles plopping to the surface.

"The river has to be freezing," Rico grunted. "They won't last two minutes in there!"

"A frozen tomb," Arias agreed glancing to the helicopter above their heads. "The news has their lead story for six o'clock."

"Damn it!" Rico cursed staring at NYPD Water Patrol boats racing through the choppy Hudson. "It's gonna take a miracle to recover the bodies."

"And," Arias grunted. "We're fresh out of miracles."

Chapter 87

Fighting Irish

MIGHTY WHITEY snapped awake.

The crash jolted him from LA LA Land.

As the SUV sank into the murky abyss, freezing water gushed through the engine compartment and quickly filled the floorboards.

"You ungrateful bootlicker," *The Santa Claus Killer* groaned struggling from the seatbelt, turning to Stefan and swinging the hatchet. "You were nothing more than a missed fucking opportunity at abortion," Santa screamed as the hatchet missed the boy and shattered the passenger window.

A surge of icy water blasted through the vehicle–like an erupting fire hydrant on a blistery summer afternoon–and knocked the chopper from Santa's hand.

Stefan attacked, grabbing Santa by the throat and pushing him underwater.

Air bubbles popped on the surface.

"I hate you!" You ruined my life you no good asshole!"

Santa kicked, scratched, and urgently fought to free himself from death by drowning.

I'm going to die right here.

He could barely make out the boy's irate face above the waterline.

So innocent, just like I used to be, and yet the violence is there.

For a moment, the Giver of Gifts considered letting go– forgetting all his worries and simply gasping a lungful of water–and drifting into the nothingness as his heartbeat waned.

Take the dive, Mammy urged. *Come into the long sleep!*

And then, Richard saw her hovering above the boy's grimace, reminiscent of her twenties. The face was peaceful, a smile twisting her lips. She was beautiful magnificently bathed in soft white light. A flowing gown draped around her body; there was love in her eyes.

Come to me, Son, Mammy enticed. *No more pain or drama over here on this side!*

Santa sensed energy departing his body as the boy's hands tightened on his throat, draining life from his soul. Slowly, his spirit drifted towards eternity, embracing the peacefulness.

Then, it felt like he was hit in the head with a ten-pound brick.

Snap the hell out of it, Son! Daddy's apparition squawked, floating beneath the water. *Since when have you taken instructions from your Mother?*

Unexpectedly, the Ford rolled over in the current and Stefan was knocked off balance.

While it settled inverted on the riverbed, Richard glimpsed an escape route.

Go for it, Sonny Boy, Daddy shouted. *Swim like a tiger shark is on your white ass!*

So Santa swam for the broken window. But the hole wasn't wide enough so he reached for the door handle and pushed his shoulder against the hatch.

It held firm.

Santa recalled reading water pressure outside a submerged vehicle prevented doors from opening until water inside filled completely.

He'd be dead long before that opportunity came so the murderer decided to face the snot nosed brat.

"Stefan," Santa begged from the edge of unconsciousness. "Please, Son, forgive me!"

Mighty Whitey hit *his father* again.

The forehead split open from the hatchet handle's blow.

The moment had been a long time coming, a planned event. He, Marco, and Darius had stalked his murdering father for years... beating his ass each time they'd stumbled upon him acting like Santa Claus.

"One day, I'll kill him," Stefan promised Marco long ago. "I'll get the courage to take his life and repay him for the pain he caused me and Mom!"

"Do you think you can really do it?" Darius asked.

"When that time comes," Marco assured his friend sitting on the apartment building rooftop, "you'll decide it's really not worth it."

As Stefan stared at his worthless father now, spread-eagle on the backseat with water threatening to drown him, he decided Marco was right.

It wasn't in his blood to kill the deadbeat.

Stefan swung the hatchet as hard as he could and watched the blunt edge smash through the window. Moments before the river filled the SUV; he took a final gasp of air and glanced back at his lousy father struggling for consciousness.

Let the river take its course, he'll be buried at the bottom of the Hudson.

Then, with a final blink, Mighty Whitey swam into the murkiness and broke the river's surface.

There, in the frigid night, he stroked through icy water with everything he had.

"Come on, kid," Rico yelled from the deck of a boat. "We got you, just keep swimming!"

Yes, baby, keep swimming, his mother's voice urged. *You did me proud down there, now swim!*

It was the first time he'd heard her whisper from beyond the grave.

I'm swimming, Mommy, I'm swimming! He cried, feeling liberty now, *freedom* in the knowledge that his father would be eaten alive in the depths.

"Over here, kid," Arias hollered, "just a few more feet!"

Stefan was losing consciousness; the icy waters of the Hudson had done their drudgery and drained the heat from his muscles.

But giving up was something he'd never embrace.

Come on, baby, do it for momma!

He owed it to his friends who never got that chance, and, most importantly, he deserved to see what life had to offer.

I love you, Stef, his mother whispered. *Always have!*

Chapter 88

Coup de Grâce

TRIBECA WAS the Hollywood of Manhattan.

It was home to Robert De Niro and hosted the Tribeca Film Festival.

Thus, the minute Deputy Inspector Harold Morrison moved into the neighborhood, residents supposed he was on the take.

"A dirty cop of the rank and file," they whispered.

It wasn't easy to pull the wool over the eyes of New Yorkers.

Everyone knew:

COPS *lived in Queens.*
THIEVES *battled for Brooklyn.*
    &
CON MEN strong-armed Manhattan.

So, when an army of Federal Agents arrived at 395 Broadway–*pushed aside the doorman*–and stormed through the building's lobby, the gossip became nods of validation.

The deputy inspector was going down.

His $1.5 million dollar World War II condo featured two bedrooms, three designer baths, and eleven foot ceilings.

Nevertheless, none of these trappings mattered one bit to Harold as he stood on the chilly floor staring through an over-sized corner window as NYPD cruisers dropped frantic cops at the curb.

"What's the matter, hon?" his wife said, peering through the kitchen, a dishtowel in her hand. "You seem somewhat distant."

Not as distant as my ass will be when the convicts are done screwing it.

His cell rang then, and when he answered it, the reality of the situation came crashing through the handset with a warning from the lobby.

"Mr. Morrison," a faithful doorman cautioned. "They're here for you, just like you always said they would be. I'm sorry I couldn't stop them."

"Thank you, Phillip; you've been a faithful vanguard all these years." Pressing the end button, he sighed and turned to the love of his life. "It's nothing important," he lied kissing her on the cheek. "I have to go into my office for a few minutes to make some calls."

She squinted with concern, "You okay?"

He grabbed her ringed hand and kissed her fingers.

"Of course, Darling, why wouldn't I be?"

Walking down a long hallway, he passed the master bedroom and pushed through a heavy oak door leading to the study. No space was wasted in the room; its walls were lined with framed front page news articles heralding a lifetime of accomplishments and storied manhunts. They hung there brilliantly, capturing moments of an extensive career in the New York Police Department.

"Damn it," Harold mumbled walking over to an antique desk that had been gifted to him by then Mayor, Ed Koch, the 105th Mayor of New York City.

Harry had been one of his best friends.

"You'll never get promoted to police commissioner under stinking Dinkins," Koch once told him after losing his fourth re-election in 1989. "But you'll always have my desk to remind you of the good old days."

Harold recollected smiling as Ed left City Hall for the final time asking a question.

"By the way, Harold. How'd I do as Mayor?"

"You did great, Mister Mayor."

Harold grinned at the memory of Koch who'd recently passed away. Sliding open the center drawer, he pulled out his service revolver and loaded six silver bullets into the cylinder.

"It's been a good run, but now it's time to take care of business and avoid the Perp Walk. The *Walk of Shame* was a common custom of the NYPD. It was a drill of walking a suspect through a public place after their arrest, creating an opportunity for the media to snap photographs and roll video of the happening. The perpetrator would always be handcuffed and sometimes outfitted with jail clothes. It was mostly associated with New York City, which originally only degraded its violent street criminals with the practice, but since Mayor Giuliani's stewardship, it had been extended to almost every defendant.

Especially, dirty, lousy, crooked cops!

Harold was snapped out of his considerations by heavy knocks at the front door. They were more like blows; deep hammering fist explosions on the outside of the apartment's entrance. He'd been party to hundreds of such arrests and knew the practice. Flipping the revolver's cylinder closed he stared at his reflection on the stainless steel barrel.

"Where's Harold?" the police commissioner's voice boomed from somewhere down the hallway. "Don't screw around, Emma, this is serious. We have an arrest warrant for first degree murder."

"Murder? For Harold?"

Funny how life turns out, Harold supposed, staring at the gun. *One day you think you're doing the right thing and the next?*

He recalled how it all began as a young captain rising through the ranks, fighting the city's crime, arresting nickel and dime street dealers, prostitutes and panhandling bums who he'd been ordered to remove from the streets.

"Harold," his then superior ordered fifteen years prior. "If you expect to raise your pay grade, then the bums have to move from the corners, the dealers get shuffled to Rikers, and the tourists must feel safe in Times Square."

So, after the meeting, he hatched a plan to rid the city of hundreds of scumbags lurking along the streets begging for money, harassing the tourists–*almost threatening them*–for spare change to aid drug induced perversions.

"The Christmas season is our shining moment," the commissioner chewed his ass back in 1999. "And what do I have up in the theater district? Bums dressed as Santa Claus stumbling along sidewalks, liquor on their breath, approaching *Out of Towners* for their hard earned cash!"

And then, it hit Harold... the *realization* that if he could clean up the streets and make the vagrants disappear from his district he'd be seen as a hero.

That's when Richard came to mind.

And so, Morrison made a deal with the Devil.

He approached Blake with a plan to rid his district of the Santa bums–and in return–Captain Harold Morrison would be rewarded by One Police Plaza for ridding the city of the Santa posers.

And, Richard would be free to pursue a life free of Attica. Prison, after all, was no place for a white doctor from Manhattan. They'd have him bent over a bunk, red Kool-Aid brushed on his lips, legs shaved, screaming in pain as they screwed him in the rump until he bled from his gaping hole.

Those images made Richard appreciate the consequences of prison life and so, soon after, he and Harold initiated *the plan* to kidnap and murder anyone panhandling on city streets dressed as Ole Saint Nick.

Nobody cared about bums gone missing.

It was a win-win for everyone, Harold thought back then. So long as he never got his hands dirty and Richard wasn't jammed-up during one of the murders.

That was fifteen years and dozens of bodies ago...

Everything had been going great–crime was down, the panhandling Santas were few and far between, and Harold Morrison was promoted to deputy inspector–until this knock came at the office door.

"Harold!" the commissioner hammered. "Open the door, the game's up, we know about Blake, about the murders!"

The deputy inspector placed the barrel of his revolver under his chin, took a deep breath, and pulled the trigger.

There would be no PERP WALK for the mastermind of death… for he was, at that moment, meeting the gatekeeper of hell where he'd find command of another sort.

There was always a position there for egomaniacs.

Chapter 89

New Beginnings

PADDY'S WAS PACKED for Rico's retirement party.

With the river dragged and the body of *The Santa Claus Killer* missing, the case was stored away for future examination by forensic psychiatrists and serial killer profilers.

The story premiered on the front pages of newspapers across the globe and the networks ran the headline around the clock. A Santa Claus serial killer was big news.

SANTA KILLER PRESUMED DEAD!
No Body Found In Frozen Hudson

There were more questions than answers surrounding the investigation and heads were rolling over the supposed role Deputy Inspector Harold Morrison had played in the conspiracy to murder innocent civilians.

Bellevue doctors were fired, directors of the psychology department were summoned before the city commission, and the mayor's office was hell bent on probation department resignations.

Kathleen Royce packed her bags and was hiding in shame, with her daughter, somewhere along the Jersey Shore.

However, in the end, time would heal all wounds; the media would move on to new atrocities and life would plod forward while the department reviewed policy and procedure.

The important thing for New Yorkers was their belief the killer had been ferried to his grave and his final victim luckily escaped the frozen Hudson with his life.

The tabloids flew off the shelves–everyone craved to learn of the killer's son who directed his father's soul to hell–and then swam for his life.

Stefan was Manhattan's newest hero, and on the television above Paddy's bar played a news conference of the mayor presenting Mighty Whitey with the Bronze Medallion, New York City's highest award for exceptional citizenship and outstanding achievement.

"Stefan's astonishing bravery," the mayor faced the cameras, "in bringing down the city's most diabolical killer and saving his own life and that of future victims, is an inspiration not just to New Yorkers, but the entire world. His courageous battle at the bottom of the Hudson is a reminder of how we are surrounded by everyday heroes in this city, and I am deeply honored to recognize one today."

Earlier, because so many were murdered in the subway, Stefan was awarded a year of free subway rides, twelve unlimited monthly Metro Transit Cards, plus various items of MTA merchandise. Also, the Walt Disney World Ambassador presented him with a week long, all expenses paid trip to Disney World and a fistful of vouchers for merchandise at the Times Square store.

"What are you going to do now?" a reporter asked the smiling seventeen-year-old boy.

"I'm going to the Disney store on Christmas Eve!" the boy beamed to the applause of reporters and dignitaries.

The *Today Show* and *Good Morning America* had already scheduled interviews and there were rumors circulating about a movie deal.

Maybe even an interview on Oprah!

Nothing got by Hollywood producers. They were like ravenous sharks; blood in the water brought them around for a sniff and chomp at the bait.

There was nothing like a good old *Cataclysm*.

But tonight, nobody talked of the horrifying case or the serious ramifications it held for the city. Here in Paddy's, the evening was all about the man of the hour, the lead head hunter, the cop who dedicated his life to law and order.

"Here, here!" Sergeant Mike Murphy raised his Jameson. "To the best damn murder cop Manhattan South has ever allowed to chase the scent!"

"Aye, aye," the mob of cops responded, "to our very own Lieutenant Martinez!"

Rico raised his glass, chuckled, and felt a stab of sorrow and loss for his departure. "Look here, fellas, I'll miss you schmucks for sure, but Miami Beach margaritas and rum runners are a pretty good trade off."

Everyone laughed.

"And don't forget about the cushy Deputy Chief position at the Miami Beach P.D.," Murphy shouted. "Now you'll be chasing cocaine cowboys and rap star, gun toting, wannabe gangsters."

"Here! Here!" the crowd hooted.

Rico smiled and held his glass high.

"To the guys who covered my six, this is for you!"

It was a term police and military personnel often muttered. It indicated the relative location of another person. In other words, a suspect could be at 12 o'clock (straight ahead) or at 3 o'clock (on the right). So, your *SIX* was directly behind you, the most dangerous enemy location.

Cover your Six meant protect your ass.

Rico knocked back his Jameson and threw the glass to the floor where it shattered. Breaking the glass represented breaking ties with the past and moving into the future.

The room of well-wishers applauded loudly and watched as Rico and Murphy moved across the room and disappeared through Paddy's exit.

"So, what now," Murphy asked pulling on leather gloves. "Have you and Liz packed up the house?"

"Yeah, the house is packed and the moving trucks arrive January first and then…"

"Miami sunsets and early morning walks on the beach," Murphy finished, "must be nice!"

"What about you, Mike? What are you going to do, stick around the department or listen to that Chinese girlfriend of yours and head to the FBI academy?"

That was the question everyone wanted answered.

Special Agent Mei Ling had publically stated to the New York media that Murphy would be a great fit at the Bureau's Behavioral Analysis Unit. They focused on serial, mass, and other types of murder, sexual assault, kidnapping, and criminal acts targeting adult victims.

"I'm not sure," Murphy answered. "Fact is I happen to love New York and the city life."

"Quantico, Virginia is a little too slow for you, eh?"

Murphy's answer was interrupted by his cellphone. Grabbing it from the holster and glancing at the screen he grunted. "Damn it!"

"What is it? We got a body?"

Murphy answered the call from Detective Operations and then turned back to Rico. "We have to go, they have a report of Santa Claus carrying a hatchet and dragging a sack through Times Square."

"Are you serious, a copycat?"

"I think its Blake," Murphy nodded. "Christmas Eve and the monster returns to take vengeance."

"Guess we didn't find his body in the river for a reason. I'll radio the chopper. We need to get to Times Square… like right now!"

Chapter 90

The Santa Con

THE GREAT WHITE WAY was packed.

It was Christmas Eve in Times Square.

Silent night! Deadly night! Kill your mom just for spite!
"Haaaaa-HA," Santa bellowed, "Merry Christmas!"

He was marching with more than fifty thousand Santas through Broadway in a boozy celebration.

This was SantaCon and it was bustling.

The event took place in 225-cities worldwide, including London, San Francisco, and right here in Manhattan.

"Drunken impersonators," Santa griped, "wannabe posers, taking in my glory!" He trudged through the crowd of costumed idiots–elves, reindeer, fairies, snowmen, and the ones who wanted his job–dragging a bloody red sack through the snow, counting imaginary victims along the way.

I could make this an international killing spree if they left me alone!

"Damn spoiled fucks, whatever happened to Mr. New Year's Eve, Dick Clark?"

He's dead and stinking, Son, Daddy boomed in his head.

Don't you read the Daily News? Mammy huffed. *He kicked the bucket years ago!*

New York was the commercial intersection of the world, at the intersection of Broadway and Seventh Avenue and stretching from West 42nd to 47th Streets. Broadway at Christmas… *on this night*… was the epicenter of the entire joyous world; a brightly illuminated hub of the entertainment industry.

Disney had taken over the show.

The square was the world's most visited tourist attraction fetching more than forty-million visitors a year.

And, some of them had to die!

Santa was on the prowl with nothing to lose.

One thing was sure, he wouldn't go down alone.

There'd be a little snot nosed brat at his side when he met the demons of hell.

Reminds me of a scene from the movie, Ghost, Mammy offered. *Where that hoodlum is hit by the car and his soul is dragged through the streets by black demons.*

"Wouldn't that be a sight," Santa cackled in response, "demons dragging the worthless, stinking bones of tourists through the city streets! Next stop, purgatory!"

They were leaping out of his way now, screaming in panic at the bloody trails tracking through the snow.

"He's got a hatchet!" someone yelled.

"There's blood on the snow!" another shrieked.

"Mommy, Mommy, it's Santa!" a little boy pointed.

Richard's face was speckled with blood; deep lacerations were carved into the skin. One of his eyeballs hung from the socket.

But it was the blood soaked hatchet that was most frightening.

"That's right, sonny boy," Santa leered. "I'm the Santa Killer and I like killing little boys, too!"

"Oh, my God!" the boy's mother shrieked, pushing her child along the street. "Somebody better call the cops!"

"Go ahead!" Santa shrieked swinging the hatchet. "Call the peepers, see if I care!"

However, calling the cops… there wasn't time for that. Everyone was too busy clearing a path for the diabolical madman hobbling down the center of Broadway.

"Jeez, get a load of this guy," a gangbanger jeered a little too close. "Whatcha doing, man, looking for your reindeer or a hit of crack?"

Santa snarled at the thug, raised the hatchet, and relieved the *Sassylipper* of his head. That round little puppy rolled along the snow until it stopped, eyes-up, where they stared, non-blinking, at his buddies.

"Anyone else have an opinion?" Santa sniggered, picking up the head and pushing it into his sack. "God damn cattle," he mumbled stomping through the snow, the hatchet swinging at his side. "I have to find the Bootlicker and send him to his grave, to end what I started seventeen years ago when I pushed my flesh into his mother."

I tried to tell you, Mammy whispered. *Pussy would be your downfall!*

"Shut the fuck up!" Santa screamed to the horrified bystanders. "Just shut your dead pie holes!"

Nobody watching ever thought they'd visit Manhattan and see a live show for free, but that's exactly what they were getting, right there in the middle of Broadway, as the psycho talked to ghosts.

Santa marched quickly through the square.

Straight ahead to the left sat the Bertelsmann Building, home to Planet Hollywood's All Star Café, the Apple flagship store, and the Disney Store.

"Get out of my way!" he roared, swinging his hatchet. "Daddy Christmas has finally arrived!"

And, that wasn't far from the truth, because New York, at Christmas, was all about the arrival of Santa.

People didn't have far to look.

He had come to kill.

And the blood was flowing.

Chapter 91

The Magic Kingdom

MICKEY, MINNIE, DONALD & GOOFY lived in the hearts of children everywhere.

But Manhattan was home.

Disney's Times Square store was a Magical Kingdom of Princesses, Fairies, Action Figures, Winnie the Pooh and so much more!

Stefan was blown away as he excitedly stepped through a series of wooden replicas of New York City skyscrapers.

Above his head was a giant twirling swing set.

"What do you think of this place?" Timothy Smith asked as his cameraman rolled on the scene unfolding before them.

Eyewitness News was chosen as part of a media pool to follow the boy as he shopped with the mayor and Disney Ambassador.

"Man, this is super cool!" Stefan shouted, glancing to Terry and Mirabel busily chatting with the mayor.

"Anything you want to see I'll be glad to show you," the ambassador stated. "This day is all about you and the heroic courage you've displayed to the city."

"Aw, thank you, but I'm no hero!"

They had shut the store to the general public for the boy and his shopping spree. The networks and newspapers formed a circle around Stefan as he pushed through the winter wonderland. On the walls were huge illustrations of both classic and modern Disney characters.

"I can buy anything? Anything at all?"

"Until your heart is content," the dignified man beamed.

Stefan had been awarded vouchers in the amount of $10,000.00 to purchase just about anything–except the fancy gold and diamond Mickey and Minnie collector's watches–those were for kids with gold American Express cards.

"We have a Marvel Superhero section upstairs," the ambassador suggested. "I understand you happen to be an admirer of comics."

It was true. He was a fanatic when it came to comic books and Marvel movies.

If God roamed Earth, Stan Lee was his name.

He was an American comic book writer, editor, actor, producer, publisher, television personality, and the former president and chairman of Marvel Comics.

Hurrying to the escalator, Stefan stepped onto the moving stairs where miniature morsels of pixie dust moved up and down the walls.

"Do you like it here, Stefan?" Terry asked, sliding his arm around his shoulders.

"It's awesome! I've never seen anything like it."

Walking off the escalator, they found themselves moving through an archway into Imagination Park. It was intended to be a magical destination, giving people the best thirty-minutes of their day. That was accomplished by fashioning a destination, engaging individuals in *a story,* and designing every detail to be a fun place where fantasy could interrupt the bombardment of everyday life outside the magical world of Disney.

And it worked.

"Wow," Stefan squealed, running to a wall of encased superhero figurines containing Iron Man, the Hulk, and Captain America.

They reminded him of Marco and Darius.

"I miss you guys," he mumbled.

Mirabel caught the transformation from glee to sadness. "Is there something wrong, Stefan?"

He sighed, blinked back a tear, and grabbed her hand.

"I was thinking how great it would have been to have Marco and Darius here with me to see this."

As she wrapped her arms around his frame, the sound of helicopter blades cutting the air caught her attention.

"This is the NYPD," a commanding voice boomed outside the window. "Drop the weapon and get on the ground!"

The reporters ran to the windows looking onto Times Square.

"It's the NYPD!" Tim shouted. "Ahmed, roll tape!"

They watched thousands of people running through the streets as the NYPD helicopter hovered above the chaotic exodus.

"Attention!" the voice again boomed. "This is the NYPD, we repeat, drop the weapon, and get on the ground or we will be forced to shoot!"

Shoot? Tim thought, *in Times Square?* From where he stood looking out the window, only frantic pedestrians could be seen running down Seventh Avenue.

"Please, folks," the manager nervously asked. "We must ask everyone to stay calm as there is an emergency on the street."

The mayor stepped forward. "Is there a back door or an escape route other than the front door?"

The manager nodded and led the mayor and his entourage from sight.

Stefan, Mirabel, and Terry stood gawking out the window with a group of reporters.

"I guess the shopping will have to wait, Stefan," Mirabel stated to the deflated teenager who refused to release his grasp on an Iron Man tee shirt.

"I'm sorry," the ambassador stated. "But we'll reschedule this for another day."

At that moment, a blood-curdling scream pierced the night and it became apparent something much worse was underway.

"Come on," Terry said. "Let's get out of here before something bad happens."

Chapter 92

Climatic Endings

A HOLLYWOOD MOVIE couldn't have done it any better. This was action! Prime time, baby… the action sequence in the final five minutes of Santa's starring role.

It is the scene where an audience squeals, covers their eyes, and peeks through fingers at the bloodshed on the silver screen.

Santa laughed at his thoughts while dodging into the doorway and out of sight of the chopper.

"Daddy's home!" he shouted up into the Disney Store while swinging the hatchet, cackling like a madman.

The blade hit the elbow of a man on the escalator. Collapsing, he gaped in shock at the sight of red arterial blood spurting from his missing limb.

"Oh, my God, somebody help me!"

There was, however, no help as the reporters all ran back up the stairs, two at a time, to get away from the mayhem.

They're pussies, all of them, Santa thought watching the tipster's frantically rushing up the escalator… running like actors in an Alfred Hitchcock film. *No good pants pissers!*

"This is the NYPD," the loudspeaker blared, "drop the weapon and come back out of the doorway!"

Santa glanced down the ascending mechanical stairs and laughed. He could just make out the helicopter's searchlight, illuminating Broadway like a Hollywood Premiere.

"Stupid idiots, why would I walk out there into the sights of their guns? Ho! Ho! Ho!" he bellowed marching up the escalator stairs "Merry, fucking, Christmas!"

"Attention! Attention!" the loudspeaker barked. "By order of the New York Police Department all pedestrians must clear the streets!"

Santa smiled at the sight before him.

"Well, look at what we have here," he shouted, his hand firmly clenching the handle of his hatchet. "My Son, welcome to the show. I brought you into this lousy world and now I'm going to take you out!"

"Oh, Terry!" Mirabel screamed. They were trapped at the escalator landing, pinned with a group of terrified reporters who pushed themselves against walls and into corners to watch from a distance.

Santa grabbed Stefan, taking pleasure in the knowledge he'd finally captured the little, snot-nosed punk... that *finally*, he had the boy right where he wanted him.

"I'm gonna cut you up real nice," he threatened swinging the hatchet back and forth to keep Terry at a safe distance.

Stefan could have sworn he heard the blade cutting the cold air beside his ear. "Leave them out of it. They didn't have anything to do with our family problems. This is between you and me."

Santa laughed. "Let's not forget that lousy mother of yours; this is about her, too!"

Pushing Stefan to the ground, he raised the hatchet.

"I'll fucking tell you what happens here, you don't have a vote; this isn't American, fucking, Idol!"

"Please, Dad. I just want to live."

"Time's up!" Santa angrily muttered... the hatchet ready to strike. "No more time to lie, cheat, or steal!!"

"I wasn't meant to die this way," Stefan struggled in his father's grasp. "I could have been somebody!"

"But you ended up nobody!" Santa spat. "Shit happens and then you die!"

Then, just as he was about to bring down the hatchet, a shout erupted behind him.

"Hey, fuck face!" Mirabel yelled pointing the old revolver she'd taken from Stefan at the bus station. "Leave *my* son alone!"

The killer turned to her, an insanely wild smile filling his face. "Hehehehe-ahahahaha-bahahahaha," he cackled. "What is it, bitch? You want to play grown-up?"

"Mirabel!" Terry hollered. "Honey, no!"

But it was too late; the anger rising within her was beyond hearing words. She was pure vengeance; payback for every mother who'd ever suffered torment of a man like the one before her.

"Come and get it, Santa Claus!" she snickered. "You are a sorry excuse for a Santa if I ever did see one! Nobody takes you seriously, dumbass!"

Santa exploded in anger, released his grasp on Stefan, and pounced, his hatchet swinging back and forth through the air while lunging at Mirabel.

"You high-class, smart–mouthed housewife, who the fuck do you think you are? You want to dance with the devil?"

"Tell him I said hello," Mirabel shouted pulling the trigger and watching as the bullets slammed into Santa's chest knocking him back onto the descending escalator. He laid on the steel staircase, sprawled in a pool of blood, gasping for breath, his vision fading.

"Yyy-you-sssssh-ssshhhh-shot me," he struggled. "Ssss-sss-son?" he called to Stefan, his jaw chattering with death's icy arrival.

Mirabel glanced to Stefan, shook her head, and marched down the steps to Santa. At the bottom, she pointed the gun at his head and laughed.

"The devil is waiting, you miserable, rotten man!"

The last thing Santa heard and felt were gunshots and the slap of steel piercing his brain.

"There goes Santa Claus," she mumbled staring at his dead body, "right down Santa Claus Lane!"

"Mirabel!" Murphy yelled running through the door just paces from the scene. "Put down the gun!" Staring into her eyes, he saw peace and an expression of knowledge that the boogeyman was no more; sent to the depths of hell where he'd never hurt anyone again.

And he was glad.

Stefan ran to Mirabel, wrapped his arms around her, and said, "You saved me. You killed my father!"

"No, Stefan, honey, I killed your NIGHTMARE!"

They embraced for what seemed like eternity.

Around them buzzed the excitement of media hounds and gawkers who peered at tragedy… and beyond them, the silent respect of two proud homicide detectives.

"I guess you're going to make it to Miami after all," Murphy winked at Rico moving towards the scene.

"I couldn't have asked for a better Christmas gift."

And then, the reporters merely shrugged, shuffled down the escalator and got on with the business of reporting.

Tomorrow was the biggest day of the year.

There was a story to tell.

And nobody wanted to miss it.

The end

DON'T MISS

RJ SMITH'S

CATACLYSM

Available Now

A momentous and violent event marked by
overwhelming upheaval and demolition;
Broadly: an event that brings great changes.

Chapter 1

EARTHQUAKE

THE ISLAND of La Palma was deadly.

It was the fifth largest of seven Canary Islands hosting a hundred thousand residents.

That meant trouble... *big trouble!*

The volcanic ocean landmass contained three ridges. One of these, Cumbre Vieja, towered four miles from seabed to summit and it was a slumbering demon.

Locals supposed the volcano was primed for catastrophe, believing one day the beast would awake in a noxious, fiery explosion of ash and lava.

When that transpired, everyone would die.

Home to the world's most sophisticated telescopes, the William Herschel stood majestically atop the caldera with its optical near-infrared reflectors monitoring the heavens.

If E.T. existed, this lens made contact.

Through a layer of wispy, fibrous white clouds, a Beechcraft Baron twin-engine airplane lined up for landing on a short blacktop runway. The plane belonged to the U.S. Geological Survey and ferried scientists to the volcano.

"This is a hot blooded monster," Dr. Tish Harriet stated exiting the plane and leading her team of six men into a bunker. "It could take out the United States."

They'd been watching the Old Summit closely due to alarming steam vents which recently erupted.

"The data is disturbing," Professor Chris Grossman agreed checking the latest AFM readings on his tablet. "If we have lahar activity, this could very well mean massive slippage of the ridge."

"We need to check the monitoring poles," Tish answered. "See if the data confirms our suspicions."

She was lead volcanologist and had spent her entire life studying stratovolcanoes' tall, pointed summits... built up by countless layers of hardened lava, tephra, pumice, and volcanic ash.

Beeeeep
Beeeeeeeeeeeep–Beeeeeeeeeeeep

"We have a problem!" Chris shouted, glancing at a seismogram display. "This is huge seismic activity."

Seismograms were records produced by seismographs calculating the location and magnitude of an earthquake.

On the graph, lines now spiked.

"Damn," Tish shrieked hurrying to the monitor.

Installed along the ridge, seismographs detected, amplified, and recorded ground vibrations before sending signals back to the bunker during earthquakes. They were securely mounted into the earth... so when the ground shook, the unit wobbled with it. As it vibrated, the device recorded motion between itself and the rest of the instrument, thus recording ground motion.

"A minor quake," Chris muttered watching a spike elevate on the screen. "3.3 is the current reading."

Then, it shot up.

Each second, it rose higher, until passing through 5.5 on the graph. Nobody here sought to openly proclaim a prediction of doom; yet privately, behind their silent stares... they nodded, winked, and made escape plans.

"Maybe Dr. May is right," someone whispered.

Dr. Samuel May was the premier researcher of volcano doomsday theories and prophesies... who, up until that point... was the laughingstock of volcanology. So, for the last couple years, he'd been hidden away in the isolated wasteland of Iceland.

Up there, in the middle of nowhere, his public predictions of disaster could be silenced.

And everyone could breathe a sigh of relief.

That was, until the bunker quaked.

That caused Tish to glance out a fortified window where the dome of the William Herschel Telescope collapsed. With a tired shrieking roar, the telescope gave up its ghost and plummeted to the ground with a thunderous crash.

"Notify the Hazard Center," Tish yelled. "Send out an immediate satellite dispatch!"

The team was clustered around an array of computer screens struggling to balance themselves in the violently quaking chamber. Rows of florescent lights flickered. An alarm WHOOPED, a siren SHRIEKED, and shelves packed with research equipment fell from cracking walls.

"It's going to erupt!" Chris hollered glancing at the quaking wall of video screens. The room shook violently, and a three-foot wide monitor blinked 8.9. "Look at the size of this! We may have flank collapse! Notify GDACS and locate Sam, immediately!"

Tish rushed to a satellite phone and punched her finger onto its dial pad. "This is the Palisades Hydrophone Station at Cumbre Vieja Volcano! We are experiencing a major earthquake!"

Then, the ceiling cracked, bowed, and collapsed onto the researchers. The wall displays broke free of their hangers and crashed to the ground.

One by one, the florescent lights exploded, thrusting the chamber into darkness.

Chapter 2

ACT OF GOD

TOM ANDERSON was the network's fluff man.

He was the correspondent *Network News* tossed across the globe when *the package* was a sidebar of public interest. His assignments were filler for dead air... to thistle down the violent coverage pouring in from around the globe. Israel, Iran, Egypt... that's where the *real* news was. Hidden away in tempestuous countries where violent threats and acts of extinction were everyday occurrences.

Unlike this event of the newly elected pope,

And his attendance at:

Nothingville!

This was filler, capital-F for fluff.

> "Good morning from the Canary Islands," Tom smiled into the camera as the *Emissary of God* stepped from the pope-mobile surrounded by cardinals and Swiss Guard. "The popular Spanish Pope, Callixtus the Fourth, just three weeks from his election by the conclave of cardinals, has arrived here at the Patron Saint of the Canary Islands for what has been dubbed the seaside salvation of souls."

The pope cut his hand through the air and made the sign of the cross, a humble expression lining his face. He'd traveled to *Basilica of Candelaria* to attend and celebrate the famed apparition of Mother Mary on the Island of Tenerife. According to legend, a statue of The Virgin appeared on this beach in 1392 bearing a child in one hand and a green candle in the other. But, it happened all right, just as sure as the day is bright. There were eyewitnesses.

Two Guanche goat herders claimed they saw Mary trudging from the sea, dragging her feet along the frothy sand. Approaching, one of the men tried to throw a stone at her, but his arm became paralyzed.

When the second man attempted to stab *The Virgin* with a knife, he ended up wounding himself.

"Papa!" an old woman cried falling at the pope's feet. "Bless me, Father!" Beside her loomed nine bronze Guanches King Statues of the aboriginal kings. These were the Menceys of Candelaria and were mounted along the seashore beside the basilica. Some claimed they had worked alongside people from another planet centuries before to build this paradise.

"Bless you all," Callixtus muttered to thousands of onlookers lining the route. "Go with God, my children."

Alongside the pope strolled Cardinal Jonathan, the pontiff's handsome Italian personal assistant. He grinned while explaining the significance and antiquity of the bronze sentinels.

Yet, Callixtus was Spanish and knew the history.

Then and there, thousands of Eurasian Sparrow Hawks flapped from nearby trees, filling the sky with shrieking, echoing cries. They were small, bluish-gray *birds of prey* who specialized in catching woodland birds.

Now, they fled in fear of something else.

"Oh, vaya, mira thos criaturas hermosas!" Callixtus excitedly exclaimed at the sight.

"Sì Padre, sono belle!" Cardinal Jonathan nodded. "They are beautiful, aren't they?"

"Strange," Callixtus muttered in broken English. "I've never seen them fly in panic before."

The reporter pointed in the distance:

"A flock of sparrows have jolted from nearby perches. They're soaring over the guardian sculptures lining the shore. With their backs to the sea and facing the basilica, these eternal monuments watch over the faithful in attendance today, just as they have for an eternity."

Then, the sculptures shook as the earth violently quaked.

It reminded the reporter of Universal Studio's Earthquake Ride in Orlando.

"It's a quake!" he yelled to his viewers, pandemonium breaking out around him, people sprinting for their lives.

"Watch out!" someone shouted. "The church is collapsing!"

Unexpectedly, the statue's stone foundations crumbled and the Guanches toppled to the pavement.

"The cathedral is shaking violently," Tom yelled into the camera. "Behind me, you can hear its bells gonging oddly inside the twin stone towers of the old stone apostolic."

At that second, a loud screech escaped the pylon and everything collapsed in a cloud of crumbling cement.

Piece by piece, the tower released its clutch on history and sent its enormous brass bells plummeting to the ground.

"Look out!" a priest screamed. "Everybody run!"

They were the last words he'd offer, as one of the mammoth carillons crashed onto his head sending his soul to Saint Peter.

"Oh, no!" Callixtus bellowed to the sky while studying the scene. "Not yet! I haven't had enough time!"

"We have to get you out of here, Holy Father!" Cardinal Jonathan shouted as guards frantically ushered them towards the motorcade.

"Quickly!" the papal protectors shouted. "Get to the vehicle, Your Holiness!"

However, Heaven had other plans.

The destruction of faith was underway.

Belief was being tested.

Just a millisecond before Callixtus reached the safety of his pope-mobile, an enormous sinkhole swallowed the holy chariot into its cavernous jaws.

Oh, Dios Mío! Callixtus thought. *The dismantling of the world has begun!*

Chapter 3

MR. VOLCANO

GRÍMSVÖTN VOLCANO hulked over Iceland.

Its icecap, Vatnajökull, loomed magnificently on the northwestern ridge and boasted the highest eruption frequency of all volcanoes in the country. Because most of its mass lay beneath ice, its eruptions were sub-glacial.

That's what held the attention of researchers the world over... *deadly, fiery, magma...* bubbling deep below. It brought survey grants because sleeping giants like this one had the ability to end a lot of things.

It threatened life on planet Earth.

Everybody agreed a super-volcano explosion could marshal in a new ice age; ash from the eruption would travel the globe and block out sunlight for years.

And, without sunshine, crops would *fail...* plant life would *perish* and food would become *scarce.*

That would cause famine, the breakdown of civilization and, quite possibly... the *end of mankind.*

In 2011, an eruption began here that continued over four days. Spewing plumes of ash and lava into the atmosphere, it complemented several earthquakes resulting in the cancellation of nine hundred flights in Iceland, the United Kingdom, Greenland, Germany, Ireland, and Norway.

Planes were forced to land, and international travel crawled to an economy crushing halt.

Airports became parking lots.

Some said it was the *beginning* of the *end.*

When natural disasters like that happened, directing airliners to their nearest tarmacs–well, money poured in and prominent researchers the globe over were assembled for predictions of doom.

Those prophecies and fears are what brought a team to Geological Base Camp *FIRESIDE* to lead the way.

The plan: to save the world from destruction.

One of the team members was American geologist, William Squire. On this morning, he celebrated his forty-eighth birthday by staring into a hole in the ground; this is what he lived for, *science.*

"Good morning, Sunshine," Will muttered to an Acoustic Flow Monitor sitting exposed in excavated earth.

He specialized in the study of solid and liquid matter that constituted the Earth, the processes and history that shaped it, and all things related. When compared to scientists in other fields, he was more exposed to the outdoors than those remaining in laboratories.

Will treasured the frontiers of hazard and thrived on the forefront of natural danger and disaster warnings.

His *thing* was studying earthquakes, volcanic activity, tsunamis, weather storms, and the technologies used to warn governments of the infrequent occurrence of those events.

Sometimes, that works just fine, he considered glancing to the towering icecap and then back into the hole. *And sometimes, all hell breaks loose.*

The rumble of an engine brought his attention out of the hole… and when he peered across the tundra, he grunted at the sight of a muddy Jeep Wrangler Rubicon. In the background, far beyond it, the volcano spewed superheated steam into the brisk morning air.

As the Jeep slid to a stop in a patch of mud beside the excavation, a British man winked at Will and jumped to the ground. He was Dr. Samuel May, a rugged crackerjack of a man, steady as the volcanoes he studied.

"You don't look a day over forty, Will," Sam grunted.

"Is that right?"

"Right as can be, dear boy!" Sam snickered, slapping his junior researcher on the back before pointing his thumb excitedly back towards the volcano. "She's all mouth and no trousers, I tell you; day six of moaning and groaning!"

"That's what you get when you mess with women."

"Huh? What's that?"

"Never mind, Professor," Will waved dismissively. "Women are women, even when they're volcanoes!"

"Oh, yes! You have learned a thing or two."

Interrupted by the sound of an approaching helicopter, Sam raised his hand to block the glare of the sun cresting the apex of the icecap.

"Bollocks! What the hell is this tosh, the newsies again? Haven't you told them to stay out of our testing area?"

A white United Nations helicopter swooped out of the clear blue sky, landed, and deposited a man wearing a U.N. GDACS bomber jacket.

Crouching beneath the blades, he hurried to Sam.

"Professor May, I'm Oscar Thomas, from the United Nations Global Disaster Alert and Coordination System here in Iceland."

"Is that right?" Sam chuckled pushing forth his hand. "You must be new at the post; your accent sounds like you spring from the Caribbean."

"The Virgin Islands, my friends call me *V.I.* for short; I was born in St. Thomas."

"No kidding?" Sam chuckled. "Well, Mr. Virgin Islands, you must be out of your element here in Iceland!" Motioning towards the excavation, he introduced Will. "Professor Will Squire and I know the U.N. well. Besides, that bird you sprang from gave you straight-away. How're the lackeys back at GDACS, huh?"

V.I. shook his head. "Not good, I'm afraid. We received word from Secretary Soma that the U.N. requests your presence in New York!"

The mention of his longtime *frenemy* brought a grin to Sam's face. "Karin dispatched you to pull my chain, eh? What's biting her rump these fine days?"

"It's Cumbre Vieja, Professor," V.I. sighed.

"The Old Summit?" Will snorted. "What's happening in La Palma, Spain?"

"The U.S.G.S. Volcano Hazards Program has confirmed seismological data on the ground. They have catastrophic seismic activity in the Canaries and are concerned the western flank of the volcano might be unstable."

"Son of a gun!" Sam exclaimed. "They've realized their *cock up* and have come to their senses? Are they actually *talking* about collapse?"

"Yes, Sir," V.I. stated pointing at the chopper. "I need to get you to New York at once!"

"Should we deactivate the AFM monitors?" Will asked, pointing at the hole in the ground.

"There's no time, Dr. May!" V.I. urgently answered. "If your past predictions of Cumbre Vieja are true, Africa could only have hours!"

"Leave them to the elements, William," Sam ordered. "Grab our bug-out bags. We have to move with the wind, dear boy."

Gathering the bags, which were always ready for immediate escape, the researchers hurried beneath the helicopter's spinning blades and climbed aboard.

"If the summit fails," V.I. asked, "Is there anything that can be done to save the Atlantic shores?"

"When she erupts," Sam answered as the chopper lifted, "the only thing we can do is get out of her bloody way!"

Chapter 4

JUST THE FACTS

THE U.N. chopper was a battleship.

V.I. pointed to a string of bullet holes peppering the floor. "This MI-24 was one of the choppers that took on heavy gun fire in the village of Kinshasa."

"Bob's your Uncle!" Sam scoffed. "It flew the Democratic Republic of the Congo? Why're bullet holes still visible in the airframe?"

V.I. shrugged. "Repairs cost more than retiring it for missions like this in non-hostile sectors of the world."

"And yet, it still has guns attached to the exterior," Will nodded out the window. "Worried about an invasion?"

"It's a dangerous world," V.I. remarked. "We never know when a rocket propelled grenade will streak its way up from the ground."

That forced Sam to consider the ramifications of such an event. "In that case, we'd be a bit shanghaied, would we not?" Following world affairs with a keen eye, he recognized disasters and military upheavals often dictated his own survival while traversing the globe's most treacherous environments.

"The U.N. security council," V.I. continued, "activated a squad of these attack-helicopters to knockout insurgent positions in the eastern Congo in November 2012, after they gained ground in heavy fighting."

"It's a *testy* planet," Sam granted. "Nobody seems to recognize we're all on this sphere together. We're fighting one unique enemy, you know?"

William cut into the conversation. "What did President Ronald Reagan say to the U.N. about the human race and aliens? He went to New York, stood before the U.N. Body in 1987, stared across the Hall and said: 'How quickly our differences worldwide would vanish if we were facing an alien threat from outside this world.' How do you like that for disclosure?"

"Aliens exist," Sam affirmed. "I could tell you stories. Their elongated skulls have been found in tombs on too many of my digs"

"I've read your papers," V.I. quickly changed the subject. "In college I heard about the possibility of flank collapse and read your theory on Cumbre Vieja. Do you really believe an earthquake will cause a tsunami?"

"It could. I was concerned in 2011 when officials on the smallest Canary Island, El Hierro, had to evacuate civilians following a series of quakes. The island experienced over eight thousand tremors during two months, and I feared a major disaster would happen then."

"But it didn't," V.I. stated.

"No, it did not."

"Do you think this quake will cause an eruption?"

"None has taken place on any of the Canary Islands since the Las Palmas in 1971, but my team has been warning the international community that a La Palma eruption could take place when her magma rises to the surface and produces a series of ruptures that will generate significant seismic activity."

Will pulled an iPad from his bag and showed it to V.I. "We don't know if magma will break through the crust, cause an eruption, or worse." On the screen played a computer generation of what might happen if an eruption did cause flank collapse.

"This is a ridge collapse?" V.I. asked staring at the video of the volcano ridge splashing into the ocean.

"It is," Sam muttered. Then, motioning for Will to turn the display off, he turned to V.I. and peered into the man's stare. "So, what do we know so far?"

"La Palma had an 8.9 major earthquake early this morning. Of the thousands of swarm tremors recorded since, only twenty or so have been noticeable to residents. However, the government of Spain is reporting the quakes are continuing across all seven islands. The volcano itself has not seen an eruption, but the Spanish have raised the eruption risk-level to *red*, the highest alert since the swarm of earthquakes began."

"Bonkers!" Sam grunted. "All seven islands are experiencing quakes! An 8.9 is enormous, it might have displaced La Palma!"

"But there hasn't been an eruption," V.I. argued.

"Not yet," Sam contended glancing out the window at the mountain peaks. "But an eruption is coming, my friend, just as sure as we sit in this bullet ridden deathtrap. Has anyone heard from my wife, Dr. Tish Harriet?"

V.I. reluctantly frowned. "The last we heard was an alert she sent out from Palisades Hydrophone Station."

Chapter 5

PREDICTION OF DOOM!

KEFLAVÍK INTERNATIONAL was the largest airport in Iceland. American tourism was big business.

V.I. stood at the top air-stair of a white Lear Jet bearing the seal of the United Nations. "Whenever you're ready, Dr. May, the pilot has indicated we're clear to push off."

"Thank you, Mr. Virgin Islands." the volcanologist smiled politely staring toward the end of the runway. "I'll be a few more minutes." He stood at the bottom stair speaking animatedly to Will. "We have to lay it all out again to the United Nations. Show them our data and the flank failure model. Convince them to close the London Underground and evacuate America's East Coast"

"Good luck with that!" Will exclaimed. "Do you really think they'll take our work seriously now? The U.S. Congress practically laughed us out of *The Beltway* the last time we went to Capitol Hill warning of this very issue."

"It's those Republicans," Sam sighed. He *had* stressed to the American leaders that the coastlines of the United States were under threat from a monster wave of Hollywood–*and Biblical*–proportions when the volcano finally collapsed and crashed into the ocean. He'd thought that perhaps bringing God into the equation might have helped–though he really didn't believe in such an entity.

"Maybe this time they'll listen," Will hoped.

Sam grinned. "This quake should bring them around." Yet, deep down, he wasn't convinced the White House could be persuaded the earthquake would cause a massive landslide sending a 300-foot wave across the Atlantic.

Will shook his head in disbelief. "We've issued countless warnings to the U.S.G.S. predicting that, in the *best-case* scenario, a tsunami would destroy the east coast from Florida to Maine."

"Maybe now they'll listen," Sam stated glancing towards an *Icelandair* commercial plane leaping from the runway and bursting through the sky.

"Don't hold your breath," Will chuckled. "People in Washington wait until the last minute to do anything."

Sam knew this was true.

Actor Samuel Jackson had even gone on the Discovery Channel and warned that of the top five *natural disasters* facing the globe, a volcanic collapse from Cumbre Vieja was one of them.

The problem was this:

Although Hollywood loved *end of the world* disaster predictions, they were slow to climb onboard another disaster, thanks to the Mayan 2012 lunacy. That END OF DAYS prediction claimed a catastrophic event would occur on December 21, 2012, and warned Earth would cease to exist thanks to a collision with Planet X. Some even suggested the North and South Poles would reverse bringing on worldwide earthquakes terminating all life.

That prediction expired on December 22nd 2012.

Sam shrugged as he emerged from those thoughts of disaster. "Nobody, including Washington's elected officials, is going to jump onto another prediction of catastrophe. Especially one that calls for a tsunami generated by a mountain twice the size of Britain's Isle of Man crashing into the sea following a volcanic eruption."

Will grunted. "We have to make them believe."

"I remember," Sam chuckled glancing at his colleague, "the first time I told U.S. officials a 500-miles-per-hour wave would wipe out the east coast."

"They were a bunch of grouchy, whining broods," Will recalled. "The National Weather Service smiled politely, and showed your British rump to the door."

Not one U.S. Senator or Congressman believed it would happen. They practically threw him off Capitol Hill.

But Sam, Tish, and Will… *they believed.*

"What about Admiral Brancor?" Will asked, remembering the saucy American Admiral. "Is he going to be at the U.N. meeting?"

Sam snorted and pushed his hands into his pockets. "I've got a two-finger salute for that chap!"

"What's that mean?"

"It's similar to the American middle finger, dear boy."

"I didn't know the British were so vulgar."

"Well, now your doorbell has been rung," Sam smiled hurrying up the air-stairs. "We'll put some *welly* into our arguments to the global community. They have to understand the severity of the crisis."

"We'll give it all the muscle we have."

"Cheerio, then; off we go," Sam grinned stepping onto the plane.

As the door closed, Will wondered if he would ever see Iceland again.

It might be the beginning of a deadly journey.

ABOUT THE AUTHOR

RJ Smith is an American Screenwriter & Novelist who blossoms in the Contemporary Horror and Thriller genres.

He enjoys twisting the mind of readers while bending the reality of his characters.

The author's been noted in multiple national writing & screenwriting competitions: The Page International Screenwriting Awards, Francis Ford Coppola's American Zoetrope Studios and the Sundance Film Festival Table Read.

He lives in Florida

www.ingramcontent.com/pod-product-compliance
Lightning Source LLC
Chambersburg PA
CBHW060146260626
47160CB00001B/142